The Inheritance Dilemma

By

Santos A. Conteh

Edited by Winston Forde

Published by New Generation Publishing in 2021

First Edition

ISBN   Paperback 978-1-80369-166-4

www.newgeneration-publishing.com

New Generation Publishing

Dedication

To my dear late parents - Komrabai Meleh Conteh and Sentho Kamara who, though illiterate, embraced education as being essential and sent me to school, I dedicate this work. I also dedicate this to Dr. Gordon M Halliburton, who graciously and generously paid my West African School Certificate Examination fees when they were not forthcoming from my parents, who couldn't afford it. I am grateful to him because he enabled me to take the examination that paved the way to reach my achievements in life.

Acknowledgements

I want to affectionately thank my family for the unwavering support over many years. I want to particularly thank my wife, Lucy E. Conteh, who over the years, has been my strong pillar of sustenance and support. I sincerely want to thank her for understanding the many times I stayed out of bed to get my thoughts together and write this story. Finally, I am grateful to Winston Forde for his invaluable contribution as my editor and literary agent, following a recent introduction.

Contents

CHAPTER ONE

Magoronwa village is unique for its able-bodied male population and its highly grandiose male circumcision festivities. The initiation of male youths into the society of manhood is a proud occasion for every father in this village. Fathers begin preparation for this occasion when their sons are about the age of twelve or shortly thereafter. When a son is ten years, in the next succeeding three or four years to the year of the grand occasion, a father will increase his farm so that he could have enough resources to send his son to the society bush. Over the years *Kayneh* Bondaa, the only surviving son of the Nwoingoha clan and the reputed chiefdom blacksmith has not participated in this occasion as he has no son. *Kayneh* Bondaa inherited his father's wealth of several cows, sheep and goats, farmlands, many economic trees of kola nuts, oranges, and banana farm. His two wives have given him six daughters but no son. He realized that he was getting old, and he knew that he could not pass this inheritance to any of his daughters as inheritance in his clan was only through the male line.

On his death, without a son, his inheritance will pass on to a nephew and he did not want this to happen. His great grandfather had accumulated this wealth which was eventually passed on to Bondaa. He too has added to this wealth. Bondaa desperately wanted a son and therefore wanted to marry a third wife who he hoped will bear him a son. But before he could do that, he decided to consult the village seer, Sago-Gbo, who lived at the other end of the village, and tell him of his intentions and to inquire what the ancestors will say. He was pondering on this while he inclined in his hammock in his verandah smoking his *Sangotho* and waiting until the village is dead quiet when everyone had gone to bed. As it was normal for his wives to leave him alone in the verandah, he sneaked out to Sago-Gbo walking in the shadow of darkness. He quietly knocked at Sago-Gbo's side door.

"Sago-Gbo it's me Bondaa. I have come to see you" he said in a low voice so as not to arouse the curiosity of the neighbours.

"Bondaa, what is so urgent that you should take me away from my wife's side at this late hour?"

"You will know when you let me in."

"Bondaa I am in bed with my wife. Can't it wait until the morning"?

"No. I must tell you now when everybody is sleeping."

"Okay wait. I'm coming out and we will go to the shrine," Sago-Gbo concluded because he knows that when people knock on his door at this time of the night it is to consult the oracles.

Sogo-Gbo took his time to come out and when he eventually did, he forgot his bag and had to go back in. A few moments late he emerged, and both went quietly towards the shrine. He performed some ceremony before he could open the shrine door and entered leaving behind his sandals made from rubber tyre at the entrance of the shrine and telling Bondaa to wait outside a moment while he performs a ritual inside.

"Bondaa, you can come in now." Bondaa went in leaving his sandals also at the shrine entrance.

"What has brought you here at this late hour when I was just picking up sleep?" He asked, and Bondaa explained.

"I must first give the kola nut and the customary shake hand to you before I say anything."

He put his hand into the breast pocket of his *ronko* and took out six large kola nuts. He put them carefully on the floor before Sago-Gbo and added Five Leones on the side of the kola nuts.

"Sago-Gbo, you know that I have two wives and they have given me six beautiful girls," he began.

"You are going to be a rich man Bondaa, because when suitors come to ask for any of your daughters' hand for marriage you can expect to receive a handsome dowry for each of them"

"That is true, but they will all go away from home to their husbands, and I will be left alone with my wives. You know I have no son and you also certainly know that sons continue with the family name, and they are also necessary in a family specially to assist on the farm. But more so for the continuation of my family inheritance. You no doubt know that not only this village but also the entire chiefdom depend on me for all their blacksmith needs. I am getting old, and I still don't have a son who would take over my clan's successful blacksmith trade, and more especially inherit my properties and wealth."

"That's true," Sago-Gbo said. "Maybe you have heard the rumour that the people of our village are greatly concerned that you do not have somebody to train. If you join your ancestors on the other side today, villagers will have to go all the way to Pelewala for blacksmith work. People from Magoronwa will have to spend several days away attending to our needs before heading back home."

"I am more gravely concerned than the villagers," Bondaa replied. "People from neighbouring villages passing through Magoronwa will ask, 'where is that blacksmith's hut?' Or will they see a heap of rubble formed from my house abandoned because there is no son to live in it and continue the inheritance of my father and his ancestors? It is for this reason that I am here to consult the ancestors whether it will be wise to have another wife who will give me a son."

"Bondaa, this is a genuine request from my natural and human perspective. But we do not know what the ancestors know and what they will say.

"That is certainly true"

"They lived their lives in this world and ex-perienced their issues before they departed. Now that they are in the other world, we do not know what they believe will happen in our world."

"It is for you to consult them and seek their pro-prophecies relating to my intentions. Should I marry another wife or can any of my present wives give me a son. What should I do?"

"I assume that none of your wives know that you want to add to their number"

"Sago-Gbo, before I get to that point, I want to know what my ancestors will say. It seems but logical and fair to them. Don't you agree?"

"Yes, I do. I will do the necessary rites and hope they will respond immediately."

Sago-Gbo reached for his bag and took several objects. Some were sheep's horns wrapped at the open end with red taffeta and tied with white thread and another was a bottle again wrapped with the same red taffeta and planted with white cowries. Then he spread a hide of leopard skin on the floor before him. He also

4

took out from the bag smooth whitish pebbles the size of an egg and placed them on the hide. He turned round from where he was seated and grabbed a mirror that was face down at his back. Next, he took one red kola nut and one white that Bondaa had given him and split them. He took a third kola nut bit a half of it, chewed it and spewed out the chewed substance on the red bottle and the horns holding them in his hand. He next mumbled a few words of incantation and threw the four halves of the kola nuts on the hide. Three turned face up and one face down. He gathered them and repeated the process. This time one half was face up and three were face down.

"Bondaa, did you have any misunderstanding with anybody recently?" Sago-Gbo asked.

"I don't really remember having any issue with anybody lately. Except the minor incident with Ngefo over my axe which he borrowed and brought back with a broken handle. I asked him to repair it, but he thought it was a minor thing and that I could do that myself. I did not think that was a fitting and appropriate response to my kind gesture because I loaned him my axe in the first place."

"You know that this world is full of mean people? They will return your good favour with evil. This is the first message I have received from your ancestors. They say that Ngefo is not pleased with what you have asked him to do."

He gathered the kola nut halves again and said, "Pa Hanwa, Pa Labilow, Pa Korwaa, Pa Kaigbo, Pa Yetima-Sandi, Yakoni, Yabuthu, Yahengbeh-na and all you ancestors of Bondaa who have gone ahead of him for your final rest, Bondaa has come to seek your approval on whether he should marry another wife as he has not been given a son. What do you want me to tell him?"

He threw the kola nut halves again on the hide. One white and one red half turned face up and the others face down. Bondaa was anxiously watching all these rites with an expectation of a positive response. When he observed that two kola nuts halves are face up, his face lightened up thinking they had an answer.

"Bondaa your ancestors seem to be evenly divided over your marriage proposal. Maybe you should talk to them directly? Sago-Gabo cautioned.

"Here take these two pebbles and speak to them, but I should not hear what you want to tell them, and they must be unanimous in their decision. When you're finished throw the pebbles onto the hide."

Sago-Gbo handed the pebbles to Bondaa who rubbed the two pebbles between his palms while muttering inaudible words to the pebbles. When he was satisfied with what he had to say to his ancestors he threw the pebbles on the hide as he had been instructed. Sago-Gbo looked at the mirror and peered into it as if looking at a figure in it. He took up all the pebbles and uttered some inaudible words whilst blowing on them and threw them on the hide. He again threw the four halves of kola nuts on the hide. This time, two white halves and one red turned face up and one red face down.

"Take any two pebbles from the hide and talk to them again as they seem to be nearing a consensus. Maybe you omitted something which is vital to the proposal. So, make your request as complete as you can, leaving nothing that is essential to your proposal."

Bondaa took two pebbles from the pack on the hide, rubbed them between his palms and uttered a short inaudible incantation again and threw the pebbles on the hide. Then Sago-Gbo took the mirror once more and repeated what he did earlier. However, before gathering the pebbles he took the bottle and shook its contents and rested it again. He took the horns in both hands and chanted something which Bondaa could not comprehend. Then he gathered the pebbles and muttered some chanting words as he shook them in his hands. He opened his hands, blew on the pebbles in his hands and then gently threw them on the hide. He repeated this with the four kola nut halves and all the four halves were face up.

"Ah! We seem to have an answer, but we have to be certain on this." So, he repeated the rites with the pebbles and kola nut halves and the result was the same but this time all four haves were face down.

"We still have an answer, but we need total confirmation." Sago-Gbo once more went through the ritual and the outcome was the same, all halves were face up. Bondaa who has been bending over the hide with intense expectation leaned over with a sigh of relief.

"Ah ha. There you are. We've had a confirmation to your proposal, Bondaa. But there may be something they may want to add to just agreeing. So, I need to listen to what else they want to say to you." Sago-Gbo said taking the two horns and holding them both before him. He chanted a few inaudible words and then asked Bondaa to open his palms and he placed them in Bondaa's palms.

While thanking them for the answer, he felt they may have conditions attached or something more than just marrying a wife.

"Talk to them as before. But this time implore them to tell you what comes with marriage. This time you don't rub them in your palms. Hold them close to your chest and speak."

Bondaa took the horns and did as he'd been instructed by Sago-Gbo. He muttered several words to the horns and handed them back to Sago-Gbo who then put them close to the bottle. He took the mirror and peered in it as in the previous occasions but for a much longer period occasionally nodding his head indicating agreement or shaking it sideways showing disappointment. Bondaa became even more tense and anxious than before as this s the most critical part of consulting the ancestors to know what conditions they stipulate to make your supplication or entreaty come to pass.

"What are they telling you Sago-Gbo? I'm curious to know what I must do if I should have a son. Even if it might be a difficult task to accomplish, just say it."

"Here is what they have for you: you can marry a third wife, but you must not send away any of your present wives. The woman you're going to marry should be light skinned, medium height with bright big brown eyes and plenty of hair. On the day you are going to show yourself to the parents of the woman you wish to marry, your present two wives must accompany you."

"But Sago-Gbo, you know that our tradition requires that before you marry another wife, you should discuss the issue with your present wife or wives. In fact, I was told by my mother that she identified her mate for my father even before he set eyes on her. Now that the ancestors agree with me to have a son to carry on the family name, I'll take the appropriate time to discuss and explain the rationale for my intention to my wives in the hope that they will understand."

"There is something they relayed to me. Your new wife will bear you a son within a short time after she comes to you. Three months after naming the child, send him and the mother to her maternal parents. They should not stay in your house beyond that period."

"Do the ancestors foresee any foul play or evil within the house?"

"I'm sure they have a very good reason for that. You send your wife and the baby away to his maternal grandparents and they should stay there until the child is two years old. After that you have to perform a special purification of your home before mother and child can return."

"That means that I have to maintain two homes?"

"Bondaa don't ask me that. You want another wife to get you a son, not so? Well, that is what your ancestors say you must do. It is what they relayed through me to you. If you want a son, the choice is yours: maintain two homes and have your family name continued or your ancestral foundations are ruined forever. So, make up your mind"

"No, no Sago-Gbo. You've gone too far. I was just pondering how I have to work much harder to do that"

"I have something else to tell you. Your son should not hunt but can climb any palm tree to tap palm wine or cut palm fruits. He should not swim in any stream with swift currents. Your son will be a man of stature and fame."

"So, I perceive that he is going to surpass me in my blacksmith prowess and dexterity".

"That was not what your ancestors revealed to me. They only indicated that he will be a person of fame. It will be your part as the father to guide him to be what he will want to be. Furthermore, he will travel to distant lands in his life and will return to fame back home."

"Are you saying that my future son will leave me alone when all her sisters would have been married and living with their husbands?"

"That seems to be the case. Sometimes we must be watchful of the attendant consequences of what we ask from our ancestors," Sago-Gbo mused.

"That's true. But I believe that he'll continue with the lineage after I join my forefathers. "What else have they got for me and my future son?"

"You have to offer to your ancestors a sacrifice for mercy for arousing them from their peaceful rest and another as thanksgiving for granting your request. Each sacrifice must be a hefty brown bull and two fully grown rams. Your ancestors have been very generous to you. It appears to me that they appreciate what you did for them while some of them were on earth."

"What season of the year did they specify these sacrifices should be offered?"

"Again, they have been liberal with that. They say that you can do them separately but within six months and you can choose the season."

"Well, that gives me much time to search around for the bulls and to prepare for the second sacrifice. "Anything more, Sago-Gbo?" Bondaa asked

"I don't think I have left out anything from what they told me. I have relayed their message fully to you and now you have to offer the sacrifices and do what they have asked of you. Now you must take me off this mat."

Bondaa knows exactly what Sago-Gbo means by *taking him off* the mat. He had to give Sago-Gbo something in appreciation of what he had done.

He dipped his right hand in his front breast pocket again and took out a twenty leones note and placed it on the leopard hide, which brought a broad smile to Sago-Gbo's face. Bondaa rose and bade Sago-Gbo good night and left the shrine walking backwards by tradition. He sauntered off to his house, without meeting a single soul on the way, listening to the constant barking of dogs. He'd received a positive answer on a matter that has bothered his life, and this filled him with much satisfaction and joy. As he approached his house, he imagined himself sharing his home with a son and not being the only man in the house. Bondaa entered his house without knocking as the door was unlocked since the wives had left him relaxing in his hammock and went straight to bed.

CHAPTER TWO

In his household Bondaa is the early bird but this morning he is awakened by his first wife who slept with him last night.

"*Kayneh* Bondaa, wake up. What's wrong today? Are you not well?"

"Um-um. Hogaii. Is it already day?"

"Yes, it is unusual for you to be in bed up to this time. Is anything the matter?"

"No, Hogaii it is just that I had an extra sleep."

"It is because you stayed out too late last night in that hammock."

"Maybe, but I am fine. Get me some water to wash my face and prepare myself to join my brother villagers on the communal road brushing."

Hogaii brought him the water in a calabash, and he quickly washed his face, walked to the right corner of the room, took his machete, and headed straight for the road leading to the next village. He found that the village head was busy cutting out equal plots for each person to brush. Bondaa chose the third plot and started to brush. He felt energized by the prospect of having a son who will in future take his place in farming. He finished his plot well ahead of anybody and the others were wondering about his extra energy not knowing that he had been motivated and inspired by the promise of a son.

"Bondaa did you take a bit of palm wine so early this morning to boost your energy and help you to finish your plot so quickly? Korthombeh asked.

"No because you know that it is too early to climb a palm tree, and you know that the town crier announced that every adult male should report here for the first task of the day. I can't afford to be fined for failing to show up at the right time."

"I guess you are right. One should keep the little resource you have instead of losing it because you failed to do a very minor thing."

"Now that I have completed my plot I must be going because I have to go to help my daughters on the farm to scare birds from picking up the little rice I have sowed. You know that I don't have a son as you who are blessed with two."

"I perfectly understand your situation and I wish you God's speed."

Bondaa left the rest still struggling to complete their plots and rushed to his farm. As he approached, he heard his daughters shouting and throwing stones at the birds with a sling. He stood still for a few moments to ponder in his mind what it will be like when his daughters get married. He must not delay any further but should start the process to get himself a third wife.

Each night when the early-teen-daughters are cither out playing with other girls in the village open play space or the younger ones are sleeping, Bondaa and his wives would review activities on the farm for that day. So, on that fateful night, Bondaa mentioned to his wives that he must visit their villages to discuss an important matter with some members of their families.

"What is this important matter? I would have thought that before you go to our families you would give us an idea of what you want to discuss with them." Hogaii posed what seemed a critical suggestion.

"Yes *Kayneh* Bondaa, I agree with Hogaii," Bendihe butted in. "I believe we know our relatives better. They still listen to us, and we certainly have some sway over some of them. We can talk to them to see your point depending on what you have in mind"

"This is an issue which affects our family. I think that all three families should know the concerns of our own family here at Magoronwa."

"What is this concern? Do you suspect any of us of harlotry around in the village?" Bendihe asked.

"Or is there a witch in the family that you want to expose?" Hogaii posed her own question.

"No… no… no... N-o-o-o, my dear wives. Neither of the two issues you have raised is the problem. You women have been so faithful to me and each of you have given me three lovely and hardworking daughters. I have never questioned your fidelity to me, nor have I experienced any hardship or major sickness in the family that I could attribute to witchcraft."

"Then what is it?" Hogaii asked again. "Is it about the upcoming initiation of the two older girls in the bondo society? I can assure you that Bendihe and I will work extra hard to make our daughters proud when they are in the society bush"

"It will also be my pride to see that they go through initiation with great dignity and satisfaction. But that too is not what I want to discuss with your families."

"I heard through your cousin that Mbaabaga is quarrelling with you over that piece of swamp where we farmed last year claiming it to be his great grandfather's?" Hogaii suggested to Bondaa

"Hogaii that is not a reason for my wish to see your families. I can assure you that I will handle Mbaabaga, he needs a much older person to narrate to him how his forefathers came to Magoronwa. He does not know much about his forefathers' motherland, or he will think twice about picking up a quarrel with me over that swamp."

"Oh, I see. I think *Kayneh* Bondaa would like to be the next section chief of Dohahun section" Bendihe intervened. "It is an honourable idea and I assure you that Hogaii, being my senior mate and myself will secure the support of our families. Is that not so Hogaii?"

"*Kayneh* Bondaa, you should not even blink an eye to doubt our total support for your aspirations if you are keen to become the next section chief. In fact, we will pledge our valuables to raise money for you, Bondaa; we promise you that faithfully."

"Yes, I do have an eye on that possibility because I am qualified in many respects to be section chief. Who follows me next when I am appointed is what bothers me. Becoming a section chief is indeed important but that is not the issue I have in mind."

"What else could be the reason for you wanting to see our families? I can think of nothing else", Bendihe said sounding somewhat irritated.

"Bendihe, you don't have to be annoyed because you have not been able to decipher what I have in mind to discuss with your families. It is not a matter that should cause any of you to be irritated. But let me ask both of you: is there anything missing in our family which every family has in Magoronwa?"

The wives looked at each other and then faced Bondaa in total bewilderment at his question. They know that their husband is not only the blacksmith of the village earning a handsome income but did equally well as a successful farmer. He's got a better house than most men in the village; he has farmlands and swamps, numerous economic trees such as kola nut, coconut, and orange trees.

In addition, he owns more sheep and goats than anybody in the village. He has two wives who have given him six daughters. Then it donned on Hogaii that her husband is the only male in the family.

"It's about the family name." Hogaii said in a low tone that suggested that something was out of place. "Kayneh Bondaa needs somebody to carry on the family name."

"What about the family name?" Bendihe asked

"Wake up Bendihe. You don't seem to get it, do you? Wake up and think straight."

"But *Kayneh* Bondaa has several close relatives who have the family name."

Bondaa realized that Hogaii has hit the nail on the head and so decided to listen to his wives and not intervene for now until they both understand the issue at hand.

"He doesn't need a close relative to carry on his family name for him. Bendihe, you have two brothers by your mother and another three with your mother's mate. Is that right?"

"Yes, I do. As a matter of fact, my father has another son by another woman who left him before my brothers were born."

"When you were chosen to become his wife, you left your father and came to your husband"

"Yes, that is what is expected of me after he has performed all the traditional marriage rites."

"When you came away, your brothers remained behind with your father until his death, right?"

"True and they have more or less succeeded him."

"Well, our husband does not have a son to do that when he's gone."

"Hogaii," Bondaa stepped in at this stage. "That is the reason why I never undertake anything major for this family without first intimating it to you two, especially you my senior wife. You have certainly figured out what I want to talk to your families about." Then he turned to Bendihe.

"Bendihe, you rightly said that your brothers stayed until your father's death and that they have stepped into his shoes. Both of you have three daughters each. You also know that the oracles have said that I will not have a son by any of you. I don't have a son that will take my blacksmith craft and continue with the family trade and name."

"What are you going to do? Adopt one of your brother's sons to be an apprentice and to succeed you after you go join your forefathers? Don't you think that is one way of solving this family name issue?"

"Yes, that may be one way, but I do not think it is the best way for either of us or for Bondaa." Hogaii said. "We both know that our wombs have been cursed by a member from each of our families; we can never bear male children, nor can we have more children. You know that both of us have consulted many soothsayers and other oracles and the message has been the same."

"Hogaii what are you trying to tell me? That *Kayneh* Bondaa has to marry a second mate to me so that he could get his son?" Bendihe questioned Hogaii in an obvious jealous tone.

"That question Bendihe is not for me to answer. Bondaa is right here with us why don't you ask him? I am certain that he will give us an answer."

Bendihe turned to face Bondaa, and she halted a moment thinking that Bondaa will answer. But he never uttered a word until Bendihe asked the question:

"Are you going to marry another wife?"

For several moments Bondaa did not respond. He bowed down his head as if thinking of something else to add to what he and Hogaii have clearly explained to Bendihe. Then he sat up straight in his hammock for all this time he has been reclining in it and slightly swinging in sideways, he removed the butt of the Sangotho he was smoking and cleared his throat.

"Hogaii, Bendihe. You both know that I love you and you also know that I have not been unfaithful or involved in any infidelity whatsoever. You know because I have never been summoned in court for *woman palaver*. I am proud of myself and am fully aware that you too have been equally faithful to me. We have lovely and beautiful daughters who are the pride in this village. The older ones are comporting themselves well under your watchful eyes and guidance. Give ourselves another three years and even before they go through the *bondo* initiation suitors will be streaming at our front door asking for their hands in marriage. And you know that the greatest wish of all parents for their daughter is for a good looking, respectable and responsible man to propose to marry her as I did for you two. When you ladies took my calabash as an acceptance of my proposal, my parents asked that you should come over to my house that very night. Is that not so?"

"It is so, and I had to come back home the next day to collect the rest of my belongings," Bendihe answered.

"Since then, have you returned home for more than a few days on a visit or when the family is bereaved?"

"In several instances the visits have been with you especially if there is an occasion in the family" Hogaii replied.

"Then shall we allow our daughters to break the norm and be permanently with us? They will all be snatched from us even before we know it. And then what do you think will happen to the three of us?"

"We shall be left to ourselves with no one to do certain chores for us. It will mean that we will find it embarrassing having constantly to ask our relatives to give us a child to take care of who will do the chores we will be unable to do." Bendihe replied as she begins to understand the issue.

"It is even more serious when I get old and unable to farm to feed us. I know you two are not asking for favours from anybody and I don't think you will want to depend on hand-outs from family members or the village community," Bondaa stressed.

"This Nwoingoha family is too dignified and proud to depend on hand-outs. You experienced that when my father was alive but old, I took over the blacksmith hut. I had already learned the craft before I married you two. I also took over the farming and other activities and I took care of him and his wives with you as my capable hardworking helpers until their death."

"You are still that hardworking man," Hogaii commended.

"Thank you, but this will fade with age. We don't have a trusted person that will take care of us in our old age with social security needs, Bendihe. You cannot rely on children of other family members, as they too may have to take care of their old folks. You should also not forget that the Nwoingoha clan has had a high reputation not only in this village but also in surrounding villages. I don't have a son and it is a dilemma for me. But particularly so for Nwoingoha as we risk being forgotten in this chiefdom as a notable clan if I, the only male heir, do not have a male successor. To save the clan from obscurity and extinction, I think the only proper legitimate thing for me to do is to take a third wife. But I cannot do this without telling you and getting you fully involved in the process. It is only when you see the rationale behind my thinking will I approach your families for further discussions."

"Bendihe, I had foreseen this coming for some time now. I could not foresee its arrival" Hogaii commented.

"This never crossed my mind Hogaii, especially when the family is united, happy and hardworking." Bendihe replied.

"In addition to those three family qualities you have just stated," Bondaa interjected, "we need continuity of this clan, its trades, values, beliefs and tenets after we are gone. I don't believe that you will disagree with me on this."

"No, we don't" the wives replied in unison.

"We can only do that through a son who we hope will have a male child also to inherit the clanship glory after him," Bondaa said.

"That I also agree with you," concurred Hogaii "and I want to give my consent for you to go ahead and marry another mate to me. There is one condition though to my consent: and that is we shall fully receive our normal rights and entitlements as your wives, nothing less indeed maybe something more. No special treatment for your new wife"

"I join Hogaii in the consent and we pray to God that He will give you a woman with the womb to give you a son who will also have grandsons. But let me say this: you don't neglect us because you would have had a young wife who will certainly not be more beautiful than any of us. To do that will be to usher in disaster in the family."

Bondaa could not believe his ears when he heard the consent given by his wives. He asked them to repeat what they'd just said.

"We consent to your desire to marry a third wife but not at the expense of our rights, respect and entitlements as your senior wives."

"I thank you from the bottom of my heart and may God and His good spirits bless your daughters so that they will have good husbands as I have been to you."

"I know that this is not an issue for our daughters to know right now but we shall prepare their minds when the time comes for your new wife to join our family," Hogaii offered. "You will no doubt agree that it is normal for children to seek the interest of their mothers in such situations."

"Hogaii has pointed out a very crucial issue," Bendihe emphasized in agreement with Hogaii. "It will be good to have a son who will bear the Nwoingoha name, but we do not want a situation where our family will be disunited because another wife has joined us. We all have a future task tempering the minds of our daughters."

"I certainly see your concerns and I totally agree with you both" Bondaa acquiesced with his wives' premonition. "I know that they don't have a say regarding my wish to have another wife, but they will have to live with her. It will be essential, as Hogaii suggested that we prepare them to accept your new mate when she comes in. They should also contemplate that a similar situation might face them in their marriages, and they may have to give consent for another mate just as you have done."

"When do you propose to see our families now that you have our consents?" Bendihe asked.

"You know that I cannot go to my in-laws to talk to them without taking the customary handshake and other gifts. It must be after we have harvested the swamp rice so that we can take a bushel of clean rice with us. Besides, the kola nuts are yet very young, and they will take another two months to mature."

"I think we have totally exhausted this issue" Hogaii concluded, "I am going to bed as I have my group of community workers coming tomorrow to help us finish weeding the swamp rice. Good night Kayneh Bondaa. Good night Bendihe. You too should go to bed as you have to prepare food for them."

"Good night to you both. I am glad that we have resolved an issue which has been troubling me for quite some time. A heavy family weight has been lifted from my shoulders. I'll sleep like a log tonight"

The two wives went in and left Bondaa in his hammock gently swinging it sideways. He took out his pipe from his breast pocket, emptied the bowl and loaded it with freshly cut Sangotho. He slowly set it alight drawing long puffs of smoke. Then he began pondering over the things he must do before meeting his in-laws of the two families. Visiting in-laws entails certain unavoidable expenditure. He must carry a sizeable gourd of fresh tasty palm wine which he taps. The palm wine is meant to enlighten the hearts of the partakers. And if it is more than the normal quality, he will receive approvals and compliments of those who'll participate in drinking it. He will also carry one hundred kola nuts since kola nut chewing is a common habit for most village people. The palm wine and kola nuts will not be a headache for him since he taps his own palm wine, and he inherited a quarter of the Magoronwa kola nut forest from his father. In view of what he's going to pose to the in-laws he must carry a fully grown and fattened he-goat of any colour except black and a bushel of clean parboiled rice. In addition to all these he must get money for customary handshake. The bushel of rice he could get from his swamp rice after harvest and his wives will parboil it and later clean it. Bondaa's remaining worry was that he must search in other villages for a he-goat because his village people unanimously agreed not to rear small ruminants as they destroy crops in their freedom since they've not been tied or confined. He has sold all his flock of goat and sheep as he had nobody to take care of them. Now he has not the vaguest clue on how much one would cost him. This is a task he must do alone as the wives will not be involved in the acquisition of the necessities for his missions. With this final thought he puffed his last smoke and retired to bed.

CHAPTER THREE

Three months have elapsed after Bondaa had the consent of his wives to marry a third wife and yet he has still not obtained all the items that he needed for his visit to in-laws. 'How will I get the money for customary shake-hand and to purchase the he-goat' he questioned himself? The thought came to him that he had inherited several farm and swamp lands from his father many of which he had not farmed for a long time. Several men in the village had asked him to allow them to farm on them, but he had refused. He feared that if they worked on them for long, they might claim to own these lands eventually. His fear was buttressed by the fact that he has no son who knows about these lands and swamps. Now that his ancestors have delivered a message through Sago-Gbo that he will have a son that will be of great fame and stature through a third wife, he felt that he could pledge one of his swamp lands to raise the money if he failed to raise a short loan. But decided that he will do so in the full knowledge of the village elders.

One evening immediately after he had his meal and drunk a few cups of his palm wine, he decided to go to Yeemor, the village trader to try his luck at borrowing some money from him. Bondaa went to his house when he was just about to lock his little shop.

"Bondaa, good evening. What do you want as I am preparing to close the shop?

"Yeemor, I hope all's well with you? I don't need anything from the shop. I just came for your personal help."

"Okay, let me lock the shop and we shall sit in the veranda to talk. Please help me draw that door close to you and press it firmly until I put the tower bolts down from inside."

Bondaa obliged. After satisfactorily locking the shop from inside Yeemor came out through a side door to join Bondaa in the veranda.

"So, how can I help you?"

"My urgent need is money. I need five hundred Leones to accomplish an urgent private family affair," Bondaa explained; Yeemor looked puzzled. "And I'm sure you do not want to know the detail and I promise you faithfully that I will repay you back next month when I harvest and thresh my rice. The village community work group will be at my swamp next *juma* to harvest my rice. If you wish, I could pay you then in kind."

"I appreciate your need Bondaa, but I'm sorry I can't help you because somebody came this afternoon and borrowed seven hundred Leones. What is left is what I have reserved to replenish my stock as you can observe my shop is nearly empty. I cannot risk lending you my reserve in the interest of my business."

"How about two hundred Leones? That will go some way to meet my need?" Bondaa asked desperately.

"Sorry, that too I cannot afford. I promise to help next time. But for tonight, I am in no position to help."

"Well in that case I will not delay you further" Bondaa conceded. "Go to bed to join your wife as you were already closing up when I showed up. Good night and we'll see tomorrow."

Bondaa left the house feeling somewhat dejected. As he headed home, he remembered that Korwaa had approached him twice for a land to farm but, he had turned him down. He could not go to his village friend, Fokogbo, because he too had approached him two days ago for a loan and he doesn't think he will have the amount of money he wanted. So, he decided to check on Korwaa to find out whether he will be interested in a pledge. He knew that Korwaa had no land because his parents emigrated to Magoronwa about ten years ago and they own no farmlands or swamps. Before every farming season he must rent land to farm. Bondaa believed that if he offered him a pledge of swamp land for five years, he would be relieved of the yearly embarrassment of being turned down by somebody. He walked to Korwaa's house and found him in the veranda sitting in his favourite reclining wooden bench, smoking his pipe.

"Korwaa, good evening," he greeted.

"Who is that?" Korwaa asked as he could not see Bondaa approaching in the dark.

"It's me Bondaa"

"Oh, Bondaa, I could not see you"

"You're right; there is no light now as the moon is late coming out."

"Please come in and have a seat." Bondaa walked into the veranda and took the bench next to Korwaa.

"Is something wrong?" Korwaa asked.

"Oh no, I just came to discuss some matter that could be of interest to you."

"Before you do that can we have some of my palm wine, which is right by my side here?"

"Why not, although I just drank some of mine before I came over hoping to go back and finish it before going to bed."

Korwaa pulled the gourd of palm wine took his improvised tumbler (a pint cut in half) from under his seat and poured out the wine. He took the first full tumbler as the custom requires and poured another from the same tumbler and gave it to Bondaa which he gulped down.

"This palm wine is great. Mine is still young and this is so mature."

"I have been tapping it for the past three months"

"That's why it is so strong and yet tasty." He handed over the tumbler.

"You said you are here to discuss something that will be of interest to me?" Korwaa reminded Bondaa as he was pouring him another glassful.

"That's true, Korwaa. How was your harvest this year?"

"It was not as I expected because the land was quite small. I could not get anybody to lease me a bigger plot, so, I had to farm what I could get from Gborni this year. However, for the next season, I plan to ask you, once more, to reconsider your stand."

"Well, I have a proposal for you. Would you like to take a pledge from me over the swamp near Rogbalan village? I am giving you the right of first refusal because I know how desperately you needed somewhere to farm this year."

"The swamp with the cane bushes?" He asked after gulping his second tumbler of palm wine.

"Yes, but if you take it, you don't harvest my cane bushes because I have a plan for them." Bondaa cautioned him. "I'm prepared to take five hundred Leones that works out at a hundred per year. But I want all the money within the next three days."

Korwaa handed Bondaa another tumbler full of palm wine.

"I want to thank you first for the thought. Second, I will accept the offer, but you will get my final answer tomorrow evening. Will that be alright with you?"

"Yes. But if I don't see you by tomorrow evening it will mean that you're not interested." He handed over again the empty tumbler to Korwaa. "But if you do show up with the money, I want us to make the arrangement in the presence of the village elders, your son and my nephew Yongaa so they can be future witnesses as I do not have a son."

"I don't think that is unreasonable for either of us. I have a son and you don't. Another cup of palm wine for you?"

"No, thank you. Don't forget I told you I still have my bit to finish when I get home. I must go now and thank you for the nice palm wine."

With that, Bondaa returned home feeling satisfied that he has nearly solved the most difficult part of his marriage requirements. He finished his gourd of palm wine and retired to bed. Korwaa came to Bondaa the next evening as he'd promised and told him that he has got four hundred Leones, which left him short by a hundred.

"I promise that tomorrow after we have concluded this before the village elders and your nephew, I will certainly bring the balance"

"You will have to confirm that to the elders and my nephew. Shall we go to Pa Kombolo who will quickly summon his elders as I believe at this time every household has had their meal."

Arriving at Pa Kombolo's house Bondaa quickly explained the purpose of their visit after performing the customary handshake of five Leones and six kola nuts of all white or three red and three white but not all red. The elders quickly responded to Pa Kombolo's call and all gathered in his veranda.

"Elders of Magoronwa, I have summoned you because Bondaa and Korwaa want to tell us something that could be of benefit to my family and our village also. Bondaa the elders have their ears opened to hear what you want to tell them."

"Pa Kombolo and elders of Magoronwa!" Bondaa said. "I have come with Korwaa and his son Gbaagor and my nephew Yongaa to inform you that I have decided to pledge my swamp land near Rogbalan village to Korwaa for an annual rent of five hundred Leones for five years. I must take care of a pressing personal need. I tried to borrow money from somebody, but the person turned me down. But then I thought it was good that he refused because when you borrow money from someone and you are not in position to pay back, you face harassment by debt collectors. I, therefore, decided to pledge my swamp. But we all know in this village that the person who needs farmland most is Korwaa. So, I approached him with my proposal, and he has accepted."

"Is that correct Korwaa?" Pa Kombolo asked.

"That is the correct Pa Kombolo. Bondaa's proposal came as a complete surprise to me as I have approached him twice before for farmland and each time, he flatly turned me down. His proposal is quite good and acceptable to me as well as my son who is here with me as a witness for the future."

"Repeat what you have agreed upon again for everybody to hear and know the arrangements because we all have a final call." Commanded elder Gbaagor.

"He asked me for an annual rent of one hundred Leones, and he will pledge his swamp for five years to me," Korwaa replied.

"Do you confirm that Bondaa?" Pa Kombolo asked.

"Yes, Pa Kombolo. He has already given me four hundred Leones and has a balance of hundred Leones"

"I want you all to know that I have promised to give him of hundred Leones tomorrow without fail and by the grace of God."

"Yes, that is the arrangement we have agreed upon and we want you and the elders to be witnesses. I have brought my nephew, Yongaa, my elder's sister's son as a witness since I have only daughters and no son yet."

"Bondaa, you need to inform us if he brings in the balance on time, otherwise the pledge years should be six months short. Is that a fair deal, elders?" Pa Kombolo asked his elders.

"That is what it is supposed to happen in all land pledges" the elders agreed.

"Bondaa, I speak on behalf of the elders," said Pa Kombolo. "You have done a great thing for Korwaa and for the village. We are grateful to you because if Korwaa has a good harvest of rice, the village has more to eat. We wish that this arrangement will work out profitably for both of you. So let us know Bondaa when Korwaa brings the hundred Leones. Good-night, everybody. I am not asking you to partake of my palm wine because my nephew brought me just what's enough for me."

"Good night, Pa Kombolo. I will bring you some tomorrow evening" Korwaa's son promised. The gathering ended and all returned to their respective houses.

When he woke up next morning, Bondaa thought about the bushels of clean parboiled rice which is the next major need for his mission. He is blessed that this year he will have a bumper harvest. His swamp rice is ready for harvest, and he must prepare for the village community working group to come and harvest it for him in the next three days. On such occasions he knew as the host farmer that he must satisfactorily feed the group and that entailed preparing good soup with plenty of bush meat. As a trap setter this did not worry him. His concern was whether the group will completely harvest his swamp on that same day. Two days before the group's arrival he checked his traps and found a big wild boar was whining and squealing in one of his pit traps. He brought in the local hunter to shoot it with his *chakabula*. In another trap, he found a deer trapped and already dead from trap's strangulation. Bondaa thus had more than enough to cater for village workers when they come to work for him. So, when the village group had its break meal, Bondaa was full of commendations and compliments. He was also applauded for making them eat to satisfaction. Consequently, the group could only leave a very small portion of the swamp un-harvested which Bondaa and his family could harvest in two days.

A few days after the harvest, Bondaa measured five bushels of husk rice to be parboiled by his wives. He estimated that these five bushels would yield him the two bushels of clean rice he needs for his two missions and a little extra for the home. He briefed his wives.

"Hogaii, I have measured five bushels of husk rice and put in that large cane basket so that the chicken and ducks will not get at it. I want you people to parboil it and clean it afterwards." He spoke to his senior wife.

"I am preparing for our visits to your families to present my case to them"

"Kayneh Bondaa, you know that rice is the least of your worries for your mission. We will do as you have directed. Though it is not my place to ask, yet what about the other things that you need?"

"Yes, Hogaii! It is your right to ask. I am working on those also. It will not be long before I finally get things together."

"You are aware that putting together all that you need is solely your task?" Bendihe reminded their husband whilst standing at the far end of the back yard winnowing some sorghum.

"However, we will do the part which we cannot avoid in doing like parboiling and cleaning the rice."

"I have no quarrel with either of you on that. I am working out some things and when they are all in place, I will certainly tell you before we go."

"What do you mean when you say, 'before we go'?" Bendihe asked.

"Do you think that I will leave you behind when I go to my in-laws on this issue? No, you must be there because they will ask you if this is with your consent. I will not be the one to give them the answer. It will best for them to hear it directly from you, Bendihe. They'll believe you if you tell them that you and your mate have agreed. Bendihe, have you forgotten that Hogaii was present when I went with my parents to ask for your hand? Did she not give a clear response?"

"I was there willingly, and I confirmed my consent again to Bondaa that night to the hearing of all present" Hogaii confirmed. "I have to do it for a second time.

The first time it was difficult for me to see you with Bondaa. But this time it is different as we have seen his reasoning and the rationale behind it."

"I think I am in the same position as you were when you gave your consent for me"

"Ladies, haven't we passed this critical stage, and do you think that it is time for me to go on the next phase? So, when do you people think the rice will be ready?"

"I think in another two days or so" Bendihe replied.

"Okay. I must be at Magaaho by a little before sunset as that is the time the boys are bringing in the goats and sheep from the field. I am going there to search for he-goats. I will be back before people go to bed."

He went in his room, took clean clothes from his wooden box, and soon set off to walk to Magaaho. He decided to have his bath at the stream crossing the road just after the village before changing to his clean clothes. He reached in time as the young boys were guiding in goats and sheep into pens. He went to a boyhood friend Simanie to whom he explained his purpose to his village.

"Well, you have come to the right village. Although we have so many small ruminants, yet we lose most of the vegetables and fruits we grow in our backyards to them. You were wise to ban the rearing of small ruminants in Magoronwa."

"However, there is a disadvantage that goes with that, and I am forced to come here to look for he-goats. From whom do you think I will get two full grown he-goats?"

"We'll go to Ngandiya. He has the fortune of rearing small ruminants, and he has several of what you have come for. But we shall go after we've had our meal and when we return you have the chance again to drink my palm wine." Bondaa and Fokogboh went to Ngandiya as they had agreed. They found him seated in his veranda with his son drinking palm wine.

"Good evening Ngandiya, I hope you are in good spirits as I see that you are having palm wine with your son"

"Good evening Simanie. Is this not Bondaa from Magoronwa? You are both welcome. There are benches over there in the corner. You have come when I am taking the last cup of palm wine."

"That's okay with us as I have my gourd still intact and we shall return to it from here," Fokogboh remarked.

"Why are you here with Bondaa this evening?"

"My long-time friend wants to marry a third wife and you know what is required of you when you already have two wives in your house."

"So Bondaa you are here for two he-goats, am I right?"

"You know exactly what my needs are. Can you help me?"

"I think I can, depending on whether we shall agree on the price"

"Ngandiya, remember what I told you. Bondaa is my friend, and I don't want to be disappointed as I have already boasted that he will get the goats from you."

"How much are you are you asking for a full grown he-goat?" Bondaa asked Ngandiya.

"It's not much, only forty Leones for a goat. I'm asking that price considering that my village brother has brought you to me."

"That is reasonable, but may I ask for a small reduction so that I can pay thirty Leones for one as I need two?"

"Ngandiya, I want to join my friend to appeal for a reduction because you and I know that he has more needs to meet before he could make his move."

"I understand that perfectly because I have been through that myself. I will accept your offer. But you know that you can't select a goat at night. So, you have to wait until the morning to make your selection."

"I agree and when I make the selection, I shall pay the price money."

"Then I shall see you in the morning. Good night"

"Thank you Ngandiya. We appreciate your goodwill and kindness," Bondaa expressed his gratitude.

They left Ngandiya and went home to do what Fokogbo had promised, drink palm wine. But Bondaa remembered that he had promised to return to Mago-ronwa before bedtime. He, therefore, told Fokogbo that he would only take a few cups of his palm wine and then would kindly excuse himself to return to keep his promise to his wives. He promised to return early in the morning before the goats are taken out to graze.

Bondaa woke earlier than his usual time to go to Magaaho to collect the goats and head back home before the village community work group begins work. When he appeared at the entrance of the village with two he-goats, some people began to question themselves what he was going to do with them. But nobody dared ask him as it would be considered an intrusion into his personal business and a rude gesture. Bondaa knew that his family was already in the farm, so he went straight to the back of his house and tied the goats where there was adequate grass for them and headed to his farm to join his family.

After his evening meal he called his wives to the verandah to brief them on what he had been able to accomplish.

"I believe that you saw two goats at the back of the house when you came in this afternoon."

"You got them from Magaaho I believe," Hogaii assumed.

"Yes, I bought them through the help of Simanie for sixty Leones. Ngandiya wanted eighty but we prevailed on him to come down to sixty."

"That was kind of him because I have heard that he is very stiff on prices for his animals, especially if he perceives that the buyer is desperate," Bendihe remarked.

"I certainly did not show any desperation. The transaction was quite normal especially with the presence of Simanie," came the assurance.

"It means that I have been able to get all I need to go to my in-laws, because I will pick fresh kola nuts from the forest in the morning of our journey. But I must visit Royeima to buy some things that I need. I will leave early in the morning to be there before the sun is overhead when it will be hot. I will be back in two or three days. But when I am away, I want you Hogaii to supervise the gathering of the rice sheaves in one place. When I return, I shall assemble all in that thatched barn."

Bondaa planned to surprise his wives with gifts as an appreciation of their consent to his quest for a son by marrying another wife. He proposed to give each wife two full dresses of *taymulay and lappa* and head tie in addition to his usual commitment to cloth them each year. So, his trip to Royeima is to buy quality cotton cloths and get a tailor to sew them into dresses before he returns.

At the first cock crow, Bondaa got up because he knew that going to Royeima is a whole day's journey. He took his *managbesse* chewing stick by his bed side and his water jug filled by one wife every night before they go to bed and went outside to brush his mouth and wash his face before he sets out. He grabbed his travelling raffia bag which contained some clean rice to give to whomsoever was going to lodge him and picked up his machete by the door. He bade Hogaii goodbye as she had just started her three-night rotation in his room. Since it was too early in the morning and there was nobody outside, he was greeted by the barking of the dogs. He ignored them and continued to walk through the village as his house is at the other end.

He reached Royeima on the hour when people were returning from their farms. This was his first time coming to this village; besides he does not speak Temne the language spoken here. He is *landorgor* and can only speak *landorgor*. But he knew, according to what his father and other elders in Magoronwa told him, that one of theirs, Pa Woroma, lived in Royeima. He, therefore, thought it reasonable to locate his house and introduce himself. Maybe the connection might cause Pa Woroma to provide him with lodgings. He stopped at the first house and asked for Pa Woroma's house, and a young boy volunteered to accompany him to the house. Bondaa could not see any movement or hear any sound as he approached the house. So the young boy went along the surrounding mud wall to the back. Then a young man came out and greeted Bondaa.

"Greetings to you pa…." the young boy hesitatingly greeted Bondaa.

"My name is Keybalee Bondaa Nwoingoha, but people just call me Bondaa. I am from Magoronwa. Is Pa Woroma in?"

"He is not in now. I am his son. Is there anything I can do in his absence?"

"This is my first visit to your village, and I know nobody. But I was told by my father years ago that a Landorgor man from Magoronwa took refuge in this village. He told me that he established himself here and got accepted by the elders in this village. So, I thought I could seek his hospitality to lodge me."

"He is on his way from the farm, but his routine itinerary in returning home includes visiting his palm wine tapper friend before he finally gets home. But please come to the veranda and have a seat. It will not be long before he will be here."

"Thank you, young man. What is your name?"

"Saibaa Kortu."

"That's a typical Landorgor name. Your father must have given you the name to remember his roots. What about your mother, she too is not back yet from the farm?"

"She is at the back, cooking. I will tell her that papa has a stranger from Magoronwa. I am sure she'll come to greet you."

Saibaa Kortu went back and returned with her mother. She was of similar age and stature as Hogaii only she was light skinned. She came close and curtsied with her right foot slightly bended and stretched out her hand to greet Bondaa in the customary manner.

"Greetings Pa Bondaa. Kortu told me that you are from Magoronwa, the birthplace of Woroma. I am Buffu, Woroma's first wife. It has been a long time since we had a visitor from there. You are welcome to our house."

"Thank you Buffu. I only hope that Woroma will equally welcome me as you and your son have received me."

"I'm sure he will. It will not be long he will be here shortly. Meanwhile let me get back to continue with the cooking."

She left Bondaa and Kortu chatting, the latter curious to know about his ancestral village. Suddenly they heard a voice asking if his bath water has been heated up and it is in the outside enclosed fence thatched with palm fronds.

"That is papa. Whenever you hear that voice asking for that water you know that he is back. The next thing he does is to put his machete in his room before he comes out to the veranda." Kortu said. True to form his father came out of the front door of his room having entered at the back door.

"Kortu, we have a stranger here? Nobody even mentioned that as I came in."

"Papa, I know that you will eventually come out to the veranda before going to have your hot bath."

He approached Bondaa and stretched out his hand and Bondaa grabbed it with warm greetings.

"My name is Bondaa, and I come from Magoronwa, and I know nobody here, but I remembered that my late father once told me that one of their brothers, Woroma, came to Royeima and settled. Before coming to Royeima, I hoped and prayed that he is still alive and that I could ask him to lodge me."

"Oh-o-o. You are the second person that has come to my house in Royeima, thirty years after I came to settle here in Temne land."

" I am pleased to hear that. I only hope that I have not surprised you unduly".

"Not at all Bondaa. Anybody that comes from Magoronwa is welcome to my house. It is the house of the Magoronwa people. You are so very welcome to my house and it's yours too"

"Thank you, I never expected such a wonderful reception. I can see that having the same roots matters to you." Bondaa took out a parcel of kola nut he had wrapped in leaves, untied it to expose the kola nuts and presented them to Pa Woroma.

"I bring greetings from Magoronwa your ancestral village."

"Thank you very much. I had longed for fresh good kola nuts as there are very few kola nut trees in the forests around Royeima. I very much appreciate having the opportunity to chew kola nuts from Magoronwa again."

"Kortu, I think you have to give up your room for Bondaa as we have no guest room. So go and prepare it. Bondaa let me go get my bath and we shall talk about Magoronwa after we've had our meal."

Indeed, after their meal Pa Woroma asked about several people, he'd left behind in Magoronwa when he left for Royeima in the prime of his youth.

"If I am not being impolite, may I ask why you came over here?" Bondaa asked Pa Woroma.

"I had to flee Magoronwa because of woman palaver. The chief at the time fined me a hefty full-grown bull to pay for woman damage I caused to one man at Mayaagun. There was no way I could afford it nor could my father. The only way I could pay that then was to become a slave to whoever provided that bull for me. I chose a better punishment. I banished myself from the chiefdom and took refuge in Sanda chiefdom where the Dohahun chief's jurisdiction could not reach me, nor could I be extradited."

"I believe they took woman damage as a very serious offence to impose such a heavy fine".

"Oh yes, it was, and it is still a serious offence in Sanda Chiefdom, but the fines are not as heavy as in Dohahun chiefdom."

"The offence is still a very serious one in Dohahun. But the old chief, before he passed away, realized that his able-bodied youths were fleeing the chiefdom. In view of that, he decided to reduce the fine for fear that he will lose his chiefdom's workforce."

"We have talked about a lot of things concerning Magoronwa and the chiefdom, but I have forgotten to ask you why you are here. I hope you are not following in my footsteps?"

"No Pa Woroma, I am here to buy and sew for my two wives who have given their consent to marry a third wife."

"Are the two not enough problems for you, my son?"

"They have each given me three lovely daughters, but I don't have a son. Upon consulting my ancestors, they gave me a favourable endorsement to marry a third wife who will give me a son. As a gesture of appreciation for their consent, I want to surprise them with dress gifts. I'm informed that you have a tailor in Royeima, an expert at sewing women's dresses. That is my purpose of coming here"

"Bondaa, you are a very thoughtful husband, and your wives will certainly be pleased. Well, tomorrow I will take you first to Babakaleh's shop to choose the cotton and then we go to Siddie, the tailor. I'll make sure we agree on his charges before I go to the farm so that he will not take advantage of the fact that you are a stranger who cannot speak Temne."

"Thank you, Pa Woroma,"

"I am sorry that I don't have palm wine for us to drink because at my age I don't climb palm trees anymore. Kortu has just tapped two new palm trees and you know that it takes another four to five days before you could get drinkable palm wine."

"Pa Woroma, you don't have to apologize for that. I perfectly understand and besides, once on a while the stomach needs to be free of palm wine."

"Maybe yours but not mine as it has been accommodating palm wine since I was five. I don't think it will be pleased with me if I didn't drink a little bit for the day. But don't worry, I will tell Kortu to ask his friends so that he could bring some for you. Good night Bondaa. We'll see in the morning."

Pa Woroma and Bondaa left the veranda together for the night. In the morning Pa Woroma and Bondaa went to Siddie the tailor after Bondaa has bought two different colours of cotton cloths from Babakaleh's shop. Seeing Pa Woroma, Siddie got up from his sewing machine to greet him and Bondaa.

"Pa Woroma what brings you here this early morning? Is anything wrong with my young friend Kortu?"

"Nothing is wrong, and Kortu is well. He has just left for the farm before me. This is Bondaa my compatriot from Magoronwa."

"You are welcome to Royeima" Siddie stretched his hand again to shake Bondaa's."

"We in Magoronwa have heard that you're famous for sewing women's dresses," Bondda told Siddie.

"Bondaa has come here to sew dresses for his two wives." Woroma offered to inform Siddie. He has bought cotton cloths and he wants you to show your expertise in sewing four dresses out of them. These dresses that you will sew are to be given to his wives as a big surprise for what they have done for him."

"I will be glad to do that for him."

"We know that, but for how much. That's our concern!"

"Well, it depends on the quality of the cotton material and the style chosen."

"Siddie, we are men. We do not know about styles of women's dresses. We leave that choice entirely to you. But remember that it's a surprise, so do your best." Bondaa stressed.

"I will ask for twenty Leones for each dress because I have to use special thread to do a little embroidery."

"Siddie, this man is my brother from my hometown. I do not want him to go back without getting what he has come here because you have charged high, and he may not have the money to pay you. Please make a reduction for my sake and your friend Kortu."

"Pa Woroma, I cannot refuse your request. And besides this is a small world. Sanda Chiefdom shares a common boundary with Dohahun Chiefdom. Who knows, either me or one of my sons might one day go across there to seek similar help. So, I will make it sixteen Leones for each dress that will total sixty-four Leones for all."

"I think that is reasonable enough Pa Woroma. I will pay that," Bondaa accepted

"Thank you Siddie for your concession. But I'm still waiting for your promise. I guess you have forgotten?"

"No, I have not forgotten. I have not been able to get the right thing. Please be patient. I will fulfil my promise."

"Okay then. I must go join Kortu and the family on the farm and leave you and Bondaa to sort out the rest." Then he left.

Siddie took the cloths stretched them open and spread them the floor to see how he could shape the floral designs to tie in with the style he wants to sew.

"When do you plan to return?"

"The day after tomorrow if all works out fine"

"For the style I want to sew these dresses, I don't think I can finish in two days. You probably have to return a day later."

"That will be alright with me. I will simply have to give some explaining to my wives for the extra day before I present them with their gifts. As for sizes, Buffu is a perfect size for my first wife. For the second wife, she is just a little taller but almost the same size."

"Then I will go to Buffu and take her measurements. You can go now, or you can stay and chat with me."

"I will stay since there is nobody in the house. All have gone to the farm, and I know nobody in this town besides Pa Woroma. Maybe tomorrow I will join them to do some work."

Bondaa stayed and they talked over things as if they'd known each other for ages. When Siddie's wife brought him food they both ate together.

Time passed so quickly that they could not believe it. At sun set Bondaa returned home and came back two days afterwards to pay and collect the dresses. But dresses are not the only things that will please his wives. He needed to buy for each wife a headwrap, *bintu el sudan* talc powder, small medium size bottle of Vaseline and sweet-smelling bath soap.

On his way to Pa Woroma's house he visited the same shop and purchased these items. Next day he was ready to return. He will have to start his return journey a little later than he left his house four days ago because he had to bid farewell to Pa Woroma and his family. He thanked them profusely for their generous hospitality and invited Kortu to visit Magoronwa soon to re-establish his family connections.

CHAPTER FOUR

Bondaa returned home late finding the whole village was asleep and he was again welcomed by the barking of dogs. He went straight to his house as the dogs were doing their civic duty by barking at strange objects. He knocked at the front door twice and there is no response, so he called out Bendihe who should be in his room. Bendihe did not ask who it was because she recognized the voice of her husband. She rushed to the door and opened it.

"Welcome back. What happened that you come so late and two days after the day you indicated?" Bendihe asked. "We were worried because we know that the road to Royeima is infested with wild animal, and we feared also for those kidnappers who capture people for ritual sacrifices."

"Nothing threatening happened. I could not do all that I went to do, and I had to take an extra day before I could accomplish my mission. I left Royeima when the sun was just overhead, and it is a far distance from there. I encountered no threats on my way and I am safely here now."

"Thank God you are here. I will dilute the warm water and set it outside for your bath. Your food will be in the room after your bath."

"Thank you". They both went into the room and Bondaa set his raffia bag on the top of his wooden box and went out to have his bath. Immediately after having his meal, he was so tired that he went straight to bed. Even after he has been out for four days from his wives, he did not notice that his wife was in bed with him. He slept like an overfed baby and woke up at his usual time and urged his family to hurry up and go to the swamp farm to scare the birds from the harvested rice. He went ahead of them to ensure that they follow immediately. On reaching the farm he was pleased to find that his wives and daughters have gathered all the sheaves of the harvested rice in one huge pile. On joining them, he immediately started packing the sheaves in the barn. The whole day was devoted to this task, and it was halfway completed when they retired back to the village.

In the evening after Bondaa has had his meal and had his palm wine, he decided to call in his wives in his room for the big surprise he has for them.

"I have just completed my three days in your room. It is Hogaii's turn to go into your room and keep your company," Bendihe protested.

"Don't I know that? You were with me last night and I slept like a log? This has nothing to do with your three-night rotation in my bed."

"If it is a family matter, why can't you tell us here?" Bendihe suggested.

"Bendihe why don't we just go in and hear what Bondaa wants to tell us." Hogaii urged Bendihe, "because we usually discuss all family issues in this veranda. I know it's my turn to join him for the next three days. If he calls us into his room maybe it's something special that he wants to discuss out of earshot of our daughters."

"You are always the more understanding wife, Hogaii," Bondaa observed. "Bendihe often looks at things with a mate's eye and does not give an open mind to certain things. That could lead you to misconstrue people's genuine intentions."

"I did not mean to offend anybody. I just thought that it could be better to talk here in the veranda."

"Are you coming then?"

"I don't think that will be respecting you and humbling myself to you if I sit out here."

"Then be the good wife and let us all go in and hear what I want to say," Bondaa said.

Hogaii and Bendihe took along their low wooden stools they sat on as they went into the room. On entering the room, Bondaa took his hurricane lamp and lighted it, raised the wick slightly up to brighten the room and set the lamp on a high platform that was on the bed side. Then he took his raffia bag and set it gently on the floor while he sat on his bed as there's no chair. He opened the bag and carefully took out the dresses and put them separately according to size on his bed. He put a head tie on each set. Then he reached out again into the bag and took out the powder and Vaseline and placed one on each set.

"You certainly are curious to know for whom? They are for you. I know that each time you weaned our daughters I presented you with dresses to change your nursing clothes to new ones before you come back to my room. Of course, I have never failed my obligation as a husband to clothe you every year and the last one I did three months ago."

"You have never failed on that, and we know that we received dresses after weaning our last daughters," Hogaii responded.

"We appreciate that very much and you make us proud and the talk of the village," Bendihe added her appreciation.

"In this village I have commanded respect because you have not exhibited mate-jealousy by quarrelling between you or with me. I am proud that over the years you two have shown that mates can live together without quarrelling or fighting and that you can raise your children in the spirit of love, unity and understanding."

"If we had not accepted our roles as wives and mates, your home will be in chaos daily. But there is a mutual understanding between us to present an enviable example for our children to emulate. That does not mean that we do not have minor issues which you often settle between us," Hogaii commented.

"Above all these exemplary qualities for which the village envies me, you recently agreed for a third wife. I think that was the best thing you have given me. It provides the opportunity for me to have a son that will inherit the Nwoingoha name and continue with the blacksmith craft. Not only did you consent to that, but you have also contributed to assembling together what I require to meet your families."

"We are supportive of your greatest need, a son, because we know what it means to you and the Nwoingoha clan," Bendihe said.

"I have bought these dresses and articles for you in total appreciation of this support. Hogaii, you take the pile on my right and Bendihe that on the left. I asked the tailor to use his best design and style in sewing them. I was able to identify women I thought fitted your sizes. You can try them on as no strange person is here with us."

Each wife took her pile and put it on her wooden stool and came back to kneel before Bondaa and clap her hands many times in the manner the culture dictates to thank him profusely. Each tried the tops of the dresses and each top fitted as if they were measured by the tailor which proved how well Bondaa knew his wives.

"I pray that your desire to have a son be fulfilled shortly," Hogaii uttered in prayer, "and that anything that wants to hinder the fulfilment of your wish will be totally cleared and destroyed; that your enemies will fail in every attempted venture to frustrate or pull you back in every area of your life. I pray that your daughters will have husbands who will surpass your character and fortitude."

"That too is my daily wish for all of them," whispered Bondaa.

"I want to join Hogaii in wishing you that our future son will excel among his peers. And that he will have one wife and not follow his father by marrying three wives but that his wife will be blessed with several sons. I pray that he will grow up and mature to a leadership position," Bendihe added sincerely.

"I also wish a good future for him and that he shall be more successful in life than me," Bondaa said in response. "I want us to go to Hogaii's family first as the senior wife in twelve days' time. We would have threshed the rice and brought every bit of it to town by then. At that time also we would have completed planting the cassava farm which will tide us over the hungry season next year. What do you say?"

"It means that we have to bring forward the clearing and burning of that piece of land I want to plant my groundnuts this season." Hogaii indicated. "But that will be all right. I will only ask you to seek the help of two young men to join you in clearing the land"

"How about you Bendihe, I guess the pepper plot will also be ready by then?"

"Yes, because it is not a big area as the groundnut farm. In fact, it is almost cleared. It remains only a small stretch which could be cleared in one day"

"Okay then, the twelve days countdown starts tomorrow. But two things I would want you two have to do. On the day we go to Hogaii's family I want you both to wear the same dress from head to toe and you will wear the other dress on our visit to Bendihe's family. It will show people that you have a good relationship with each other. The second thing concerns your daughters. Though they are young, yet you two must explain the rationale of what I'm about to do and that it has your total support and concurrence. You are in a better position as women to explain the issue giving them the justification behind it."

"Leave that task to us. As you have said we are better placed as mothers to assuage them of the issue," Bendihe said assuring Bondaa on his concern. After that assurance to Bondaa, Bendihe left the room as it was Hogaii's turn to be with Bondaa over the next three days and Bondaa retires to bed immediately.

It will be out of custom to surprise in-laws on any family issue except sudden death. It is the norm to send a message or a messenger to the in-laws indicating the day you want to visit them and indicating that it is an important issue that needs the presence of most family members. The best person Bondaa will send is his nephew, Yongaa his eldest sister's son. Four days before the visit, Bondaa called him just after meals to his house as Yongaa's house is a short distance from his and discussed his plans with him. Yongaa fully understood his position of inheritance in the clan and accepted the fact that he cannot inherit his uncle's lands and properties because he was not of the Nwoingoha clan male line.

"I want you to send you to Mindorwa to Pa Fundorwa, Hogaii's father to tell him that I will be visiting him and his family in three days' time. Tell him it is not anything that should worry him or cause concern but a proposal that I will be presenting to his family. On your way through Mabiama tell Pa Sandikenju, my mother's senior brother that I will be passing through his village three days from tomorrow. Also tell his son, Sandima-toko, that I will be grateful if he can reserve a big gourd of good and tasty palm wine in a cool shrub for me. I need this to take to my in-laws. Know this Yongaa, that in visiting your in-laws the first thing you present is a gourd of good palm wine that will enlighten their hearts to talk more openly to you or discuss an issue you may present to them."

"But you have very good palm wine as the one we drank yesterday by the swamp farm. Why don't you take that? I will carry it for you on the day of the journey"

"If I take mine from here, by the time we reach Mindorwa it will be hot and sour. Old people like Pa Fundorwa, who have been drinking palm wine for ages, dislike sour palm wine. If I take mine from here, it will mean serving them sour palm wine. I don't want to let myself down to my in-laws, not one bit, especially when I am going with an important proposition."

"I forgot that palm wine gets sour when exposed for a long day. I see your point. I will stress the importance of your request. Well, let me leave you to smoke your *Sangotho* and finish your palm wine."

"Thank you Yongaa. But don't forget that the distance is far. It means you must start very early in the morning so that you will be there before sun set. I will tap your palm wine in your absence. I'll clean the gourd and extend the tapping drain. Have a safe trip." Yongaa left Bondaa relaxing in his hammock slightly swinging from side to side. After taking his last gulp of palm wine he went in.

Yongaa returned two days after he left and two days before the planned journey. A day before, Bondaa asked a young boy in the village who can climb a tree to accompany him to the forest and pick some his kola nuts since he has passed the climbing age. He had already earmarked the trees which have mature kola nuts, and he took the boy straight to them. They picked a good quantity, peeled them from the pod, put them in a basket and returned to the village. In presenting kola to in-laws, you should choose big, fresh, and mature nuts. So, he sat on his chair and picked out the best one hundred nuts with the skin and wrapped them in green banana leaves to preserve their freshness.

The traditional ritual in the village was that, on the eve before embarking on a few days' journey to pursue or discuss any important subject matter, the ancestors must be informed by making an offering. An offering of white rice flour dough, two kola nuts one red and one white and water in a clean transparent tumbler for them to drink after they have partaken these items. In the morning Bondaa had requested Bendihe to prepare the dough before sun set. As sun set approached, Bondaa asked for it. Bendihe brought the dough in a small calabash with some water in another bowl. She also brought along two small wooden bowls and set all before him. Bondaa set about kneading the dough with honey and water while uttering guttural inaudible words as he was kneading. When he completed kneading the dough he divided it into two equal halves, moulded each half and placed each half in the wooden bowls. Then he took one white kola nut and placed it at the top of one dough mould and put a red on the other. He went to his room and brought out his improvised pint bottle-cut tumbler and poured clean drinking water into it. The final act was to put all these items underneath the head side of his bed until early in the morning when they should be removed.

The D-day arrived and Bondaa and his entourage must set out early so that they reach Mindorwa before dusk when people are returning from their farms. He instructed his youngest daughter to bring out the sacrificed elements from under his bed. He gathered all the items to be carried on the journey except the goat and placed them in the centre of the house. He checked them to ensure that he has not omitted anything. In his room he checked the balance money left after the purchase of the goats and the dresses for his wives. He was satisfied that it is more than enough to take care of any omission. While in his room, Bondaa pondered on how will the items be conveyed to Mindorwa?

He decided that Yongaa will tote the bushel of rice. He will pull the goat behind while Yongaa follows close behind so that he could gently nudge the goat's dangling balls to make it move along in case it wants to be stubborn. The eldest daughter, Hopanda, will tote the raffia basket that will contain the rest the items and their apparels. When he collects that palm wine gourd from his uncle at Mabiama, he will sling it on his shoulder. His wives will follow behind because he knows that they are slow-paced walkers. He led the journey and everybody else followed apace and not lag far behind.

About midday the entourage reached his uncle's home village, Mabiama, and made a stop at the house as he had planned. The uncle and his son were waiting for them.

"Bondaa you are welcome. Is everybody well and fine in Magoronwa?"

"Yes, Pa Sandikenju. Everyone is okay in the family?" We've left the young ones at home and as you can see my wives are with me on this journey."

"Sandima-toko," Pa Sandikenju turned to his son who was seated next to him and said "call your mother and tell her that the strangers she is expecting are here. I believe she prepared food for them."

His wife answered the call and after the salutations she ushered Bondaa and Yongaa into one room with the women in another. It is the custom that husbands cannot dip hands with wives and daughters in the same bowl to eat. After the meal Bondaa and Yongaa joined Pa Sandikenju and Sandima-toko while the women join their kind at the back until they are told when they should resume the journey.

"Bondaa, I need to ask: what is so important that you're taking your wives to Mindorwa? Has Hogaii done anything wrong after so many years without any dispute between you two?"

"No. Hogaii is a faithful and hardworking wife. She takes the utmost care of all our children including her mate's. No, I don't have any issue with any of them."

"That is rare to hear from most men nowadays. It is the blessing of your mother that she obtained from being obedient and submissive to your late father that is following you."

"You know that I have six lovely daughters from my two wives. But you are also aware that I have no son to inherit the Nwoingoha name and all that is associated with it. Don't forget also the trade I inherited from my late father. I consulted the ancestors and they have given the green light for me to take another wife who they say will give me son that will be a man of stature and fame."

"I see your dilemma, but have you discussed this with your wives and what did they say to that?"

"They are totally supportive of the proposal and have given their unreserved consent. I have responded to their consent appropriately."

"I'm happy for you. So, your trip to Mindorwa is to present the issue and to confirm Hogaii's consent in the presence of his family?"

"Yes, it is. After Mindorwa I have to make a similar journey to Dendehun and visit Bendihe's family."

"I know this is certainly costly, but you need to do this if the Nwoingoha clan should continue to flourish as I have known it. Before you resume your journey, Sandima-toko has a small gourd of palm wine to pep you up."

"Pa Bondaa, I have got the gourd of palm wine to take to your in-laws and this small one is for you to taste what you're taking." Sandima-toko allayed Bondaa's fears about the palm wine.

"Thank you for the food and palm wine. We must continue as the journey is still long." Bondaa expressed gratitude. "We will be back in two days, and we hope to stop again." Immediately after that expression of appreciation, Bondaa and entourage continued their journey. The walking pace was getting slower for everybody as they neared Mindorwa. What slowed them down was the goat which became stubborn at one point and refused to walk. Bondaa had to tote it on his shoulders for some long distance before it set down again.

It was almost sun set when they reached their destination. But before entering the village Bondaa made sure that the gourd of palm wine was concealed as it is meant to be a surprise to his father-in-law. When the younger siblings of Hogaii saw her approaching they ran to embrace her and welcome her. The rest of the family women folk basically swarmed on her, and she was overwhelmed by the welcome that she broke into tears of joy. Bendihe, who was close by comforted her. Meanwhile Bondaa and Yongaa were being welcomed by Pa Fundorwa, his *komaneh*, and the men. These customary welcome groupings later split to welcome the opposite sex and it was a big joyous family reunion. Hogaii and Bendihe were absorbed at the back to the chatter of the women led by Ya Yeneba, Hogaii's mother. Bondaa asked to be excused to see a friend, but in fact he was going to bring the gourd of palm wine he hid before they entered the village. He made sure that it was not seen by Pa Fundorwa.

Bondaa was lodged in an outside room next to the Fundorwa's second son, Sebeh-woro, who lodged Yongaa as he was still single. Bondaa and Yongaa were given warm water for bath moments later as it was approaching time for the evening meal. They had their baths quickly and returned to their respective lodgings. Shortly after, Hogaii's younger sisters, one with food in a special bowls reserved to serve notable strangers and the other with a bowl of water for Bondaa and Yongaa into the room where Bondaa was lodged.

"Pa Bondaa, here is food for you and your nephew". The elder of the two sisters said. They set the food bowls and the water on the floor and left closing the door behind them. Bondaa immediately called Yongaa for them to eat. When Bondaa opened the soup bowl it was groundnut stew full of chicken pieces and fish. Such delicious dishes are normally prepared for highly respected strangers. After the meal they returned to join Pa Fundorwa and his son at the veranda. Bondaa brought with him the gourd of palm wine and presented it to his brother-in-law, Sebeh-woro.

"*Komaneh* (meaning brother-in-law) Sebeh-woro, I cannot come to my father-in-law without bringing him something to quench his thirst. This is a small gourd, and I will ask in advance for his pardon if it does not taste good." Bondaa handed over the gourd.

"Thank you *komaneh* Bondaa. I pray for your safety in climbing to tap the palm tree from which this wine came or any palm tree. Papa this is what *komaneh* Bondaa has brought for you." He lifted the gourd for his father to see.

"I will just add to your good wishes that he will live long to bring more gourds for me" Pa Fundorwa added. "And that he will get what is closest to his heart."

"Anima" Bondaa answered. Sebeh-woro went to his room and brought out his palm wine. He poured out a full cup and gave it to Bondaa who gulped it down without pausing. He then poured out another full cup and handed it over to Pa Fundorwa who also drank 'bottoms up.'

"Um. It's a long time since I drank such good palm wine. I wish the distance was not that long so that I could have this every day," he handed over the cup to

Sebeh-woro. "Bondaa it's a long time you came to us," Pa Fundorwa observed.

"You're certainly right. It is because you gave me an industrious and faithful wife. I have no complaints to come to you or any other person in your family. I am thankful to you." Sebeh-woro handed his father another cup.

"How are my other granddaughters as I have seen the eldest?"

"They are growing fast and good looking too. Not too long you will have great grandchildren if God preserves your life."

Fundorwa gave back the cup to Sebeh-woro who filled it for himself. The next cup he gave to Bornor who had walked in to visit. Then he poured out a cup for Yongaa who was in the company.

"What about the blacksmith hut?" Pa Fundorwa continued "Is it as busy as I used to know that people from various villages crowd there to get their farm implements forged by your great skill?"

"It is even busier now that we have more young able-bodied men in the chiefdom."

"Do you cope with that?"

"I manage to cope. However, before I used to forge ten hoes or seven machetes a day, but now it takes me two to three days."

"You need somebody to train and help you because you are getting old."

"That is true, and I need to do so quickly."

"How do you want to do that?"

"We will discuss this in the morning."

"All right then." He received another cup from Sebeh-woro.

"How was your farm this year? Pa Fundorwa?" Bondaa asked.

"Maybe I can talk for him since I am his worker," Sebeh-woro butted in to answer.

"Yes, Sebeh-woro is right," said Bornor. "He did a great job this year for his father."

"We can't complain because we had a fairly good harvest this farming season," Sebeh-woro said.

The company discussed general things concerning the two villages as they drank the palm wine. When it was finished Pa Fundorwa thanked Bondaa again for his tasty palm wine and everybody retired to their rooms for the night.

CHAPTER FIVE

Morning in Mindorwa is not like Magoronwa's because you are not only awakened by cock crow but also by the baa-baas of sheep and the bleating of goats. Bondaa was awake on the first cock crow and never went to bed again. He sat on his bed rehearsing what he must do and say. Shortly after, the house was bustling with the women and children engaged in the daily chores. He came out and sat in the same bench he sat on last night. Just after that, Yongaa and Sebeh-woro joined him.

They exchanged morning greetings and Sebeh-woro asked to be excused because he must tap his palm tree before going to the farm.

"Sebeh-woro, please go quickly to tap the palm tree, but do not continue to the farm as I have an important issue I have come to present to the family. You need to be here as the son"

"I forgot that you sent Yongaa three days ago. Okay, I will make it fast. I will tell the women to bring you water to wash your face."

Pa Fundorwa opened his door and he came out to join Bondaa and the others with his plastic water jug in his hand.

"Sebeh-woro I hope you will tap your palm wine as fast as possible and return immediately. You know Yongaa brought a message three days ago from Bondaa stating that he has an important issue to present to the family?"

"He has just reminded me, and I will be quick." With that, he left through the house and to the back.

Not long after, a girl brought a bowl of water for Bondaa and Yongaa to freshen their faces. Pa Fundorwa was busy brushing his teeth with his *managbesse.* He then washed his face and took back his water jug to his room. He immediately returned to the veranda and sat in his hammock and hollered one of his younger sons to come to the veranda. When the youth came, he sent him to call three relatives of Hogaii's mother to come to his house as soon as they can for an important family meeting. The same message he sent to his own important relatives and to his long-time friend.

Before these summoned could assemble, Sebeh-woro had returned from tapping his palm wine. He later brought the gourd to serve when all were assembled. He started with the older folks as he did not think that the palm wine would be enough for everyone present. But before this was emptied another gourd was brought by Hogaii's cousin who said it is for the strangers from Magoronwa. So, everybody had one glass and the older folks had seconds. It appeared to Pa Fundorwa that the notable male family members were all present. He sent Sebeh-woro to tell his mother, her mate and his older daughters to come to for the family meeting. Ya Yeneba and the rest of the women picked up low wooden stools and benches they were seated on and joined their men folk at the veranda. Satisfied that all those required at the family meeting were present and seated, Pa Fundorwa opened the proceedings.

"I greet you all present here this morning. I am fully aware that we all have some tasks to do this morning on our various farmlands before the sun gets too hot. I believe that some of you were already on your way to tap your palm wine before going to the farm. But three days ago, I received a message from my son-in-law, Bondaa. His message was that he will be here to present to us a matter of importance to Nwoingoha clan but involves the *Gbendepoga* family. This is the reason I have summoned you all so that we can hear him."

"Before we can ask him to speak, did he bring the customary gourd of palm wine for his in-laws"? Inquired Hogaii's uncle, Foambo.

"Yes, he did but it was after our evening meal that he brought it out as he came in just a little before dusk. I know that usually after our evening meals we partake of our palm wines as a relaxer to send us to bed for the next day's hard work. Therefore, I did not bother to call you Foambo. I hope you will understand and overlook that."

"Sure, I understand. That is a minor thing to hold against my brother-in-law. We have had more palm wines together than we can count."

"Did Hogaii come with him as she did not go to greet me," asked Hogaii's aunt.

"Aunt Ya Hengbenna I am here." Hogaii responded immediately. "I apologize that I did not go to you. I was too overwhelmed by the welcome here that I totally forgot to go to you. But I told my mate that I would want us to visit you after everything is over. Please understand that it's a long time since I left Mindorwa."

"You are forgiven my dear. I have something to give to you before you return"

"I will sure go there to see my cousins and pick up what you've kept for me"

"Well, I think those questions were quite pertinent in this gathering," Pa Fundorwa commented. "Shall I proceed to ask Bondaa why he is here?"

"Yes, let's hear him," the assembly answered almost in unison.

"Bondaa, we open our ears and hold our breaths to hear what you have purposed for us." Fundorwa invited Bondaa to speak.

As a principal courtesy of respect for the elders, Bondaa got up from his bench and stood by its side and cleared his throat and offered an immediate apology.

"Pa Fundorwa, Pa Foambo and Ya Hengbenna and all elders and in-laws gathered here this morning. I wish to thank you for scarifying your valuable time to come here. I understand that this is the busiest month of the farming season. For you to come listen to me demonstrates the love you have for your daughter, Hogaii, whom you were so gracious to give me to marry. She has been a faithful, industrious and hardworking wife and I am blessed to have married her."

"Those are reasons enough for you to visit the in-laws more often and bring us palm wine and some of the fruits of her hard work," Foambo interrupted.

"That is true, but distance between our villages is the reason that I don't visit Mindorwa as often as I should. But I promise that after the issue I am about to present is resolved, my visits will be more frequent."

"We'll remember that" Sangeetha Hogaii's brother noted. "Continue with your presentation".

"Before I continue, I want you Sangeetha to come close to me as I want to formally shake the hands of my in-laws." Sangeetha took his bench and came sat near Bondaa.

Bondaa reached into his breast pocket of his gown and took out a red handkerchief tied with money. He untied the handkerchief and took out two

Leones. "Komaneh Sebeh-woro this two Leones represent my gourd of palm wine for Pa Fundorwa as I cannot get fresh Palm wine since I slept here last night. He took another five Leones and gave to Sangeetha. "I want to shake his hand with this five Leones and hope I meet him well. I will be remiss in my observation of the custom if I forget the town chief. So here is two Leones for the town chief to report my presence in his village and I pay my respects to him. Next these ten Leones is the shake hand for all the men in the family. Equally, I give you another ten Leones for the women. I should not end without thinking about the young ones who sweep the house and compound. Lastly I will give you five Leones for anybody or group I've forgotten to formally shake their hands."

"Komaneh Bondaa, these are generous boraas and I want to thank you from the bottom of my heart. I pray that the source of this money will be replenished twice over; that evil people will fail in their evil plans against you and your family, I pray that you have long life to see the benefits of your children. "

He moved forward towards Foambo, who was seated close to Pa Fundorwa.

"Uncle, I hand over these boraas from *komaneh* Bondaa to receive your blessing and for onward delivery to papa Fundorwa."

"Sangeetha, I want to thank you for passing these boraas through me. I want to join you in your sentiments and wishes for him. I pray that whatever he wants to present to us will be resolved without any obstacles. Komaneh Fundorwa that is the message I have received from Bondaa." He turned to Pa Fundorwa and handed over the money to him.

"I want to thank you Foamba for passing on the message. May you still be with us for such occasions. I also thank Sangeetha for receiving the boraas and pray that he will live to bury us the older ones. Bondaa on behalf of all those present, I want to thank you immensely. This is what is expected of a son-in-law, and I am proud to have you as my mine. I pray that your star continues to shine and that no witchcraft forces will succeed over you and your family. I wish you prosperity and success in your farming and blacksmith crafts-manship. I also pray that your ancestors will always answer your entreaties favourably. I shall pass your message to the town chief this evening as I believe he's gone to his farm. Proceed with what you wish to present to us."

"Hogaii is not only hard-working, but you all also know that she has given me three beautiful daughters and they are nicely growing up almost ready for initiation into the bondo society. I have another wife, Bendihe, who is here also, and she is equally faithful and hardworking. She too has three lovely daughters with me. I am blessed with six daughters"

"They usually say a man with many beautiful daughters is a rich man, as suitors will bring dowries to ask for their hands in marriage."

"That may be true for some people but my wish for my daughters is for them to have husbands who will not only love them but also be faithful and industrious to sufficiently provide for their families. I'm not enthusiastic about what dowries will be paid but I pray that my daughters will have such husbands."

"I agree with you Bondaa. That is the wish of every father that wants his daughter to have a peaceful and successful home," Pa Fundorwa concurred with Bondaa.

"As I said, I have six daughters and they are all doing fine. But I am growing old, and these children will eventually marry and join their husbands in the respective villages. My blacksmith business is experiencing a sudden increase by the number of young men coming to forge their farm tools. It takes me more time to do certain jobs which I did for less time before. Above all, I do not have a male heir to succeed me, and you know that the customary inheritance law recognizes only a direct male son. That may mean that the *Nwoingoha* family name could be lost to history if I don't have a male successor."

"The chiefdom will cringe if that happens. We would be dismayed to see that to happening to our *Gbendepoga* clan or any other family clan," Foambo remarked.

"This has been my anxiety and dilemma for quite some time now," Bondaa continued. "I have sought and secured the ancestors endorsement of my plan to marry a third wife. But the ancestors are not the only ones to give consent to my quest for a son. I discussed this with my dear wives, and they too gave their unreserved support to my proposal but also cautioned me on a few things which I have borne in mind. So, Pa Fundorwa, Pa Foambo and Ya Heng-benna and all gathered here this morning, I am here to tell you that I want to marry another wife and I have my wives' total support on this. I have come through the usual customary way to seek your blessing and support." He gathered the edges of his gown before him and sat down.

"Bondaa, we thank you for seeking our customary blessing on your quest for a male inheritor. We are in sympathy with you that at this your age you have no son to help you farm or in your blacksmith hut. We are even more worried about your clan's survival, and we are prepared to consider your predicament. But let me ask my daughter Hogaii, since she is here, and the entire family is also present: 'did you and your mate give this a very serious thought and all that is involved before granting your consent knowing the temperament of women'?"

"Papa, my mate, Bendihe and I discussed this issue thoroughly with Bondaa and reasoned with him," Hogaii replied. "I gave my consent based on the reality of the situation. I know that when our daughters are gone and we are old, we will be on our own and not able to do much. But with a son in the home, we that are hopeful that he will be our security for our sustenance and provision. So yes, I gave my total consent. I do so now before all who are here."

"My daughter, Hogaii you did the right thing for Bondaa and for yourself," Ya Yeneba spoke. "I know it is not easy for a wife to consent to her husband marrying another mate. But as you rightly said you realistically assessed the situation and granted your agreement. I support you and I pray that the woman who will join you will bear the son that you so crave for in the family. I will counsel you though, that you, being the eldest and senior wife, will have more longsuffering to endure. And for you Bondaa it is a love sacrifice that Hogaii has offered you and she should not be rewarded by neglect."

"Foambo, as the uncle of Hogaii have you anything to say concerning what you've just heard from Bondaa and Hogaii?" Pa Fundorwa asked.

"Komaneh Fundorwa, we know that in our tribe, particularly among the Nwoingoha and *Gbende-poga* clans, succession is through a male off-spring," Foambo began his contribution. "What we men fervently hope for and expect when we marry is to have a son who will inherit not only the wealth or position passed over to us by our fathers but also what we added to it. I am in sympathy with Bondaa who is the head of the Nwoingoha clan now and yet has not a son. More important perhaps to me is the fact that our daughter has assented to his plea for a third wife. I will, therefore, support her and her husband and wish them success in the search of an heir."

"Ya Hengbenna it is your turn to say something before I end this assembly as we have to go to our farms." Pa Fundorwa asked his sister-in-law.

"I thank you Fundorwa for asking me. When my sister and brother have reasoned and given their blessing, I don't have much to say. I only want to caution Bondaa against favouritism towards his new wife at the neglect of the older wives, who have given him the consent to marry another wife. My appeal and supplication on their behalf is that you will be respectful and the new wife submissive. I pray that she will be fruitful and have a son. Hogaii, I admire you and your mate for such a great courage. Hogaii, please embrace your mate when she joins you just as you have embraced Bendihe. That is all."

Pa Fundorwa lifted himself up from the hammock where he has been reclining and listening to what the various relatives have been speaking and sat up with his legs dangling. He ensured that he had everybody's attention by making a deliberate pause as if to pronounce a judgment and then cleared his throat.

"I want to thank you all again for answering my call this morning. I am sure that from what you have heard from Bondaa and the comments thereafter you now accept the importance of this call." Pa Fundorwa spoke. "We agree with you, Bondaa, that a man of your stature would want a son to succeed him after joining your ancestors. Nobody will envy you in your search for a wife that you hope will give you the son you desperately want. There is an unfulfilled portion of a successful man's life if he has not a successor. By every standard in this chiefdom, you're a successful man especially in your craft. You've consulted the oracles and your ancestors' endorsement, but you have also secured the complete consent of your wives as we heard it from Hogaii. Your ancestors' endorsement and your wives' consent were all you needed to proceed with your intention. However, you've only come to us to pay the customary respect of informing us about your justifiable intention of marrying a third wife. "

"Let me say *Komaneh* Fundorwa that Bondaa has so much respect and regard for this family and for custom sake he has decided to honour us with his intention? That is what I call a man of character," Foambo interjected

"I totally agree with you Foamba. And we thank Bondaa for the respect and regard he has for the family and especially in bringing such a sensitive inheritance matter for our endorsement. To continue I would advise you Bondaa to consider very seriously the cautionary comments made by Ya Yenkeni and Ya Hengbena. Those are genuine and legitimate concerns of women whenever we husbands take another wife. The issues raised are the sources of conflict in the family especially when we fail or neglect to fulfil our marital duties without bias. I will go along with the other members of the family that you have justifiable intention and I give my approval also."

"*Komaneh* Fundorwa, don't forget that Bondaa is from the most prominent clan and that is something we should note." Foambo reminded Pa Fundorwa.

"That was one reason I gave him my daughter to marry. If I think differently about this proposition, the Gbendepoga clan could be accused by the Nwoingoha clan of withholding or frustrating their endeavour for the continuity of their clan. I will not stand that accusation and will not want any of you either to face that. Besides these two clans have so many intermarriages that it is difficult for us to refuse such a request."

"The chiefdom's strength is hinged on these two clans and their continued existence is vital not only to the members of the clans but for the entire chiefdom." Foambo stated

"My other advice to you, Bondaa, is that you tread cautiously in your search. I think that things might work out favourably if your wives can be involved in the process. I pray that you find the right woman to give you a son that will fulfil your dreams. I also call upon the good spirits to grant you peace and harmony in your home as it will not be easy to have three wives. We are all in support of your endeavour to have an heir to succeed you and wish you well and a safe return to Magoronwa." Pa Fundorwa concluded.

"I want to you profusely thank all you who are here this morning for the precious time taken from your farm work. With your endorsement, I have partially surmounted the third huddle in my quest, and I am very grateful to everybody. Your support has given me

71

hope that the *Nwoingoha* clan will have somebody that will continue to uphold the clan's reputed high tenets and principles. I hope that this son will hold high the bright touch and continue to run the *Nwoingoha* race. My dad once told me that, if you want to see the entrails of the black sugar ant you must be extremely patient to carefully open its belly and do all that is necessary to see those entrails. So I have to do similarly what I have done here to the family of Bendihe my other wife. Thank you all and goodbye. We shall return immediately."

"I want to join Bondaa to thank you all for favourably endorsing my consent and hope that our expectations will materialize to the satisfaction of everybody." Hogaii expressed appreciation and expectation.

The assembly slowly dispersed to have their several private pockets of talks and consultations. Pa Fundorwa stepped down from his hammock and went to his room and came out with his cutlass indicating that he was heading to his farm. Pa Foambo and Ya Hengbena left the house together as they headed to their homes. Ya Yeneba and the rest of the women including Hogaii and Bendihe returned to the back of the house to finish what they'd left the girls to do. Pa Fundorwa came back to the veranda and found Bondaa, and his nephew Yongaa still seated.

"Bondaa, I believe we have resolved your issue with everybody agreeing with you. So, I am heading to the farm. We still have some rice to harvest, and we don't want the birds to harvest it for us. You notice that Sebeh-woro has already gone. I know that you will return with some consolation that a major concern to you will soon be solved. Have a safe trip back to Magoronwa."

"I cannot thank you enough for this," Bondaa said. "My wish is that you live a longer life to guide us. I pray that we the younger folks, who observe you through some of these delicate customary issues, will learn and appreciate the tribe's culture and traditions. May you live long enough to see your great, great grandchildren? May your enemies' nefarious plans against you and your family totally fail."

"Thank you for every Leone you gave this morning. I leave you now and hope to see you soon with another gourd of palm wine." Pa Fundorwa left Bondaa and Yongaa still sitting in the veranda and headed for his farm.

Bondaa got up at last from his bench and told Yongaa to call Hogaii who responded promptly.

"Hogaii, have you seen all your relatives here before we depart"? Bondaa asked. "If you have not, please do so now so that we can get ready for the return journey. We are already late in starting because of the meeting and you know that the distance is far. I don't want us to be too long in darkness as the moon is not shinning now."

"I have to see auntie Ya Hengbena who has promised to give a few things. I'll go to her right now and I will be back shortly. But let me tell Bendihe to pack other things that have been given to us." She left Bondaa and went to the back of the house again.

In a short while she returned from her auntie's house, with a child toting a bowl containing groundnuts, sesame, millet, and some cocoa yam and showed it to Bondaa.

"Auntie Ya Hengbena has given this produce as seed so that we can plant them next season to produce seeds and help us tide over the hungry months before we harvest our farms. She requests that if the yields are good, we think of sending her own share of the crop."

"I thank her so much and her request is certainly in place. We will make sure that she receives a fair share"

"My mother and I were discussing common marital affairs and I told her a little secret about you that you love to eat *pehmahun* rice. So, she said 'in that case let me give you some new variety of pepper and garden eggs which are ingredients. I got these varieties from a friend who just came from far away Kombu, and they are not in Magoronwa.' It means that you have a lot of land clearing for me to plant these seeds. I know that it is too much for you and that is why I am glad my family has endorsed your request."

"Go now and let's try to leave as soon as possible. All the key people in the house are gone to the farm except your mother, who I believe wants to see her daughter to leave home once more in a happy mood."

Hogaii went to the back of the house to assist Bendihe finish packing. Bondaa had told her that he would not want them to travel for long in darkness as the moon isn't now shining. Soon all were in front of the Fundorwa house bidding final goodbyes to the remaining household members and they set off for their return to Magoronwa. Bondaa veered off to see Pa Foambo and Ya Hengbena to express his final appreciation and goodbye.

The entourage set out almost at midday and this means that the latter part of the journey will be in darkness. Despite this Bondaa had an obligation to brief his uncle Pa Sandikenju at Mabiama and so they made a stop there. Since Bondaa had told his uncle that he would return in two days, Pa Sandikenju was anxiously waiting in his hammock. Again, food was ready waiting for them. Bondaa and Yongaa had their food in the same room they ate two days ago, and the three women had theirs at the back veranda. Immediately after the meal Bondaa came out to the front veranda where Sandikenju was still relaxing in his hammock

"Well, how did things go at Mindorwa?" Sandikenju asked. "I hope your in-laws didn't ruffle or upset you in presenting your case."

"I know that in rare cases like mine, you should expect several questions and comments. However, I was totally surprised that the entire family elders reasoned with me. The fact that their daughter confirmed in their presence her consent, made it easier for them to endorse my quest. Their comments were more cautionary advice than caustic or negative."

"The truth is that any reasonable man, thinking about the continuity of his family name and faces an inheritance dilemma, will empathize with you. Bondaa, you and your wives will be pathetic at your old age without a hardworking and thoughtful son to step into your shoes. You need a son who will support you when you will no longer be able to do any physical work."

"I think I have just achieved one positive step towards that uncle. I propose to go to Bendihe's family shortly as I want to accelerate matters."

"I wish you the best of luck with that too. Well, it is yet a long way to Magoronwa and you'd better resume your journey."

"Thank you, uncle, and please extend my greetings to Sandima-toko and tell him I missed his palm wine."

And with that they continued their journey to Magoronwa where they arrived much later than Bondaa had expected because of the time they departed. When they arrived the village was quiet, and they were greeted by the barking of dogs. They too walked quietly to their home. The children were not only excited but happy to see their parents back. Hogaii's children asked about their grandparents and other relatives. Hogaii told them they were glad to see her after a long period of absence and they sent their loving greeting to them even though they have not seen them. "They all wish you to grow up to be good girls who will attract worthy husbands as your father."

"I hope you were able to achieve the objective for your journey to Mindorwa." Little Adamsay, Hogaii's third daughter, asked with a tone of concern.

"Yes, my dear daughter, we did" Bondaa proudly answered. "It was achieved with the prior assistance and understanding of your mother which I appreciate so much. Thank you for asking. It shows that you and your sisters are concerned about the welfare of this family. I hope you all behaved yourselves while we were away and that there were no petty quarrels."

"No papa. We were too busy working on the plots for planting the groundnuts to quarrel and when we come home, we were too tired to even play with the rest of the village girls". Bendihe's first daughter said.

"I'm happy to hear that. Did you keep any hot water for my bath, and did you keep any food for us as I am hungry?"

"Yes papa. Your water will be diluted in the bucket to your usual liking and taken to your place of bath. Your food is in your room. That for our mothers and sister is in the usual place. We had a separate dish for uncle Yongaa which I will take to his house now."

"Thank you, children. I am proud of you." After having his hot bath, Bondaa had his meal and went out to relax in his hammock and smoke his pipe of Sangotho, which he did not take with him on his trip. Reflecting on the outcome of his trip he felt happy that one huddle in his quest has been successfully skipped over. While pondering on his next moves he dozed off and almost fell off the hammock, so he decided to retire to bed.

CHAPTER SIX

When the farming season starts farmers have little time for other issues as crop planting is time specific. So, when Bondaa woke up in the morning, he discussed with his wives what would be planted and where. There is no doubt that the main activity is working the rice swamp which is the main source of food and other needs. But Bondaa knows that the swamp rice farm cannot sustain the family and all its needs. Supplementary farming activities usually undertaken by his wives provide other food items which complement the rice. They decided to plant groundnut as the next major crop on the land adjacent to the swamp so that energies will be concentrated in one area. Besides these, Hogaii must multiply the seeds that her mother gave her at Mindorwa and that meant that plots for these should also be close by.

"Bondaa, you have to make some heaps for me to plant the garden eggs and pepper seeds that Mama Yayenkeni gave me", Hogaii indicated. "I can't keep them beyond this farming season otherwise they would not germinate because they would be dead."

"I have not forgotten that Hogaii. She also gave us some millet which I know is the next best substitute for rice. I cannot afford to ignore planting that millet this season as I know it will be our staple food for three months before the rice is harvested."

"Bendihe you will be responsible for the groundnut farm though I will ask the village men community to do the brushing and the ploughing." Bondaa told Bendihe.

"But you'll ask your village women folk to help you do the seed planting, weeding and harvesting."

"I have already alerted them, and they are willing to make their input at each stage of the work" Bendihe replied. "But don't forget that during each stage we have to provide one meal for them"

"I'm fully aware of that. Let that be my worry. When the time comes the Great God who has provided us the land will feed them. That said, it means that we all know each other's farming responsibility this farming season. But before we go into all these, we need to clear all pending activities so that nothing will hold us back when we start. One such activity is the visit to Bendihe's family to do exactly what I have just accomplished with Hogaii's family."

"When do you want us to go as the rains will soon start" Hogaii asked.

"In the next five to ten days but not later than ten days because I have already asked the village community co-operative workers to come brush the swamp in fifteen days' time from today."

"I will go ahead and parboil the rice we shall take to Dendehun. It should be ready in two days. Do you agree with me Bendihe?" Hogaii offered.

"Yes, I do."

"I am going to see what the girls have been doing on the groundnut field while we were away." Bondaa told the wives and he departed immediately to return at dusk.

Two days later when husband and wives were discussing farm and family issues, Hogaii informed Bondaa that the bushel of parboiled rice is ready as she had indicated.

"In that case we shall make the journey to Dendehun two days from today," Bondaa said, "because I already have all the necessary items. This time Bendihe, your daughter Yagoro, will accompany us to her grandparents."

When the visit day arrived, Bondaa went to tap his palm wine to take to his in-laws. Arriving at his tapped palm tree he found out that his gourd was leaking. When he climbed up and touched the hanging gourd, he noticed that there was no palm wine. He remembered that when he tapped the previous day, the tapping gourd slightly hit against a stone as he turned the palm into another gourd. But he did not consider the slight crack a serious problem. So, he hung it back on the tree to collect the palm wine. He was hoping to take his own palm wine this time to his in-laws instead of someone else's. He immediately went to Yongaa and explained what has happened and to ask him for palm wine.

"Uncle Bondaa you just missed my friends who normally come to my palm wine site. We have consumed every drop of my wine and I don't even have a bit to take with me to the village."

"Who do you think could possibly have good palm wine this morning?"

"Before you came to tap, did you leave Korwa in the village?" Yongaa asked Bondaa.

"I'm not sure, but I think I heard his voice in his compound, but it could have been his son's."

"Why not try your chances and go to his palm wine sites since he has currently two palm trees. He normally goes to the one farthest from here. If I, were you, I will wait for him at the second one not too far from mine because I have not heard his whistling this morning"?

"I need to do that at once otherwise we won't have any palm wine to take to my in-laws at Dendehun and that will be totally out of customary procedure and embarrassing."

"I am going to the village to get ready for the journey while you sort out the palm wine issue."

"Okay, I will join you shortly immediately I get any. Please find the goat and tie it for the journey and tell Hogaii and Bendihe to get ready before I get back."

"I will do that uncle. I hope you see Korwa."

Yongaa left Bondaa and headed towards the village. Bondaa took Yongaa's advice and went to the Korwa's second palm wine site to wait for him. Shortly he heard a whistle at a distance and guessed that it must be Korwa as he was the only man that loved to whistle in the village. He was whistling the most popular song that was number one when he, Korwa, went to through circumcision initiation. As he approached, the whistle grew louder and Bondaa was now certain that it was him. When he came to his palm tree, he found Bondaa sitting on the bamboo cane bench where Korwa and his friends meet with their gourds to drink their fresh palm wine.

"Bondaa, what's wrong? Why are you here? You have never ever come to any of my sites for palm wine and I know that you're a tapper of good palm wine."

"We have a saying that says: 'it is trouble that makes a monkey to chew hot pepper.' I am not really in trouble, but you can call it so. I have go to my in-laws at Dendehun. You know of course that one must carry the customary gourd of palm wine. I came this morning and I found not a single drop in my tapping gourd because I ignored a small crack caused when I hit it against a stone. I did not take the crack to be serious. So, I hung it to collect the wine only to find it dripping this morning. Yongaa could not help because by the time I got to his site he and his friends had consumed all his palm wine. He suggested that I wait for you here as he did not hear your whistling this morning. So, I am here to ask to you to save me from serious embarrassment before my in-laws."

"Bondaa when I think of your generosity to offer me a place to work so that I can feed my family, this request is a small matter. When one thinks that palm wine's effect is only temporal and sometimes harmful there is no reason for one to be greedy over it. Take these two gourds I have now. One is for you to drink and the other you will take to your in-laws"

"That's so kind of you. Thank you so much. I hope I will remember this someday."

Bondaa took the two gourds of palm wine and left Korwa to tap. When he reached home, he did not find his wives ready. Hogaii, he was told, had gone to collect a debt owed to her by a quarrelling woman who was known to refuse to repay loans but very persuasive in putting her problems to lenders. Bendihe, he learnt, had gone to fetch a new head tie she left behind in the groundnut plot the previous day. He couldn't see Yongaa anywhere near the house. So, he furiously sat in his hammock waiting for them. Then Hogaii showed up.

"I thought I sent Yongaa to tell you be ready before I returned. How can you go and waste your time to that woman when you know very well, she won't pay you? You shouldn't have loaned her the money in the first place knowing that she has a terrible creditworthiness."

"We had packed and have been ready long time ago. Because we did not see you, I decided to go quickly to that woman and get my money back from her and I was able to get at least half of it. Bendihe will be back soon. She went to the groundnut plot to look for her head tie." Bendihe appeared even before Hogaii rested her defence and closely following from the other end behind Bendihe was Yongaa.

"Now that everybody is here, we'd better get everything together so that we won't forget something vital. Yongaa, have you loosened the goat from its feeding ground ready for the journey?"

"Yes, I have untied it and it's in front of the house." Yongaa replied, "Bendihe, is Yagoro ready for the journey?"

"She is very excited and anxiously eager to go see her grandparents."

"It'll take me a few moments to get ready and we shall soon be on our way." Bondaa went into his room packed his usual travelling raffia bag with his clothes and this time he made sure that he packed his pipe and Sangotho. Soon he moved out to the veranda where everybody had gathered including all the daughters. He addressed them to comport themselves as well as in the previous time when they went to Mindorwa. He confessed that he made a mistake the last time they left them for the trip. He did not request an elderly woman to keep an eye on them. However, this time he has asked Yagbathor the next-door neighbour to watch over them and see what they do and come to their aid when they need support.

"Papa, I promise I will take care of my sisters and Yagbathor will have nothing negative to report when you return," the eldest daughter, Hopanda, promised. "As long as they listen to me and carry out simple instructions, we'll be fine. When are coming back?"

"The day after tomorrow, if everything works out as they did at Mindorwa."

With that Bondaa went out, untied the goat, and told the rest of the entourage to follow him in the trail as they travelled. The road to Dendehun was not like the one to Mindorwa. There's a river to cross before passing through two other villages to their destination. Reaching the banks of the river the canoe was not on their side to cross them. They saw it anchored on the other side, but the canoe man was not in it.

"Bockarie" Bondaa hollered loudly. "We are here and ready to cross over."

He waited for a response. There was none nor could he see any movement from the other side. He shouted again even louder. Yet no answer.

"Bockarie please cross us over," Yongaa decided to call. Then there was a faint feminine voice from the village so inaudible that Bondaa couldn't hear what she said.

"We did not hear and understand what you said. Can you please repeat?"

"Bockarie is not here right now. He's gone to work on his cassava plot not far from the village. I have sent a message to him," this time the voice was audible and clear.

Having no choice Bondaa and his entourage had to sit and wait until the boat man showed up. But the waiting was too long and little Yagoro spread her *lappa* to lay down and sleep. Long moments passed and Bondaa once again got up and shouted for Bockarie.

"I'm coming. Please be patient. I'll be there soon to pick you up," apparently the voice of Bockarie.

"Of course, we have been patiently waiting because we have no choice."

Bondaa shouted back in response. Then he saw Bockarie emerge, untie the canoe, and sit in with his oar. He rowed as fast as he could and soon landed on Bondaa's side. When the canoe touched, Bondaa realized that the canoe cannot take the entire group including the bushel of rice and the goat in one trip. It meant they must cross in two groups. So, he decided that the first group should be the wives and Yongaa with the bushel of rice. He and Yagoro will follow bringing along the goat. Yongaa helped the women to board the canoe and soon they were over on the other side.

Bockarie rowed back fast to collect the remaining passengers. Bondaa carried Yagoro and placed her into the canoe. Next, he picked up the gourd of palm wine. Finally, he went and toted the goat on his right shoulder though it was bleating and put it in the middle of the canoe. He shortened the rope and held it in his left hand. As they approached the other end, the goat moved to the edge of the boat to drink water. This tilted the canoe and caused an imbalance. Yagoro grabbed his father by his short gown. Bockarie stopped rowing and came to the aid of Bondaa. He pulled back the goat and the canoe regained its balance. The wives and Yongaa were very frightened and terrified when they saw this happening. All were glad afterwards that they'd crossed safely.

Bockarie charged no fees for taking people across. He performed a community service, but passengers were free to give him anything in appreciation. For his services Bondaa gave ten Leones and they continued their journey. They arrived just before sunset.

Since Bendihe's Nwoinbonga family house was at the extreme end of the village, Bondaa and his wives had to greet and shake the hands of villagers on the way to the house. During this greeting of villagers Bondaa bumped into his long-time society friend, Simanie. They warmly embraced each other, and people watched them with amazement.

"What are doing here in Dendehun?" Simanie asked.

"I should ask you what you're doing here as this is not your home village."

"You're right. The next village is my home, but I married Pa Gbangbawa's daughter and the old man has not a son. So, he convinced my father that I come over and take care of him and his farmlands."

"Good, that is very considerate of a son-in-law. I am here to see my in-laws too. I don't want to be in a similar plight as Pa Gbangbawa. I'm here to continue the process of overcoming that situation."

"I empathize with you, and I wish you success in your search. I see you carrying a gourd and I know it is for your in-laws. Don't you think that palm wine will now be a little sour? I will give you a fresh one tomorrow morning for your in-laws. Let me keep this one. Go meet your in-laws and come back and meet friends while we drink this. Will that be alright with you?"

"Simanie, I have no reason to doubt you. I will do as you have suggested." He handed over the gourd to

Simanie and continued his walk to the Nwoinboga household. On reaching the house he was told by a young boy that his parents were not in.

"Papa and mama have gone to attend the funeral of a close relative in the next village, and they would be back in the evening" the young boy told him.

"What about your eldest brother, Limamee?"

"*Kothor* Limamee went to bring his wife back from her village. His wife fled almost a month ago after she had a heated quarrel with *kothor* Limamee who had claimed that she had been unfaithful and should 'name' the man. The wife denied any such thing and *kothor* Limamee threatened to beat her to confess. So, she fled for refuge to her parents for protection."

"Will he be back tonight?"

"I'm not sure. That will depend on how they settle the matter and if the wife feels safe to come back"

"What about your stepmother?"

"She went to her potato plot to see how it is progressing and to find out if it is due for weeding. She will be back soon."

"Where has your sister, Bendihe, gone? We just arrived moments ago?"

"She has gone to see uncle Koilondo because I told her that there is no room to lodge the male strangers in the house. I believe she wants that settled before it is dark."

"Yes, Bondaa, I went to greet uncle Koilondo and also to fix rooms for you and Yongaa as Keybalee told me there is no room to lodge you two." Bendihe showed up from behind Bondaa who did not sense her approaching. "Since Mama and her mate, aunty Chando are not home, auntie Nendaywa has decided to take her sister's role and cook for us so that mama will not be bothered again when she comes."

"Was uncle Koilondo curious to ask why you are here?"

"No, I guess papa has told him of our pending visit since you sent an advance message of our coming some time ago. Aunty Nendaywa did not ask either. They probably are all aware of our coming. I believe the funeral at Mabureh must be that of a very close relative to papa. I think the suddenness of the death must have caused him to forget about our coming, because he made no arrangement for lodging you. I am told that Limamee went to bring back his wife.

"I hope he comes back this evening as he is key member of the family."

"The village where he's gone is not far from here. Somebody will be sent to inform him that we are here if he does not come tonight."

"Meanwhile, while we wait for their return, I am going to see a friend called Baitheh. He has relocated here from his village because he had married a wife whose ageing father has no son. His father-in-law has asked his parents to allow him to come over and take care of him. Please send Keybalee to call me at his house when your parents return from the funeral."

He left to go join Baitheh and his friends. When he arrived, he found three men sitting in the veranda apparently waiting for him. He walked in and his friend introduced him. Bondaa shook hands with all three as is customary. Baitheh went into his room and fetched the gourd that he had taken from Bondaa and gave it to him with a cup. Bondaa sat down comfortably on the bench that had been reserved for him. He turned the first cup for himself and drank all of it as the accepted norm demands in palm wine drinking.

It was obvious from the discussions during this occasion that the other men wanted to know his purpose in Dendehun. Bondaa did not consider this as intruding into his business as his friend, Baitheh, is a living example of a situation he wants to avoid. It did not bother him to tell the purpose of his visit to his in-laws. The three men sympathised with him stating that if they were in a similar situation they would do likewise. While Bondaa was telling the three men Baitheh went again in his room and brought a gourd bigger than Bondaa's.

"I told you I will replace your palm wine because I want you to feel proud that you brought good and fresh palm wine for your in-laws. Give me the cup and let me drink a cup from it before you take it." As this was going on, Bondaa saw Keybalee approaching the house. He knew immediately that his in-laws have arrived, and he should go at once.

"Simanie, you and your friends have been wonderful, and I hope we'll meet again before I return. But for now, I must go to my in-laws as Keybalee has been sent to call me." He left the rest of the group to finish his palm wine. He gave the gourd of palm wine to Keybalee and instructed him to take it to Limamee's room until he sends for it. He then followed the young boy. Approaching the house, he saw his father-in-law relaxing in his hammock. Bondaa went straight to him and as he stretched out his hand, Yeemeh-chorgoh got up and sat in the hammock with his legs dangling on either side of the hammock and warmly took Bondaa's grip.

"My son-in-law, I am extremely sorry that you came to Dendehun and did not find me. I believe that you have been told the reason."

"Pa Yeemeh, I perfectly understand that such circumstances are beyond our control. And when it occurs, one had to do the inevitable customary condolences. Only a hard-hearted man will not symp-athize in such situations."

"You are welcome once more to my house and your house also."

"Thank you, sir. I hope I see you well and healthy?"

"At this age my son I can only thank the Creator for giving me this body and energy to still do some farm work. Many of my contemporaries are either dead or cannot move out for long distances, much less work. How was your harvest this farming season that has just ended?" he asked Bondaa.

"I cannot complain because it was a good year for me considering the fact that I am the only male in my household." Bondaa replied adding a statement as if to prepare his father-in-law's mind about what comes tomorrow. "I intend to work the same swamp in the coming farming season."

"Limamee was not so fortunate because his farm was invaded by grasshoppers a month after sowing. Then later in the season, rodents infested the farm that he had to hire men to fence the whole farm. Otherwise, he would not have harvested a seed."

Immediately after this remark Limamee appeared at the far end not seen by Bondaa but by Yeemeh-Chorgoh. "Talk of the man and he appears." Bondaa turned around and saw him walking in. They greeted each other in the most courteous manner as brothers-in-law.

"You must have been informed that I went to bring back my wife from her parents. I hope you will excuse me for not being here to welcome you."

"There's no need for an apology as that is normal in marriage life. I hope you were able to bring her back?"

"She will be here tomorrow as we all agreed."

"Can you please tell Keybalee to bring what I gave him to keep in your room? Thank you." Limamee went by the side of the house calling Keybalee and disappeared to the back. He later reappeared with his brother holding the gourd to his stomach and his arms around it. He put it down in front of Bondaa and left knowing that he should not be seen around anymore.

"I am here to honour my message that I will visit my father-in-law and his family. I cannot be here without bringing the usual goodwill palm wine to him."

He presented the gourd to Limamee who thanked him and passed the word to Pa-Yeemeh Chorgoh who in turn expressed his appreciation. He stood up and reached for a pint-sized cup that was stock upside down under the grass thatching of the house. He sat again and poured out a cup for Bondaa who had the first cup as the custom requires. Then he poured out another for his father who drank it bottom up. He belched loudly indicating contentment that he has taken good palm wine. Then he handed the cup back.

"I have always known you for bringing good and tasty palm wine. Limamee call your mother and stepmother so that they too can have a cupful each of this delicious palm wine. They have their place on such occasions."

When the two wives came, Limamee served them, and they left the men immediately after drinking their cups. The three men then took cups in turns until the gourd was empty. While drinking Bondaa took the opportunity to indicate to Pa Yeemeh-chorgoh and Limamee that he would want the family to gather in the morning because he has a request to make.

"I certainly did not forget to tell my brother and sisters and the relatives of my wives that you will be here. However, since I had no clue as to the purpose of your visit, I did not tell them to gather here in the morning of your arrival. Nevertheless, I will summon them this night for tomorrow morning before they set off for their farms."

"I will go round this night and tell them," Limamee offered to summon them. "I am not sure that your friend, Pa Kobba, is around because when I passed by his house to greet him while returning home, I was told that he's on a short trip to where I came from."

"I will surely miss his usual wise contribution, but we'll go ahead without him, I will brief him later when he returns. I have to go in now after that tasty and refreshing palm wine and rest my old bones for tomorrow." With that Pa Yeemeh-chorgoh left the others and went to bed. While Bondaa went to where he was lodged, Limamee went to inform relatives about tomorrow morning's meeting.

In the morning the relatives had reminded them of the meeting. Shortly after, all the relevant relatives gathered including Pa Kobba who returned late in the night when everybody was asleep.

"My humble greetings to all present here this morning. I could not possibly ignore the fact that we all have some tasks to do this morning on our farmlands before the sun gets hot. Some of you were about to step out to tap your palm wine. About four days ago, Bondaa, my son-in-law sent a message to me saying that he will be here to present to us an important matter relating to his Nwoingoha clan but somehow involves the *Nwoinbonga* clan family. I have summoned you all so that we can hear what he has to say. You should know that last evening after my meal he presented me with the customary in-law gourd of palm wine, and it was one of tastiest palm wine I have consumed for quite some time. Bondaa we are gathered to hear this important matter you have for us."

"I thank you Pa Yeemeh-chorgoh for summoning your family this morning when they should be getting ready to go their farms. I want to extend my appreciation to all who are gathered here this morning and I will be very brief in my stating the reasons why I am here. But before I state my case, I must conform to the traditions of such gatherings. So *komaneh* Limamee please come close to me for I have greetings I want you to convey greetings to certain people."

"Why me? Why not Keybalee, who is younger and could run faster than me?"

"It's because although he can run faster, yet he does not have enough wisdom to know how to hide when danger shows up. Besides, if I make a mistake in extending my greetings you are wise enough to correct me."

"I see your point." So, he took his bench and sat close to Bondaa.

Bondaa stood up and put his right hand in his front pocket and pulled out his red handkerchief which he never leaves behind on travels. He untied the part of the handkerchief which contained money and placed it in his left hand as it is convenient to pick out the money with his right hand. Then he went through the same ritual of token boraa greetings as he did when he visited Mindorwa. After completing he said to Limamee "please express my sincere regret that I couldn't do more because we all know that many of us were harshly hit by poor yields from our farms."

"Komaneh Bondaa, with such generous greetings, even for the little children, you don't have to express any regrets. I wish to thank you for passing these boraas through me. I now understand why you chose me to come by your side because you omitted one group of people and that is the friends of papa and mama who both contributed to the upbringing of your wife"

"I regret my omission. It is not out of spite but a genuine omission. And because of that, here are twenty Leones to cover any other boraas I have omitted." Limamee took the money and gave ten Leones to Pa-Kobba and ten Leones to Yakargor the respective friends of the father and mother. Limamee put all the money together and went to the next person in the gathering older than him and said "kothor Daawaa, I believe that you heard the various boraa that *Komaneh* Bondaa presented to me. I now pass all over to you for your blessing and comments before you pass them on to the next person." The passing over of the boraa continued until it finally reached Pa Yeemeh-Chorgoh who gave his blessings.

"Bondaa, I believe the elders are ready to listen to what you want them to hear and deliberate on." Pa Yeemeh-Chorgoh said. "So, the veranda and all inside are listening."

Bondaa got up from his bench not only to respect the elders but also that he would be clearly heard by all and sundry.

"I thank you Pa Yeemeh-Chorgoh. I want to start with an encounter with my long-time society friend, Simanie. I believe everybody in this veranda knows why he is here in Dendehun although his village is a short distance from here. I am in a move to avoid the Pa Gbangbawa's situation because I already have six lovely girls, three from your daughter." Then he went on to state his case as he presented it in Mindorwa to Hogaii's family.

"Bondaa, why not take one of your sister's sons to be by your side and groom him to succeed in your trade as well as your inheritance?" Pa Kobba-Wa asked. "He will still be family line."

"I appreciate your suggestive question. But Pa Kobba-Wa you do have a son who will succeed you after you've gone to join your ancestors, correct?"

"Yes, I do. In fact, I have three." Pa Kobba-Wa replied.

"They will certainly succeed you and your inheritance which all fathers long for. Am I correct?"

"You are definitely correct"

"Well, the option of taking one of my sister's sons to groom and succeed me would be the last option if what I am trying to do fails to yield the intended result."

"Kobba, you have been my lifetime friend and I always appreciate your input in occasions like this," said Pa Yeemeh-Chorgor. "But you seem to underplay the importance of male succession in our society. Your father's first wife gave him a boy and that is you, and she got another, your brother Komrabai. When your

95

old man died you stepped into his shoes. If you join him before your appointed time because of any reckless action, your brother steps in. If he too joins you in eternity, then who next succeeds you? It will be one of your sons. Bondaa has no son now. Don't you think he should do something to normalize the issue?"

"You heard him say that his wife, Bendihe, cannot have more children because her womb has been bewitched and cursed" stressed Bendihe's aunt. "The only natural way to get a son is by having another wife whom he hopes will give him the revered son he desires"

"What about her mate sitting right here?" asked Kobba.

"My position is not different from Bendihe's. For this reason, Bendihe and I consented to allow Bondaa to have another wife as we empathized with him and we too desire continuity in the Nwoingoha clan"

"Bendihe, what have got to say in all this?" his father asked.

"Papa, Hogaii and I discussed this issue extensively with our husband and we agreed with his reasons. We both decided to support his efforts towards achieving his desire. What else could I do as a wife but to assist my husband to realize his dream which I consider a worthy vision?"

"My daughter, I am only trying to ensure your happiness in your marriage, because I know what it is to have three wives. I also know what it means when you're old. Bondaa will be incapable of doing any more farm work and you have no young man to care for you until you go to your creator."

"Yeemeh-chorgoh, it is not easy for a committed wife to decide to accept a mate, much so a second,"

Bendihe's mother interjected. "Hogaii and Bendihe have both consented that their husband takes a third wife if that will fill his inheritance void. Bondaa is their husband, and the next wife will be their mate in the mix of six daughters. I will join her in agreeing to Bondaa's inheritance succession endeavour and I wish her well. I hope that their husband will be rewarded for his efforts."

"You will all expect me to summarise what we have discussed here this morning." Pa Yeemeh-chorgoh said. "But I cannot do so without the wise words of our friends Kobba and Yakagor. These two have been with me and my wife through kith and keen and have never forgotten what friendship is. I will want to hear what these two have to say because I did not call them only to listen if I don't seek their own wise input in this sensitive matter."

"Often times we think we have a perfect explanation to certain critical issues when in fact only those who are directly affected have the appropriate solutions to the problems." Kobba commented. "Bendihe and her mate Hogaii have taken what I believe is the only natural approach to surmounting Bondaa's inheritance hindrance. Yeemeh-chorgoh I would advise that we give our blessings to Bondaa's wish."

"I have very little to add to what has been expressed here this morning," Yakagor said. "I know it is not easy for a wife to succumb to the idea of a mate. But our society allows that. The situation which faces Bondaa and his wives is not unique. We have not only heard but witnessed more complex cases than this. I will support you in giving your blessings."

Since there was nobody else with comments when Yeemeh-chorgoh asked the assembly, he got up from his hammock to sum up the deliberations.

"Thank you Yakagor and Kobba for your wise comments and I want to thank all who have made meaningful contributions to this important issue," Pa Yeemeh-chorgoh started his summation. "It is the wish and desire of every married man in this our society in Dohahun that he has a son to succeed him no matter what his position in the society. When there is an obstacle to achieving this, the man will do what is humanly possible to overcome that obstacle. Bondaa's obstacle is that his two wives can no longer bear children and so he needs to marry a third whom he hopes will give him his heart's desire. Because his two wives have already consented to his plans and the parents of Hogaii have given their approval, we in Dendehun do not want to fall foul with the Nwoingoha clan by hindering their endeavour and effort to have a successor to their clan. Bondaa, in summarizing the comments of all those present here this morning, we give our blessings to your heart's search for a son to succeed you in your trade and continue the honourable legacy of your clan."

Those last words of Yeemeh were the golden words Bondaa had been longing to hear. He got up from his bench and moved a little from it and wasted no time in expressing his appreciation to all who were present but particularly to Yeemeh-Chorgor.

"Pa Yeemeh-Chorgor your words are so precious to me that I can't allow them to fall on the ground. He took out a fifty Leones note and gave it to him. These fifty Leones are to make a comfortable and reliable place for them to rest. I want to thank you all family members and friends for your thoughtfulness of my quest. Your endorsement has overcome the final huddle to the next stage of my search. I promise you that I will not neglect my marital responsibilities to my present wives even when I have a third."

"Bondaa as a married old man I can tell you that what you have promised isn't easy to achieve," Kobba proffered to advise Bondaa. "We human beings admire things that are lovely, young and beautiful and all men like young, beautiful and lovely looking women. What I can advise you is this: always get your present wives on your side, and you can be assured that the third will fall in line. Alienating them, however, will create a totally dysfunctional home and you may never achieve your objective."

"I have told you often Kobba that because of your wisdom I will always guard our friendship. That is the reason I cannot have any deliberations relating to my family without your presence." Yeemeh-Chorgor said.

"Your wise advice, Kobba, I will keep in mind and will endeavour to do so," Bondaa promised.

Before dispersing a few senior family members privately expressed their support or misgivings to Bendihe and to Bondaa.

However, overall, the atmosphere was one of approval and support for husband and wives. Since it was still morning Bondaa decided to return with his wives immediately to Magoronwa so that they will not be late to catch Bockarie, the boat man, to cross them.

Indeed, when they reached the banks of the river, Bockarie was just rowing back to their end. This time the entire entourage boarded the boat as there was neither the goat nor the bushel of rice. The crossing was relatively better than two days ago.

"Thank you Bockarie, we pray that you have a successor knowledgeable of this river as you are. We'll see you the next time we are at this end. Goodbye."

The return journey to Magoronwa was without any hindrances that would delay their early arrival home. However, when they reached home sooner that they'd expected, they found only their two youngest daughters, Mayilla and Yehuleh, in the house.

"Where are your sisters, Mayilla?" Hogaii asked her daughter in a stern tone indicating anger and anxiety.

"Nbaiinbeh and Posseh have not come back yet from the groundnut planting. Tikidankay and Yadoweh went to purchase cooking salt yesterday as we expected you to return today." Mayilla answered.

"Are you sure of what you saying? Haven't they gone to that bondo dance which I hear from here?" Bendihe asked sounding sceptical.

"No mama. Have we ever lied to you?" Yehuleh answered." You will see them soon and you will judge for yourselves."

Bondaa decided not to take part in this conversation as he knew that the guidance and nurturing of his daughters was the responsibility of the wives and he intervened only when matters are referred to him by either of the wives. So he went straight to his room, changed his clothes, took his machete, and went to his palm wine site. He returned just after sunset and after having his evening meal he invited his friend Fokogbo to join him in drinking the palm wine.

"Where have you been in the past two days, Bondaa?" Fokogbo asked him.

"I went with my wives to Bendihe's family at Dendehun. You know why I went with them because I explained the reason to you when you asked me the same question when we returned from Mindorwa. I am glad to tell you that the way is now clear to get another wife. The two in-law families have endorsed my pursuit for a male successor, that's why I have invited you to celebrate with me."

"Good. I am so glad for you. The major obstacle on your first step towards your pursuit has been lifted and cleared out of the way. Now the next step is finding the right woman to be your third wife. Obviously, you will be looking for a young virgin girl that has never been touched by any man."

"That I cannot dispute, Fokogbo. But it is not easy for me to get such a girl at my age with two wives and six daughters."

"You might not agree with me, but my advice is to let your two wives find their mate for two reasons: They are initiates of the bondo society and they have total access to any bondo bush where young girls are initiated. Secondly, they will be choosing their own mate themselves and not you."

"Fokogbo that makes a lot of sense and for the second part you have re-echoed what one of the Mindorwa elders advised me." He poured out another cup of the palm wine for Fokogbo. "But how am I going to tell them when it was an arduous and demanding task to tell them in the first place that I wanted a third wife."

"Bondaa, if you found courage to tell them about marrying a third wife, you will certainly find the same courage to tell them to find their mate. Take a few days to muster your courage and face your wives."

"I will take your advice and handle this cautiously lest it blows apart my quest."

"Any other way will not be wholly acceptable to your wives. And jealous acrimonies will be less when they bring in their own mate. The new wife will have it at the back of her head that she is in the house through the consent and goodwill of her mates."

"Okay my friend, I have told you I'll take your advice because I believe it is reasonable though it is a formidable task." Bondaa said as he poured out the last palm wine for Fokogbo. They talked over other matters affecting their village and how they thought these could be solved through united and collective action of the entire village.

"I must go now and join my wife in bed otherwise she might begin to develop some jealous ideas" Fokogbo said. "When you have one wife you cannot afford to displease her at night, or you will plead the entire night for you know what. So, thank you and don't forget what I have told you."

As Fokogbo left Bondaa entered and shut the bamboo cane door of the house.

CHAPTER SEVEN

The following night Bondaa was reviewing the day's farm activities with his wife and planning what's to be done the next day when suddenly Hogaii burst in an agitated voice "Bondaa, tomorrow Bendihe and I are going to the Bondo society dance at Gargbow. You know that is a big occasion for women in the surrounding villages. We are taking Hopanda and Yagoro with us so that they will have the opportunity to witness the celebrations for the first time. They too will soon go through the society. Tomorrow twenty-six young girls will be graduating from the society. It will be a shame if we don't attend that ceremony."

"You know what it entails for us women and for parents and would-be husband of those girls." Bendihe added. "I believe you wouldn't mind if your wives and two daughters have a break from farm work and have some fun with other women for two days."

Bondaa turned this over in his mind and decided this is a good time for him to tell his wives what Fokogbo had advised last night.

"You definitely have a point, and I don't have any objection to that. In fact, I also know that you two will meet old society friends and relatives whom you've not seen for years. It is a day for women to chatter and gossip about others."

"This is also the day that single young bachelors could identify possible wives from those graduates," Hogaii said.

"I wish I were young and single. I could have gone too to look for one" Bondaa said. "But if I ask you two to be my eyes to look among those twenty-six young girls, you will take it as an insult to your humanity and femininity. But I sincerely mean it. Maybe you might be attracted to one you think could be an accommodating mate."

"Is that the reason why you readily agreed to give us a break from the farm work?" Bendihe asked in a raised tone. "If that is so I may decide not to attend."

"Do you want to miss this important and joyous occasion because Bondaa tells us to be his eyes for his third wife?" Hogaii asked Bendihe. "Your daughter will miss it too, and she has to learn something from witnessing this for the first time."

"You are always on this man's side. I wonder what secret *juju* potion he deceptively gave you that turned your heart to support him on his third wife proposal"

"Bendihe, I just want to remind you that we both have consented for him to have one and our families have endorsed our consents. It may serve us better if we do what he has asked because we both considered that it was the right thing for him to do. We reasoned that with a son in the family, we will be somehow assured of sustenance in our old age when we will be incapable to do any work"

"I think I was just reacting naturally as a jealous wife would. Don't blame me for my reaction, Hogaii"

"I perfectly understand that, but also I was just stating the obvious facts. And you know what? We should from now on begin to face reality as we are deep knee high in it."

"It is not my intention to spoil your attending the dance by mentioning that." Bondaa tried to ease what seemed to be a tension. "I know it is my place to find the woman I want to be your mate. But I thought I could give you the first opportunity because I believe that you will know the parents or at least the mothers of many of the graduates and that these could give you some insight as to the character of a girl." Bondaa was trying to state his case without antagonizing his wives and making them to understand their position on this issue.

"You certainly will not spoil our leisure trip to Gargbow, but we shall keep in mind what you have asked us to do. We are not promising you anything. We are going to have some fun and that's it." Bendihe said.

"I'm not forcing anything, and I hope you will have great fun and dancing. But please don't come back with swollen feet as we have just started our farm work," Bondaa advised them.

"We'll keep that in mind too." Hogaii replied.

"When is the dance and how long will it last?" Bondaa asked.

"Actually, the dance will start in two days' time," Hogaii replied. "But the society's graduation ceremonies have already begun. We will leave here on the day the dance starts and return a day after because the dancing ends at sundown. You don't expect your wives and daughters to travel at night with most of the men returning home after the final ceremony."

"I don't expect you to return at night because I have never let go to any far distance at night without me at your back. Go to your bondo society dance and take care of your daughters. Make sure they don't leave your sight one moment because I know there will be a throng of people to fill that village. Come back after four days from the day you leave here."

"Thank you for allowing us to attend. We promise that we will be back on your specified day," Bendihe expressed appreciation with a promise.

"However, Bondaa you have omitted one major thing that will make us feel good when we are there," Hogaii said. "We need to hold some money in hand to shower some of the graduates with some modest cash gifts. So, think about that before we depart."

"I will do that because I will not let you go there to be just dancers and spectators but also active participators. I will give you, Hogaii, fifty Leones and you will use your judicious judgment how to spend it."

"Now we know that we are truly going to that dance, and I can go to bed satisfied," Bendihe remarked

It was not only Bendihe who was eager to go to bed, so also were Bondaa and Hogaii. They all decided it was bedtime. While he was on his bed reflecting on what he has promised to give to his wives, the thought occurred to him that, if they decided to identify a young girl amount the graduates for him, they will need money to introduce themselves to the girl and her parents and show their interest. They must create curiosity in the girl and the parents. Therefore, he decided to double the amount.

On the morning of their departure the women plaited their hair befitting the occasion but with each having a different hairdo. The mates decided to take along their newest dresses that Bondaa had sewed for them at Royeima. They put these and a few other clothes with the *bintu el sudan* talc powder to dab on their faces in one basket for the days they will be away. Hogaii did not forget that during such occasions where you have a multitude people, one would need food unless one had relations or friends in that village. With that contemplation she ensured that they took adequate rice, palm oil, fish and other ingredients that will last them until they return. Then they dressed appropriately for the journey. When they completed all their preparations, Hogaii and Bendihe and the two daughters came to bid farewell to their husband.

"I see you have one basket only." Bondaa observed.

"No, we have one more basket inside. It contains our basic food needs," answered Hogaii"

"Hogaii two days ago I promised to give you fifty Leones. I have changed my mind and I am going to double the amount to hundred. There might be a pressing and important issue for which you might need to spend some money. I do not want my family members to be embarrassed in a situation that could be solved with some money. I know that will not be fine for you and me. So, here's the money." Bondaa gave hundred Leones notes. "Please take care of my daughters because I have confidence that you can comport yourselves well and I'm not too worried about you.'

"Thank you very much. You are so supportive of our going. I promise that I shall give details of every cent we spend because I know how hard we all work to earn this money." Hogaii expressed gratitude and appreciation.

"Hopanda and Yagoro, you two are attending your first bondo dance. I know that your mothers will guide you while you are there. But I want you to behave as good girls and never leave your mothers' sides as they have attended many of these and they are fully aware of things that can go awfully wrong on such occasions."

"Papa we'll do what our mothers tell us, and we promise to comport ourselves," Hopanda promised her father. She went into the house took the other basket containing the food items, put it on her head and said goodbye to his father and other sisters. She followed the others who were already on the way.

Bondaa and the rest of his daughters stood at the veranda and stared at them until they disappeared from their view before they could go in.

When Hogaii and her entourage arrived in Gargbow they found the village was already overflowing with dancers and observers. They wondered where, in this situation, were they going to find a place to lodge for the duration of the celebrations.

"Hogaii, is that you?" somebody called from behind them and Hogaii turned to see who it was. To her greatest surprise she saw her long time *bondo* society friend Nanday from a village much further than Magoronwa.

"Nanday are you also here for these celebrations? You mean you travelled all that distance to attend?"

"You know when you walk in a group, and you have fun on the way, the distance is not noticed. I am here with ten other women. So how are you and your family?"

"I am here with my mate Bendihe and our first daughters. We want our daughters to have a first-hand experience of what this is all about."

"You have beautiful daughters. Who lodged you so that I can visit you and we can have reminiscence of our youth years?" Nanday asked.

"That is our problem right now as we have just arrived, and I see that the town is full to overflowing. I was just wondering where we could put up."

"Well, if you don't mind you could join me at auntie Yakwendeh, and we will all make ourselves comfortable by spreading our mats on the floor."

"We wouldn't mind the least" Bendihe said. "We are not here to be comfortable but to dance and at night we have a place to lay our heads and rest our dancing legs."

"I will take you to the house so you could rest or maybe you might want to do something else?"

"Oh no", Hogaii said. "We'll go with you and do exactly what you have said. We'll cook something to eat and get ready for the beginning of the dance." Nanday led the way to her auntie's large round mud house and a small out-hut at the back surrounded by a mud wall. The compound was seriously overcrowded with other strangers. Men were lodged outside the house but in the compound as this was the dry season and no fear of rain.

"How on earth are we going to sleep with such a crowd tonight" Hogaii thought to herself while she curiously looked at Nanday who perceived what Hogaii was thinking.

"I can see from your face that you are curious to know where we will sleep on your seeing this crowd. Don't worry my aunt has reserved the back hut for me and we all can sleep there comfortably on straw mats on the floor." That eased not only Hogaii's fears but also her mate's. "Let me introduce you to my auntie before I take you to the hut and you'll decide whether you want to stay or find another place." Followed by her guests, Nanday weaved her way through the crowd from the entrance of the compound through onto the hut.

"We all will sleep here if you decide to stay."

"Hogaii, do we have much of a choice." Bendihe said. "We do not have any relative or a friend here. We can't keep on moving from house to house finding a place to sleep. Don't forget that our two daughters with us. We cannot afford parading them in this multitude. This place is fine with me and my daughter. But if you have somewhere in mind then you can leave us here and you can find us here later before the dance starts."

"What have I commented that should warrant these remarks from you, Bendihe? I don't believe I deserve those because Nanday was and is my best bondo society friend. Besides, you know what it means to turn down an offer like from a long-time friend in such situations? It means that you do not revere the friend-ship."

"Hogaii, I did not mean to offend you. May be my words were out of place considering the circumstances that we have walked a long distance coming here and we still have not had a rest nor a meal."

"I want you mates to rest yourselves and your children. Maybe you will think of something better," Nanday tried to cool down tempers.

"Nanday, can we have two pots and some firewood as we would like to cook some rice and groundnut soup as we are famished," Hogaii asked her friend. Nanday went to her aunt, and she soon brought what was requested and showed them the cooking site under a tree as there was not kitchen. Bendihe instructed their daughters to cook as they brought all that was needed to cook such a meal. Being strangers in the town, the girls asked a resident to go with them to fetch water from the stream which they were told was a distance from the town. However, Hogaii was uneasy with this and did not feel the girls will be safe with such a large male presence in the town. So, she kindly asked Nanday's teen male cousin to accompany the girls to the stream. The three left in haste and came back shortly after and the girls set to cook. They were soon finished and called their mothers who were in the company of auntie Yakwendeh and Nanday reflecting on their own days in the initiation bush.

"I hope you girls dished a bowl for Yakwendeh and Nanday?" Hogaii expressed some concern as it will be discourteous to cook in a housewife's compound without giving her a dish of your cooking. Besides you will be branded as a greedy somebody.

"Mama, you have long taught us that it is not only greed but disrespect to the person," Hopanda answered her mother. Satisfied that the girls have followed what they had taught them relating to cooking in a strange environment, they went on to have their meal for the day. After that they had their baths and went into Yakwendeh's room to dress up for the dance. Hogaii and Bendihe agreed to wear for the first day the better of the two dresses that Bondaa had bought for them from Royeima. Wearing the same dresses during such occasions indicated that the wearers were sisters, friends, or mates. In this case the latter was true. They wanted to openly express their closeness to each other. Hopanda and Yagoro wore the only dresses which their father bought for them almost six months after the harvest season. These they will have to wear until the end of the dance as they have no other dresses to change into when these are sweaty or dirty.

Before they finished dressing, Nanday joined them in the room, and she too powdered her face and back with Hogaii's powder. There being no mirror to check how they were dressed, they acted as mirrors for each other to correct what was inappropriate or incomplete. They

111

giggled freely as they did so. Satisfied that they are well dressed and powdered, they streamed out of the room to the main veranda attracting the eyes of both men and women not only in the house but standers-by in the compound. As they came out, they observed that the dance was approaching their area. They walked briskly to the advancing dancing throng that and joined in the dance.

In the forefront of the dancers were six well-dressed women with large size talking drums tucked under their left arms and on the right, they had a small drumming stick.

They drummed to a rhythm that harmoniously blended with the song which the lead drummer sang. Immediately following these were the new graduates called *Shaymas*.

On graduation the *shaymas* were dressed in specially fashioned attire. Each girl's head was neatly plaited with a unique hairdo. Strings of colourful tiny beads were skilfully tied from the brow so that the beads beautifully hung from the forehead to slightly cover her face. The strings of beads were tightly secured by a white headscarf yet displaying the strings. Their pointed firm and taut breasts with tantalizing nipples were left bare indicating their virginity. However, below the navel and down beyond the knee they wore skirts tailored specially for this occasion. At the seams of skirts, tiny jingles were tied so that when a *bondo shayma* walked the jingles announced her on-coming.

In the dancing procession, which is predominantly women mingled with few young boys, the lead drummer sang, and the rest of the women took up the chorus. She sang a stanza three times or more and the chorus followed. She paused at the end of each such singing and led the rest of the drummers in beating a special rhythm that will make the crowd go into rapturous and ecstatic dancing. The procession continued in a slow pace in circles from house to house until each front house was visited. The dancing stopped when the drummers decided to take a break to refresh themselves with palm wine or the local brew, *omole.* They resumed with extra vigour. During this break many dancers sat in the verandas of the houses and waited the return of the drummers while others attended the call of nature so as not to miss the invigorating and exhilarating sessions. On the resumption, dancing continued until the sunset, when it dispersed as the women had to cook for their families and visitors. It resumed the next day around midday when the women had refreshed themselves and had a change of clothes for those who can afford it.

Hogaii and the rest of her group were close to each other so as not to lose sight of each other. They were in good spirits and seemed to be enjoying not only the dance but the entire occasion. The new dance step was unknown to them, but they soon picked up and fitted completely with those who had known the steps before this occasion. Hogaii and her entourage retired to their accommodation and had a rest.

"Yagoro, I see that you are enjoying the dance so far, because I see that all your top dress is soaked with your perspiration?" Bendihe asked.

"Bendihe, you need not ask the girls they are certainly enjoying this dance. But the time will soon come when uninitiated young girls like them will similarly dance to their graduation from the society." Hogaii commented.

"We witnessed such dances before we went into the society bush. I agree with you, they seem to be enjoying their first dance."

"Whatever you mothers may say it doesn't matter. We are having a wonderful first experience of such a dance and we are certainly enjoying it." Hopanda responded. "Yagoro, are we not? I believe that we have a lot to tell our younger sisters when we return."

"That is quite true, and they will be eager to have their turn. I hear the drums again. The dancing has resumed. Mother, are we continuing the dancing?"

"Oh yes. Let's go back and finish the day's dancing." Hogaii responded. They walked briskly to join the dancing again. This time they forced their way close to the new graduates and the drummers, a place most dancers crave to be so that they could be in the heart of the action. This was not without some pushing and shoving to the displeasure of some dancers. The dancing tempo changed somehow because the lead drummer seemed to be getting out of rhythm with the singers. So, she paused so that harmony could be sustained. During this stop Hogaii had a good look at the graduates and recognized one of them to be the daughter of another friend, Kargor, who visited her a little over eight years ago bringing this daughter along. She became curious as the mother or aunt will normally be behind her daughter to celebrate her graduation. So, she looked again behind the graduates, and she saw this friend almost at the back of the daughter. She edged herself through the graduates to meet her.

"Kargor! Why did you not inform me that Makalay was going to be initiated?" Hogaii scolded her friend without any exchange of felicitations. "For such an important event for women in our society," she continued, "you need to inform not only your relatives but also your close friends. But you didn't inform me because I am not a close friend?"

"Hogaii, I apologize profusely. I beg you to come to our house and I will explain why I couldn't. This is not the right arena. We talk better and I believe you will understand."

"Congratulations anyway that your daughter has graduated, and she looks so beautiful in her regalia."

"Thank you but it was certainly not easy at all. We'll talk more in the house." The two friends then danced side by side as the drumming resumed.

As promised, after the dance Hogaii accompanied Kargor to her house where he met the husband for the first time. They exchanged greetings and the women went through the house to the back yard and took low stools and sat down to chat.

"Hogaii, on the very night that the town crier announced the date for the initiation, I was not in the village. I went to see my parents. In the morning my husband told me about the announcement. I was excited about it and with that excitement I went to plant on my groundnut plot the whole day with extra energy. I was filled with excitement. But during the night I was so cold that I had to ask my daughter to light a fire right at the centre of the house and I had to spread a mat on the floor close to the fire to warm myself."

"You must have overworked yourself with that excitement."

"I don't think it was overwork because the cold got so intense that I could hardly get away from that fire.

Then I developed a rash over my body. I was told that the much-feared village dwarf who is never seen touched me. It lasted for days, and I could not walk in public. I had to rely on my husband, Sandima, to inform my relatives and friends. It means that he forgot to tell you because I could have seen your hand as a friend in the process."

"He could have told Bondaa to have father-to-father or husband-to-husband conversation. But that too must have skipped him with you on the sick bed."

"He tried to do so but the young man he wanted to send also fell ill of dysentery and that is a disease that can drain a person in a day. With all these obstacles we could not get in touch with you. Please understand and accept my apology."

"I now know that circumstances beyond your control prevented you from informing me, because I could not imagine you deliberately ignoring me on such an important event as the initiation of your only daughter. Despite that here is sixty Leones as our help to you and your husband. I know things will be very tough after such expenditure. We forgive you and let's put your oversight behind us."

"Thank you very much Hogaii. I never expected such generous help from a friend who did not even know that we're doing this. You came to dance and did not expect to become involved in a graduating ceremony. I will certainly show this to my husband, Sandima, who I'm sure will send his appreciation to Bondaa"

"Now who is the fortunate suitor for Makalay?"

"Surprisingly not a single man has showed up to propose to us even before she went in for initiation as we had in our own cases before joined the society."

"What could be the reason if I may ask?"

"We really do not know what the reason could be."

"Sometimes men are very hesitant in making moves to propose to parents about their daughters. They must look at the parents' position in the community they belong, and they also must examine their own means and standing too in addition to their physical stature and build. The latter is fundamental especially if they want to propose for a beautiful girl like Makalay. Although the parents can accept a proposal, yet in the final analysis it is a relationship between husband and wife. We have witnessed cases where the young women divorce within a very short time after they join their husbands."

"Of course, we have witnessed such cases. I pray that Makalay's beauty does not scare away men to propose for her because we are not prosperous or wealthy. We are but an average hard-working family. We do not intend nor desire to give her to a man who she will abandon because she senses that the husband is not her type."

"Has your husband somebody in mind because husbands sometimes may fancy a hardworking young man who may not be attractive to the daughter?"

"I don't really think so otherwise he would have mentioned it to me."

"In that case I may have somebody in mind, but I have to consult with two people. Meanwhile, I want you to use your feminine persuasive endowments and prowess to mention this to your husband. I will kindly ask you to send a coded message to tell me his reaction and I will certainly revert to you as soon as I get the message. I can't tell you who the possible suitor will be. This is the time for you to use the coded messaging we were taught in the society bush".

"Hogaii I will do my best to tell my husband about this. I believe your intentions are genuine realizing the fact that you never knew that Makalay was going to be initiated. I believe he'll give it a thought"

"In that case I will be looking out for a messenger with your coded message"

"Yes indeed." Satisfied with this discussion Hogaii returned to join Bendihe and their two daughters who had gone home without her.

She immediately called Bendihe aside away from the hearing of the group and explained where she was and what she has suggested to Kargor. Based on their unanimity in granting Bondaa the go-ahead she felt they must get a joint agreement on her proposal.

"Hogaii, you have done it again for Bondaa. You are too full of kindness for our husband. I don't think I have any objections to your proposal. However, I think that we should give him the freedom to find his third wife just as we gave him the consent to marry another wife. I say so as a precaution because if something goes wrong and Bondaa does not have his heir, we'll be in big trouble. We'll be blamed for life by the Nwoingoha family. Are you also aware of that possibility?"

"Yes Bendihe, I am. I believe that that was the risk we took, when we reasoned that it will be to our mutual benefit during our old age to have somebody to care for us until our ancestors call us home."

"What then is our next step into this unknown?" asked Bendihe.

"We tell Bondaa who we have seen and who are her parents. He knows Makalay as she came with Kargor when she visited us some eight years ago."

"I agree with that but from then on, we must let go and observe what he will do next."

"Accepted, and I promise you that I'll no longer be involved until the new wife, whoever it might be, comes in."

The next day Hogaii and her group danced closely to Makalay and her mother for reasons unknown to all three children except the mothers.

The atmosphere oozed with happiness and hilarity as every dancer in the throng danced away on this last day of the ceremony. Graduates as well as their *shaymas* and relatives were having the last dance. An event like this will take place in this village until perhaps another five years or more when other girls here would have reached the age to join the society. The occasion came to a happy ending when the town chief announced that the dancing will continue in twenty days from now in another village where other girls will shortly graduate.

CHAPTER EIGHT

The following day Hogaii and her group joined other Magoronwa villagers on their return home, sapped of energy from the dancing. But Hogaii and her mate were not tired as during the dancing they'd sneaked out to rest and have a drink of water. So, they were walking back home normally. They reached home at sun set when women were usually busy preparing evening meals for their families. As the younger daughters spotted their mothers and their sisters approaching their house, they sprinted to meet them and walked home with them. They asked their parent nothing about the dance as they knew that their elder sisters will be just too glad to tell them their experience. All that is expected from them is to greet their mothers and show how happy they were to have them home again.

When they reached home, they found the rest of their daughters busy preparing the evening meal.

"Children we know that you did not expect us today. But here we are here, and it means that you have to replace that rice pot on the fire with the bigger one because we are famished." Bendihe commented.

"It was intuitive that I told Yayneba-goro to clean some husk rice in case you people showed up after meal hours and we would have to cook rice for you," Sentho said. "Yeneba-goro, bring the rice you just cleaned up and we'll add it what I want to cook."

Hogaii and Bendihe went in to change their dresses and join the children at the backyard until food is ready. They knew that their husband could not be home yet as his normal return journey home from the farm takes him through his palm wine tapping. After tapping he will have a few cupsful and bring the balance of the palm wine home to share with his friend and wives. As they were pondering over his return, Bondaa usual guttural sound was heard just by the side of the house. He walked to the centre of the backyard and stood there as if to say, 'I am here ladies.' And all four women who had attended the dance went to greet him one after another starting with the youngest in the group.

"I was not expecting you back this evening but tomorrow afternoon when the dance would be over." Bondaa showed his surprise to see his wives and two daughters.

"Are you not happy to see us earlier than you expected?" Bendihe asked.

"Bendihe don't get me wrong. I am very happy to see you it's just that I did not expect you back today. I hope you are all well and not worn out by the dancing because tomorrow we have a group of volunteer workers coming to help me complete making the heaps for the potatoes and cassava."

"We know that our break period is over and farm work must resume in earnest." Hogaii observed. "We're all well and fine and I believe we are ready to resume our farming tasks. We shall report to you after we've eaten, and I hope you brought enough palm wine because we did not taste a single drop of palm wine while we were at Gargbow."

"I brought one and half gourds hoping to spend the evening with my friend Baitheh who is here visiting his in-laws. I am sure he will not mind sharing with you when he sees that you're back because I told him that you have gone to the bondo dance at Gargbow with your eldest daughters."

"Then we'll join you after our meals." Hogaii said.

Bondaa left the back yard and went into the house to change from his farm clothes and then relax in his hammock. Shortly after, his youngest daughter brought him a bowl of drinking water followed by his steaming-hot meal which had just been dished out.

"Yeneba-goro what sauce did you girls cook tonight for the rice?"

"Your favourite dish papa, cassava leaves cooked with the dried meat of the hare you caught in your trap three days ago. It put enough pepper and palm oil in as we know that you love licking your fingers when you enjoy the meal."

"Thank you my dear. You girls are learning so fast from your mothers."

Yeneba-goro left her father making no comments as she knows that her sister does most of the cooking, but she has not yet started to cook. She came back with another sister with rice bowl and sauce. Bondaa washed his hands and sat to have his meal alone.

Before eating he cut some of the rice and put it in the cover of the bowl from which he will add more whilst eating; later he would put the remainder into the soup bowl after eating and the women will decide what to do with it. As he ate, he reflected that during his teenage years he and his late brothers always had their meal with their father; within the clan young boys were expected to eat with their father to learn eating manners. He recollected that when fish or meat was put on top of the rice mould, the young dared not reach for it. If a stranger was having a meal with them, the father made sure that he did not put meat or fish in the bowl. He reserved it in the soup bowl until the meal is over and then he will share it according to their age. In most cases he gave Bondaa aa the bones to suck the marrow being the youngest son. But here he was eating alone without a small boy to have his meal with him. He hoped that this lonesome eating will end one day soon. He finished eating and called Yeneba-goro to come back for the bowls. Then he lay back in his hammock waiting for his friend Baitheh to show up.

Suddenly he heard him talking to somebody not far from his house. He took out his *Sangotho* pipe from his pocket, knocked out the ashes from it, loaded it with fresh *Sangotho* and called Yeneba-goro to bring a live firewood to light his pipe. As he was drawing the first puff from the pipe, Baitheh walked in with a hilarious salutation. But Bondaa could not immediately respond to his greetings as to speak would make him choke and cough on the *Sanotho* smoke causing considerable discomfort to the smoker So, he made a sign to him to seat on his favourite bench he has always used for the past few years while visiting Bondaa. Then he cleared his throat as if he was throwing up and blew his nose openly whilst hanging over the wall of the veranda.

"I have long warned you to stop smoking that *Sangotho,* but you have ignored my advice. One day it will choke you so that you'll never want to smell the smoke again." Baitheh admonished him. "I am speaking from experience my friend."

"You were smoking the damn thing too much. It was always in your mouth, even when we are working on the farm or making heaps. You were never parted from it. I smoke my pipe only at night to relax from the hard day's work."

"Okay. Remember the saying that 'the grass which is sweet to the goat will give it a running stomach'."

"I hear you. Let me bring out the palm wine but tonight we are going to share with my wives who got back just before dark." He went to his room and brought the two gourds of palm wine and two cups. As he was pouring out the first cup, he invited his wives to join them in the veranda. He emptied the first cup bottoms up as is the custom in palm wine drinking and then burped loudly relishing the drink. The next cup he filled and handed over to his friend. Before he could take another Hogaii and Bendihe came with their special low stools and sat on either side of Bondaa, and they exchanged pleasantries with Baitheh.

"Bondaa, it seems unusual that you should send your two wives away for a week to attend a bondo dance. If I do that, who will cook for me and who will warm my water to bathe? And above all who will warm my back in bed?"

"Don't forget my friend that we have six daughters and there is only one now still learning to cook." Bendihe responded. "All the others are good cooks as their mothers. As for warming his back, Bondaa knows that there are certain days in the month when neither of us will lie behind him"

"Also, we needed to take a little break from the daily farm work to have a little fun with my mate and our lovely daughters," Hogaii added.

"I concede. I think I opened my big mouth too widely. However, I welcome you back and I am happy for my friend."

"I know that I have capable wives who can defend themselves anytime against such comments. I know each one's strengths and weaknesses just as they know mine,"

Bondaa said. "But I understand your concern for me. However, you've heard their explanations." He poured out another cup for himself after his wives have each had a cup. Before drinking it, he asked Hogaii, "was the dance well organized?"

"I thought that must be one of the best organized bondo dances I have attended. Don't you agree Bendihe?"

"I certainly do. There were loads of dancers singing new melodious songs with matching choruses that all the women loved so much."

"I suppose that there were many young bachelors looking for new graduates who had not been engaged to men?" Bondaa surmised.

"That did not concern us," Hogaii confessed. "We were there to dance and have as much fun and for our daughters to have their first bondo dance as they will soon be initiated too."

"However, I observed that the graduates' bodies were round and healthy and were well dressed in their petticoats" Bendihe added. "They looked so beautiful in their various outfits, and I did not recognize any ugly ones among them. Parents and fiancés must have spent considerable sums of money to present those girls in such beautiful dresses."

Bondaa poured each wife a cup and took one himself. After pouring the last wine from the first gourd he opened the other and filled the cup which he handed to Baitheh. His wives were still holding on to their cups as they cannot do bottoms up as the men do with Bondaa's cups. They must go a second time to empty the cup before handing them to Bondaa.

"Was there anything particularly noticeable that you would like us men to hear?" Baitheh asked the women.

"There was a man who tried to disguise himself as a woman, tied his head with a beautiful headscarf and adorned himself with colourful beads on his neck," Bendihe proffered to answer Simanie's question. "But his cheek bones and his gait revealed that it was a man in woman's clothing. He was dancing as the women were dancing but certainly without the finesse and the rhythm that matches the drumming and singing looking so out of place, but he seemed to enjoy himself despite the pushing and shoving by the women and the ridiculing from the watching crowd. He seemed determined to create as much fun."

"I noticed among the new graduates that one of them was Makalay, Kargor's daughter," Hogaii craftily interjected. "You remember Bondaa that Kargor, Sandima's wife, visited us eight years ago with her daughter, Makalay? The eight-year-old Makalay who visited us has reached the age of maturity for initiation into the society. I was surprised, though, to see her with the graduates. I scolded Kargor for not informing us that they intended to initiate Makalay into the bondo society. She gave a very valid and excusable explanation and I accepted it."

"So, we missed out in supporting them materially as family and friends would like to do when informed about an intending initiation of a daughter?"

"Well, Bondaa out of the hundred Leones you gave me for our trip, I gave sixty Leones to Sandima and Kargor as our help towards the expense. She did not complain, on the contrary she expressed her deepest appreciation because they never informed us."

"Since Baitheh is here. I will take up the rest of the story," Bendihe jumped in. "I was not with Hogaii when she went to see Kargor in her house because I was too exhausted with the dancing. But when she re-joined us, she called me aside and explained what she had done. Hogaii told Kargor that she had a suitor in mind for her daughter. She then told me that we should suggest that you propose to take Makalay. I did not immediately agree with her because I believed that the choice of a third wife should entirely be yours and that we should not be involved in any way. I have my fears that if something goes wrong in getting your heir we will be blamed for the rest of our lives by members of your clan."

"I told Bendihe that we can only suggest to you. But the decision to go for Makalay is entirely yours. You can accept or ignore our suggestion. What follows your decision can only be ascribed to you and not to us. We are glad that Baitheh is here as a witness in making this suggestion to you."

"Hogaii and I have decided that since we both gave the consent to take a third wife, we may as well suggest somebody whose parents we all know and then we let go for good."

"Let me add this," Hogaii continued, "I promised Kargor that I will get back to her the moment I get coded feedback from her on her husband's resp-onse to my suggestion. It means that if your choice is to pursue her then I will send my coded reply"

"Baitheh did you hear what Hogaii, and I have said? You are our living witness in the future for as long as we live." Bendihe asked.

"I hear you two clearly" he answered. "Certainly, that goes beyond my imagination that you two can go so far.

It is because you both care for yourselves and your husband. Yes, indeed the decision to accept your suggestion and the consequences thereof are entirely Bondaa's. Bondaa your wives have stated their case. What do you say?"

Before Bondaa could respond he emptied the second gourd of palm wine into the largest cup and set it down and so that the rudiments could settle down before he drinks later. He leaned back and made another loud burp.

"Thank you for asking me. I accept that my dear wives have done more than I asked of them and I'm grateful. I also accept that the decision to marry a third wife is exclusively mine although I had sought the consent of my wives because it was the right thing to do for harmony in the home."

"We accepted your reasoning behind it, and we gave our consent. As to which woman you will marry is your choice. All we have done so far is to suggest a candidate which you have the absolute right also to reject." Bendihe butted in to make things clearer to Baitheh.

"I agree without any buts. I want to thank you both wholeheartedly and unreservedly for the suggestion and I will make my decision known to you in the next few days. That said, did you observe any other thing or incident of interest that will help us when our own daughters go through the initiation in the not-too-distant future?"

"Well, we have to brace ourselves to work harder as graduation attires are becoming prettier but more expensive," Hogaii mentioned recognizing the fact that soon her first daughter and Bendihe's will be initiated.

"I have never seen such a crowd of dancers before." Bendihe said. "It appears that more people are attending the graduation dances and having great fun."

"You know Bendihe," Baitheh offered to comment on that, "the attendance of crowds at graduation dances very much depends on the year's rice farm harvest. If it is poor, few people can't afford to buy new clothes to go dancing. Also, if the parents of a mature girl experience a poor harvest, they will be forced to postpone the initiation for another year in the hope that their fortunes will be better."

"That is quite true," Bondaa said. "And that only tells me that I have to work extra hard when the time comes for my daughters, and I will count on you as my friend for help at that time."

"He has always been by your side whenever you needed him. I'm sure that he will do likewise when we need him the most," Hogaii offered some assurance regarding Baitheh's help.

"I hope that when that time comes, I will be healthy and strong to aid my friend," Baitheh said as he got up. "With that Bondaa I want to thank you very much for entertaining me with your Palm wine. I am going to sleep early because tomorrow I'm expecting fellow village workers to make heaps for my cassava farm. To you women, please continue to take care of my friend and your daughters. May the spirits of prosperity and peace be with you? Goodbye" He shook Bondaa's hand first.

"Be safe on your way home." Bondaa bade good night to his friend.

Then he courteously shook the hands of the wives and left.

"I want to welcome you back from your break which I believe you thoroughly enjoyed." Bondaa turned to his wives. "However, tomorrow we must complete the bit of the potato vine planting that is left. The earlier we finish it, the better for its germination and good yield." The wives went in and left Bondaa lying back in his hammock with his lighted Sangotho pipe in his mouth.

Four months have passed without a word from Bondaa after the return of his wives from the Gargbow nor did the wives inquire as they had clearly emphasized that they were totally excusing themselves from this somewhat delicate task. But Bondaa has been pondering over this issue from the first night this had been mooted to him. His first reaction was to reflect on what Sago-Gbo, the village seer had told him when he consulted him. He clearly remembered the words: "*The woman you are going to marry should be light skinned, medium height with bright big brown eyes and plenty of hair. On the day you are going to show yourself to the parents of the woman you find later to marry your eldest wife should go with you.*"

Indeed, he remembered well that Kargor's daughter, Makalay was light skinned, and she had brown eyes though not that big. With the height at the time, they visited his home, she only could grow to an average height; and certainly, even though her hair was platted all the days they were visiting, he noticed that the braids were thick indicating that she had plenty of hair. She was also beautiful at that tender age of nine. But more importantly Sago-Gbo had also indicated that Hogaii should go with him when he goes to show himself to the parents. Could this be a coincidence that Hogaii identified Makalay, her friend's daughter? To him this seemed to be confirming all that Sago-Gbo had said.

He discounted this and took it off his mind for three months during which time he visited neighbouring villages far and near hoping he might see or be told of an unmarried young woman that matches Sago-Gbo's specifications. During one of these visits to Makargow late in the afternoon he saw a woman ahead of him on the road toting a *sukublai* raffia basket balanced on her head. As he drew closer, he observed that she had a light skin and average height. He walked faster so that he could pass the woman and face her to see her face but as soon as he passed her, the woman asked him to help her put down the *sukublai*. She told him that she had walked a long distance and needed a rest before she could continue. Bondaa was certainly more than pleased to oblige the request. He helped the woman, and he rested the basket on a flat stone high enough to make the lifting up easier later.

"Where are you from and where are you going?" Bondaa asked the woman while observing her facial features.

"I am from Garbabra the village on the left side of Magaylorma" the woman replied with a subdued tone of fatigue.

"Where are you heading with this heavy basket?"

"My journey is almost done as I am going to the next village."

"Are you *a markit (market)* woman? I mean, do you sell things in these villages?" Bondaa observed that the woman had tiny eyes like a far easterner. This one feature disqualified her for a possible match.

"No, I don't sell anything. My husband sent me to bring something for her relatives in this village." That statement hit the final nail in the coffin and Bondaa knew that he could not pursue his advances anymore.

"You want me to help you to place the basket back on your head?" Bondaa asked.

"I would have liked to, but I have not rested enough, and I do not want to hold you up. I'm hopeful that some other person will come by and help me. If not, you were kind enough to set the basket on that high stone where I could easily lift it unto my head. Thank you. But before you go what is your name?"

"I am Bondaa, the blacksmith from Magoronwa?"

"My name is Beh-Siamba (meaning 'do not touch') and my husband is Pa Nyangulay." Bondaa recognized the name immediately as he is a renowned hunter in the chiefdom. He knows that nobody can mess with a hunter's wife let alone with intention to marry that wife. He took his leave from Beh-Siamba and continued his journey to Makargow.

Despite this encounter he made several visits to other towns and villages with the same purpose, but the results were mainly similar even some were outright rejection with a threat to name him as somebody making advances to married women. He doesn't want to defame his family or his clan's reputation to be accused of chasing other people's wives. What then could he do now as he continued to grow older, and increasingly cannot undertake the blacksmith or farm work with the same vigour and strength as he did in his prime? He was aware that he can no longer talk this over with his wives because they have told him that they will not be involved anymore. Should he go to Sago-Gbo again to consult the ancestors? But Sago-Gbo has given a description of the woman he should marry and under what conditions. Makalay fits all the attributes given him and he is fully conscious and mindful of the fact that Makalay is probably only two years older than Hopanda, his eldest daughter.

Above all, Hogaii happened to have identified her. Her parents are of average means, and he knows them to be admired and contented couple with no record of problems with the village or section chief. He also acknowledged the fact that they were respected in their local community. These are encouraging background credentials for the parents of a woman that a man like himself would want to marry. He assumed that Kargor might be working on her husband to accept Hogaii's proposal although she knew not the suitor. His fear was that even though the parents might accept him, Makalay might reject him she already knows that he has two wives, and she might not want to be a young third wife in a family dominated by women. This fear of rejection gripped him to the point that he was hesitant to mention this to his wives.

But the positives seem to point at Makalay. Realizing this he concluded that a marriage proposal has only one response 'yes or no.' He also knew that there was only one way to get a response and that was by proposing. He decided to tell his wives that he will propose for Makalay. One consolation he has is that Hogaii and Bendihe will be by his side when he goes to propose in the morning.

After meditating on this for half the night he got up earlier than usual and went to the potato plot after tapping his palm wine. His wives and daughters followed much later to find that he had made over twenty long heaps that early morning and he was still energized. His decision to propose and the palm wine gave him extra vigour to work that morning.

"Good morning Bondaa and thank you. However, we are sorry to say that we only have cassava to cook for you to eat with pepper and red palm oil. We did not expect you to work so hard this morning. We know that such energy used up so early in the morning needs more replacement." Bendihe shouted to him

"I hear you, but that too is a good energy booster especially if the cassava is soft when it is boiled" he shouted back while still working with his big hoe. "Did you people bring enough vines to plant in all the heaps I have been able to make for the past four days?"

"I think we have more than enough for those heaps and even for the heaps you will make in the next two days" replied Hogaii.

"Alright then. Start with the first heaps because they will be cool inside now after three days and you work your way up to the latest."

The women complied and he continued to make the heaps until he was told that the cassava is ready, and everybody should take a break and have some. The family continued its work on the plot until sundown when he decided to call it a day and go to his palm wine site and tap before heading home. Today he decided to take a hot bath at home after his hard work. He had to go home early to tell his wives to warm some water for him so that he could have his bath before his evening meal. Consequently, when his friend came by, they only drank two cups each. He took the two full gourds home because he knows his wives also worked hard today, and they deserve to be treated with appreciation. After the meal he rested for a moment and then called his wives to join him for a drink of palm wine.

"I have called you so that you can have some palm wine with me. I am sure that you would like to sleep off the hard day's work by drinking some palm wine."

"Your friend did not join you at palm wine site to drink with you this evening?" Bendihe asked.

"Actually, he did come, but we only had two cups each and I told him that my wives need a treat for their hard work today."

Bondaa told his wives although he had another agenda in mind. Bondaa has planned that this was the night he should disclose his decision relating to Makalay, but he should do this in a relaxed atmosphere. Thus, he has invited his wives to join him this night so that he could have their final view though he is fully aware of their position on this issue. But he's aware of the fact that he cannot go to Gargbow without Hogaii as advised by Sago-Gbo and also that she spotted Makalay and came up with the suggestion. Bendihe too cannot be left out of this as they she too would want to know what his decision is as she in fact told him their agreement to tell him about Makalay. He thus remained committed to telling both wives his final decision and that he will pursue it from this point onwards. However, he could not just bluntly tell them, so they reviewed the day's work.

"I wonder if you women planted all the potato vines you took today" he asked while giving a cupful of palm wine to Hogaii.

"We did our best to plant all but we couldn't because the children were tired and we had to put the little that was left under the palm tree and covered it with some palm fronds," answered Hogaii as she received the cup from Bondaa. "We have to draw more vines from the old farm to add to it so that we can cover the unplanted area including the heaps you made today." Bondaa poured out another cup for Bendihe and handed it to her.

"The area left to make heaps is still big." Bendihe said as she took the cup from Bondaa. "By the time you complete the area by yourself alone the time might be too late for the vines to germinate healthily."

"I thought about that myself this afternoon. I'll ask the village communal working group for volunteers to help me for two days to cover the entire plot. We should have some food for them when they come"

"Since the entire village is largely feeding on cassava, we shall make them cassava portage with some of that dried rabbit meat" Hogaii proposed.

"It is better than giving them just cooked cassava and pepper in red palm oil," Bendihe said.

"I don't expect more than six adults to join me each day. I'm hopeful that within the next two days we should be able to complete the rest of the plot. Having reviewed our farm work there is something else important I want to tell you ladies. I have held this back for longer than necessary and it needs to be dealt with immediately." Hogaii and Bendihe had no clue as what this important matter might be. What came to their minds was the heir issue and therefore the third wife. This time, however, none of the wives was willing to question their husband. They simply listened to him to reveal this important issue which he has put off for longer than is necessary.

"The night you returned from Gargbow and suggested that I should consider proposing to the parents of Makalay. I have been debating and meditating on it. I have even been exploring alternatives. My self-debate was whether it will be morally good for me to marry a girl almost the same age as my first daughter, and whether I should marry a girl who is the daughter of my wife's best friend. I was searching for a woman much more mature than Makalay and who you would treat as an equal adult when she is in the house. But all my advances were rejected and in one case the woman threatened to tell her husband if I should ever talk to her again about that.

"Don't forget who you are in this society for some foolish women to cast aspersion on you from your genuine point." Hogaii reminded her husband.

"I have maintained my dignity and respect in this community. I do not want anything to tarnish it. I have considered all the alternatives and have come to the decision that Makalay is the only choice. I need to mention this for the first time. Makalay fits the description of the woman Sago-Gbo said I should marry if I should ever have a son. Also, Sago-Gbo specifically said that I should go with my senior wife when proposing to the parents. Under the circumstances how could I propose to Macaulay's parents without Hogaii who identified her and proposed to her parents? So, I have decided to propose to the parents of Makalay to be your mate."

"Your decision comes at the right time." Hogaii said. "Yesterday I received a coded message from Kargor indicating that Sandima is willing to consider the suitor I had in mind for his daughter. Remember I did not tell her it was you because I needed to know your decision before disclosing the suitor. Now that you have declared your intentions, I will send another coded message to her revealing you as the suitor. If that seems acceptable to both parents and of course Makalay, then she will revert to me soonest. I will emphasize to her that it should be done quickly so that Makalay will not have a change of heart if action is prolonged."

"I would have thought that you Hogaii should go to Gargbow and explain things better to them all" Bendihe suggested.

"I don't think that will be a wise approach even though Kargor is my friend", Hogaii replied. "But I believe Bendihe that you are the right person to go because she knows you are my mate. When they see you, they could only conclude that this is an understanding among us three. They will know that if we do not agree on this, you could not go to disclose Bondaa as the suitor."

"Do you think I should ask Baitheh to join Bendihe on the trip?" Bondaa asked.

"Not this time as this is the most delicate point in the whole process. This is the moment when everything will either break down or succeed." Hogaii countered.

"I suggest that you go to Gargbow and stay with Yakwendeh" Hogaii advised. "She is the oldest and most respected woman in her community. She is not only the community's celebrated and legendary herbalist but most of the womenfolk in and around Gargbow seek her counsel on several issues ranging from marriage disputes to childbearing worries. Tell her your mission and ask her to join you when you go to Sandima and Kargor. As an elderly woman with long experience, she knows how to tread in this delicate terrain. In fact, let her be the spokeswoman when you go."

"It sounds a reasonable plan. Bendihe what do you say?" Bondaa asked

"Hogaii, I told you we should let go of this issue with Bondaa, now you want to drag us back into it. What we agreed upon was to let go."

"I certainly agree with you on what we decided. But it has come to the critical point where our suggestion will be realized only if we step in again. I am sorry that this time it must be you. It is not deliberate; it is a circumstantial coincidence." Hogaii said.

"Hogaii we are getting deeper and deeper into this third wife affair much to my discomfort. Why do we have to take the lead from this point?

"If the proposal should succeed then the preliminaries have to be planned and executed properly, don't you think so?"

"I grudgingly see your point but only because I want this issue behind my back and to begin my life as the second of three wives. I will go and lodge with Yakwendeh."

"I will suggest that Hopanda goes with you to keep you company. Do you agree with me Bondaa?"

"It's fine with me. I do not want Bendihe to be alone on that long stretch to Gargbow."

Satisfied with the arrangement Bondaa poured the remaining palm wine enough for each to have a full cup. When the wives emptied their cups, they left Bondaa in the veranda sitting in his hammock. He tucked up the gourd up-side down at the corner of the veranda to prevent ants and other insects from getting into it. He reached for his pipe to smoke some Sangotho before retiring to bed for the night.

Two days later Bendihe was on her way to Gargbow, on a very delicate mission that could positively impact their future lives or be a humiliating embarrassment not only to Bendihe but also

Yakwendeh. Before she left on this task, Bondaa gave her three hundred and forty Leones to take along for all necessary transactions: hundred Leones for all customary *boraas* that Yakwendeh might think appropriate and hundred Leones for the naming the suitor to the parents and Makalay. He also gave Bendihe forty Leones for Yakwendeh as the spokeswoman. The rest she should spend as she thinks appropriate to make the mission successful.

On arriving in Gargbow Bendihe went straight to the house of Yakwendeh as agreed.

"We have some unfinished business we started here, and I'm here to complete what we started." Bendihe tried to ease the surprise on her face.

"I hope you were not attracted to some mean-spirited man when you were for the dance, and you have come to see him"

"Far from it, Yakwendeh. I am attracted to something else, and I am here to get closer to it."

"Could you be referring to the wonderful mortar and pestle that Dowlowma makes here? Have you come to buy one?"

"I will tell you tonight after meals but only for your ears."

"This must be a very important matter because I believe that your husband gave you permission to come."

"You are absolutely right on that."

At night Bendihe went into Yakwendeh's room. With the two ladies in the room, she spoke in whispers so that walls will not hear what they were discussing. She first gave her the forty Leones from Bondaa before she gave her the background but more importantly their consent for Bondaa to marry.

"It is not easy for mates to agree to do a thing like this, Yakwendeh." But consider that at some stage in our lives we need to rest from hard work and depend on your children to take care of us. We do not have that sufficient coverage. All our children are girls and when they marry, they will go away with their husbands, and we shall be left struggling to survive until we join our ancestors. This thought made us to rationalize Bondaa's suggestion to have a third wife. We know we are taking an immense risk because we do not know what would be in the womb of the wife-to-be. But more important perhaps is the fact that if we did not consent to his proposal, we could be blamed by the Nwoingoha clan as terminators of their clan's continuation by not giving Bondaa a chance to have a male heir."

"I definitely do not envy you mates," Yakwendeh expressed. "On the contrary I admire your courage and resolution to go down the road with Bondaa up to this point. I can't remember in my lifetime two mates with such understanding and mettle, consenting for their husband to marry a third wife. You went incredibly further to identify the wife-to-be and suggested to him to propose to the parents. You mates are special. You are not of the stock of jealous wives even where the wife does not love the husband."

"What you have said is all true. But we have resolved to do our part and let the rest take care of itself in due course"

"I guess it's no use questioning or probing your joint decision because you mates have dared to bravely embark on a proposal the outcome of which you have no clue. I will go with you to Sandima and

141

Kargor to state your case and reveal Bondaa as the suitor that Hogaii had in mind."

"We all thank you for accepting this task."

"I will now send a message to them to say that I wish to see them early in the morning to discuss an important matter and that they should not go about about any normal business before then."

In the morning just after the early morning chores, Yakwendeh asked her husband for a few kola nuts good enough for the usual traditional boraa. When her husband asked for what purpose, she told him that she and Bendihe were going on a special woman's mission which will be known to him only when it is accomplished. Receiving the kola nuts she and Bendihe went to meet Makalay's parents in their house. Sandima and Kargor were indeed waiting as it is not normal for Yakwendeh to send word to them. They suspected that this should be an important matter knowing her distinguished standing in Gargbow and the surrounding villages. They warmly welcomed the two women into their house

"Good morning Yakwendeh. Welcome back to Gargbow, Bendihe." Sandima greeted them. Please take that bench just by the entrance and sit comfortably. They two women grabbed the bench and made themselves at ease.

"Getting a visit from Yakwendeh is an honour and I have to reciprocate that honour. Here are the traditional welcoming kola nuts. Added to that, I rose early this morning to tap my palm wine. Let me pour you some if you don't mind," Sandima was quick to offer them some palm wine.

"Sandima, thank you for the thought, but first things first. Can we four meet in a place where no one else can hear what we are saying to each other?" Yakwendeh suggested.

"In which case let's go to my room," Sandima said. Kargor offered to lift the bench to the room as it will be discourteous and disrespectful to allow them to carry it. When all were comfortably seated, Yakwendeh unwrapped the kola nuts which were wrapped in green leaves and loosened the leaves. She handed the kola nuts on the leaves to Kargor as the traditional *boraa* before one could say anything. Husband and wife thanked the gesture and Sandima took one kola nut and split it into two and gave one half to Kargor. They both bit pieces and chewed.

"Yakwendeh, what is so important that you should disrupt your morning entry to the bush to gather your herbs to come to us with Bendihe from Magoronwa?" Sandima asked.

"When you want something, there are certain things one has to sacrifice to get it. Yakwendeh replied. "I know I had to go to the bush to get some herbs for some people, but this is more important. I can go to the bush later and get what I want. The herbs are always there if the bush remains. Bendihe has a delicate mission here and she has solicited me to speak on her behalf."

Yakwendeh praised the couple how they are the least heard of in Gargbow relating to petty quarrels and how they are not involved in the village gossip because she is privileged to hear most gossip. She also admired and applauded them for successfully initiating their daughter, Makalay, even though Kargor was very sick one month to the ceremony.

"You parents made your daughter proud and del-lighted when I watched her dance during the graduation," Bendihe added to the praises. "She was one of the four best attired of the lot. It was must have cost you some expenses for both of you, but you did it with dignity. Is she around?"

"No. She has gone to the stream to fetch some water for cooking and drinking. She will be back soon" Kargor replied.

"That's all right. I was just curious to see her again."

Yakwendeh reached to her bosom and untied from her waist a piece of cloth where she had secured the money Bendihe gave her and took out a fifty Leones note and gave it to Kargor for her husband. She followed that with another fifty Leones to Kargor herself, explaining that these *boraas* are with a message. Both husband and wife generously thanked Yakwendeh and Bendihe.

"This is a very generous *boraa* under normal conditions, Yakwendeh." Sandima expressed. "It appears to me that this handsome *boraa* could have some challenging message for us. But let me not prejudge you even before delivering your message. What is your mission?" He calmly asked.

Step by step, Yakwendeh proceeded to state the Nwoingoha dilemma as embodied in Bondaa case as was eloquently and justifiably explained by Bendihe. But she stated the case in parables quoting wise old adages and proverbs to buttress the case as she presented it. Then she came to the point where Kargor disclosed, during a conversation with Hogaii, that their daughter Makalay, had no suitor. She said that during their conversation, Hogaii indicated that she had somebody in mind but had to consult two people. She stated that Hogaii promised to get back to her and that she, Kargor, was to talk to Sandima about it and send Hogaii his reaction.

"Is that correct Kargor?" asked Yakwendeh.

"Yes, that is what we discussed and agreed upon. I sent Hogaii a message a few days ago after I got Sandima's reaction to her suggestion", she answered.

"That's fine then. So, our presence here this morning is a follow up from your messages," Yakwendeh said.

She reached again to the piece of cloth round her waist and took one hundred Leones and handed it to Kargor.

"The message from Hogaii and Bendihe the two mates are this: Bondaa their husband wants to ask for your daughter Makalay to be his third wife. This money is to deliver the message to you the parents. If you accept his intention and you discuss this with your daughter and she too is agreeable, then he will come to do the appropriate and fitting proposal," Yakwendeh concluded.

"I want to emphasize that all three of us are in total agreement on this proposal. Bendihe stated to allay the fears of Sandima and Kargor. "I am doing to Makalay what Hogaii did for me before Bondaa proposed to marry me and I pray she will not let me down and send us back in shame."

"Thank you again Yakwendeh and Bendihe, for such a generous message delivery." Sandima said as he received the money from his wife. "We are not too worried that Makalay will get a suitor. Our anxiety or let me say, our uneasiness is whether she will get a husband who will be with her until their ancestors call them home. I know Bondaa, our renowned chiefdom blacksmith who forges our farming implements, and he is a fine and respectable man of honour."

"When I visited Hogaii some eight years ago, Makalay accompanied me." Kargor revealed. "So, she will have a recollection of who is Bondaa, and she will respond appropriately. Our daughter is now mature and can make her own decision on who she chooses as a future husband though we may give parental advice."

"I know times have changed from what we knew before about marriage in our culture" Yakwendeh will recollect. "When I was young, I remember that you the girl had very little choice as to who will be your husband. The day you were born a man would give the mother a token sum of money and say I put my hand on this baby girl as my future wife. Then he will make periodic visits to the parents bringing gifts or in some cases a gourd of palm wine for the father.

"And the parents are committed to that arrangement until the girl is due to be initiated into the bondo society and the husband-to-be will confirm his intentions by proposing to the parents." 'Bendihe added.

"You the girl had not the choice whether you loved the husband-to-be or not." Yakwendeh continued. "Your parents' acceptance was a fait-a-compli. But I have witnessed dramatic changes during my lifetime because our society has become more civil and now respect the rights of the girl to say something when a marriage proposer shows up."

"That was exactly what happened in my case. I was fortunate that I was passing through Kargor's village when I was told that a woman had just delivered a cute baby girl. So, I took the opportunity to meet the mother and the lady who delivered her and gave a token sum to say the new-born was my wife-to-be. The rest is as you explained. But each time I visited I made sure that

I bought something special for my wife-to-be and I tried to make Kargor know who I was even though she was young. I believe my frequent visits developed an acquaintance"

"Yes, and when you proposed I gave my positive answer as if I could have gone against my parents' years of commitment to you." Kargor interrupted to conclude Sandima's story. "But as you said things have changed so much beyond our imagination."

"I know," Yakwendeh said. "Well, we will leave the matter in your capable hands, and we await your answer before Bendihe returns tomorrow."

"You will certainly hear from us this evening" replied Sandima.

"Bendihe, my daughter and I will talk as mother and child, and we will sure give you an answer this evening."

"Thank you and I look forward to seeing one of you this evening."

Yakwendeh and Bendihe rose to leave but Sandima reminded them of his offer of palm wine. So, he went into his room to the foot side of his bed and pulled out the gourd. He went to the veranda to fetch his cup. He poured out a full cup and drained it in one long gulp. Next, he poured another cup and gave it to Yakwendeh who drank it with a short break. Then he poured out a third to give to Bendihe who said,

"I don't think I should partake of this wine because I should have brought a gourd of palm wine from my husband as the tradition requires."

"But your generous *boraa* has covered that. So don't feel any guilt if you drink mine as I need to reciprocate also." He passed on the cup to her, and she hesitatingly took the cup and drank it slowly not showing any delight in drinking it. Finally, she turned to his wife and poured her a cup full. She too drank it with a break. As she handed the cup to Sandima she thanked Yakwendeh for her timely action to heal her through the roots and herbs. However, she reminded her that she had some more herbs to give her.

"That pox almost disfigured my face but for your prompt intervention. Thank you so much, I don't even know to how to reward you enough even with what I have started."

"There is the belief, Kargor, that if you don't give an herbalist a satisfactory reward for healing you, a small portion of the illness will return. You certainly don't want that to be your fate," Sandima said.

"Yakwendeh knows that I already have some quite remarkable things for her, and I am certain I will do what it takes to make her satisfied."

" We herbalists have a moral obligation to heal the sick that seek our help and often do not charge a fee," she remarked as she received another cup from Sandima. "Rather we leave a quantum of appreciation to the patient who knows what he or she had been cured from by our herbs." She handed to Sandima the empty cup after drinking its content.

"Thank you, Sandima. Your palm wine was tasty. I have not had such good palm wine for several days now because my husband has tapped his for over two months and it is strong for me. Bendihe, we leave after you have finished your cup as I have to go into the bush to get some herbs before the sun is hot." And indeed, the two left immediately Bendihe finished drinking the cup but again reminding their hosts they had promised to get them an answer by night fall. Bendihe was apprehensive of the situation and on their way home, she asked for Yakwendeh's opinion.

"You know nearly every family in Gargbow and no doubt this family. Do you suspect that there is somebody else ahead of us? Or did you receive strangers lately that could have been on the same mission?"

"If there was anything of the sort, I would have known from the gossip line, because the ultimate terminal of that gossip will be me and I will know the latest in the village. I can tell you that no strangers have visited them since the end of the graduation dance. I know Makalay as a serious and hard-working girl and she is not the type that associates with cheap company."

"As the village herbalist have you ever treated Makalay for any serious sickness relating purely to women?"

"What I can remember administering an herb to Makalay to deworm her when she was about two or three years old, as we do with all growing children. Since then, they have not brought her to me for any illness nor have I received complaints from her either."

"Are you aware of any sickness that you think is hereditary in the family?"

"Except that she has bulging big brown but beautiful eyes. She inherited them from the great grandmother whom I knew when I was young, and I admired her eyes"

"I apologize for asking these questions. But you know that Hogaii and I have risked our necks out to the Nwoingoha gallows. It will be tragic for us if Bondaa does not have male heir by Makalay should she accept the proposal."

"I perfectly understand your predicament. But not even you knew that you were going to have children until you slept with your husband. So why don't you and Hogaii wait until Makalay sleeps for three days in Bondaa's room when it is her turn?"

"I seem to be fast tracking myself when the first step is yet in the balance. But we made one thing clear to Bondaa when we introduced the Makalay proposal. We specified to him in the presence of his best friend that the decision to propose was entirely his and the consequences of that decision will solely be on his shoulders and his alone"

"Why then are you so apprehensive."

"Any negative outcome will point to the initiators of the proposal and that is Hogaii and I"

"That's why we wives should leave our husbands alone to pursue their quest to marry a second, third or whatever wife they choose. In this our culture it is their right. When they do, they bear the ultimate consequences. You don't assist them as you can never foretell the future outcome"

"It is a mistake Hogaii, and I will live with that for the rest of my life."

"However, I am hopeful that Makalay will deliver you two from your transgression into men's sole exploitative escapades in marrying more than two wives." They reached home not realizing it as the question-and-answer session preoccupied their attention. Immediately Yakwendeh changed clothes to go to the bushes to get her patients herbs and roots. Bendihe asked whether she should accompany her although she knew that it is not usual for a stranger to accompany an herbalist to the bush. But Yakwendeh politely turned the offer down as herbalists are only accompanied by relatives who under study the herbalist and are shown the various herbs and roots, their names, and what diseases they cure and how they are administered. Eventually this pupil herbalist will take over on the demise of the present herbalist but not until then can that pupil practice because the responsibility for administering a wrong herb or root will be that of the administrating herbalist. No two herbalists can treat a patient for the same disease at the same time with the same prescribed herb.

Almost at night fall Yakwendeh returned from her searches with a basket full of leaves and roots from which she concocts and blends her cures for her patients. She found Bendihe sitting on the same bench at the same place.

"You never moved one foot from this place since I left?"

"Yes, I did. I went to the back to chat with the women while they were cooking. But Sandima sent a few moments ago to enquire if you have returned from the bush. The women sent back to say that you will be back shortly as nightfall never finds you in the bush. I came to the front to look out for you. That is why you have found me in the same spot."

"All right then. Let me set this basket safely in my room and I will send to say I am back." She went in and immediately called one of her granddaughters and sent her to Sandima's house to report on her return. A few moments later Sandima, Kargor and to their surprise Makalay also showed up. Yakwendeh made them comfortably seat in her room as this was still a matter that should be confined to the people closely involved. Yakwendeh and Bendihe exchanged warm salutations with Makalay and welcomed her presence.

"We are here as we promised. We have come with Makalay around whom everything hinges and revolves. We've had our family discussions and she has a word for you," Sandima said.

"Yakwendeh, my parents have explained to me *thara* Bendihe's mission here in Gargbow and specifically to them." Makalay said. "I know that when I choose a husband, I should be the wife of that husband and hope to be together until death parts us. But with the same token" she continued, "I must listen to the cautionary advice of my parents who in their hearts want to see me comfortably married. I have reflected on these and told them I will give Bondaa a chance to prove himself."

"Yakwendeh and Bendihe you have heard it from her mouth" Kargor said. "We have nothing more to add but to say we look forward to seeing you again. Remember, however, that Makalay is uncommitted for now."

"Sandima and Kargor, we are pleased with what we've heard", replied Bendihe. "It's up to us on our side to act appropriately and fast. We should not give the opportunity anyone younger man who could be more favourable to nudge us out of this race."

Before Yakwendeh could speak she got up from the edge of the bed where she sat, went to   Makalay took her hand and sat by her side as she was sitting on a long wooden bench.

"I have heard your word and I applaud you and admire your courage to give Bondaa a chance to prove himself of what he can do. During all my years in Gargbow I have not heard or experienced a young girl in this village giving a man who already has two wives a chance. I know several who agreed to be a mate to another wife but not be a third wife. That is the most admirable and courageous statement I have heard in my lifetime in such matters. I am enthused and delighted by that. She lifted the head side of grass mattress and took out the one hundred Leones and gave it to her. This is to give weight to our 'thank you'. Sandima and Kargor you will hear from us very shortly. I thank you two for guiding and counselling your daughter to reach her decision. Such decisions are not easy because I know I have had my moments too in that regard."

"We want you to remember that our daughter is in her prime and although she had not a suitor before her initiation to the society, yet there could be admirers out there who will try their chances too." Sandima cautioned his hosts.

"I certainly see your point. Bendihe was here specifically for a word like this, and she will be very delighted to deliver your daughter's word immediately. She leaves early in the morning so that she can reach Magoronwa before it gets hot."

"We will leave now, but I just want to reiterate that the door for our daughter's marriage is still wide open," Sandima made a statement of caution and may be indicating that Bondaa should act soonest. "We want our daughter out of our house with a decent man that will take care of her more than what we have been able to do as parents."

"I note with complete clarity your statement," Bendihe said. "Any man who sees Makalay now will want her to be his wife. And if she has given Bondaa the first chance it will be up to him to initiate immediate positive steps to seize the opportunity now knocking on his door."

"Have a safe trip back to Magoronwa and please give my special regards to Hogaii and your daughter who were with you during the graduation dance." Kargor bade farewell to Bendihe. Both husband and wife left to return to their house.

Immediately the couple left Bendihe jumped with jubilation for a successful mission in view of her pessimism. She feared that she might go back with disappointment. She feared that not only will the parents but also Makalay would reject the proposal. She warmly embraced the old woman until she said, "My bones are creaking, Bendihe. You might break them, and the next person won't need me if they are broken."

"I'm sorry Yakwendeh, but my heart is over-joyed, and it is you that I have to profusely thank for your wise approach. I pray that you live a little much longer to get people like me out of shame and humiliating dilemma. Thank you so much. But for the distance to Magoronwa I would have left this night to return if I had a male escort. But as you said I will leave tomorrow. In fact, I will be out at the cock's first crow."

"That will be too early as it will still be dark and some of the evil forces will be returning home. So, I would not advise you to take young Hopanda out during that ungodly hour." Yakwendeh cautioned Bendihe.

"I'm going to prepare some of my herbs before mealtime and you will help me later to scrape the roots before you go to sleep. There is no restriction scraping the roots for me"

"I'll be so glad to do that when I consider what a marvellous thing you've achieved for me." Bendihe followed Yakwendeh to the main floor of the house where the old lady had conveyed her basket of herbs and roots from her room. They both began scraping the roots and were later joined by Hopanda. This lasted for some time after the evening meal and Yakwendeh noticed that it was getting deep into the night. She urged Bendihe and Hopanda to go and sleep as their return journey starts very early in the morning. Both got up before midnight and bade good night to Yakwendeh who seemed determined to complete the scraping.

CHAPTER NINE

Bendihe and Hopanda got up early just after the first cock crow, bade farewell to Yakwendeh and started their return to Magoronwa. They reached the village by mid-day and headed straight to the family potato plot as they knew that the rest of the family will be there to finish the planting of the vines. Although they were busy planting, yet when the women saw them approach, all were excited to see them so early in the day. Bondaa was in another part of the plot trying to complete the fallow section of the plot where heaps have not yet been made. He was completely unaware of the arrival of Bendihe and Hopanda on site. It was only when Hopanda shouted to greet him, and he recognized his daughter's voice did he raise up his head and stopped to respond.

Nyanday Hopanda! Are you people back so early? We were expecting you by sun set. Anyway, you are welcome back."

"We left Gargbow just after the first cock crow. And since the weather was cool, we walked faster without the fatigue that someone normally experiences when the sun is very hot," she replied.

"Well, how was your trip?"

"We have come back without any obstacles on our way. But if you want to know the outcome of Mama Bendihe's mission, you know I am not privy to the reasons why we went to Gargbow. So, you must ask your dear wife. I have not the slightest clue. But she doesn't seem to be excited or thrilled."

This did not sound good to Bondaa who stooped for a moment to clean his hoe. "All right my *nyanday*; go join the others to plant those vines. We must complete the entire plot tomorrow. I will see you in the village then."

He resumed his heap making pondering on what Hopanda has just said that Bendihe doesn't seem enthusiastic. Something must have gone wrong somehow. What could this be? Has his decision taken too long that somebody has edged him out? Or could it be that the parents do not want their daughter to marry a much older man like him? Maybe Makalay does not want to be a third mate in a house where the only male is the husband and there will be bickering among the women. Could it be that Yakwendeh turned the request to be the spokeswoman and therefore Bendihe went to Sandima and Kargor on her own? Maybe Bendihe could not assertively and convincingly plead his case enough to persuade both parents and daughter? Or could it be that the parents were out of town and Bendihe could not wait?

These were the numerous questions that crossed his mind, and he could not put a finger on any one definite obstacle. He wanted to discard these thoughts, but he could not as this issue is vital to solving the Nwoingoha dilemma of a succeeding heir. He will leave every thought in place until he hears his wife's report on her mission. There is only one response to a proposal for marriage: a "yes or no" answer. If it will be a 'no' answer, then he will have to start all over again to identify the woman who fits the perfect description from Sago-Gbo.

This dampened his spirit considering the humiliating rejections some threatening on tarnishing his eminent position in the Nwoingoha clan. He didn't want to stain his prevailing excellent reputation in the Magoronwa and chiefdom community. Whatever the report will be, he must face it as a man and find the next best alternative approach to overcoming his dilemma.

He ended his pondering and resumed his work again. Today he will stop work early so that he could go and prepare a fresh palm tree to tap since one of his existing palm trees is now producing too strong palm wine that intoxicates with only two normal cups. He speeded the completion of the last heaps. Cleaned up his *paybayli* hoe and put it at the back of his shoulder so that the handle drops at his back. He picked up his clean clothes and his empty palm wine gourd. Then he shouted to his wives telling them that he was leaving earlier than usual. He wasted no time but went directly to tap his palm wine.

As he approached his palm tree, he observed that the gourd was unusually overflowing with froth. He noted that such a thing has not happened to him for quite a long time. He could remember that the first time this occurred to him he narrated the incident to his father who told him that when such a thing happens it's an omen which is either good or sad depending how full the gourd is even though it overflows.

"If you find the gourd full and it is dripping fast with palm wine, then it is a good omen." He had told him. "It indicates that something good and beneficial is coming your way. However, if the gourd is half full of froth and the drip is just trickling then it is an evil omen which indicates that some important event has failed to occur or the death of close member of the family."

He reflected on what his departed father had told him. Which of these omens could it be? He could only find out when he climbed and checked his gourd. In either case he was anxious to know. So, he placed his clothes and *paybayli* hoe down on the cane raft bench he had made just a distance from the palm tree trunk. He loosened his *baii* climbing rope so that he could put it around his waist and the trunk to climb. He tied his usual large empty gourd he had below to the climbing rope so that it will not fall and shatter pieces when it reaches the ground. He anxiously climbed the palm tree.

When he reached the top, he shook the gourd to see if it is full, something he didn't usually do when up there as the appearance of the gourd was normal. He shook it for the second time to ascertain the contents of the gourd. The gourd was certainly more than half full but not completely full as usual. He poured the palm wine in the empty gourd and noted to his dismay again that the gourd is not as full as it should be. This seemed to confuse him even further. The gourd is neither half nor full but far more than half full. So, if it is far more than full and if he relates this to his father's interpretation, it means that the good omen is incomplete and therefore an important pending event coming his way is still in the balance. He completed the tapping and descended. Before going home, he decided to take his bath at the village stream and not bother his wives to warm water for him to bathe. He changed into his clean clothes and took the half full gourd of palm wine, his *paybayli* hoe and proceeded to the village.

Bondaa's family completed planting the heaps that Bondaa had made with the help of some village men with an obligation to return the favour the next time they too will need help. Bendihe told the children to go ahead to the stream, wash and get some water to cook. It was a way to send them away so that she could have a freedom to narrate the outcome of her mission. They decided to seat under the large wild mango tree on the wayside to the village.

"Bendihe, how did it go?" Hogaii asked anxiously.

"You were right to send me to Yakwendeh. She is a woman of considerable experience, and she is a sweet talker. At first, she questioned our decision and said we should have left Bondaa to pursue his objective. Her exact words were 'we wives should leave our husbands alone to pursue their quest to marry a second, third or whatever wife as they choose.' But she was wonderful. She convincingly presented Bondaa's case with many parables and examples. Sandima and Kargor were persuaded to our reasoning with Bondaa. I think that they in turn must have given more justification to the circumstance because I was totally amazed at the response from Makalay herself. Makalay said in our presence and that of her parents that she 'will give Bondaa a chance to prove himself'. Those were her exact words. I was overjoyed she said that."

"What did the parents say before she made her decision?"

"She was not present when we went to the parents' house. She had gone to the stream to fetch water for her mother. So, she was not even aware that I was in the village. Kargor and Sandima promised to talk things over with her but reminded us that times have changed when parents decided for a girl who she will marry. They indicated that they would get back to us before nightfall with whatever her response will be. And indeed, they did not only come before nightfall,

160

but they came with Makalay. I believe they wanted us to get it from Makalay's lips. She said that I believe on her own assessment of who she should marry. I also believe that she also accepted the cautionary advice of her parents and decided to give Kayneh Bondaa a chance. Her words were 'I told them I will give Kayneh Bondaa a chance to prove himself'". Is that not all we want from her?"

"Certainly. Our role is ended in resolving Bondaa's dilemma. From now on we suggest nothing and do nothing until he tells us what to do."

"You can say that now but when he comes up with something it will be you who will first jump into his rescue. From now I am going to adopt Yakwendeh's advice and leave Bondaa alone to pursue the marriage of his third wife."

"Bendihe this time I am totally on board. No more rescues or interventions. We must wait for his next move."

"His next move has to be fast as the father told us that there could be secret admirers and that the door for his daughter's marriage is still wide open."

"So, are you going to tell him tonight?"

"I will be too tired to sit down and report after that long walk from Gargbow plus the work we have just finished on the farm. I think Bondaa can wait till tomorrow night. I will go to sleep immediately after we've had our evening meal. Besides I am experiencing a slight headache which means I need rest. After all, Bondaa took four months to think over our suggestion. So, one more night won't create any problem."

"Then I shall tell him nothing because you are the best person to deliver the message. It will be inap-

161

propriate for me to say anything. Let's go home and let's leave it at that." They got up from under the mango tree and proceeded home

Bondaa reached his house and he put his gourd of palm wine in the usual corner. He took his hoe to his room and returned to the veranda to relax for the first time since he left this morning to work. He then waited for his meal for which he didn't have to wait too long as Hopanda brought it and set it before him and left immediately. She told him that her younger sister will bring the drinking water. Even though the meal was his favourite rice and *jackitomboi* cooked with some dried bush meat from his traps, yet he did not have the usual seal when one is hungry. He lost appetite as he was pondered over that omen. He did not eat the food, instead he decided to drink his palm wine and sleep off this omen. He waited for a while and then called back Hopanda to take it away. Hopanda was surprised to find that his father had not eaten his food.

"What's wrong papa? Are you not well because I was told this afternoon that you only ate a small quantity of boiled cassava and ground raw pepper with salt as your mid-day meal?"

"I am okay my daughter. It's just one of those days when you lose your appetite, and you don't feel like eating anything."

"Or could it be that in our absence you and mama had a quarrel, and you want to show your displeasure by not eating her food?"

"No, my dear everything was fine between me and your mother in your absence. She did nothing to displease me. I just don't have the appetite tonight. Take the food back to them and let them share it among your younger sisters. Tell your mother thanks for the *jackitomboi* but I will only drink my palm wine tonight and that will be good enough for me. Tell her and Bendihe to join me in the veranda to drink the palm wine when they finish eating." Hopanda was not convinced as she looked her father straight in the eye and asked "Papa are you sure? Can we keep the rice and heat it up for you in the morning?"

"Yes! I'm sure and you should know by now that I don't eat stale rice in the morning."

"All right papa I will tell her" And she took the food away.

After the evening meal only Hogaii came to the veranda to join Bondaa.

"Where is Bendihe?" Bondaa asked Hogaii.

"Bendihe complained of headache and fatigue from the journey and the potato vine planting. She has asked me to tell you good night and she has gone to sleep. You should know that I have one more night with you before she can join you in bed."

"I can understand that." Bondaa said. "But she could've come to tell me so."

"Please forgive her tiredness" Hogaii pleaded on her behalf. Bondaa brought the palm wine from the usual corner and took the cup down from the same area. He sat in his hammock and poured out a full cup and gulped that as usual bottoms up. Then he poured out one for Hogaii and as he passed the cup to her, he asked "did Bendihe tell you the outcome of her mission?"

"She has not. You know that we're busy planting the vines and now she's gone to bed."

"Can you guess what it could be from her body language or the tone of her voice since she came back?"

"Nothing, whatsoever. I am also confused and equally anxious to hear her story" she lied thus keeping the promise to Bendihe not to tell him anything before Bendihe does so. She drank her cup in two breaks and handed the cup back to Bondaa who poured another cup for himself. Before drinking it, he revealed to Hogaii the omen on his palm tree and what could be its interpretation. Hogaii could not contribute anything to the possible interpretation as Bondaa told it.

"I was thinking of consulting Sago-Gbo to explain the omen."

"My advice is to wait a few days for the good part of the omen to come to pass. I will also suggest that you offer some sacrifice to avert the negative part."

"I will consider that, and I will tell you what type of sacrifice to offer. Meanwhile I will wait to know what comes up next." Bondaa poured out another cup full for Hogaii. This time she was slow in drinking it as if she was meditating on something while she drank it. When she finished, she said she has had enough, and she thanked her husband for the palm wine. She then asked for permission to go to bed as this was her third night with Bondaa before Bendihe takes her turn.

Bondaa was left alone in the veranda to finish drinking what remained in the gourd. After that he decided to have a smoke of his *Sangotho* before retiring for the night. But as he smoked, he pondered on the fact that he was in a state of uncertainty: uncertain about the actual manifestation of his palm wine omen but more disturbing perhaps is the uncertainty about the outcome of Bendihe's mission to Gargbow. Or does the omen relate to the Makalay issue because things seem to be unclear and doubtful as he has not seen Bendihe since she returned from her mission? Could the bad omen be that Makalay has rejected his proposal and Bendihe finds it hard tell him? But she must report he said to himself?

Whatever the answer, she must tell him because it was her obligation as an emissary to report to the sender. He resolved to wait until Bendihe took her turn tomorrow to sleep with him in his bedroom. If she said nothing by then, he will demand a report from her. But he didn't think Bendihe would withhold such vital information from Hogaii since they all agreed to send her on this mission. Only one option was left to Bendihe and that was to report to him and Hogaii after tomorrow's evening meal. So, he settled down to waiting until the next evening when he hoped Bendihe will reveal result of her.

However, this will be emotionally tormenting for him before then, but he knows that there is nothing he could do about it. He recognized the health of his wife is equally important to the family. He smoked his *Sangotho* without the relishing pleasure he used to get out of it when all is well with him. He smoked anyway to wile time away until he slept, and it was the fall of the pipe that startled him.

He did not know how long he had slept in the hammock, but he realized that it must have been some time because the entire village was very quiet and eerie. He picked up the pipe and went straight to his room and to bed.

It was morning the family must resume the potato farm work which needed to be completed so that the vines could take advantage of the early rains to germinate and have good yields. Bondaa went through his palm wine tree as is the routine itinerary before going to any place of work on that day. When he approached, he again observed the same froth on the tapping gourd. "What can this really be"? He asked himself. "It could only be a double confirmation of either a good omen or an ill one" he answered his own question. He climbed up and tapped the wine. Again, it was a little over half full just as it was yesterday. Again, he poured the palm wine into the receptive gourd, dressed the palm wine's dripping channel, and climbed down with the same despondence as last evening. He will have to ponder through this the whole day. He wished he had not come to tap and be so reminded of the emotional pondering. He reached the plot without realizing the distance he had walked.

"Good morning, everybody and thank you. You have covered a lot of ground. Well, I think we will finish this work today at the rate you are planting. I will go finish making the heaps on the plot that still needs heaps. I think I will do that before mid-day and you ladies will plant and we are done." He sounded amusing and optimistic shadowing his emotional tormenting feeling within.

"We thought you will not come today because you are late, and this is not your usual time to show up at work" Bendihe commented. "What held you up?" she asked.

"Nothing really. Maybe I slowed my walking pace. And besides, I had to take a few cups of palm wine to pep me up to start work."

"Hogaii has explained to me that you observed an omen at you palm wine tree last evening? What are you going to do about it?"

"I think we'll discuss this when the children are not around. Don't you think so?"

"When would that be?"

"This evening, if your headache does not persist after work."

"Okay. Did you hear that Hogaii?" Bendihe asked Hogaii.

"Yes. I heard all. Bondaa! I only hope you will come with a proposal that will either celebrate the good omen or avert the evil one."

"Bondaa, you know of course that in either case you need palm wine to pour libation for celebration of the good or aversion of the evil." Bendihe reminded Bondaa. "So, make sure you and your friends don't drink all the palm wine in the bush before you come home. Besides it's been several days since my lips touched your palm wine and I don't know how it tastes now." Bendihe was building a scenario wherein they will celebrate the incredible result of her mission when she reports tonight. She was keeping her husband out in the dark until tonight.

"I'm with you Bendihe" Hogaii supported her. "Please bring some for us tonight if you don't intend to celebrate or avert the omen."

"I am not sure what I want to do concerning the omen," Bondaa said "but I'm sure that I will bring some palm wine for you tonight. I will bring some from the new palm tree I tapped a week ago. Its palm wine is much tastier than the old one which is now strong. Let me go and finish making the heaps on that remaining small piece of land."

He walked briskly to the plot and started work with every amount of seriousness that depicted a conscientious husband and father. A little after mid-day he finished the plot and told his family that he was going near the village to clear a place to plant the pepper and eggplants given to Hogaii by her mother during their last visit to Mindorwa. He took the direction leading to the village and left the rest of the family to finish planting the potato vines on the heaps including the ones he's just made. He completed clearing the area and went to tap his palm wine.

As he went, he was uncertain what he will find again after the repetition of the omen this morning. Hesitantly, he approached his palm tree only to find that it was no longer foaming. He climbed up and found the gourd was full and if he had delayed coning it would have overflowed. He knew that the second foaming was a confirmation of the first. He briskly tapped the tree and immediately descended. Now he must do something about the omen soonest because delay can be dangerous and sometimes disastrous. He must work fast to avert the evil omen and facilitate the good soonest. Tonight, he will discuss with his wives, and he is glad he has a full gourd to take home for the purpose. While pondering on this he heard a rustling sound of somebody approaching. Indeed, it was his village associate, Korwaa, who had rescued him by giving him a gourd of palm wine to take Bendihe's parents.

"Hello Korwaa, are you going to the village?"

"Yes, I am."

"But I don't see your gourd by your side. It is rare to see you like that. What's the matter?"

"You may not believe what I have to tell you. In all my years of palm wine tapping I have never lost my gourd from the tree. I went to tap my palm tree. You know that when we move towards our palm tree to climb it, we look for the hanging gourd at the top to see if it's still there."

"Indeed, that is true, because you want to know if the gourd is collecting the sap of the tree."

"But when I looked up, I could not see my gourd up there. My first thought was that some thief has come from another village to steal our palm wines because this has never happened to anybody in this village."

"Did you look down to see whether it fell off the tree?"

"Sure enough, I did and saw my gourd lying shattered on the ground. It means that I did not secure the gourd properly to the frond. So, I have not only lost my tapping gourd but have no wine to drink this evening. I'm here to have a cup or two to quench my burning thirst for palm wine."

"You are fortunate that this didn't happen yester-day"

"Why do you say so?"

"My gourd was half full yesterday, that's why. I found it foaming and I assumed that it was full but when I went up it was half full. You know what that means to any palm wine tapper."

"An omen?"

"You got it right my friend. It happened again this morning, and I could only say that it was a confirmation of the first."

"You can delay a little the facilitation on the good omen, but you can't afford to wait to avert the evil omen. What are you doing about it?"

"I am going to have a family discussion with my wives this evening and this will go well with the exchange of cups of palm wine. I have reserved this for this evening. But I cannot afford not to give my buddy a cup or two. Sit down and I will pour you some."

Bondaa poured out three full cups for his comrade and friend who took moments to enjoy the drink.

"Thank you Bondaa. We can now go home". The friends left for the Kathabai River to have their baths before heading home. When they reached the village, each man departed for his house.

CHAPTER TEN

Bondaa went straight in and put the gourd of palm wine in its usual place. He coughed loudly and cleared his throat as usual to announce his presence. As an acknowledgement his daughters came to greet him in turn.

"Do you need warm water to wash?" Bendihe asked him.

"No. I have had my bath at the Kathabai."

"Your meal is ready when you are ready for it." Hogaii told him.

"I will have it now as the cassava portage this afternoon only dented my appetite. So let somebody bring it to the veranda. Then I will like you and Bendihe to join me later after you have completed all your chores. Remember we promised to discuss tonight on what to do about the omens of my palm tree."

"Call us when you are ready, and we shall be there." Hogaii replied.

Bondaa went to the veranda and shortly Hopanda brought his food. This day he has given up to whatever the outcome of the omens. He has prepared to brace up with whatever report Bendihe has to present. He therefore had his food with a great appetite and left a little for Hopanda who brought him the food. He hollered her and she came promptly to pick up the basins.

"Papa you almost finished your food tonight," Hopanda expressed delight at seeing how little he'd left over in the basins. "Your appetite has returned. I'm happy for you. I feared that you were getting sick"

"Tell your mother that I am ready for them," he told her.

"Yes papa." and she went off to inform her mother who was getting ready to go to her room. She diverted her direction towards the veranda and told Bendihe that Bondaa was ready for them in the veranda. Bothe trooped to the veranda and found Bondaa reclining in his hammock. They took their normal sitting positions on either side of the door but closer to Bondaa's hammock.

"Did you finish planting all the mounds with vines today?" he asked.

"There is none left. In fact, we have surplus vines. Maybe you must find another small spot to make some heaps so that we can plant all the vines," Hogaii replied.

"Okay, I will do that tomorrow," he responded. "Last night Bendihe had a headache. Maybe it was a result of the long walk from Gargbow and joining immediately to plant the heaps. I hope you are much recovered. Before we discuss what to do about the omen, I would want Bendihe to give a report on her mission."

"Before Bendihe gives her report, are you not forgetting to do something? You know that the traditional custom is that when you send an emissary on an important mission, the sender must welcome back the messenger with something before the report whether good or bad is delivered." Hogaii reminded Bondaa.

"Thank you Hogaii for reminding him. He knows that I will not say a single word of whatever my report will be. He has to welcome me in the correct customary manner."

"You are right Hogaii. It's my omission. I will correct that now." He went into his room and took a ten Leones note from his safe box and returned to his wives. He handed the money to Hogaii and said "please give this to Bendihe for her journey to and from Gargbow and for whatever ordeal she might have endured during her mission. I wish to welcome her formally and kindly ask her take a rest before she gives us her report."

"Thank you Bondaa for this gesture. We cannot forget to follow the good traditions our people have passed down to us. Bendihe your husband who sent you says, 'take a rest and report'" and she handed over the ten leones to Bendihe. "Bondaa has suggested that you give us your report before we discuss the omen. I have no objection with it. I agree with him as I am equally anxious to know what we have stepped into."

"I thank you Hogaii for reminding Bondaa of his obligation as the sender. Thank you also Bondaa and I pray that God puts His blessings upon what we are working towards; and that all evil forces will be impotent to derail your objectives or place any obstacle against our objective."

"How did it all go at Gargbow?" Bondaa asked Bendihe sounding anxious.

"Well, let me start from the beginning. When we reached, I complied with your advice that I put up with Yakwendeh. She welcomed us generously and gave us a comfortable room for me and Hopanda. In the night I explained the purpose of my mission."

"How did she receive that?" Hogaii asked so that Bondaa can know how much they have bent backwards to accommodate his passion for an heir.

"When I explained to her, she was furious that we should be involved in your quest for third wife. She thought it to be weird. She couldn't comprehend how two wives and a husband can agree to get a third wife. 'You mates are special. You are not of the stock of jealous wives even where the wife does not love the husband.' Those were her exact words. She thought that we should have left you alone to pursue your quest to marry your third or whatever wife you choose" 'You don't assist them as you can never foretell the future outcome,' she said. However, she was a bit palliated when I explained our rationale for granting you, our consent."

"Did she consent to go with you?" Bondaa asked.

"Though not completely convinced, yet she took over the mission to Sandima and Kargor"

"With that hesitation I wonder whether she did her utmost to plead my case." Bondaa expressed doubt.

"You will know that when I conclude my report. As I said she took over the mission and led me to the house. She displayed her wisdom and experience because she was wonderful. She forcefully and convincingly put forward your case with all sorts of parables and examples to persuade them. During our meeting Makalay was not in the house. She had gone to fetch water for their evening cooking."

"But were they persuaded?" asked Bondaa.

"After several exchanges on the matter this was what they told us 'Our daughter is now mature, and she will make her own decision though we may give her parental advice as to who she will choose as a future husband'. But Kargor added to say that she will have a talk with her daughter when she returned from the stream. And they promised to give us an answer by the evening. We left with that promise."

"Some people will tell you that as a way to get rid of you." Bondaa observed.

"That did not seem to be the impression we got from them. They seemed sincere but couldn't commit their daughter because times have changed from our days when we did not choose our husbands. You remember Bondaa that my parents consented to you marrying me and not the other way round?"

"Yes, I do but I believe that you've had no regrets since? We have been a happy family with you having three beautiful daughters, the envy of the village."

"No, I have no regrets and those three daughters came from the womb of a beautiful mother which you can't deny."

"What then can I say about myself and children?" Hogaii butted in. "why do you two want to take us back to things we had put behind us. I will suggest we hear Bendihe complete her report because I'm getting tired and sleepy."

"You are right Hogaii. I will continue. Sandima and Kargor kept their promise. They came to see us bringing along Makalay. I was worried that things might have gone awry and therefore they brought Makalay to explain herself to us. They were relaxed and looked somehow in a bright mood though I was tense with anxiety. We went into Yakwendeh's room and shut the door so that no other person could hear the conversation. When we were all settled Sandima said that they have brought Makalay along so that she can tell us directly what she told them after discussing your proposal with her. She did not appear as someone who had been pressured into acceding to something she disliked. She addressed us in a composed and gentle voice that was clear and emphatic. This is what she said: 'I have to listen to the cautionary advice of my parents who in their hearts want to see me comfortably married. I have reflected on these and told them I will give Bondaa a chance to prove himself.' My heart leapt with joy within me though I could not express my emotions before the rest of them."

"It's delightful to hear that. It is good to maintain good relationships with devoted friends," Hogaii expressed her emotions as if she was hearing this for the first time.

"Hogaii! That is my report from my trip to Gargbow. I just repaid your debt when you went to intimate my parents about Bondaa's intention to marry me."

"Thank you for a successful mission. There's no better way of putting it," commented Hogaii "Bondaa, you have heard Bendihe's report. I'm sure you have something to say and do."

"Let me add the warning of the parents before he says anything." Bendihe continued. "They said that Makalay is uncommitted for now and that there are men out there who might also propose to her."

For a moment Bondaa was speechless not believing what he just heard from Bendihe. He started reflecting on the palm tree omen. "So, this is what the omen was all about. The more than half full gourd means that the good omen is incomplete and therefore the thing coming my way is still uncertain since Makalay has only said she is giving him a chance to prove myself. If I don't measure up to the expectations of Makalay and her parents within the shortest possible time, I might miss my greatest opportunity of preserving the survival of his clan. My wives have done all within their ability to facilitate the preservation of the clan lineage. There was nothing more they can do for me on this issue. The approach I must adopt in solving this dilemma is now entirely mine. This I must approach with urgency." Then he ended his mind wondering by asking Bendihe the question "Did you say that Makalay said that she is giving me a chance to prove myself?"

"She said nothing more after that sentence."

It then dawned on him that challenge to marry Makalay is open: who will go first to make a formal proposal for Makalay and be accepted? He is no doubt the first to make the approach and he has been given the first opportunity to formally follow up this informal show face. The next step must be something more colourful and acceptable to both the uncommitted spinster and her parents. The next step must be something more colourful and acceptable to both the uncommitted spinster and her parents. But first things first. He must thank Bendihe in a special way for her willingness to go and her endurance of the tension of uncertainty. So, he got up from his hammock where he has been sitting all along with his legs dangling and went again to his room. He opened the same box, took hundred Leones notes from his savings, and returned to the veranda. He handed the money to Hogaii and as he was sitting back in his hammock he said "What Yakwendeh said about you two women is quite appropriate, and I appreciate it very much. It is certainly rare for mates to collaborate so much to help their husband in an issue what is entirely his dilemma to solve. This money is for you and Bendihe. It is a token of my appreciation for your extraordinary and amazing support to me over my dilemma for an heir. I thank you very much. Your daughters will be blessed because you've been supportive of my quest."

Hogaii was surprised at this unusual gesture of gratitude from their husband as she received the money but said nothing. She simply handed the money to Bendihe and said "Bendihe we have hundred Leones from Bondaa as a token of his gratitude to us for our peculiar but remarkable support to him."

"I want to thank you Bondaa. But I think you should do more for us if you appreciate our uncommon help to you to get an heir. A hundred Leones notes is fine, but I think you should demonstrate your gratitude in a more concrete way. What you will do we will leave that to you. Do you agree with me Hogaii?"

"I wanted to give you the younger mate the chance to say something first before I come in. Bondaa, you surprised us. This is unexpected and I am pleased with this as a token of your high appreciation of our actions on this issue. I pray that your quest will be accomplished. But I totally agree with Bendihe. It is an exceptional act that we have done for you, and you know it. As you have just said it is very uncommon for mates to agree to help a husband to get a third wife. Yakwendeh said we should have left you alone to pursue your quest for a third wife. But we did not. I will suggest therefore, that if all goes well for you and you marry Makalay, Bendihe and I deserve a decent house roofed with corrugated iron sheets (pan house) to spend the rest of our lives in it. We are not asking for an appeasement or concession edifice. When you do this, you would also silence the critics about our singular action in this affair. Besides you will be the envy of the village and probably the entire chiefdom. Don't you think so Bendihe?"

"That is why I like about you as a senior mate. You think ahead and big too. What else could be a better proposition? And this is not a big deal for Bondaa as we know you can do something extra in the Blacksmith workshop. We'll be here to help where we can."

Bondaa seemed taken aback by the Hogaii's proposal. He has been thinking about constructing a decent house roofed with corrugated iron sheets. He was thinking ahead that if he cannot have a son that will succeed him then he needs to have such a house that will be admired. He knows that old aged he will not be able to cut the grass and tote it down from the hilltop to mend current thatched house when it leaks. It is a sheer coincidence that he and Hogaii have been thinking on long term family interest. He has been funding this thought with some savings earned from his workshop to purchase corrugated iron sheets undisclosed to his wives as he wanted to surprise them. But it has now surfaced as a common need for the family that will stay when all the daughters would have married and gone to the respective villages of their husbands. Should he reveal his plans to them or only promise to consider their request as leverage for their help when it really needed.

"I have heard you and I don't think it is an unjustifiable request" Bondaa said. "I think you are right. We need to have a house where we shall have less worries about leakages at night when it rains or worse perhaps fire to gut our grass house. We shall all work on this together. Now about Makalay. I'm worried about the parents' warning that there are suitors out there who might also propose to her. I need to double my efforts and leave no stone unturned to get this issue concluded soonest. I intend to follow up these five days from tonight. I think I can do this if you ladies are still with me. I believe we all want to see the final chapter in solving this critical dilemma. Can I still count on you?"

"You can. We will help in your preparation by cleaning the rice and making the palm oil to take to the occasion," said Hogaii. "We shall offer no more suggestions or plans. But we shall do what is in our capacity to do. Don't you think so Bendihe?"

"I have told you before that you speak as a senior mate. I agree with you. We have done far more than what we should do. From now on we will listen to you and do what is within our social responsibility as wives."

"I hear you and I accept your position from this point," Bondaa yielded to his wives' stand. "I want you to go to the farm and take some rice from the barn thresh it, parboil it and clean it for the trip to Gargbow."

"When will this be?" Bendihe asked.

"In five days', time"

"So soon?" Hogaii asked

"Yes soon. You heard the warning from Makalay's parents. I cannot allow the momentum to slip through my fingers. My father was repeatedly telling me that the black goat which you cannot find during the day you will never see it during the night. I need to fast track this whole issue as I have delayed too long since you two suggested to me about Makalay."

"We shall do as you have instructed. How many bushels do we thresh?" Bendihe asked she will have to lead the children in threshing it.

"It has to be six because two bushels of husk will give you one and half bushels of clean rice. We shall take one full bag and whatever remains shall be for our consumption."

"It shall be done as instructed."

"Tomorrow I shall go to Ngandiya to buy a he-goat from him for the journey," Bondaa informed his wives. "The next day I shall go to Royeima to get some decent gown sewn for me for the event. The day following my return from Royeima we shall proceed to Gargbow."

"I think we have so far concluded tonight's discussions. I must go to bed as I'm now sleepy" Hogaii said getting up from her bench bidding her husband a good night.

"You are right Hogaii. We're done for the night. Good night senior mate" she said as she's about to start her three nights with Bondaa. She too got up and went in leaving Bondaa as usual reclining in his hammock.

CHAPTER ELEVEN

Two days later he went again to Ngandiya to buy another goat. He returned late in the evening and told his wives that he was going to see Pa Woroma at Royeima early in the morning. He explained to them that he had found a self-banished Magoronwa man there and established a very cordial relationship with him. He did not want to disclose the actual purpose of the journey which was to sew another set of dresses for his wives and a gown for himself. When he arrived at Royeima, Pa Woroma was surprised to see him so soon for the same purpose. He explained that for the exceptional part his present wives played in the search for his third wife, they deserve special thanks by sewing another set of dresses for them and this should be a surprise to them. So, in addition to his gown, he ensured that tailor Siddie sewed nice cotton dresses for his wives as the previous ones. He also bought new head ties to match the dresses.

This time tailor Siddie expedited the sewing so that he returned a day after he left Magoronwa. The following night he again planned to surprise this wife for the second time as an appreciation of their wonderful and remarkable support to him. After the evening meal, he summoned them to the usual evening family discussion on pending or recent issues that need to be addressed appropriately. This discussion he purposed should be on the Makalay proposition and it will be in his room because he did not wish intruders to interrupt their private family discussion. He had brought enough palm wine for this meeting. When his wives came into the room, he was having a cup of palm wine. After finishing that he served Hogaii first as the custom demands and then Bendihe. As he poured out another cup for himself, he told Bendihe to pull out his travelling raffia bag from its usual place and take out what is in it.

"You have never asked me to do so before, how come you are asking me today to open your bag?"

"To everything there is a beginning or a first time." he replied.

Bendihe got up from her bench and fetched the bag and carefully opened it so as not to disturb whatever delicate things are packed in it. She took out the first dress laid it on the box close to her.

"Take out the next one and all the head ties in there." Bendihe obeyed as instructed and put everything on the box.

"The dresses are for you both. I needed to express my high appreciation and indebtedness to you in a positive way. I have sewn those dresses for you. You will observe that it is the same cotton material, and the style and pattern are also the same. That is what you women call

Ashoyebi. In this society we know that it is the husband who cloths the wife. So, by sewing an *Ashoyebi* for you at least people will evidently see that I am not partial in my relationship with my wives. Of course, the sizes will tell whose which is. I would plead with you to wear those dresses when we go to Gargbow to propose to Makalay." Bendihe unfolded the dresses to see which size is hers. Having seen it she gave the rest to Hogaii, and she returned to her seat.

"We have known over the years," Hogaii remarked "that whenever we positively accomplish a task for you, we are somehow surprised with gifts. Let me on behalf of Bendihe and on my own behalf thank you for the dresses. They are beautiful and neatly sewed. Thank you very much and may your daughters be blessed to get husbands like you."

"I will only add by praying that no obstacle will impede achieving your desire," Bendihe said. "We know how desperate you are to solve this dilemma. It surrounds the survival of the Nwoingoha clan and its traditions. I believe that the oracles are in your favour because from the day Hogaii and I agreed to accede to your request things seem to be working perfectly. I can confidently say that the final solution to this dilemma rests with the Makalay."

"I would like to ask you Bondaa, 'will our two eldest daughters be joining us to Gargbow?' I ask this question because we are not going to tote the rice and other things, we are taking to Gargbow. I know though that your nephew, Yongaa, will be around to take the heavy stuff like the 5-gallon tin of palm oil or the two bushels of rice. If the answer is yes, then they will need to put on some decent dresses. I am sure that you don't want your daughters to be dressed in old raggedy dresses while their mothers are adorned in latest styles. Don't you think so Bendihe?

"I would hate to perspire in my new dress because I have to carry my heavy stuff and may be this cotton colour will run off with the sweat and so spoil the beauty of the entire dress," Bendihe remarked. "Hopanda and Yagoro have to go with us. But if for anything else they need to witness, hear, and see what our ancestors left with us for nuptial arrangements.

They too need to know what we expect as parents when it is their time to marry. We needn't only build their characters and attitudes but also to build up their minds through witnessing and observing those norms and traditions which will make them good wives tomorrow. You, husband, will take all the honour, though the primary responsibility of bringing up a girl to womanhood is the wife's. We also know that if a girl grows up discourteous, disrespectful, and uncivil it is the mother who takes the blame. I would therefore support Hogaii that Hopanda and Yagoro should accompany us to Gargbow."

"This never crossed my mind," Bondaa confessed, "because when I was proposing to each of you, only my uncle Sandigi Kenju, my elder sister and my aunt accompanied me. While I was in Royeima to sew your clothes I thought about that. But I wanted to know your take on this because I thought I should go only with my wives and Yongaa to carry the rice and palm oil. Now that you have expressed with tangible arguments the rationale for Hopanda and Yagoro to go with us, I will send Yongaa tomorrow to Royeima to sew a dress for each for them. You will choose the style for each."

"You leave that to us," Hogaii said." We will talk to the children tonight because we know Yongaa will leave very early in the morning to cover a greater part of the journey before it gets hot," Hogaii said.

"When then are we going to make the trip with this new development?" Bendihe asked Bondaa.

"It now has to be in two days after Yongaa returns from Royeima, because I know that the tailor will not sew the dresses today even if he arrives at Royeima early. It will take the tailor almost the entire day to sew those two dresses. Knowing the hazards on the road between Magoronwa and Royeima, I will advise him not to risk returning late whenever the tailor finishes."

Bondaa called Yongaa and gave him instructions to leave very early in the morning for Royeima to sew dresses for his two daughters. He told him that Hogaii and Bendihe will give explain to him what styles the children would have chosen. He directed him to go directly to Pa Woroma and to refer any issue to him as he is a son of Magoronwa and a relative. Yongaa left early as expected but did not return on the day he was expected. This worried Bondaa reflection on Sandima's warning that the door for their daughter's marriage is still wide open. More delays could be losing the opportunity he has to be the first to propose for Makalay's hand. What could have happened? Could it be that Yongaa fell a victim of muggers and stripped of the money? But if he was unhurt, he could have returned to report this. Could it be that the money was insufficient, but he told him to refer any issue to Pa Woroma? Or could it be that the tailor was out of Royeima that he had to wait on his return? Or was he sick and unable to walk back soon? These were bothering thoughts. Should he go after him to find out what happened, or should he still trust Yongaa's discretion to do the right thing? He decided to do the latter, but he had to nervously wait for additional four anxious days. He was very apprehensive.

Yongaa return late in the evening when the village was almost asleep. When he heard the knock on the door and Yongaa announced his arrival, Bondaa jumped from his bed and rushed to open for him.

"Yongaa, how are you, my son. I was so worried about you because I cannot afford to lose a hardworking nephew like you. What happened my son?"

"Uncle, two unfortunate issues confronted me. When I arrived, I was informed that the tailor had travelled that same day with his wife to visit relatives in a village almost afar as Magoronwa is from Royeima and they will return only after two days. He indeed returned in two days but then he said his legs hurt as it had been many years since he'd walked that distance, and he could not pedal his machine in another two days."

"And he is no young man like you. I understand such situations and I pity him"

" But that was not all. On the day he was to sew he could not trace his machine shuttle as he had to remove it to prevent the use of the machine in his absence. He could not find it for the whole day and that meant another day added. Even when he eventually traced it, he did not have the right colour threads for the different cotton cloths I bought."

"He is getting old, and he hasn't a son to learn from him and take over from him when he can no longer sew or when he dies. Yongaa, you realize that this is the same dilemma I face right now with the blacksmith shop. Who will take over after I'm gone and who will carry on with the Nwoingoha clan name? You are my nephew, but your father is of the *Gbendeponga* clan. According to our clan's sacred traditions and norms, of which you are aware, my trade can only be taken over by a male *Nwoingoha* son."

"I now understand why you are preparing to propose to a younger woman whom you hope will give the son. I wish you success in this venture as we all stand to benefit from a fruitful outcome. I have brought the dresses for Hopanda and Yagoro. I hope they will like the sewing since they chose the styles"

He handed over the dresses to Bondaa.

"Thank you Yongaa. I cannot express how much I appreciate you especially for the fact that you're now playing the role of a son. Thank you very much. I have some palm wine for when you finish eating the food reserved for you as I had instructed my wives to reserve a dish for you every day."

"Hopanda get up and give Yongaa his food" He shouted to his eldest daughter. Yongaa had his meal and took the palm gourd with him as he left.

In the next two days Bondaa and his wives put the last touches to the travel arrangements. They made sure they had all that is required in making a marriage proposal especially for a girl in another village because for in-village marriage certain requirements are waived. Hopanda and Yagoro plaited their hair for the occasion but also to captivate the attention of young men. The previous day Bondaa had gone to the forest in the morning to pick some fresh kola nuts for the occasion and later that same day he went to pick up the he-goat from Ngandiya. Hogaii and Bendihe measured the cleaned rice to ensure that it is a full bushel (12.5 kg) and made sure that the red palm oil is a full five-gallon tin. Hogaii had gone to the local market at Pelewala to purchase the calabash into which items symbolizing the elements of a successful marriage are placed.

Early in the morning of the third day after Yongaa's return, Bondaa woke up, hurriedly washed his face, took his two gourds, and went straight to tap his palm wine to take to Gargbow for the occasion. As he approached, he heard the repeated coo-coo of a dove. But as he drew closer near the palm tree the coo-coo stopped. He looked for the dove, but he couldn't see it. Then the coo-coo started again and Bondaa heard the coo-coo right on top of his tapped palm tree. He looked up and saw the dove. He thought to himself "my father had told me when I was a youth that whenever you hear the coo-coo of a dove on your palm tree you want to tap or kola nut tree from which you want to pick some nuts for specific purpose, it is announcing some good fortune." He smiled as this is the sort of good omen, he wanted to hear for today a momentous day for him and his clan. He said to the dove "thank you, may that good thing you have announced come to pass." The dove coo-cooed again three times as if to say you are welcome.

Bondaa took his climbing rope and tied it around the palm tree and hung the two gourds on his left shoulder. As he took the first three climbing grips, the dove flew off, but Bondaa continued to climb until he reached the gourds with the palm wine. He quickly tapped the wine and descended as fast as he could. He was aware of the fact that it was hot season and if you are going on a long journey on foot, you better start it early when the sun has not risen, and the morning is still fresh and cool. Reaching home, he found that the women were ready, but Yongaa was not there. He inquired but was told they have not seen nor received a word from him. He was perturbed because Yongaa must carry the rice and if he not available it means he would have to tote the rice and pull the he-goat behind him, and this will slow their journey. He was worrying over this when he heard Yongaa's voice greeting another person.

"Thank God he is coming," easing his tension.

"I will get ready soon and we shall start our journey," he told his wives.

He gently set down the gourds of palm wine close to the bag of rice to ensure their safety and so that he might not forget them if they are far from the rest of the things. He rushed into his room and key-opened his box to take out the special gown and matching pants he has sown to wear for the occasion. He tucked them in his travelling raffia bag. He also slipped in his hand-woven hat of multi- colours complementing his gown. At the right corner of the box, he took out an old 'woodbine' cigarette tin, opened it and took out the money he had saved for the marriage, inserted it in small compartment of the raffia bag and buttoned it. He turned round and picked up the neatly wrapped kola nuts at the right corner of his room. He stood for a moment and looked around to see if he's omitting something that could jeopardize the outcome this important journey. He was content that he has taken all that is needed but as he approached the door, he saw his machete on the floor. He picked it up as he knows that a man cannot go on a journey like this without something to defend himself and family in an attack by robbers or wild beast. When he stepped out of his room found Yongaa drinking palm wine.

"I went to tap my palm wine as you too will not be here to tap it for me. That is the reason you did not find me when you returned from yours. I have had enough cups for the journey, and I am sure you need some too. I am positive that you did not have some from your palm as that is what we are taking to Gargbow."

"You are absolutely right. I could not have even a cup as the gourds on the palm tree seemed to have gathered just enough palm wine to fill those two gourds" he said pointing at the gourds near the bag of rice. As he sat down putting his raffia bag close to him, Yongaa poured him a cup and handed it to him. He gulped it with some relish and gave a big belch giving up the gas that had accumulated in his belly overnight.

"That is good palm wine, Yongaa. I wish I had tasted this before; I would exchange one gourd for yours as my wine is beginning to get stronger." Yongaa poured another and again he gobbled that immediately and handed the cup back to Yongaa who poured the last and set the cup on the floor so that the dregs would settle down before drinking it.

"Thank you Yongaa now I feel good to start the journey."

"Before we do that, I prepared some *pehmahun*

for you to eat so that you feel better after that palm wine", Bendihe disclosed. "We cannot start a journey of that distance without having something in your stomach. We have already eaten ours and we're only waiting for you and Yongaa to have yours. Yagoro bring the food for your father and Yongaa. Don't forget that you bring the water first before bringing the food."

"You are very thoughtful, and we are grateful," Bondaa expressed his appreciation. When they finished eating, he went back to his room and fetched small three-legged pot containing water, twenty cowries and four kola nuts (two white and two red). He called everybody in house including those staying behind to squat round the pot and touch the edge of the pot so that he could tell his ancestors goodbye and to seek their support for his mission.

"Pa Guhun, Pa Hanwa, Pa Yeemeh, Ya Yehuleh, Ya Fayngray, Ya Digba, Ya Ndemore Chapaa, Pa Koilowdo and all you other ancestors who I have not called". Bondaa started his offer of sacrifice for ancestral spirits intervention. "You all have gone before me and left me as the only son to continue with the traditions, customs and trade that are sacred to the Nwoingoha clan. I need not state that you require me to pass on these sacred Nwoingoha rites and customs to another son. But you all know that I have been blessed with six beautiful daughters but no son. When I consulted Sago-Gbo, you revealed unto him that I will have a male child but under certain defined conditions. I have fulfilled those conditions to the best of my capabilities. Today I am about to embark on a journey that is the first important stage of the solution of the dilemma I face. I am going to Gargbow to ask for the hand of Makalay, the daughter of Sandima and Kargor. She is a young girl and hopefully she will be a virgin that she will bear me a son. I, therefore, come to you to grant me a favour and remove all obstacles and barriers on this journey. Make a clear and easy path for me. Destroy all the plans of the evil ones, all witchcraft manipulations and make them impotent in derailing my plans. That is my request this morning and we leave under the protective shadow of your spirits."

When he finished everyone got up and dipped the tip the fingers of their right hands rubbed the water between their hands and wiped their faces from the brow to the chin with the wet hands. He poured some of the remaining water on the floor outside of the front door. Those who were going on the journey stepped on the spilled water and never re-entered the house again but continued the journey.

Before Bondaa and his entourage reached Gargbow they rested at the stream some distance from the town so that they wash of the sweat and dust and change to clean clothes before taking the last lap of the journey. They reached before mid-day because of their early start. Bondaa had decided days before their departure that he will not ignore Yakwendeh who was his intermediary and negotiator with Sandima and Kargor. Therefore, he had sent an earlier message of their coming and requested her to lodge him and accom-panying family members. On arrival they went straight to Yakwendeh's compound where they were warmly welcomed by her and her husband Krikoma. She had made prior arrangements to lodge any extra strangers they could not accommodate in their compound. Bondaa was lodged in the front room of the house. Hogaii and Bendihe were given a room inside the house although one of them (whose turn it is to sleep with him) will join Bondaa later. The two girls were told to join their equals at night in the main parlour. Young Yongaa was lodged in a neighbouring house. After completing lodging the strangers, Yakwendeh sent a word to Makalay's parents that they should expect visitors at eve time and that they should sum-mon all close relatives and elders of the village at his residence. After the evening meal Bondaa briefed Krikoma and his wife the purpose of their mission. It was not a surprise to wife. But to the husband it was a total shock. His wife had kept visit from him because she knows her husband leaks out secrets when he has partaken enough cups of palm wine to make him spill out secrets. Krikoma was curious to know why Bondaa should go for a girl almost half his age and a little older than Hopanda, Bondaa's first daughter.

Since Bondaa wanted him to be his spokesman for this important stage of his endeavour, he laboriously explained to him the reason for his decision to marry Makalay. To forestall and pre-empt an obvious question that Krikoma would ask, Hogaii voluntarily told him that she and her mate are in full agreement with their husband, and he has their complete support. Bondaa's explanation and the confirmation by Hogaii persuaded Krikoma. He willingly accepted the honour to be the spokesman to convincingly present Bondaa's proposal to Makalay's parents.

"Well, well, well Bondaa how am I to approach this issue?"

"Is there any other way rather than the way our forefather fashioned and adopted? Has Gargbow added something unknown to me and which is necessary? I think we need to clear this before we rise up to go."

"Oh no, nothing spectacular, just that present day Gargbow is becoming a little more sophisticated. They now require a bottle of schnapps gin in addition to the palm wine."

"I wish I had a fore knowledge of this. I could have sent to buy it at Kanunwa. In the absence of this can we make a cash substitution for the equivalent value?"

"Oh yes, although they would prefer the liquid itself. What else do we have to take?"

"The usual contents in the calabash. Hogaii can you please bring the calabash." Hogaii went and fetched the calabash covered with a fitting hand-woven raffia fan and on the top is a small mat made from small raffia and straw. The calabash and the top contents were tied with a white shirting. Hogaii gently set it before Bondaa and returned to her bench.

"First there are one hundred kola nuts," Bondaa started to list the items in the calabash, "fifty white and fifty red to indicate that I come as a peaceful man to give life to all the relatives of Makalay. Then there are fifty bitter kolas which when chewed are bitter but when swallowed leave a sweet after taste. I need Makalay to know that in a marriage, bitter moments are to be chewed with endurance but after which pleasing and delightful moments follow. In the calabash there is a pod of alligator pepper to indicate my intending wife that marriage can be hot. We all know that when one chews the seeds from this pod one's mouth is hot as if one chewed hot pepper. Next is a small bottle of honey. There is no explaining what this denotes. Then there is needle and white thread pointing out to Makalay that my clothes and hers will wear out and might be ripped. We should mend each other's clothes so that the public will not see our concealed and shameful body parts. The calabash is to be used to wash the rice she will cook by removing all grains of sand so that I will unnoticeably chew them and make the rest of the eating unpalatable. The fan covering the calabash, Makalay will use to cool any hot food she will serve me to eat so that I don't have a sore mouth from eating hot food. The mat is for us to sleep on. The entire calabash is tied with a white piece of cloth signifying that the intentions are pure and wholesome."

"Don't you think you have forgotten the most important item when your new wife comes to your room for her first night? Krikoma observed.

"No, I have not. I have deliberately reserved that item to the end of this list and that is the one-piece white shirting. This shirting will show the virginity of the wife when the marriage is consummated."

"What about the dowry money?" again Krikoma asked.

"As for the dowry money, I have not placed it in the calabash. I will give it to you at the right moment when you ask for it. I have done so to ensure harmony in my household in case everything materializes tonight. I am taking the identical approach about the dowry money as I did when I went to marry my second wife Bendihe. I believe, Krikoma, that you will adopt the same tactic if you were in this position."

"I guess I would. But I don't think I will go again for a second wife. Yakwendeh has fulfilled all I need from a wife in my life. There is no reason for me to want another wife." Krikoma said.

"Yakwendeh, you have heard the list of things that Bondaa has placed in the Calabash. Is there anything in the eyes of a woman that we men have omitted? We need to know now so that we could remedy it before we head to Sandima's house?"

"I don't think he has skipped anything. I believe he has perfected the list after two wives," she replied. "I commend his decision not to put the dowry money in the calabash, because his wives sitting right here will not be glad if they know that Bondaa has paid more dowry for Makalay than he did for either of them. We know that the amount of the dowry is a secret kept within the immediate blood relatives."

"I will also give you enough money for all the *boraas* and other unforeseen issues that may need to be taken care of." Bondaa told Krikoma.

"Good, then we shall go after the evening meal." Krikoma confirmed the earlier message that Yakwendeh sent to Sandima and wife.

Indeed, after the meal, the wedding troupe of Bondaa and his family and Krikoma and his family headed out to the Sandima compound. The mission is to carry out a ceremony that will either break the Nwoingoha clan inheritance chain forever or solve the dilemma that faces this clan. Before heading out the tradition dictates that the calabash must be toted by a young girl aged between five and ten years. She should be dressed in white clothes from head to toe. This is to signify the genuineness and purity of what is being taken to the in-laws-to-be.

Krikoma led the way followed by Bondaa and the rest of the entourage followed behind. The women were singing a low-pitched known tune in the community that denotes that the troupe is heading to a wedding ceremony. The walk was deliberately slow but systematic and rhythmic. About twenty yards from their destination the singing was halted, and they walked quietly to the house. When they reached the compound, it was barred with a makeshift bamboo cane fence thus preventing any authorized entry. The gate can only be opened from within. It was unusual because the Sandima compound is never barred. But this time it was because the message that Sandima received from Yakwendeh was specific and he did not want any intruders in his compound. But this worried Bondaa as he believed that the message was a goodwill one and did not understand why the barrier. Bondaa has probably forgotten that he encountered the same deliberately planned obstacle when he went to Mindorwa and Dendehun to marry Hogaii and

197

Bendihe. He was too anxious to get this through that he now viewed this as an impediment to the solution of his dilemma. He has forgotten that such hurdles are created deliberately to test the resolve of the intending paramours as to how much they want the woman. The entourage will be taunted and sometimes ridiculed to assess their love and determination to marry the woman they want in the house or compound.

"Knock, Knock, Knock" Krikoma shouted the top of his voice which anybody inside the compound could hear. But there was total silence within, not even a dog barked. He shouted again, "Knock, Knock, Knock. Can anybody hear me?" Again, the silence was even deafening. But Krikoma cannot give up as he knows this is part of the ceremony.

"If anybody is living in this compound that hears me, please open this gate?" He shouted once more.

"Who is that trying to break through the gate?" a response came from the compound. "What do you want at this late time of the night?"

"It is just nightfall, and we are strangers that have travelled a long way to visit the family in this compound."

"Sorry mister, at this time of the night, we do not open our gate for strangers especially for those who come from afar. When you say it's just nightfall, you might be a thief or violent person trying to sneak into the compound."

"On the contrary I have come with women. If I am what you think, I would not come with women and young girls and ask if anyone is in the compound. Just open the gate slightly and examine our faces that you should be able to recognize in the slight darkness even though we might miss voices."

"What? I must be an idiot to stick my head out. That gives you an opportunity to chop it off and then you can have easy access."

"But wait a moment. I know this voice to be that of a man in this town."

" But I don't know yours, mister. Yours is strange to me."

"Bawunda," Krikoma called. "This voice talking to you is Krikoma's."

"Krikoma, I don't remember voices at night and sometimes you don't want to hear some voices that will keep you awake for the rest of the night."

"I perfectly understand, but please open the gate knowing that it is me, Krikoma, your neighbour. I have come with an entourage with a message of peace and love"

"But why come during nighttime?"

"This is the best time as everybody would have returned from their farms or swamps and would have had their evening meals. This is the time when families sit together to review their farm work and plan the next. You also know Bawunda that this is the time family disputes are discussed and settled. But more importantly families receive messages from credible messengers too. And I am one of those messengers with a message that will be hard for you to refuse to hear."

"But why do come with an entourage of women and children?"

"They are the witnesses to my message as they too will share the joy of my message"

"Alright Krikoma I will allow you to come in with your entourage. But get this, you don't have the whole night here. You have only a brief period to deliver your message."

Bawunda opened the gate and let in Krikoma and his entire train of followers Bondaa closely behind him. When they came in, they noticed that the compound already had several people seated. On one end of the compound Sandima and immediate family members were seated on wooden chairs. Other close relatives were not far from them. The women were in the opposite side of the men and prominent among them was Kargor dressed appropriately for the occasion. However, Makalay was nowhere to be seen. What could have happened? The worrying thought came to Bondaa. But now he remembered that in an occasion like this betrothed woman should not be in the mist of people. She will be seated in a separate room dressed in complete white from head down to her toes. Certain seats had been reserved for the strangers and they were accordingly ushered to their seats. However, before sitting the visitors exchanged handshakes and hugs with laughter all around with the hosts. When everybody was comfortably seated, Krikoma got up and took the small wrap of kola nuts and the two gourds of palm wine that Bondaa had brought for this purpose and beckoned to Bawunda to approach him. He handed over to him the items.

"Bawunda, I want to report to you that we are strangers for this family. You know who I am but tonight I am standing in for the late father of the man who has sent me. I am here with my supporting followers with a goodwill message for this family. That wrap contains kola nuts to indicate our peaceful mission. That is accompanied by the two gourds of palm wine to lighten the hearts of those who will hear this message"

"I thank you Krikoma. May God water the trees from which these kola nuts were picked, and may God also give more sap to the palm trees where this wine was tapped? May the end of all that we are about to hear from you be rewarded." He turned round and gave the items to Sandima's uncle Pa Kokokutu who was sitting close to Sandima. "I'm sure that you heard Krikoma words" Bawunda said. "I pass this message to you for the head of this family." On such occasions the actual head of the family says the last word. In the interim he normally designates a senior blood relative to handle the procedures. This night it is uncle Kokokutu who is designated.

"I share your thanks to Krikoma" Kokokutu replied. "May he achieve his mission here" He then bowed down and picked up by his side a cup with four kola nuts filled with drinking water almost to the brim and handed it over to Bawunda.

"Tell the strangers that they are heartily welcome, and we give them water to drink as we are sure they are very thirsty after their long journey." Bawunda in turn handed over the cup and its contents to Krikoma.

"As we drink this water to quench our burning thirst," Krikoma said "we pray that there will always be water of peace and love to quench any fires of discord and disruption in this home. Bawunda please stand close to me because I want to send special greetings through you to various people in this gathering. But first let me start with you as the man whom I believe is the Sababu (intermediary) between us and your family. Here are ten leones for your intermediation."

"May God bless and multiply the pocket from which this came" as he received the money and put it in his pocket.

"It will be totally unwise for strangers to come to a village and intend to conduct an important event without paying their respects to the village head. You could be fined for breaking tradition. Here are ten Leones as we report to the village head our presence in his village. Where there is no worship and regard to a higher being there is disorder and confusion. I believe that there is a pastor and an imam that lead the people in this village to prayers. It is God who rewards them. But here are ten Leones each for the pastor and imam."

"Neither of them is here but we'll pass the message to them in the morning," Bawunda responded.

"That will be fine as long we have not ignored them in the process. I want to greet all the little children in this house because they are a joy to their parents. Here are five Leones for them. I will follow this with another five Leones to greet all the young boys and girls in this house as they sweep the house and fetch clean water for the house and for strangers like us to drink. I will not stop there as I believe that there are young men and women in this house who contribute to the farm work and carry out other chores thus contributing to the welfare of this family. For them here is ten Leones. I cannot conceive of any house in Gargbow where I was born and lived all my life that does not have grown and mature men and women. I greet them with thirty Leones. I stop here for now until I receive their responses."

"Receiving these greetings on behalf of all you have mentioned is gratifying to me. I wish to thank you, but I cannot say what will be their response except I pass them over to our senior elder in the family Pa Kokokutu" Again he turned round to face Sandima's uncle and handed over the moneys.

"Bawunda, through whom these greetings have come, I personally thank you. I also thank you on behalf of the entire family. Tell Krikoma that the family members to whom these greetings go express their gratitude to him and the sender of these greetings. We pray that the purse or pocket from where this money came be replenished double-fold and never falls empty. Now that we have received all these greetings, can we ask, "What is his mission to our compound this night?"

"Krikoma, the ears of those who live presently in this compound and of those that gone ahead are wide open to hear your message of peace and love as you call it. Please speak up so that even the departed can hear you."

"Bawunda, I am here to ask for the hand of a beautiful young woman in the family of Pa Sandima and Ya Kargor to marry my son, Bondaa, seated on my right hand. Every farmer in this chiefdom knows that he is the master blacksmith of this chiefdom who maintains their hoe or machete, or knife used on their farms."

"I believe that besides the Paramount Chief Kandeh Bai Bargarma, he is the most popular man in the chiefdom."

"Alright then, let us continue" Krikoma said as he beckoned again to Bawunda to come closer to him.

"I have more greetings to send to the immediate relatives of the beautiful woman. Here are ten Leones as our greetings to the sisters and ten Leones to the brothers. I will follow this with twenty Leones each to the uncles and aunties and twenty Leones each for the unknown far distance relatives on the paternal side of this woman and the maternal side. It will be disrespectful for us to show up here and not greet the grandfather and grandmother of this woman because we know that grandparents care for the children when the parents are engaged in the farm work. So, hold, these thirty Leones for grandpa and thirty Leones for grandma as our special greetings to them. I will wait until you pass on these greetings before I continue."

Bawunda complied and passed them over to Sandima's uncle. "As long as we receive such greetings from you, we'll continue to thank you and bless you and your entourage" the uncle said. "Let's progress so that we can move towards the crux of your mission."

"I totally agree with you Pa Kokokutu. But there are two key people I have still to greet, with all due respect to you sir. I said earlier that I have come to ask for the hand of a beautiful young woman in the family of Pa Sandima and Ya Kargor. Let me extend my humble hand to greet Pa Sandima with fifty Leones and to his wife another fifty Leones. They gave birth to a girl whom they have nurtured and raised to become a beautiful woman that has totally captured our admiration to the extent that we love her and want to marry her.

"Who is this woman, Krikoma" Bawunda asked, "because we have several beautiful girls in this house"

"We know this, but one that has just recently graduated from the bondo society. Her name is Makalay."

"Makalay? Which Makalay" a voice from the midst of the men host asked. Such questions often pop up on wedding ceremonies as this. It is usual that one of the distant male relations that poses such questions would get something to shut him up. "You mean my dear lovely 'wife' (*not really*) I have nurtured from childhood?"

"But you know that you were not the only playmate husband of Makalay," came another voice in the same area. I am the real playmate husband of Makalay, and you know it Kamanda. Pa Sandima and Ya Kargor, do you want to tell me that you want to betroth my Makalay to another man?"

"Sandima and Kargor, that is not a question for you to answer," Krikoma interjected. "I know that Makalay probably has many playmate husbands. They have helped to groom this playmate wife to become so beautiful. I know that they picked and gave her ripe mangoes she could not pick. Others helped to prepare the backyard to enable her to plant some vegetables. Some even brought palm wine. Bawunda, please take these forty Leones. Kindly thank those paramours for what they did for Makalay. These were all in the background. But tonight, please ask them to let go and tell them that somebody with a large love bug has come openly to marry Makalay. To convince them with these forty Leones"

"Playmate husbands, I know also that you are all young men of Gargbow," Bawunda said. "You grew up together with Makalay under our watchful and caring eyes as parents. You contributed in your various ways to make Makalay who she is today because you wanted her to have this night. Krikoma whom you all know is pleading to you all to release Makalay from your secret proposals. Here are forty Leones as his token of his sincere thanks to you all." He walked over to the first voice Kamanda and gave him the money.

"Thank you, Bawunda. Let me say that on behalf of Komra, who challenged me, and all the other unknown playmate husbands I accept your plea. My rivals and I are willing to let you proceed without any more interruptions from us. Is that not so mates?"

"Yes, we agree," was the response from almost five voices.

"Bawunda in that case let me proceed. As I said before being interrupted by the playmate husbands, the woman he wants to marry from this house is Makalay. She is light skinned, medium height with bright big brown but shining eyes and plenty hair. She must be in her late teen years. She is the first child and daughter of Sandima and Kargor."

"Do you mean my daughter who fetches water and warm it for me to bathe?" Sandima spoke for the first time in the evening. "Are you saying Makalay who helps her mother to all the house chores and farm work? You want to handicap us by taking her?"

"Yes. Sandima it is your daughter Makalay I want for my son, Bondaa." Krikoma answered. "You cannot hold on to your daughter when she is of age to marry. In your heart I know that this is a momentous night for you and your wife. I also know that the ultimate choice is invariably Makalay's. But I believe that before we came to this point tonight some back-the-scene softening of positions has been done"

"You are right, but a father would be expected to make such comments. They show that my daughter has been a very helpful and hard-working woman. At any rate proceed and we shall see."

Krikoma went to his seat and conferred briefly with Bondaa. Bondaa dipped his right hand into the front pocket of his gown and took out the dowry money tied in a white handkerchief. He gave it to Krikoma. Krikoma turned to Yakwendeh and motioned to her to bring the calabash which has been wrapped in a white shirting. The young girl that toted the calabash and the calabash itself were seated in front of Yakwendeh. She gently took the calabash and gave it to Krikoma. She untied it and slightly lifted the raffia fan that covered the calabash slightly so that only she and Krikoma saw what was in it. Krikoma slid in the white handkerchief from Bondaa and tied the calabash again as it was before. Yakwendeh returned to her seat leaving the calabash with Krikoma. While this was going on the entire gathering watched without anybody uttering a word except coughing and sneezing.

"Eh...eh...eh." Krikoma cleared his throat loudly as if to say I am ready. "Bawunda, please come closer to me." Bawunda responded and stood facing Krikoma who stood up delicately holding the calabash in his two hands. He stretched the calabash to Bawunda and said, "Please hold this bundle which is our token of our devoted proposal to Makalay, daughter of Sandima and Kargor, to marry Bondaa of the Nwoingoha clan from Magoronwa."

"Krikoma, I cannot thank you as I did before. This is totally beyond my mediation role. I will not even hang on to it for long because I don't know what is in it. It could contain an explosive device in it. I'll immediately pass this on to Kokokutu who will probably thank you."

"It contains nothing dangerous or harmful. The calabash contains items that remind a husband and wife how marriage should be lived" Krikoma calmed Bawunda's fears.

"Whatever it contains I still will not hold on to it. Kokokutu here is a calabash tied with a white cloth. Krikoma says it is harmless and it is for Makalay. I am not competent to deliver this present to her while you his uncle are seated here." He gently handed the calabash to Kokokutu in the same delicate manner as Krikoma handed it to him. Kokokutu took the calabash with confidence without fear as expressed by Bawunda. He set it before him on the ground before him.

"Bawunda let me allay your fears and tell you that Krikoma and I were born on the same day though of different parents" Kokokutu informed Bawunda. "Not only do we regard ourselves as twin brothers but the people of Gargbow know us as the twin brothers" he continued. "I therefore do not believe that he will give me anything dangerous or harmful. All gifts to each other have been beneficial not only to us the recipients but also to our families. I do not think what he has given to you for Makalay is anything different. I know he means well and nothing less." He stood up and faced Krikoma and Bondaa.

"My twin brother Krikoma, I want to thank you immensely. As you and your entourage came here in good health, I pray that you return in good health. I implore the spirits and watchful eyes of your ancestors continue to hover over you and protect you from witches and wizards and from every harm. Ask that their blessings increase and pass over to your children. Let all evil planned against you totally fail. I pray that witch guns fail to fire their evil. I pray that you achieve what you've come to do. This is a great night for this family. I will reserve further comments afterwards." He turned to the women's section where

Kargor was prominently seated. "Kargor, is your daughter Makalay in the house?"

"I'm not sure. I have not seen her this evening" was the immediate answer to Kokokutu's request.

"Please find and call her. She has a present here wrapped in white brought in by a stranger from Magoronwa called Bondaa. Please find her to pick up this present before me."

"Bowarah," Kargor called the niece of Yakwendeh. "Please find Makalay and tell her to come here and pick up her present."

"Ya Kargor, Makalay is not in the house," said Bowarah a friend of Makalay "I understand that she is gone to Masorie-Lol to our friend Ballu. I need transport to go find and bring her." This is a joke, and it is part of the process to put the proposer in a state of uncertainty. It is intended to get something from the proposer."

"We will provide you with adequate funds to take whatever transportation means you need to travel to Masorie Lol as long as you bring her here" Krikoma said. "But we don't want her to be sandwiched by some young men in a *poda* (public mini-bus). So, here are ten Leones. Take whatever means and go now." Krikoma gave the money to Bawunda who in turn handed it to Bowarah. She disappeared into the house immediately she took the money. A few moments later she returned and said that the vehicle she hired has no petrol. Again, this is a ploy to get some more money as everybody knows that a vehicle cannot move without fuel. She was given another ten Leones. Once more she disappeared and for some time neither the messenger Bowarah nor Makalay appeared keeping everyone in suspense. Then suddenly Bowarah surfaced running.

"I don't know what is wrong with this trip. We were making good progress but unfortunately about four miles from Masorie-Lol, the tyre fired. The driver successfully brought the vehicle under control, but I need money to patch the tyre as the driver gave the money I paid to the vehicle owner. I got a ride back to recover my money from the owner, but he was nowhere to be found. He seems to have disappeared into thin air." This was yet another believable joke and of course earns her more money.

"I pray that we overcome all these obstacles on our way. We'll be here soon." She received another ten Leones and she sprinted into the house once more.

A few moments later she appeared alongside a small girl with her face covered with a head tie. "Is this the Makalay you sent me to bring," she asked Bawunda. Krikoma approached the little girl and uncovered her face.

"No……no…...no she is not" However, little girl, here are ten Leones. Your turn will come when you reach the marital age."

Bowarah went into the house and again returned with a tall fat woman with her face covered and presented her as Makalay. For the second time Krikoma unveiled the woman's face."

"This Makalay is too mature and has seen some years." Krikoma said. "I believe that the bags of rice she has eaten over the years, would prove too much for her to carry them from this compound to my house in a month." Everybody burst into laughter. "Nevertheless, we like her but let her return to where she is now and hold fast with all sincerity." He gave her ten Leones. Then she turned to Bowarah and gave her thirty Leones and said "I know that you have more 'Makalays' in there you want to show. "I give you this money so you can hold back all the other Makalays in there and bring me the real one. When I see my Makalay I shall not hesitate to perform what I want to do. Can I trust you to do that?"

"I can't say that. I'm not sure if I can because she might have slipped out of the house again"

"Do whatever you can to trace and bring her here right now; that will be acceptable to me as long as you don't coerce her."

"I won't promise you anything, but I will try my best."

"Accepted." She left Krikoma standing in anxious anticipation. But he was not alone in this anxiety. Bondaa and his entire entourage were equally on edge and all eyes were focused on the front door of the house. The thought was "is Bowarah going to dress up another 'Makalay.' Indeed, she came holding the hand of another person who walked awkwardly without any gait. They stood before Krikoma.

"Is this the Makalay you are waiting for to collect your present?"

"Well, let me see the face." He again unveiled the face. Her face was exposed and the whole gathering erupted into laughter as they saw a coarse bearded young man dressed in a woman's clothes. Krikoma himself could not hold back the amusing site. He also burst into laughter. When the laughter died down Krikoma said "wonders will never end as long as one is alive. This is the first time that I have seen a woman with a face covered with such coarse beard. Thank you Bowarah because you have made me witness such an amusing spectacle. If this woman trims the beard, she will be more attractive. Here are ten Leones to help buy the blades."

"Don't blame me. When I reached Masorie-Lol, Ballu told me that Makalay had returned. On entering the house, I found so many faces covered and could not uncover any face as it will be insulting to the covered faces. I must bring them one after the other. You see the dilemma I face in there. But there are two more faces covered. So, I'm going to bring the next in line. I hope this one will be the right Makalay. But the hurricane lamp in the house has run out of kerosene and the place is dark"

"Look, take these fifteen Leones for three pints of kerosene. But make sure that this time you come with her."

"Are you threatening me?"

"No-no-no. It will be foolish of me to threaten you the messenger the family trusts. I was just saying please bring her."

"You really want me to search and bring the Makalay you want for your son?"

"Yes indeed. I do want you to bring her.

"How prepared are you and your followers to receive her?"

"You fetch her, and it will surprise you what you will see."

"Demonstrate that to me." Krikoma reluctantly dipped his hand into the pocket of his gown and gave her five Leones.

"You will have more, I promise, when she is here."

"I hope you will keep your promise," she said and went into the house. Within a few moments later Bowarah came out holding the hand of a woman dressed from top to bottom in white lace and slowly walking before her. The woman's face was covered with a transparent white veil, but the face could not be figured out. The woman in white walked slowly but with great dignity, gait, and poise. The two stopped right in front of Krikoma.

"You requested me to bring Makalay, but I'm not sure if this figure in white is the one you want me to bring?"

Don't worry. I'll make sure of that." He moved straight to the figure and lifted the veil. "Yes. This is the Makalay I've been longing for to stand before me. Thank you Bowarah you've been a diligent and devoted messenger. Now you have earned your reward. Receive forty Leones for your shuttling to search and bring Makalay to me. Now that you have brought her, I will now return to my seat with confidence on seeing Makalay and to wait for what I am expecting."

"Bowarah turned to Kargor and said "You asked me to fetch Makalay here. She is standing here before Bawunda. My role here is ended. I must disappear" Bowarah said, and she left.

"Pa Kokokutu, you asked me to call Makalay and appear before you," Kargor said. "Here she is standing before you."

"Thank you Kargor." He turned to Makalay. "I have before me sitting on the floor a present wrapped with white shirting. This present has been brought to you by Krikoma my twin brother. He is a stand-in for the deceased father of a gentleman called Bondaa. Krikoma says this present is from Bondaa and he is proposing to marry you. Do you know Krikoma?"

"Yes, Uncle Koko'" (the young folks cut the name short)

"How about Bondaa?"

"I know him, sir. I met him for the first time when mama and I visited Ya Hogaii, mama's bosom friend, eight years ago. I was about eight years then."

"Do you know who he is?"

"He is the master blacksmith of the chiefdom I was told then."

"Is he married?"

"I know that the time we visited Ya Hogaii she had a mate."

"Do you know whether he has any children?"

"He had four daughters when we visited them."

"Do you know to which clan he belongs?"

"According to what my parents told me he is the only surviving direct bloodline male of the Nwoingoha clan at Magoronwa."

"Makalay, this man who is from the Magoronwa Nwoingoha clan, has two wives, and now has six daughters and the chiefdom's master blacksmith, wants you to be his third wife. The calabash tied before me he has brought to propose to you to marry him. If you want this man despite all you know about him, take this calabash. It's all yours. You retain it for yourself, or you can give it to whosoever you please. This calabash contains your dowry price and all the elements that will show you how to live a married life. Or you can just walk away, and we shall respect your decision though it may have consequences. The choice is yours to make."

Makalay stooped with the left knee higher than the right and gently picked up the Calabash and gave it to her father Sandima. The moment she picked up the calabash to give her father, Krikoma and his adult followers, except for Bondaa, rose from their seats and showered Makalay with ten and twenty Leones notes as an expression of appreciation and joy for accepting the proposal. The women from the Krikoma entourage suddenly burst out with a common wedding chorus: *"we yawo fine-o, we yawo fine-o. How you manage so tay we yawo fine-o."* When the showering stopped, Makalay walked to Sandima her father, stooped again, and lifted the calabash towards him.

"What is this you're giving me?" Sandima asked.

"This is a calabash that contains a dowry price for me and other items, papa."

"For whom is this calabash?"

"It is for me, papa."

"What is the meaning of this calabash?"

"It is the betrothal proposal gift from Bondaa to me."

"Why then give it to me? It's for you and not me."

"I want you to accept this gift as I have decided to be Bondaa's third wife."

"Are you sure of what you've just said?"

"Yes papa. Please take the calabash. Use its contents for yourself, mama and the rest of the family and very close friend of the family who have contributed in various ways to make me who I am tonight."

"Did you say that I should use the contents as you specified?"

"Use the contents just as I said."

"But you know that I am a poor farmer. I have no plantation of any sort. When I share the contents of this calabash with my wife, family relations and close friends, remember that I have no resources to refund anything in this calabash should you decide to leave Bondaa for unjustifiable reasons. Bondaa is no longer a young man. May be after a few years you will think that you made a bad decision to marry this old man and you see a *'yenki'* boy you will love to marry instead."

"I'm aware of your position and that of the family. I have no intention of doing what you have just mentioned. I propose to endure the marriage trials and live a peaceful and fruitful married life."

"Kargor, did you hear my questions and answers session with your daughter?"

"I heard every bit of your questions and her answers too," answered Kargor. "She has freely chosen to marry Bondaa. He is the husband she has chosen. It is her decision. We go with her choice. This is what every parent desire for her daughter: to marry good husband and have children. My advice as a mother to you Makalay is to exercise considerable patience and endure the torments and trials that face you. I'll stop here for now as mother and daughter have more to discuss about marriage life."

"Thank you Kargor." He then settled to address his daughter who was still stooping before him. "Makalay, you have made a noble decision to marry a man of your choice despite all the marital facts you know about him. You know marriage is good, but it has bitter and sweet aspects. The sweet is nice, pleasurable, and delicious. But the bitter is not easy to endure. You must set your eyes while you swallow bitter and unpleasant aspects of marriage just as you take a bitter liquid medicine, but it will cure you. There will be jealousy from all sides: from your mates as they are human; from your mates' children in various taunting ways; from your in-laws and of course from husband, Bondaa. This is a fact of life because where there is no jealousy there is no love. The way you handle jealousy is what makes you a good wife. Follow what your inner

216

heart tells you not what your head thinks. My dear daughter, hold on to what is good and lovely and avoid and despise the evil things. Do you hear me?"

"I hear you clearly, papa."

"You will be taunted by people for deciding to marry Bondaa." Kokokutu jumped in to give his own advice. "You're young and beautiful, why marry a man twice your age who already has two wives and six children? They will ask. Make sure to cork your ears to such taunts."

"I will add by saying" Bawunda joined in to add to what the two have advised. "That the best facilitator of a successful marriage is having free discussions with your husband and mates. Be a good communicator. Tell your husband and maybe your mates what bothers you and which you believe could affect a harmonious home. Failure to communicate is a recipe to be suspicion and misunderstanding."

"Let me tell you the little I know as your auntie with several years' marriage life experience," an aunt joined in the bandwagon of advisers. "Make sure your husband eats good food every day when it is your turn to cook. Good food is one sure way of gaining the love and admiration of your husband. Even if it is not your turn to cook or sleep with your husband, give him something he will appreciate eating. 'Don't forget that a hungry man is an angry man'. When men are angry, they can do a lot of irrational things which some regret afterwards. Therefore, feed your husband and make him happy."

"Thank you, auntie I'll remember that." Makalay responded.

"Well, my daughter let me conclude my advice in addition to what you have received from your mother and other relatives." Sandima said. "Respect and honour your husband at all times not some of the time when you please. Don't argue with your husband in public. Suppress your feelings on contentious matters. At night when he has had his meal and had his palm wine and you think your mates should share it, then bring it up and discuss in a civil way. If it is an issue between you and him, wait until you join him in bed. But please do not prevent him from performing his night obligations as a husband. Do not withhold his night's pleasurable duty. Withholding that can escalate matters to the level you don't want. Do you get that Makalay?

"Papa, I get it sir" still stooping.

"I don't know you for foul language up to this night. I don't expect you to begin to use foul language on any member of your household, worst still against your husband. My daughter, as much as it lies in your capabilities, live at peace with all people within your house and outside it. Give respect to who respect is due and by doing so, you also earn respect. Respect your mates because they are senior in the marriage, and they are much older than you; and they in turn will respect you. However, maintain your dignity as a respected wife. When you honour every person, you too will be honoured. Before I stop let me ask you one more time: Do you accept the gift?"

"Yes papa. I've already told you that I do"

"And I should use the contents of the calabash for myself, your mother and close relatives is that right"

"You are right"

"Kokokutu and all family members and friends here present, you have heard what Makalay has said, and you are witnesses to this marriage ceremony. I therefore accept the calabash from Makalay." He set it on the floor before him.

"*Heebee, heeb-e-e. Marade day yah*?" (Is there a wedding here?) A lady shouted from the women's side asked.

"*Marade day*" (Yes there is a wedding) was the immediate response from almost everybody and there was boisterous laughter everywhere. When the talking and laughter subsided, Sandima got up and in a high-pitched voice so that everybody in the gathering could hear him.

"I thank you, Bawunda as our mediator tonight. You did a marvellous job. Krikoma may God bless you and add more years to our life. May God protect and deliver you and your family from evil doers. May He grant your every wish and continue to make you fruitful and prosperous. I pray that God crushes all your distractors. I say these prayers because you have brought our two families together by taking my daughter for your son. May they have more boys than girls?" A prayer that Bondaa desperately desires.

"It is I who is extremely happy, because I have not been let down and I'll not be ridiculed by some people who rejoice at others' failures." Krikoma replied. "I have only one statement for Bondaa," Sandima continued. "Makalay is now your wife, but I want her to be your first daughter also. In other words, please take good care of our daughter as your wife and daughter. Thank you for asking for my daughter's hand."

"Sandima, I take your last remarks as having accepted Makalay's betrothal to Bondaa," said Krikoma. "If this is so Bawunda please take these hundred Leones to receive his word. Also, it symbolizes our humble request take Makalay with us tomorrow on our return home."

"Krikoma, it's your justifiable right to request Makalay join you tomorrow," Kokokutu replied. "You can even ask for your wife to go with you this night and we cannot refuse it. However, we will kindly ask you to delay her coming over for another two days. The parents must give her a fitting send-off by providing her basic domestic utensils. I am sure you wouldn't mind another two days which will be good for her."

"We accede to your request. But only for two days as we love to see her join us soonest."

"Be assured that it will not exceed two days. I am guaranteeing any consequences for any extra day. I know that I could be summoned to the local court for unduly withholding somebody's wedded wife"

Sandima turned to Kokokutu and motioned to take calabash. "Let Bawunda and Kargor join you into my room and check the contents of the calabash. Make sure you secure the door and keep other persons from joining you as only the close family members should know what's in it. Come back and report if you are satisfied with the contents."

He moved over to Krikoma, and they exchanged warm handshakes. He walked over to Bondaa and warmly embraced him as a loving father-in-law would appreciate a son-in-law. "You are a renowned man in your profession, and I know you as a respectable man. Makalay is now your wife and a daughter as she is only two years older than your first daughter. I plead with you to treat her both as a wife and daughter"

"*Komaneh* (meaning father-in-law) Sandima, I promise to be faithful, devout and loving husband and a caring father to Makalay. I give you my word to treat her both as a wife and daughter."

"I take your word as a man of the head of the gbangbani society" Sandima said. At this point Kokokutu came back and reported in a whisper that he was overwhelmed with what was in the calabash, especially the dowry money. Before Sandima returned to his seat he announced to the gathering that they will be entertained. He barely finished announcing when women with trays and bowls filled with various dishes streamed out heading first to the visitors. When the visitors were satisfactorily served, the service continued to the rest of the gathering. The entire crowd within the compound was served. People ate to their fill. As they finished eating, they thanked the parents and wished the new couple a happy, peaceful, and fruitful marriage life. "I pray that the evildoers who are planning to disrupt the lives of this couple woefully fail," prayed one. "I pray that Makalay gets boys who will work with their father to provide for their mother" prayed another.

Yet another prayed that Makalay will have children so that he could be invited in the naming ceremony. Two sisters wished Makalay and her husband lots of fun with no sorrow. Each time somebody thanked and prayed a wish, he or she left the compound immediately and very shortly the compound was empty of supporters and witnesses. But the Krikoma entourage stayed put because there is one final act to perform. Therefore, Krikoma rose from his seat and strolled to Bawunda who was with the rest of the male family members.

"Bawunda, the strangers you did not want to enter your compound are about leaving. You now believe when I told you that if I entered the compound, you will be glad that I did. We are going as we have got what we wanted from this compound. Aren't you glad we did?"

"Of course, I am. However, I had to be certain for whom I open my compound gate at night."

"You are so right. Please take this money and convey our deep thanks and sincere appreciation for the wonderful reception and delicious food. Bid the entire family goodbye on our behalf. Bawunda took the money, waved goodbye to the visitors and took the money to Kokokutu.

"Krikoma, I want to thank you and all those who accompanied you," Kokokutu responded. "I wish you a safe trip back home and we promise you that your wife will follow you in two days' time. Once more thank you and good night."

CHAPTER TWELVE

Krikoma returned to his house with the troupe with joy. Yakwendeh was the happiest of the women because she had approached Sandima and Kargor on behalf of Bondaa. They owed the successful ending entirely to her and this made her proud. Hogaii and Bendihe were not only glad that things worked out beyond their expectation but also for the fact they now have a third mate whom they hope will bear Bondaa a son who will be their provider in their old age. They now have a mate who they hope will help guide and teach their younger daughters in cooking and other domestic chores. However, they also must face the fact that they now have a mate with whom they will share Bondaa's bed. They nonetheless must accept this as it was what they bargained for when they granted Bondaa permission to marry Makalay.

Krikoma immediately called an after-event meeting with the key players in this wedding; Bondaa, his two wives and Yakwendeh to assess their performance. He started by congratulating everybody for a successful mission. "The ancestors did not forsake us. They were totally with us all the way through. It was too smooth to believe because I have witnesses contentious ones. I have even witnessed two which were inconclusive"

"Krikoma, you know the background history of the Nwoingoha clan," Yakwendeh spoke. "You also know Sandima's parents and grandparents. Both families are reputable ones in this chiefdom. Did you expect anything different?" she asked. "I am happy that I have not been let down as the initiator of all this to Sandima and Kargor"

"Let me say here now that Bendihe and I have completed our support to Bondaa to marry Makalay. We are happy at this success. We look forward to her joining us and pray that we shall all have a harmonious, peaceful, and happy marriage life of what remains in us. Do you agree with me Bendihe?"

"I have often told you Hogaii that you're a wise and understanding mate" Bendihe said. "We have not held back our support to Bondaa to this point. As Hogaii said our support has ended tonight. The rest of what follows is his sole responsibility"

"What have you to say Bondaa?" Krikoma asked

"Krikoma, Yakwendeh, Hogaii and Bendihe, I want to thank you all most sincerely. This night has overcome half of my succession dilemma. But let me truthfully say that I owe the success of this night to my wives. They did all the back scene manoeuvres. They even advised me on the steps I should take to reach this night. I say thank you very much for your support. It is very rare for two mates to have a common under-standing for a husband to have a third wife. But their support shouldn't end tonight as our focus on this entire exercise is to achieve the common goal for which you granted me permission to marry another wife. I am aware that we have a common objective, and we should work together with Makalay to achieve it."

"I remember telling Bendihe when she came to me with the proposal that their action was a little queer and unique," Yakwendeh said. "But the reasons she presented to me were justifiable and I was converted to the cause."

"This whole thing was the brainchild of Hogaii. Let's give her the honour she deserves. She initiated it when we were in this village for the last bondo society graduation dance. It was she who reasoned with me on her move, and I saw merits in her action. So, it is to her that Bondaa should express his thanks and appreciation.

"I take your point Bendihe," Krikoma said. "But if you had disagreed with her, she wouldn't have proceeded with her idea. Isn't it so?"

"That is certainly true," Bondaa responded. It was because you both agreed that we should pursue the proposal. Therefore, both of you deserve equal honour tonight."

"As a wife my advice to you Bondaa," Yakwendeh opted to give her own advice, "is that you do not hold Hogaii and Bendihe in lesser esteem as before when your new wife comes in. Your respect and love for them should in no way be diminished because of Makalay. How you will play that balancing act is your sole and entire responsibility"

"I endorse what she has just advised." Krikoma said. "Let me add however, this: the way you maintain a good relationship with your wives is what will determine the peace and harmony in your family."

"I totally accept the advice you two have offered. I will try to do all that is humanly possible to maintain the unity and love in my family."

"When do you want to return?" Krikoma asked.

"We'll leave early in the morning after the first cock crow. You know the distance is long. I don't want to travel at night with four women to be protected against the unforeseen"

"Is there anything you'll want me and Yakwendeh to do before or after your return?"

"Not really. Only follow up the promise of Kokokutu about my wife's departure."

"It is my responsibility to see that he fulfils his promise."

"Thank you once again and we'll wake you up in the morning to say goodbye. Until then, good night, wonderful couple." Bondaa left for his room by the veranda outside.

Bondaa was already awake when the cock crowed. He nudged Bendihe to wake up as it was day and told her to wake up the others.

"I am going to wake up Yongaa. When I return, I hope that all will be ready." Indeed, when he was back all the women were ready. Krikoma and Yakwendeh were also there to see them off. Bondaa warmly shook Krikoma's hand with his two hands indicating unreserved appreciation and then stretched out his right hand and gently shook Yakwendeh's hand. Hogaii and Bendihe also shook hands with the couple. At the end of the handshakes, Bondaa and his family trooped out of the house on their return home. They were greeted outside by the barking of dogs. But they ignored them and continued to walk through the village.

Just about sunset they reached the outskirts of Magoronwa much earlier than the time they arrived at Gargbow. They did so because they carried no loads as they did on their way to Gargbow. Bondaa and Yongaa branched off to go tap their palm wine trees. These will be overflowing as they haven't been tapped for two days. Hogaii and the rest went straight home to the surprise of the daughters who stayed. When they saw their mothers and sisters, they ran out and surrounded them with hugs and greetings.

"Where is papa and Yongaa" the youngest asked.

"They branched off a few moments ago. I believe that they have gone to tap their palm wine before they finally get home" Hogaii answered.

"We know that you girls were not expecting us at this time of the day and therefore, you did not prepare food for us." Bendihe said. "So, get to work and cook some food for us. We're famished. Use two fireplaces to cook the sauce and rice separately. Be fast before your father comes home."

Bondaa reached his palm trees and as expected the gourds were dripping with palm wine. He climbed the first, tapped it and descended. But before he climbed the second, he poured out a full cup and gulped it quickly because he was both thirsty and hungry. He took the next empty gourd and climbed the second palm tree. He descended with another full gourd. He was satisfied that he has two full gourds. He decided to take both home and treat his friend Fokogbo tonight. On his way to the village, he took his bath as he normally does at the village stream, the Kathabai. He hid his bath soap in a concealed tin under a thicket where people would hesitate to look, for fear of coiled snakes underneath. He was happy with all things so far. He took his two gourds and headed home. As he approached the house his four daughters ran out to welcome him home. One took his raffia bag that was slung on his right shoulder; two took a gourd each and the youngest Bondaa picked up in his right hand and walked alongside him to the house. It was a moment of joy to have their father back home.

After the evening meal, Bondaa invited Fokogbo and Yongaa to join him and his wives to drink palm wine. It is to demonstrate his gratitude and appreciation to his wives and celebration for a successful mission. When Fokogbo and Yongaa arrived, he welcomed his friend and guided him to his usual spot in the veranda.

"Bondaa, what's going on? I don't think we have seen each other for two days. Did you go somewhere?" Fokogbo inquired. Before he could answer the question, he poured a full cup of palm wine and drank it as usual without pausing. Then he poured a cupful and handed it to Fokogbo.

"You remember Fokogbo the discussion we had about six months ago in this same veranda about marrying a third wife?"

"Yes, I do remember it was one night when the moon was bright, and the children were playing hide and seek in the village courtyard. Yes, that was about six months ago. It was when I witnessed your wives condescending to your request to marry another wife. So, what about that? What is on the floor now?" Fokogbo questioned Bondaa. He drank his palm wine as he waited for a reply.

"I don't want to answer that question myself. I will give my wives the singular honour to answer as I believe they are more competent to do that."

"Alright, if you say so. Hogaii what is on the floor concerning Bondaa's quest for a third wife?"

"I will be straight to the point Fokogbo. Your friend married a young and beautiful girl as his third wife."

"Really. When was this?"

"Last night, at Gargbow. She is the daughter of Sandima and Kargor my friend."

"It was an easy wedding as Hogaii, and I had laid a strong foundation." Bendihe added. "We were even surprised that things worked out so smoothly"

"I don't want to believe this. Bondaa, you mean you went all the way to Gargbow to marry and you never mentioned a word about it to me? You can't confide in a friend like me?"

"Before I answer your question have another cup. It is not a bribe." He handed him the cup. "You see Fokogbo certain secrets are better confided in your wives. Sometimes not even to your blood relatives because not everyone may have a pleasing attitude towards your progressive plans. Besides I was warned by Sago-Gbo to keep things as secretly as I can until everything is concluded. If I failed to tell you it was because I was taking Sago-Gbo's advice. Please take it as an awful omission on my part. I apologize. Please forgive me. I have called you here to be the first person to hear the news. It is a way of amending my omission."

"I see your concern and I accept" and he handed over the empty cup to Bondaa. "Where is the new wife?"

"She is expected in two days from tonight," replied Hogaii, who had just finished drinking another cup. "You know that mothers don't send their daughters to the husbands without a proper send off. She will be here."

"What's important that happened in the village during my absence?" Bondaa asked.

"Nothing serious or important. But several minor things happened yesterday which do not affect you directly, but it concerns the village." He went at great lengths to explain what happened. The conversation surrounding these events lasted until the two gourds were exhausted. Shortly after Fokogbo asked to leave because he must travel early in the morning on an urgent mission.

"I hope you are not going to compete with me by marrying a second wife?"

"What's wrong with that? You now have three. If I decide to have one more there is no offence to that. No, I am not going for a wife. Candidly I am going to settle a dispute between my cousins who are fighting over a farmland."

"Well, I wish you God's speed and handle that dispute judiciously. Good night"

As soon as Fokogbo left Bondaa asked his wives what is the next step?

"We have to make a place for Makalay when she comes. Hogaii said. "I suggest that Hopanda and Yagoro move over to the other two girls and free the room for her. My last daughter will sleep with me and Bendihe's with hers too."

Why not the empty room outside? It is spacious for them." Bendihe suggested.

"It could be ideal if it is the only space free and available." Bondaa said. What about security? Besides, you don't want your girls quietly sneaking at night and get entangled with boys of doubtful character that will deflower them and we bear the shame. Do you want that?"

"I am terribly sorry. I totally skipped that fact." Bendihe conceded.

Hogaii called the rest of the girls and briefed them why they went to Gargbow and what will shortly ensue in the home. She pleaded as their parents to show respect and understanding to Makalay when she joins them.

Bondaa told them that their senior sisters will join them in their room as they must vacate theirs for Makalay. With the placement of Makalay settled, Bondaa bade good night to the women who went into their respective rooms for the night. Bondaa remained reclining in his hammock in the veranda to smoke his Sangotho pipe. He soon followed the women when he started dozing.

A day before Makalay was to join her husband, the parents decided to provide her with basic cooking utensils. They took part of the dowry money and purchased two pots (one for cooking rice and the other for soup); two enamel basins with lids (one into which she'll dish rice and the other the soup); one wide open basin for storing water; a bucket to fetch water; four bowls of various sizes; three sizes of plastic utility bowls while cooking and two plastic drinking cups. They made sure to purchase a new wooden mortar and three pestles. She was given four wooden ladles by one aunt, and another gave her two straw mats woven with colourful raffia. Of course, she will take along the calabash and the other items in and outside except the kola nuts, the bitter kolas, and the *alligator* pepper. Sandima had given instructions to Kargor to parboil and clean a bag of rice for Makalay to take. He had secured 5-gallon tin of palm oil for her also.

All these items were intended to give her a head start in her marriage life. They are aimed at giving her those basic utensils and food items so that in the early days she will not ask for everything to cook. Above all, the mother was aware that the lack of these basics could be a source of frustration and may be friction. Taking along these items will also add to what was already available in the house. Sandima and Kargor did not only provide her with these items, but they also gave her some of the dowry money for her immediate needs as a woman. Kargor went into her wooden box where she kept all her valuable dresses and took out a beautiful oku *lappa* which Sandima had bought for her before weaning Makalay as the first child as dictated by the custom.

"I am giving this *oku lappa* to you as a special gift so you can use it whenever there is a major occasion. Also take this set of gold earrings and chain which your grandmother gave me when she got married to father."

The day has arrived when Makalay was to go to her marriage home at Magoronwa. She went to the house of every relative to say goodbye and each one of them gave her their small pieces of advice accompanied with some small gift of rice, groundnuts, bottle of palm oil, cowpea, live chicken to rear or whatever that was available and will be useful to her. She brought all these gifts and her mother helped her to put them together for the journey. The other items had already been assembled and were ready for the journey. Sandima was aware that neither he nor Kargor can accompany their daughter to Magoronwa. So, he called on Bawunda and his wife to take Makalay to Bondaa. They willingly accepted the mission and prepared for the journey. But to tote the items assembled, he needed four young men to do that for him. So, he called on Kamanda and Kumawa the two *playmate* husbands to ask two more playmate husbands for the task as their last act of playmate courtship to Makalay. Kamanda was able to convince two more friends to carry Makalay's things to Magoronwa.

Since Makalay was leaving their house to join her husband, Sandima gathered the household and called Bawunda and his wife to join them for final farewells to Makalay. He brought a white enamel bowl containing water with cowries, two pieces of silver coins and equal number of red and white kola nuts underneath. He called Makalay to squat and hold the bowl in both hands. He summoned everyone present to squat or stoop around Makalay and touch the bowl. Anyone is who cannot touch the bowl should touch someone who does. When all were set, he started to offer sacrifice to the ancestors for the wellbeing of Makalay in her marriage.

"You good spirits and you great people who have gone to the other side. You are listening to what we say and watching what we do. Makalay is leaving this home today to join her husband Bondaa of the Nwoingoha clan. I ask you to watch over her and prevent any evil spirit that wants to disrupt their marriage. Let all distractors fail in all their ventures to infiltrate into her marriage life. Let the witches and wizards be caught in their own plans and be destroyed. Shut the mouths of gossipers and backbiters against Makalay. Make her womb fruitful? Protect her babies from witchcraft operations and scheming. Those who want to harm marriage, let them fall into their own traps and be destroyed. Let ruin be the portion of those who will wish them evil. Success shall be their lot and not failure. Be with them always and surround them. *Amina*" Sandima concluded his sacrificial prayer.

Everybody present dipped the tip of the right hand into the water, rubbed it between his/her two hands and wipes his or her face. It is believed in their society that in this sacrifice anybody who drinks water and washes his or her face with water and intends to do evil to the person for whom the sacrifice was offered will have the full wrath of the sacrifice.

Kamanda and his team of playmate husbands came and took the bulky and heavy items leaving lighter and smaller ones for Makalay and Bawunda's wife to carry. Bawunda also took one item but not of the same weight as the young men. Everybody streamed out of the house except Makalay and her parents. Sandima then poured out the water in the bowl on the floor before the front door and asked Makalay to walk on it. She was not to turn back or enter the house again but to continue her journey. So Makalay and her escorts journey to Magoronwa to join her husband.

They arrived just about sunset, and they headed directly to Bondaa's house. When they entered the village, there were few men in the verandas of their houses. Some had gone to tap their palm wine and others have not yet returned from their farm plots. Those who were around greeted back as the strangers greeted them asked them from where they have come. Also, the women and teenage girls were busy preparing the evening meal in their backyards. They could not know what went on in the front of their houses... It was the youngest of the Bondaa's daughters who was playing with other girls of her age that saw the approaching company to their house. She ran into the house and out to the back and with such cheerfulness and shouted to the hearing of everybody at the backyard: "they are here, they have come"

"Who are they?" Bendihe asked

"But mama, you and papa told us that we should be expecting strangers today," the young girl replied.

"But how are sure they are the strangers that we are expecting?"

"I see that they are carrying several loads on their head as if they are accompanying somebody and they are approaching our house."

"Bendihe let's go and see who these strangers might be," proposed Hogaii. Hogaii and Bendihe got to go see the strangers were indeed approaching their house. They were followed by the rest of the children.

"Oh, she is right, it is Makalay and her escorts. Let's go welcome them." They walked hurriedly and took the loads from the women.

You're all welcome to Magoronwa" Hogaii said as they marched with the entourage to the house.

When they'd entered the verandah the strangers were asked to make themselves comfortable on the benches."

"Makalay you are welcome to the Magoronwa and our home," Bendihe said

"Thank you."

"Bawunda, you are welcome. I hope your journey here was easy?"

"Yes, we did. Where is Bondaa?" He asked.

"You know where you men go during this time of the day. He's gone to tap his palm wine after we finished weeding the cassava farm." He will be here shortly as this is his usual time that he comes in. Besides he is expecting strangers from Gargbow to bring Makalay. Hopanda please fetch some water for the strangers as they must be thirsty after this journey. Meanwhile, let's leave now so that you can rest, and we can get the children get some water for you all to wash." Hogaii and everybody else left the strangers and returned to the back to continue the preparation of food which was a special for the strangers. All the children went to the stream to fetch water, which they warmed up for the strangers.

Before the strangers could say anything among themselves, Bawunda saw Bondaa approaching the house and he told the rest. As Bondaa drew closer to his house he observed that his veranda was full of people. Immediately he knew that it is the delegation that has brought his wife and his heart leapt with joyful delight. He walked faster than before holding one gourd of palm wine on either hand. As he entered his house and extended a hearty welcome to everybody before he placed his two gourds in the usual sport. He then walked to Bawunda and shook his hand with his two hands.

"Bawunda, you are most welcome to Magoronwa and to my house. How was your journey here?"

"We had no problems. They women surprised me at the rate they walked. They did not show any fatigue one bit." Bondaa went to shake the hand of Bawunda's wife who was seated close to her husband. He then went to shake the hands of the rest of escorts. As he stretched his hand to shake Makalay she got up from her bench and kneeled as she kneeled before her father when she gave him the calabash and she took Bondaa's. Bondaa shook her hand in the most genteel and courteous manner a man would shake the hand of woman he has longed for. This was the first physical contact between these two and their body language betrayed them.

"Makalay you are welcome to Magoronwa and to this home"

"Thank *Kayneh* Bondaa."

"I have a message to deliver to you after the evening meal." Bawunda told Bondaa.

"I hear you clearly." Bondaa answered.

He then turned round and took excuse so that he could go and arrange lodging for the strangers because he had only one extra room in which he will lodge Bawunda.

"You're perfectly excused." Bondaa left to arrange lodging for the male strangers. He was not bothered with the women strangers because he knows that Hogaii will handle that without him telling her. By the time he returned the strangers have all had their baths and they were back to the veranda. He asked the male strangers to accompany him so that he could show them the houses and rooms they are lodged. Not too long they all returned to the veranda again. Hopanda and Yagoro took food into the room outside and Yagoro stooped down and told Bawunda to go into the room with the male strangers and eat. Bawunda's wife and Makalay were asked by Bendihe to go into the room opposite and have their own food. Bondaa waited for his in the usual place. Before he could settle down to have his meal, he sent one of his daughters to tell his friend Fokogbo and Yongaa to come to his house after their own meals.

When they'd finished eating, all the elders of the family intuitively gathered in the veranda again and instinctively found benches to sit on, but no one spoke. Bondaa came out of his room which he entered immediately after the meal to take something for the strangers. He found everyone seated and quiet. Before he took seat in his hammock, he took out twenty Leones from his pocket and gave it to Kamanda.

"Kamanda this *boraa* is for Bawunda as head of this delegation. I welcome him and you who accompanied him to Magoronwa and to my house. That money represents my hand of welcome before I ask you the purpose of your visit."

Bondaa said even though it was obvious to him the reason Bawunda is in Magoronwa. Kamanda thanked Bondaa profusely and handed over the money to Bawunda.

"We highly appreciate your hand of welcome Bondaa, and I want thank you. I didn't expect this kind of gesture from you so soon after what you spent at Gargbow. But it isn't much of surprise to me knowing the man you are in our chiefdom. You don't need to ask me the purpose of our presence here. I have a message for you"

He reached into his gown's chest pocket and took out twenty Leones.

"Yongaa you were with Bondaa when he went to Gargbow. I will pass this message through you for Bondaa. I have been sent to you by Kokokutu, Krikoma, Sandima and Kargor; but Kokokutu because it was, he who requested you to leave your new wife for just two days. The two days ended yesterday, and he has asked me and my wife to bring Makalay to you. The money is to symbolize this. Also take this ten Leones as a token of our release of Makalay to Bondaa." He got up and gave Yongaa the money.

"They are aware that Makalay is beginning a new life as a wife, and she needs certain domestic utensils and items to prepare food for her husband. Based on that Makalay has brought some basic utensils, a bag of clean rice and a 5-gallon tin of palm oil to join her mates in starting her marriage life."

Yongaa thanked Bawunda and said "I cannot pass this message direct to my uncle. His best boyhood friend is here. I will ask him to deliver the good news." He passed the money to Fokogbo. "Fokogbo that's the message for the attention of Hogaii and Bendihe." And he took his seat.

"Yongaa, I bless and thank you for passing this message so pleasing to hear and I'm sure so also are you. This has not come as a surprise to me anymore. I have been informed about this two days ago after the return of Bondaa and his wives from Gargbow. I pray that everything henceforth relating to Bondaa and Makalay will be one that is acceptable to our departed. That God will bless and make their marriage peaceful and fruitful; that the enemies fail to achieve their diabolical plans against them. I pray that the relationship between Makalay and the current mates, Hogaii and Bendihe, will be harmonious and cheerful. I pray that they will do things in one accord for the good of the family and that Makalay will appreciate and understand the children too." He looked in the direction of Hogaii and Bendihe and said, "My conscience tells me that I should pass this message with due respect and honour to Hogaii and Bendihe." He went to Hogaii and gave her the money. "I respectfully request you and Bendihe to pass this delightful message to your husband"

"Fokogbo, I thank you very much for the honour. But I will be remiss in my role as the senior mate if I do not ask Bendihe to say something before I pass on the message. Bendihe, do you have a word to say?"

"Hogaii, I am your younger mate, but I thank you for your decency and high regard you always have for me on such occasions. Very few senior mates show such respect to the other mates. You're one of a kind. You are special. May our children learn and emulate this relationship between us? It is gratifying that we now have a third wife in the home. It relatively means that my activities will be reduced since we have additional two hands, two feet and two eyes and two ears. I also know that we have one more mouth that not only speaks but also eats. My hope is that the additional mouth will speak wise things soothing to the hearers. I welcome you Makalay to the home. Hogaii, I give you back the message."

"I appreciate your comments Bendihe" Bawunda said. "This is forthright expression of your feelings and that frees your conscience. Thank you and I hope Makalay heard that."

"I wholeheartedly endorse Bendihe's comments," Hogaii said. "However, I will add to what she has just said. First Fokogbo you forgot to mention that our endorsement and endeavours to Bondaa to have a third wife have come to a fruitful end with Makalay joining us tonight. What Bendihe and I have done is unprecedented in Magoronwa and we are proud of it. Is that not so Bendihe?"

"You're perfectly right and we are not ashamed of what we've done."

"Makalay has come at a time when we are ageing and therefore our energies fading. Let me stress here that this family has been to a very large degree homogenous, and we want it to remain that way. It is my belief and hope that your presence will further solidify this oneness. Do you agree with me Bondaa?"

"I totally agree with you and the credit goes to you two." Bondaa commended.

"Bondaa is your husband, Makalay. He is ours also. The children are our children. They are his too. But now that you have joined us, they have become your children also. So, we have one husband and six daughters. This means that even before you start having you own children you already have six lovely daughters. Hopanda and Yagoro are you here with us?"

"Yes, mama we are here"

"Good. Tell your younger sisters that you now have a younger mother to take watch over you and teach you things we omit to teach you. Makalay our children are hardworking," she continued, "as they have no brother—younger or older. We believe that your presence will bring great relief to the dilemma facing this family. I cannot tell you much about your husband. Over time you will better understand him. But for the moment let me say this: Bondaa is not only a master blacksmith and head of the Nwoingoha clan in Magoronwa. He is also a good husband who does not neglect his responsibilities to his wives. May be this is a result of our respect and humble attitude to him and the men of this village. We are your mates now. All relationships among us three should be dependent on mutual respect irrespective of age. Don't consider us as hostile competitors for Bondaa. We've been here long enough to know each other's concern."

"I believe that is the secret of your beautiful daughters" Bawunda's wife said

"In addition to the fact we are also beautiful mothers" Bendihe added

"Let me end my comments by saying that we your mates welcome you to the home with open hands. Having said that I now pass over the message to the man for whom it is intended." She got up and walked to Bondaa and handed him the money. "The message from Kokokutu and the others is that Bawunda brings your new wife to join you"

Bondaa who was reclining in his hammock got up and received the money. He sat upright in his hammock with his legs dangling down. He cleared his throat in preparation to respond to the various comments and advice.

"I thank you Yongaa through whom this message was passed before it has finally reached me." Bondaa started to speak. "You have been my faithful messenger and helper in all this. I thank you Fokogbo my good friend. You've been so understanding and helpful. My heart is too full of joy and that is owed to my dear, faithful, and supporting wives. You are indeed a special pair to me. I can boast in Magoronwa and maybe in the entire chiefdom that I have unique wives and cannot be compared with none. I appreciate my wives and I'm totally thankful for what you've done to make this marriage happen. I unquestionably owe it to you. Thank you, thank you, and thank you. I will not stop thanking you here verbally. Things will happen. You know what I'm capable of doing on such situations." He turned to Bawunda and his wife." You couple are amazing. I thank you for accepting the task. It is an honour to me. I pray that your home continues to prosper. Let all the enemies perish with their evil plans against you and your family. I pray that in due course you too will receive a delegation like this. May the spirits of our ancestors protect you during your return to Garbow? Please take this message to Komaneh Sandima and Yaywore Korgor that I have received their daughter in good health. Reassure them that I'll do all I can to fulfil all the promises I made to them there days ago. Makalay will be well looked after as my wife. I will make a welcoming address to my new wife while you're here. Makalay please come before me." Makalay rose from her bench and walked to Bondaa. She was dressed in a multi-printed cotton *taymulay* and *lappa* which revealed all her beautiful body features. The curvature of her buttocks was tantalizing through the lappa which she tied. Even though the hurricane lamp was dim, yet it could be seen that she fulfilled all the descriptions of Sago-Gbo: was medium height, light skinned with bright big brown eyes and had plenty hair. She was in her prime. Her features were exactly as Sago-Gbo has described. She walked gently but boldly to Bondaa. She stooped down just as she did before her father when she gave him the calabash.

"I am here Kayneh Bondaa," she said.

"You are welcome to my home as my third wife"

"Thank you Kayneh Bondaa.

"I do not have much to add to the various pieces of advice that you received three nights ago; nor do I have much to add to what you have just heard this night. Your mates have spoken out. You have joined us to add to this family. You made your choices to marry me knowing all what I am. It is up to you to make your choice a reality because I and your mates are prepared to make you achieve it. Feel free to communicate to all in the family. That's how we have lived so far, and it has worked. We are prone to make mistakes as we are human. But what matters is how we forgive those who have wronged us. The children are yours. How you handle them will determine how they will respect and obey you as their stepmother. There is no simple rule, but your tactics will determine it all. All other marital issues we'll discuss when we are together. So welcome again to this home."

He stretched out his right hand to Makalay, took her right hand and raised her up from her kneeling posture. She returned to her bench. There was a moment of quietness in the gathering. Then Bawunda's wife said "Bondaa, I have been kindly asked by *thara* Kargor to take back the white shirting inside the calabash after tonight."

"Bondaa, I guess you know what my wife is trying to say?" Bawunda said.

"Yes, I do. She will surely have it."

"Fokogbo and Yongaa, before you leave, please join me and Bawunda to drink my palm wine. Yongaa kindly bring the gourds from their usual place and pour us some." Yongaa brought the gourds which were overflowing with froth from their necks. Bondaa went into his room and brought four white enamel cups which he uses only when he has respectable and reputable guests. He handed them over to Yongaa who poured the first cup and handed it to Bondaa as he tapped the wine. It is the palm wine tapping ritual that he who offers the wine should be the first to partake of it. This is to prove that it not poisoned and that it is safe. Bondaa gulped the cup in one stretch and handed the cup back to Yongaa who waited a few moments before he poured another cup and gave it to Bawunda. He poured the other three cups and gave to the rest according to age hierarchy. Age is highly respected in this society. Ignoring the age hierarchy is considered a social crime for which one could be penalized. While the drinking was going on, the discussion was centred on the next big social event- the pre-male circumcision society dance. This season's initiation gathering will be in Magoronwa. Neighbouring villages will bring their youths due for circumcision to the village that has the highest number to be initiated. Every man and woman in the veranda agreed that it will be the biggest gathering because of the large number of young boys to be initiated in Magoronwa. They also agreed that initiation period is the time that many parents cannot afford to let their sons miss the time especially when their peers will be initiated. They also realized that many who are ill-prepared for the occasion go into debt by pledging something to raise the funds. But they noted the fact that it is the norm in the community and the tradition must be maintained and preserved.

"Let us hope that this big occasion will meet us in good health to celebrate that day. It's one that makes every participating parent proud when some graduates." Bondaa concluded the discussions and at the same time Yongaa set down the last cup on the floor and announced the gourds were empty.

"I guess my presence here is over," said Fokogbo "I must go sleep as I have helpers coming to assist me in my farm clearing the pieces of wood that were not burnt. Before I go, I must congratulate you Bondaa for the new wife. I wish you couple well. Bawunda, have a safe return trip with your wife and escorts. Goodnight, everyone."

He departed. Yongaa who has been quiet since he passed on the message to Fokogbo got up to leave.

"Uncle Bondaa, I believe that at this point you have almost solved your clan's dilemma. I am happy for you, and I wish you success in ridding yourself of this difficulty. I must go now. Goodnight, everybody."

He left the veranda with two of the young men who brought Makalay's things that lodged with him. The other two young men also left for their lodgings.

"Bondaa, I think I will follow suit and go to bed" Bawunda said. "You know that the distance between our two villages demands an early start in the morning. Good night. I will see you in the morning."

He went into his room followed by his wife. Bondaa remained in the veranda with his three wives. The first to say goodnight was Hogaii. Before Bendihe could leave she said "Makalay my three nights rotation sleeping with Bondaa has just ended after taking over from Hogaii. I think that this is the right moment for you to start your three nights with Bondaa. I am sure he has no objection. I'm sure that you won't object either as our mate. So good night and have a wonderful first night."

She entered the house and left the two in the veranda. Bondaa after a few moments also went in and Makalay followed him apprehensively. This was the first time she is entering a room alone with a man when all was quiet at night. When she entered, she was confused and did not know what to do. She sat on Bondaa's wooden box far away from the bed. Bondaa was already in bed which was neatly spread with the white shirting that was in the calabash. He was anticipating her to join him. But moments passed and Makalay was still seated on the box.

"Makalay, are you not tired and sleepy and you are still sitting on that box?"

"Of course, I am."

"What are you waiting for then? Come join me in bed." She got up from the box and walked slowly and hesitantly towards the bed. Bondaa asked her "are you coming to sleep with your pretty dress on? You need to take it off. I am sure you will be more comfortable. I had bought you a nice cloth with which to cover."

"Where is it?" she asked.

"Lift the lid of the box you sat on, and you'll find it right on the top." She went back to the box opened it and picked up the cover cloth. She turned her back to Bondaa. She took off the top of her dress and laid it on the box. Then she tied the cover cloth to cover her breast and untied the lower *lappa* of her dress. She folded it and put it on top of the other. Apprehensively, she walked again to the bed and climbed to the back of Bondaa who was lying in front. There was a moment of silence and not a word from anybody. Then Bondaa turned to face her.

"How do you feel about coming into bed with me?" he asked.

"I don't know."

"Have you ever had sex with any man before?"

"No, I haven't"

"Alright I will prove that now."

There was again a moment of silence and then Makalay uttered sounds of pain which could only be heard in the room. Then there was total silence in the room until the morning. Makalay was the first to get up and go to the wash yard after what happened in the room in the night. Bondaa had struggled a bit to get Makalay through last night, and to confirm her virginity and satisfy his curiosity he inspected the white shirting that was spread to see any traces of blood on it. Sure enough, there was enough blood on Makalay's side. This was adequate proof that she was chaste. He was glad that it was he who had deflowered her and hoped that whatever issue springs from this will be pure Nwoingoha blood. He neatly wrapped the shirting cloth and tucked it at the foot of the bed. He walked out of the room and washed his face quickly. He picked up his two gourds and went to tap his palm wine before Bawunda and entourage depart. As he approached his palm trees, he observed that the gourds up the palm trees were with frost but not dripping. He knew from the previous experience that it was some omen that was revealed to him some time past. This time he knows exactly what to do without any further inquiries. He knew the meaning and what to do. He climbed up and tapped the first and moved on to tap the other. On his way home he took a bath as it is his routine. On his returned, he found Bawunda sitting in the veranda anxiously waiting for him.

"Good morning Bawunda."

"Good morning Posseh. I hope you had a restful night out of your comfortable bed and room in Gargbow." Bondaa responded.

"Yes, we did, under the circumstances we are here."

"I had to rush to tap my palm wine so that you could have some to prep you up for the journey"

"That was thoughtful of you."

"Bondaa how was your night?" Posseh asked.

Bondaa was a little bashful to answer. But he must answer as his reply will indicate what message she will take to Kargor about her daughter. He turned to Bawunda and said "It was wonderful. Please tell *komaneh* (father-in-law) Sandima and *yaywor* (mother-in-law) Kargor that their daughter was not tampered with. It was a virgin that was with me last night. That is what parents want to hear about their daughters."

"I am happy for both of you." Posseh said. "I am particularly happy for the parents. But where is your proof?"

"I will give it to you when you are about to leave. I hope Hogaii and her mates have prepared food for you to eat? I would hate to see you start your journey on an empty stomach."

"Yes, they did, and we have already eaten. Thank you. We were just waiting for you to take leave of you." Bawunda replied.

"I will call your men so that you all could have some palm wine." He immediately left to call the four young men. When they were all gathered, he called his three wives to join them partake of the palm wine. He brought out the four enamel cups and handed them to the youngest of the four young men the honour to pour the palm wine. The young man poured out the first cup and handed it to Bondaa who drank it without pausing. Before the second cup was poured, Bondaa said

"Bawunda, with your permission and not a disregard to the age hierarchy can the next cup be given to Makalay in appreciation of what happened last night."

"I do not have the least objection. Go ahead. Let her have it." The young man poured out another cup and handed it to Bondaa who in turned called Makalay and handed the cup to her. She bowed in the usual kneeling position and drank the wine.

"Thank you *Kayneh* Bondaa. This is one of the best palm wines I have ever drunk. Your palm wine is compared to my father's." She handed back the cup to the young man who had already poured the other three cups and handed them out to Bawunda, Posseh and Hogaii in the age hierarchy. He filled the cup which he has just received from Makalay and gave it to Bendihe.

He made sure that everybody in the veranda had at least two full cups. When all the palm wine was exhausted, Bawunda asked leave to return with his escort to Gargbow.

"Before you go let me give your wife the white shirting. It will reveal that Sandima and Kargor performed their parental protection and guidance excellently. Thank them on my behalf and tell them that Makalay and I will visit them shortly." He then gave the cloth to Posseh who wrapped it in another cloth.

"Well, Bondaa we should leave now." Bawunda said. "You accorded us a wonderful reception. We are glad that everything has been so smooth and satisfactory. I pray the end of all this will be achieved; and that your house will be a peaceful home for all who live in it. Thank you very much and goodbye." He shook Bondaa's hand first and then the hands of the senior mates. When he took the hand of Makalay he steadied to say something to her.

"Makalay, you have made your parents very proud by what Bondaa said a few moments ago. Continue with that and remain faithful, obedient, and respectful. Remember, your parent will no longer provide for you nor watch over you. Your welfare is now the husband's full responsibility, but with your co-operation and support. This is now your home and family."

Posseh followed what her husband. She took her hand and said "you have disproved all the false assumptions and gossipers about you. You've have made your parents proud and shamed all the gossipers. Continue in that vein and you'll find that your marriage will be peaceful and fruitful. Please give honour and

respect to your senior mates. You can learn considerably from their experience with your husband."

"Thank you, uncle and auntie. I will do best to heed
to all the numerous advice I have received in the past
four days. Tell papa and mama that though I am not
with them in person, yet I'm with them in spirit. Thank
them for me for their love and unfailing care and
protection. Tell them that I love them dearly" she
ended with choking sobs. Posseh held her close to
herself and stroked her back to encourage her.

"Don't forget to give my high regards to Bowarah
my bosom friend. Tell her that I hope she will follow
the path I have chosen."

"I will give them your message. Bye now."

The couple stepped out of the veranda for their
return trip to Gargbow followed by the four young
men. Bondaa and wives watched them go until they
disappeared from the village.

CHAPTER THIRTEEN

Three months have elapsed since Makalay entered the rotation cycle of sleeping in Bondaa's room. The mates were closely monitoring her attitude and eating behaviour. They noticed that in the past months she has been eating sour fruits or sucking a lime ever so often than before. Sometimes she will not eat the food prepared for everybody. She will instead cook some soup with plenty of pepper. There are moments she will throw up what she eats. Hogaii and Bendihe knew exactly what was going on with Makalay as they too have gone through this phase. But they were reluctant to ask her as they thought she really might not be feeling well.

One evening when the children were playing outside and Bendihe had gone to Bondaa's room for her three nights. Makalay ventured into Hogaii's room. Hogaii was sitting on her bed folding her clothes and her daughter's that she'd washed that morning.

Makalay rapped gently on the door and asked, "May I come in?"

"Why do you ask that question Makalay? You know my room is always open to you. Come in."

"I'm sorry I asked" Hogaii stopped folding the clothes.

"Please sit down"

Makalay sat down on a stool bench not too far from the wooden boxes that were in the corner of the room. She bowed her head and fiddled with the edge of her *lappa*. For a moment she did not speak. "What is wrong? Do you want to tell me something?"

"Tha (a title for a woman much older than the speaker) Hogaii, I don't know how to explain this."

"Tell me whatever it is, I'm sure I can help."

"For three months in a row I have missed my period. I don't know why? I feel like vomiting and many food items are no longer palatable to me. I feel sleepy each time I sit quietly."

"Is that so? In that case, congratulations!"

"For what *Tha* Hogaii?"

"What you've just told me bears all the hallmarks of pregnancy. It means you are pregnant."

"What do you mean? Have I taken in?"

"Exactly. You should be expecting a baby in the next six months."

"What shall I do then?"

"You take care of that baby in your belly."

"Bendihe and I will help you through this. But you must begin to eat something healthy, not those foods you were cooking for yourself lately. Then take care how you work on the farm. Don't push too hard and don't lift any heavy stuff. Things that are heavy you must ask somebody to help you with things that are heavy. But let me ask, am I the first to whom you have disclosed this?"

"Yes, *Tha* Hogaii. I have not even told Bondaa be-because I was not sure about what was happening with me. Besides, I thought a woman's menstrual peri- ods are a woman's concern."

"You are right, they are. But in this case, you must tell him when next you're in bed with him. I am sure he will be delighted to hear that. Tomorrow I will go to the bush and get you a few herbs which I will boil for you to drink because I observe that your feet are a little swollen.

"Thank you, *Tha* Hogaii. I will send a message to mama to inform her?"

"This is not a message you send with somebody you don't trust. Some people are wicked and only want to watch the misfortunes of others. I will go myself and deliver the good news to her."

"Thank you again and good night"

She left Hogaii's room and went into hers. She lay down on the bed with her face up looking at the thatched roof as the house had no ceiling of any kind. She thought to herself: "I'm going to have a baby?" Then she recollected the housewife and motherhood education she had received in the *bondo* society. She remembered they were taught how to do domestic chores and what would happen when they have sex with a man. They were told what would happen when you are pregnant and have a baby. They were given useful guidance on motherhood and how to take care of a young born. She was reflecting on all society instructions when she fell asleep. When she woke up, she felt some relief within her now that she knows it was pregnancy sickness that made her feel uneasy and lose her appetite. She resolved to face the reality that she must carry this baby until she gives birth to it. Meanwhile she will carry on with her normal chores as if everything was normal until it is becom-obvious, and she can conceal it no more. She concealed the pregnancy from the public until she was seven months. It was only then that curious eyes were beginning to focus on her.

But soon after, these curious eyes ceased to look at her as she spent less time in the public than before. In consideration of her state, she was excused from much of the farm work. Instead, she was given the schedule of preparing food at the farm hut for those working. In one afternoon while she was cooking, she started experiencing birth pains. She thought these were just normal stomach pains until they became more severe. Then she noticed a water trail between her legs. She removed the pot she has place on the fire stones and asked Bendihe's youngest daughter, who was instructed to stay with her by her mother as a massager for such occasion, to run fast and call Hogaii and Bendihe.

"Tell them to drop all work and rush to the hut as fast as they can. Tell them I am having severe and terrible pains."

The little girl ran out of the hut to the field where the rest of the family were working. When she approached her mothers who were working far away from the rest of the family, she shouted "mama, mama."

"Why are you here Yaymbeh?" Bendihe asked.

"Sister Makalay has sent me to hurriedly call you and mama Hogaii quickly. She says she is having severe abdominal pains."

"Oh…oh…oh" exclaimed Bendihe. She rushed quickly to Hogaii. "Makalay wants us now at the farm hut. She has sent Yaymbeh to hurriedly call us. I believe that she might be due to deliver."

The two women ran to the hut without telling their children or husband. This conversation was not overheard by Bondaa. He was on the further end of the farm cutting down and removing shrubs. They speedily reached the hut. They did not stop to question Makalay, instead they went immediately to assist her. Moments later they assisted her to deliver her first baby.

"Bendihe, our consent given to Bondaahas borne the fruits that we desired."

"This will shut the mouths of reckless gossipers who talk behind our backs about giving our assent to Bondaa for a third wife."

"Bondaa will be overwhelming joyful to hear that he has a boy, at last." They were too keen to know the sex of the baby that they failed to notice that Makalay had fainted after she delivered. They immediately went on to resuscitate her drawing from their own maternity experience. When she fully regained consciousness, she asked for her baby. Hogaii had wrapped the baby after cleaning it and gave it to Makalay.

"It's a boy, Makalay. You have delivered the second male in the family." Hogaii told her. "Lie down and rest. I will finish the cooking and Bendihe will prepare a special dish for you."

"Makalay, we're happy for you because you have given us a boy to reduce the woeful gender imbalance in this family. Congratulations and I give you joy"

"Thanks to you two for coming quickly otherwise I would have had to deliver this baby on my own."

"We are glad that you didn't have to endure that." Rest and as Hogaii said I will prepare a special dish for you to eat. Don't bother with that man for now when he cries. He must cry to open his lungs. That is his job for now. Later you can suckle him." She left to join Hogaii at the back of the hut.

It was time to rest from the morning's work and to have some food to replace lost strength and energy. So Bondaa shouted for someone to go for the food as he could not see the others at work. Two girls went for the food. When they reached the hut, they did not notice that Makalay had given birth as both the mother and child were sleeping. They just thought that she was having her usual afternoon nap as an expectant mother at that stage. Neither of the older Mothers revealed the news to the girls. They want it to be a total surprise to everyone when they finally retire to go home. Hogaii, Bendihe and the two girls returned to the workplace. Bondaa was still busy brushing in the far area where he's been that he did not notice that his wives had left the workplace for a short time, nor did he notice when they returned.

Suddenly, Bendihe shouted out to tell Bondaa that food has been brought. When he came, he wanted to know why Makalay did not bring the food.

"Why is Makalay not here with the food?" he asked.

"You are asking an obvious question. When we were in the stage, she is now we did not do what you are asking her to do. She is resting we understand"

"Ask the girls you sent for the food to confirm what I have said."

"Papa, we found sister Makalay resting in bed when we went for the food"

"Okay, I was just curious to know her state."

"Don't worry, she's alright" Hogaii assured him. Her tone did not reveal anything as to what has happened. "I want us to break off early today because of Makalay. I would suggest that we leave now so that night fall does not meet us on our way home." Hogaii had the new-born baby in mind and not Makalay because she still does not want Bondaa to have an inkling.

"I agree" Bondaa consented. "We go home when we finish our present plots; I will not make any more plots until tomorrow, and we will return to complete our plots after we've finished eating."

One after another they completed the work on their plots. Those who completed their plots quickly assisted those who lagged.

As usual they walk home in a convoy to ensure that nobody is left behind in the bush. As double security Bondaa normally brings up the rear. He is usually not too close to the rest of the convoy. The wives and the girls were far away from Bondaa. As they reached the hut, they heard a baby crying. They asked their mothers which suckling mother could possibly be in the hut.

"It's Makalay." Hogaii answered. "She has given birth to a baby boy. Yaymbeh came to call us this afternoon and told us that Makalay was having birth pains. We rushed to the hut and assisted her to deliver. So run and see your baby brother."

Hogaii and Bendihe slowed down their pace so that Bondaa will catch up with them. When he did, he asked, "Why did the children run to the hut? I saw them in great haste. What has happened?'"

"Relax Bondaa" Hogaii advised him. "Bendihe, I give you the honour to tell the news"

"Bondaa, we want to tell you that Makalay produced a bouncing baby this afternoon."

"What baby?" He paused for a moment. "Another girl?" he asked in a rather dejected mood as he noticed no excitement in the voice of either wife.

"Eh….eh…eh…eh…eh…eh." Hogaii dragged her response to build up Bondaa's anxiety.

"What is it Hogaii? Tell me whatever it is. I will accept the clan's fate."

"Makalay has a baby boy" Hogaii revealed.

"That's not true"

"It is true" the two wives pronounced in unison.

"Is it really true, or are you just trying to control my disappointment over another girl?"

"Yes, it is true. The baby is a healthy-looking boy with your features.

"He is not dark as you. He took Makalay's fair skin."

"I give God the praise and the glory. He has answered my ancestors' pleading. I thank Him for hearing the Nwoingoha clan cries for a successor. Let me go see and behold my son. They all walked towards the hut; the women unable to keep up with Bondaa's pace. When he entered the hut, he found Makalay sitting on a mat cuddling the baby and the six daughters surrounding them. On his entry all the kids burst into various ways of telling their father.

With a broad smile on his face, he profusely congratulated Makalay for the delivery. He knelt to take the baby from Makalay's bosom. He lifted the baby above his head and said:

"Mighty God, I thank you for this boy. I lift him back to you and present him to you for all I desire for him" Then he lowered the baby to the level of his mouth and uttered inaudible words to the child's right ear and then said loudly "All you ancestors whom I cannot name, your message through Sago-Gbo has been fulfilled. Your clan will continue to exist in life if God protects and guides him. Your great, great ancestors will not let harm come his way since your desire is that the clan should continue into perpetuity."

Hogaii and Bendihe who found him making this dedication stood behind him indicating support for him at this awesome moment. They showed him the high bench in the hut to sit with the baby.

"We are happy for you and this family." Hogaii said. "We have been able to grant you through Makalay what we cannot give you through our wombs. Our ultimate hope is to see us reap the intended reward years later when we're frail and can only depend on somebody to care for us."

"Indeed, we are glad for the outcome of our unflinching support." Bendihe added. "We pray for long life for this boy. To me he is our social security to care for us if our lives are prolonged. We know that very soon all our daughters will get married and will be gone to various places which may be far from Magoronwa. We may not even see them again before we die."

"It was based on this conviction and the fact that I need a son to take over my trade and continue with the clan's culture and tradition that I asked for your consent. Today this has paid off. Thank you both for your endorsement and backing to solve my clan's dilemma." Bondaa remarked. "But the solution is still incomplete. There is more work to do. We must all nurture this baby to be a man in the way of our family and the Nwoingoha clan. So, let's go home before the sun sets." All trooped out to return to the village with Hogaii carrying the baby in a basket large enough to contain him comfortably.

The customary child naming should be performed seven days after birth. It is a big event in the village especially when the child is the first male. Bondaa sent Yongaa to Ngadiya to buy a white ram a day before the occasion. He has already sent Hogaii to Gargbow two days ago before the naming occasion to give the good news and to invite his in-laws. So, on the morning of the appointed day the village elders gathered in the fore front of the house with Sandima, Kokokutu and Kargor prominently seated. The items for the ceremonial rites were assembled in the centre of the front forecourt. These included 100 kola nuts (50 white and 50 red) placed in a white basin containing water. Also brought were freshly milled rice flour, some honey in a bottle and a glass of water. They placed a bench for Bondaa to sit close to his in-laws. Before he sat, he took the rice flour, honey and the water and placed them in front of him. He poured some water and honey on the rice flour and started kneading into dough with both hands. While kneading the flour, he invoked the spirits of his ancestors and soliciting their presence with their next heir. He prayed that no evil forces succeed in harming him or hindering his progress in life.

He then called Hogaii to bring Makalay and the baby to the ceremony. A mat was spread close to where Kargor was seated. Makalay sat on it with the baby held to her chest while rocking it left to right. Bondaa took the bowl containing the rice flour and honey and cleared his throat as usual when he wanted to speak so that everybody could pay attention.

"I welcome you all gathered here this morning for this naming ceremony. I want to particularly welcome in our midst my in-laws *komaneh* Sandima and *yaywore* from Gargbow. This is a unique and important day for the Nwoingoha clan which I believe you elders of this village will agree with me"

"We perfectly understand your position and we are happy for you," commented Sago-Gbo.

"Thank you, Sago-Gbo and I want to thank you all for coming. I call on you all to join me in making this sacrifice and prayer for long life and prosperity for this my son." The village elders and his household surrounded him. Those closest to him placed their hands on his shoulders. Those who could not, touched the shoulders of those who did until everyone was connected. When everyone was quiet, he started his supplication. "Let the witches and wizards fail."

"Hm" was the unison response from the crowd around him. In making such sacrifice prayers those who participate will respond in agreement by just saying: 'hm'. So, he continued with the crowd responding.

"All guns aimed against him by witches should fail to fire"

"Hm"

"Instead let those guns backfire and kill the shooters"

"Hm"

"I pray that anything poisonous he swallows, or eats shall not harm him."

"Hmm"

"Let it be converted into nourishment for his bones"

"Hmm"

"May he grow to be humble yet someone that will stand for what he believes in is right and just."

"Hmm"

"Grant his needs and just wishes in life that will enhance and benefit his home and our Magoronwa community."

"Hmm"

"I pray that he becomes a prominent person in this society."

"Hmm"

"And that he contributes to strengthening the inter-marriages in the community."

"Hmm"

"Grant him favour in the eyes of men of prominence and stature."

"Hmm"

"I believe that you have heard and answered my prayer you departed ancestors"

"Hmm"

Thank you." And everybody in the gathering shouted: "way-ray."

Satisfied that the rice flour is properly mixed he moulded two lumps from it and left the greater portion in the basin. He set each of the two lumps on a saucer-like plate. He put one white kola on one and on the other lump a red kola nut. In the Nwoingoha clan, the naming is incomplete without shedding the blood of a lamb. Yongaa knew that after the rice flour mixing was over, the next ceremony is the actual naming. So, he brought the lamb with a sharp knife in his hand. He handed both to Bondaa who was assisted by Yongaa and Fokogbo to lay the lamb on the floor for the slaughter. Bondaa prepared the lamb's throat for the knife. As Bondaa lay the knife at the lamb's throat to slit it he named the boy Kewalie (named after Pa Kewalie, founder of the clan) and simultaneously slit the throat and the blood spilt on the floor. Pieces of the skinned lamb were distributed to the elders present. The lamb's skin was stretched and pinned inside up with small sticks for it to dry. It will be needed later for another important occasion. When this was over Bondaa took the dough basin and distributed it in small balls to the children in the crowd. With the last bit in his hand, he pinched a tiny bit and placed it in his baby's mouth and gave the balance to the mother. He also distributed whole kola nuts in the basin to the elders and the remainder he split each into two halves and gave to the young men and women.

After everybody dispersed, Bondaa took the saucers containing the dough lumps and placed one saucer far from the other. He set the glass of water equidistance from the two saucers. The saucers and the glass of water were place under the head side of his bed.

"This is your share of the sacrifice elements. The saucer that has the red kola is the men's and that with the white kola is for the women. I know you will have no objection to drinking from one glass because we inherited that from you."

Bondaa was very careful to observe the taboo in the clan that men and women do not eat from the same bowl. The clan's belief is that ancestral spirits will partake of the sacrifice elements at night. The evidence that they agree with the sacrifice and therefore partake of the elements is that in the morning tiny ants will be seen swarmed all over the dough. If there are no ants, then it means that the ancestral spirits rejected the sacrifice.

Before he emerged from his room, he opened his wooden box and took out a bundle which contained clothes for mother and son. When he emerged Makalay was still sitting on the mat with Kewalie. He bowed down and handed the bundle to Makalay.

"This contains clothes for you and Kewalie. I hope that you will like what's in it."

He took the child from her lap, put it on his left arm and stretched out his right hand to lift her up. They walked to the house. The rest of the family followed.

"Bondaa, thank you for inviting us to this cere-mony," Sandima expressed appreciation. "We feel very honoured and proud. Now that it's all over, we have to leave."

"Komaneh Sandima, the day is far gone. It's almost mid-day. May I crave your indulgence to spend the night and depart in the morning?" Bondaa pleaded. "The distance to Gargbow is by no means short for people of your age. You need to start early in the morning, so you'll not be caught by night fall before you reach. Besides, I believe *Yaywore* Kargor will like to cuddle her first grandson a little more. So please spend the night."

"I guess you're right. We'll stay the night but will leave early in the morning."

It's a little over three months after the birth of Kewalie and the baby was in good health. He has put on weight to the point that some people think that he was six months old. However, several days the boy woke up after midnight and intermittently cried until day break. This was bothering Bondaa and the rest of the family. During the day Kewalie was cheerful and playful. He suckled well and took naps during the day. But the continuous crying during the night could not be explained. They were all puzzled as to the reason. Then Bondaa remembered what Sago-Gbo had told him when he consulted him. Sago-Gbo had advised him that when the boy is three months old, he should take mother and child to the maternal grandparents and that they should not return until after two years. Recollecting the advice, he decided to take Makalay and son to Gargbow the next day. Neither he nor Makalay was to tell any member of the family much less a member of the village. She was to get her clothes and the baby's together for the journey.

Bondaa woke up early in the morning just after the first cock crow. When he got up, he told Hogaii who was with him, that he's taking the child and mother to the 'thothogbeh' man to find out the cause of the child's night cries. He did not know which 'thothogbeh' man or his location.

"You are taking the right approach. I agree with you" Hogaii said. "The poor child and her mother do not sleep well at night. Sometimes I get disturbed to hear him crying. Go safely with them and we hope to see you before sun set." And she went back to sleep. Bondaa went to Makalay's room and took her bundle of things she had put together. Makalay gently strapped the baby on her back and covered his head with a piece of cloth as protection against the morning dew. They stepped out of the house quietly without waking up anyone except Hogaii. As they stepped out with Makalay ahead, they were greeted by the barking of the village dogs. They ignored the barking and went through the sleeping village with no one in verandas or backyards. They headed straight for Gargbow to Sandima and Kargor. When Bendihe and the children woke up and noticed that Makalay was not in her room with her baby they asked themselves.

"They've gone to see a *thothogbeh* man," Hogaii eased their concerns. "But which one, Bondaa did not say, nor did he tell me when they will back. But since he went with them, I don't think they will make a long stay." She further allayed their worries. "Let's get ready to go to the farm and resume where we stopped yesterday."

Bondaa and his young family went directly to Gargbow just in time as people were returning from their farms. Bondaa now leading the way went directly to his father-in-law's house without stopping to greet anybody. Kargor was in but Sandima had not returned yet as he had to pass the tap his palm wine. Kargor was curious to know why Bondaa with Makalay and her baby were in Gargbow.

"Bondaa are you here on a surprise visit or is something significantly wrong?" Kargor asked.

"We are not here for a family visit. But please be patient. I will explain everything this evening when *Komaneh* is here."

Indeed, when they had their evening meals, Bondaa explained why they were in Gargbow.

"For nearly ten days the child has woken up after midnight, crying. He continues to cry with intermittent stops until daybreak. We could not tell the cause. But I was warned by Sago-Gbo that three months after the child is born, I should bring him and the mother to you, the grandparents. He said that they should not return to Magoronwa until the child is two years old. So, I am here with them. They will be with you and under your protection and control."

"Bondaa let me assure you that we will care and protect your son. We are fully aware of your concern for him and the attachment to him. I know that he is the lifeline for the continued existence of your clan. He is also special to us just as he is to you. He is our first grandchild."

"All I can add is that you brought them to their second home at the right time." Kargor added. "When I reflect on the prayers you offered at his naming ceremony, he will be protected to grow up and be a man of stature. So don't worry yourself too much about their welfare. We'll do our utmost best to nurture him and cherishingly take care of him."

"Thank you, my in-laws. I should really not burden you people with this responsibility at your age"

"Don't call that a burden." Sandima protested. "It will be our delight to see our grandson grow and be a man in the community."

"What I want to tell you also is that nobody knows that they are here with you in Gargbow. Not even her mates. I barely told them that we are going to see a *thothogbeh* man. I did not tell them which one, or where. I told them that we will return immediately after seeing him. Their stay here is absolutely a secret to all in Magoronwa. I certainly want it to stay that way if you don't mind?"

"I will secure the consent of the village headman for the village crier to make a special announcement to that effect. He will announce that anybody who discloses this secrecy will be under the curse of the Magoronwa *Gbangbani* and *Kofoe*. This will be repeated for three straight nights in a row. It will be the responsibility of those who will hear the announcement to relay it to whosoever in their household was not present to hear the message."

"Oh, that will be highly appreciated."

He dipped his right hand into the front chest pocket of his gown. He took out a piece of red cloth at one corner of which he tied money. He untied it and took some money of it and gave it to Sandima.

"I did not bring anything for their feeding as this was a secret trip. I am conscious and aware of the fact that this raining season is always a bit difficult and lean. Please accept this for their feeding until I make the next visit. I hope it will be next month."

"Bondaa you need not do this. They are our flesh and blood, and we should care for them. Please take back the money. We'll do our best to care and provide for them."

"It is no disrespect to you. But you and I know that in this raining season things rapidly deteriorate. So, I beg you, please take it."

"Alright I will accept this. But let it not be repeated."

"I appreciate it *Komaneh*. Thank you for your understanding. I will return early in the morning."

"I guess you want to go to bed now against your early wake. Before you do so I want you to have some of my palm wine. It is an old man's tapping, so it may not be as tasty as yours."

"But I partook of your palm wine after the wedding. It was very good and tasty and I'm sure that this will taste likewise."

Sandima brought out the gourd from his room. He poured out a full cup and drank it before he filled it for Bondaa. When the palm wine was exhausted, they both parted to their separate rooms. On his return Bondaa informed the rest of his family that he had left them with the *thothogbeh* man on his advice. The name of the *thothogbeh* man nor the village he never disclosed.

CHAPTER FOURTEEN

Bondaa never reneged on his promise to visit Gargbow to see his wife and son. He constantly took the trip on a scheduled basis. Each time he visited he brought a 25kg bag of rice and a gallon of palm oil. He had arranged with a well-to-do farmer in a village not far from Gargbow to buy rice and palm oil for him so that neither his family nor the Magoronwa village would know where he was going. He would only tell his other wives that he was going to visit Makalay and the child at the *thothogbeh* man's. He had some time ago told them that he had left them there on the advice of the *thothogbeh* man. He never disclosed the name of the *thothogbeh* man nor his village.

For two years he has been visiting his family at Gargbow. During those two years he has seen his son grow healthy and good looking. Bondaa now believes that grooming the successor to the clan inheritance should start at an early age. Realizing this as crucial in the lineage question and considering that Sago-Gbo had advised that the mother and child should return after two years, he decided that it was time to bring his family back to Magoronwa. So, he went back to his in-laws to ask for the return of his wife and son.

"I have not enough words to express my sincere gratitude for what you have done for me and my family," Bondaa told his in-laws. "Your parental care was first manifested in your daughter. And now you have started an enviable one with your grandson. You are an amazingly marvellous, loving, and caring couple. Thank you very much. I highly appreciate your great care. I want you to please accept this token sum of hundred Leones as a sincere manifestation of my appreciation. Komaneh Sandima, please do not consider this an insult or disrespect. I know you can do without this, but I cannot just express my gratefulness with empty words. This is the only way to substantiate my gratitude."

"Kargor you've heard what Bondaa has said. We cannot hold them here any longer than he wishes. We pray that the boy continues to grow in health and wisdom. I'll miss him very much because at this age he's always by my side asking curious questions. The hallmarks of a smart child who wants to know and learn. He has enormous curiosity to know things. I believe we've given some parental nurturing to our grandson."

"I'm happy to hear that." Bondaa said.

"He does all the easy errands for his grandfather," Kargor reinforced her husband's comments. "Sometimes he sits by his mother's side while she cooks and does the small chores for her. I shall also miss him."

"We'll leave early in the morning if you people don't mind."

"No, we don't at all. It's always better to start this journey between our two villages early".

So, after the first cock crow Bondaa and his family took to the return trip back to Magoronwa. Although the boy could walk and run about yet he could not walk the distance. This time it is Bondaa's turn to carry the boy. So, he put behind his neck with the legs resting on the upper part of Bondaa's chest. To support him in this position he propped him up at his waist with all his fingers interlocked into each other behind the boy's waist. Also, instead of Makalay leading the way, she followed behind for the obvious reason of protection.

They rested halfway through the journey so that the boy could ease himself and have some yams which her mother cooked at night for the journey. Besides, Bondaa needed a little massage on the back of his neck for the rest of the journey. It was just before sun set; they reached the outskirts of the village. The first to see them was Yongaa who was on his way to tap his palm wine.

"Welcome back uncle Bondaa. Your wives told me that you went on a short patrol. And now that I can see a little boy at the back of your neck and Makalay following you, I guess you went to bring them from where they were secretly sheltered and protected."

"Yes Yongaa. You are right. I went to bring them back as I want my son to be close to me from now on."

"I perfectly understand your concern and the precautions you took for your son."

"Thank you for your understanding. How is my home? Are they okay?

"Oh, they are fine, and everything seems normal there."

"Well let's reach home and join the rest of the family." They took the last lap of the journey. Yaymbeh spotted them as she saw her father approaching. She shouted for the rest to hear.

"Papa is back with a little boy seated at the back of his neck and sissy Makalay with him."

The rest of the children turned to where they know will be the only way they will come. As soon as they spotted them, they all ran from the back yard, where everyone was gathered cooking the evening meal to meet and welcome them. But they were particularly glad to see their brother two years after he and his mother somewhat disappeared from the home. When they saw Makalay and their brother they were convinced that they have returned for good. Hopanda took Kewalie from his father and toted him by her side. She did not bother to find out whether the boy walks or not. The rest of the children followed Hopanda as they walked ahead of his father with joy. The children walked back to the back yard to tell the good news of the return of their father, Makalay and Kewalie to their mothers. The mothers were not enthused as they knew that one day Makalay will return with the baby. They knew in the Magoronwa community, when the life of a baby is threatened by witchcraft, the father will take baby and mother to a secret location unknown to even the rest of the family. However, they were glad that they have returned home looking healthy. So, when Makalay came to greet her mates, they heartily welcomed her.

"Kewalie you've grown to be a big boy. Look at you" Hopanda said as she put him down.

"But I am not a big boy. I am just a little boy" Hanwa replied

"Alright you may say that, but we say you have grown to be a big boy because the last time we met you were crying for sissy Makalay to breast feed you. Now you can talk."

"I'm happy to see you. Welcome back. The last time I touched you was when you were three months old." Yaymbeh said. "We are happy because we have our little brother to play with, once again, and send around to do small chores for us."

"Makalay, I hope that Kewalie did not give you too many worries while you were in hiding." Hogaii mused.

"Oh, not much. There were two anxious moments when he had serious cause to worry over his health. Other than those two occasions, everything was fine with us. My mother knew this was my first child and helped me a lot. He looks healthy from eating rice pap and fundi and red palm oil as his cereal."

"Since we did not hear news about you two," Bendihe said, "we concluded that you were safe and well. During your absence Yaymbeh constantly asked me about your whereabouts as she missed playing with Hanwa."

" I missed her also. She was my errand girl and a great help at the farm hut when I was preparing the meals. She is excited to see her brother after two years. She now has a partner to play with."

"She is the youngest daughter, and he is the first son in the family. They will be lovely playmates." Bendihe agreed with Makalay.

All the children gathered around to make their brother welcome and feel at home. Bondaa came to formerly tell Hogaii and Bendihe that he has brought back Makalay and Kewalie.

"I'm sorry I could not disclose where I took them for reasons which I am sure you know. It was not a slight to you women, but experience dictated my actions. Please forgive me if you feel slighted or ignored on the welfare of your mate and only son."

"You don't need to apologize." Bendihe said. "We perfectly understand. We would have scolded you if you did not take that action."

"You remember the morning; you were leaving I told you that you were taking the correct stand" Hogaii reminded Bondaa. "So, there is no need for you to apologise for not disclosing the details to us. On the contrary we want to thank you for bringing them back looking so good and healthy"

"Well, what can I say? Thank you very much. I'm going to tap my palm wine. He entered the house and picked up his gourds and headed out straight to the site.

"Thank you mates for keeping up the farm work. Well, I'm back to continue though not from where I left off."

"You're most welcome. You have returned at the right moment. After many years farming the swamps Bondaa has decided to brush a bush that he has not farmed for nearly fifteen years since I have been with him."

"I know that brushing a bush involves several farming operations as against swamp farming which has few activities before harvest. I guess he has a good reason for choosing upland this year."

"If the vagaries of the weather are favourable without many threats of pests, we should expect a rewarding harvest, because the land is fertile being fallow for nearly fifteen years" Hogaii proffered to explain Bondaa's rationing.

"Mama Bendihe the rice is ready for dishing." Hopanda announced.

"Remove it from the fire and prepare the bowls" instructed Bendihe.

CHAPTER FIFTEEN

Fourteen years later Kewalie has become a teenager and a great helper to his father. One area of major relief was the bird scaring from the fields just after sowing and when the rice begins to bloom on the straw before harvest. Before him his four sisters had to position themselves at almost equidistance places to scare the birds. In this community women were not expected to swing slings but knew how to swing the sling. It was considered to be a man's job. Bondaa realized that the sling is an effective weapon to fight both wild animals and scare birds. He made several slings with rope made from palm fronds and taught his son how to use them. When the rice field was sowed and plowed it was Kewalie's place to scare the birds picking up the seeds. Also, when the rice stalks sprout out of the stems, birds must be scared off. Doing this wasn't easy as he had to get up early with the first chirps of birds and walked the distance to the farm. If he woke up late birds would have swarmed the field by the time he'd reached the farm. Whether it rained or not in the morning he still had to go. Oftentimes when it rained, he shaded himself with a broad banana leaf as his umbrella. This wouldn't last as it often flip over and soon shredded into several pieces. Many times, he reached the farm drenched in rain. There was no fire to warm him. He couldn't light a fire as it was impossible to carry a lighted firewood under the rain. Safety matches were a rarity. His clothes dried on his body. As soon as he reached, he went to the various spots where he has piled the appropriate sizes of stones. He picked up one and put it in the sling and swung it three or four times to develop velocity and power. He released the other end of the sling and flung the stone in the direction he spotted birds. He moved on to another spot and repeated the scaring.

When he's satisfied that there were no birds on the field, he climbed up the raft-like dais constructed in the center of the field with sticks where he will stand to watch. From this vantage point the entire field was in his view and each swing of his sling reached to any point he aimed at. After slinging several points, he sat down on the raft dais and play his xylophone-like instrument made from sticks shaped as the chords on a normal xylophone. He sat flat and spread his legs forward. The flat shaped sticks were arranged according to size and sound on his thighs. With two small drum sticks he beat a tune and sang a chorus to the top of his voice. He beat and sang loud for another thirty to forty minutes. Playing the xylophone had two basic reasons. The first was to keep him awake from the sleep he lost by waking early than usual. The second was to make his presence known to the birds. After a reasonable period when he sensed that the birds were cooing on the field, he again swung stones to various parts he observed the birds clustering. He repeated this routine xylophone playing and scaring the birds many times during the day.

A little after mid-day he saw Yaymbeh approaching from afar. Seeing her sister meant that she has brought some food for him. What she has brought he could not foretell until he uncovered the bowl. He waited until she was closer, then he said "Sissy Yaymbeh you're late today. What happened?"

"Are you so hungry that you even forget your manners to say good 'afternoon'?" She scolded him.

"Yes sissy. These pestering birds have sapped all the energy from me, and I need to replace it with something solid not just with water I fetched from the stream. Even that is exhausted.

"Okay, Hungry man. I brought some cassava and potato porridge cooked with palm oil. This is what everybody at home had this afternoon before I brought yours."

"I hope it is enough to keep me up until the sun sets when the birds retire for the night"

"You're such a glutton. You know how much is in the bowl. You haven't opened it to see. You might not even finish what's in it. Here. Take the bow and open it" she said as she gave it to him. He took it and lifted the lid.

"Good. This will sustain me until I also retire this evening. Can you please get some water for me from the stream? I can't eat because I know that the porridge is spicy hot with pepper. I don't want to choke and cough with pepper when it burns my mouth. So please go quickly."

"I don't know where it is?"

"Go towards that tall palm tree you see on your right. Pass it and take a left turn towards the small cotton tree. Just underneath the tree is the stream with clean running water."

She left to follow the directions. After taking a few steps she observed that birds have clustered in her direction.

"There are birds near the tall palm tree you pointed to me" she shouted to Kewalie.

"I hear you. Don't go any further. Let me sling some stones there first because I don't want my loving sister to be hurt."

He placed a stone in the sling and swung it several time before releasing it to the direction of the palm tree. Many birds flew from the area. "You can continue now. I will throw in other spots."

The moment Yaymbeh came with the water, he quickly washed his right hand and dipped it into the porridge to have a mouthful. He quickly went for a second while he was still munching the first.

"Take your time to eat or you will choke yourself with this spicy food" Yaymbeh, who was observing him, cautioned him as he was going for the third handful.

"Sissy, I agree but I am really famished under this hot burning sun." He took the water jug and drank deeply from it as the pepper was hot in his mouth. He followed that with rapid succession of handfuls until the bowl was empty. He licked the inside clean with his fore finger until there was no needed to wash the bowl

"Now I have regained some energy to enable me to swing the sling again. Thank you, sissy, for bringing the food."

"You're welcome. But next times please take your time to eat, and you'll enjoy the food."

"I take your advice. But when you are really famished, you don't eat to enjoy the food but to eat away hunger."

"Alright! Hand me the bowl and let me get back home. Mama is waiting for me to clean the husk rice for this evening meal." He handed over the bowl and he said, "I'll see you in the evening." Immediately she left, he got up and threw stones to the farthest spots of the farm.

Satisfied that there were no birds, he sat down again to his pastime entertainment of playing his xylophone.

However, since there was still more time before sunset, he decided to set a bird trap at the spot where the birds are a real menace. He brushed inside the bush close to the farm outskirts. He looked around for a special small flexible but strong thorny twig that is used for this trap. He saw one not too far from where he brushed. He cut it and removed all the little branches from it and tested its flexibility. Since the hour during which the birds rain on the field was drawing closer, he decided to complete the trap setting the next day as it takes some time to set it. He went to the dais and resumed the birds scaring until sunset before he went home.

The next day he resumed his bird scaring. After scaring the first wave of birds, he decided to complete the trap setting. First, he brushed some grass with seeds he knows is attractive to the birds and brought it to the trap site put it on the edge. He sharpened two pegs and firmly anchored them in the ground about six fingers apart. Some ten steps from these, another peg was anchored at the opposite end so that the twig will form a semi-circle. He tightly tied the big end of the flexible twig between the two pegs and tied a long rope to the other end of the twig. He spread the grass at the middle to ensure the birds will gather there. Then he bent the twig to a semi-circle and placed it lightly behind the opposite peg so that the slightest pull of the rope caused an easy release of the rope. The long rope he will take to the edge of the farm where he'll not be seen or heard by the birds at his approach. The trap is to hit as many birds as possible on the sudden pull of the rope and the release of the thorny twig. The sudden pull of the rope will hit and kill any birds in its path.

Satisfied with the trap, he returned to the dais and observed that the birds were already beginning to drop down on the field. He resumed his swings of the sling. He knew that towards sun set birds would eat more voraciously than they did in the morning. So, he gathered more stones to throw with his sling. At sun set when he was confident that no more birds were on the field, he too will return to the village by way of the Kathabai stream and took his bath before finally heading home. He went into the veranda where he found his father relaxing in his beloved hammock.

"Good evening, Papa"

"Have you allowed the birds to pick up the seed rice from the field?" his father welcomed him with a query.

"How can I allow them? They are a real menace though as our farm is the only one in the area."

"I know that. Thank you for your effort. You know that this will be your daily activity until the birds are no longer able to uproot the young rice shoots."

"Papa can you please ask the father of one of the young boys in the village to assist me? The farm is too big for me to cover on my own. I have to be constantly throwing stones and my arm already hurts."

"You have to cope with it. I did it for several years when I was your age. Besides this is the busiest farming month and everybody is engaged in farm work. I know that you can do it. You only need to focus on it.

"Yes papa, I will do my best."

"Has the rice started germinating?"

"Yes, and it is doing fine. I wish I can make it to grow faster as I want to get out from there and find something else to do."

"Oh yes! Something else to do. Well after you're done on the bird scarring you will join me in the blacksmith hut. You have to begin to learn how to forge farm implements from now on."

"Are you going to teach me?"

"It is my place to train you to take over from me. This is a trade that has been passed over from father to son for generations in our clan. It is a trade that cannot be passed over to any clan other than the Nwoingoha clan. I inherited it from my father, who in turn inherited from his father and so on. Now it is your turn to learn and eventually take over from me even if I am still alive."

"If you say so, I guess I have not much choice but to tow the clan's inheritance line. But, one thing I know papa, is that every farmer in this chiefdom knows you. They all come to you to make or repair their farm implements."

"Yes, my child. Being a blacksmith is an honour able profession. You don't only help individual farm-ers, but you help to develop the chiefdom through their farm output. I'm sure that you will be proud to be one."

"Let me into the skills first and we'll see whether I will like it or not"

"It is not whether you'll like it or not. It is a liveli-hood profession which you can depend on solely to take care of your family depending on its size. I decided to supplement the blacksmith earnings by farming when I had your fourth sister. It's a trade that earns you constant income. If people farm, they will need to buy new implements or repair broken ones"

"What if in future I decide to do something totally different?"

"The Nwoingoha clan has never abandoned the trade as I was told by your great grandfather. It has been temporarily put in abeyance in the past but never abandoned"

"Alright papa, when do I start?"

"As I said earlier, after your bird scarring is over you will join me the next day. But before you step into the workshop, I must purify you and protect you through a special ritual just as my father did, and his father, and so on."

"There is something else you need to learn."

"What's that papa?"

"How to climb palm trees to cut palm fruits for palm oil. And of course, you have already tasted palm wine because I have been building your taste through mine. I'll show you how to make your first climbing rope and your cousin Yongaa will teach you the rest. You will learn faster from him because I may not be as patient with you as he will be over inexcusable mistakes."

"You are going to call him over for discussions on this?"

"It is an important and honourable thing for him to undertake. Yes, I will discuss with him". At this moment Yagoro came from the back yard to announce that food is ready.

"Bring it, my dear. I'm sure your brother is as hungry as I am."

After the meal Bondaa told Kewalie to retire to bed as he must wake up early in the morning to go to the farm

Ten days later the scarring ended and Kewalie was much relieved from this task. He is now happy that he could complete his sleep till the morning. However, he had to nurse the pain in his right shoulder for several days yet, a pain that is a direct effect of swinging the sling. When he told his father about it hoping that he would obtain some remedial herbs, his father dismissed it.

"That is not a sickness. It is a pain that is temporary. It will disappear in the next few days. It is a direct consequence of swinging the sling. What I will do tomorrow is to get some herbs to steam wash you with them before you join me in the smithy. I told you days ago that you have to be purified and shielded from evil people who envy us for this trade and want to destroy us so that they could take it over."

"When will this be?"

"Seven days after I set the herbs and they have gorged their potent potions. The night before that day you keep to yourself and not with your playmates. On the day itself you shall drink no palm wine. "Do you get that?"

"Yes papa. Is that all I have to do?"

"You will know the rest when the purification ritual is in progress." Bondaa kept to his promise, He got up early in the morning and went into the forest and surrounding bushes to fetch the root herbs and leaf herbs even before he went to tap his palm wine. He came back late morning with a huge bundle of various herbs and placed them on the back veranda.

"Makalay, do you have anything in your 5-gallon cooking pot?"

"No, I don't."

"Do you intend to use it in the next seven days?"

"No. I don't have any plans to use it soon. I don't know whether my mates do."

"I don't have any plans to use it" said Hogaii. "I don't know about Bendihe"

"Neither do I." replied Bendihe.

"Then wash it clean and set a fire separate from your normal fireplace and half fill the pot with clean water."

"For what may I dare to ask?"

"Preparing to cleanse and shield your son before he joins me in the smithy."

"Oh, I'm sorry I asked."

"You don't need to apologize. You are right to ask. He's our only son. Everything concerning him, you wives ought to know. He should start to learn the trade of the clan."

"You should have done this two years ago. Why now?" Hogaii asked.

"Yes, that's true but then his muscles were not yet developed to lift even the smallest hammer in the hut."

"Don't you think that was the appropriate moment to develop his muscles?" asked Bendihe.

"Because women are forbidden to enter the workshop, neither of you know the weight of the smallest hitting hammer in the workshop. Two years ago, if Kewalie was to lift that hammer he would have farted each time he did so. It would be shameful, and he would not earn the respect of a blacksmith. Besides I did not want him to break his arm. I want to train him better than my father did to me"

Before this conversation ended Makalay had washed the pot and half filled it with water and was making a separate fire place a distance from the normal cooking place.

"When you're done, please give me the rubber bowl to wash these herbs." Bondaa told Makalay. "Also, I will need a smaller pot to boil some herbs for him to drink". Makalay diligently went for the bowl and then brought water in a bucket. Bondaa placed the broad leaves and roots into the bowl, washed them and put them in the pot which was already over the fire. It is against the ritual rules for a woman to touch any of the herbs. He threw the water in the bowl and poured in fresh one to wash the tiny roots, leaves and crawly ropes with leaves. He put all these in the small pot.

"You have to make another fire to boil this too" he told Makalay. "The two pots should boil for some time. When you observe that the water is getting black, put out the fires but don't take the pots from the fireplaces. Remember one thing: Don't touch the leaves or water in the pots at any time. If you do so you will defile the entire ritual and you would not want that for your son."

"I'll be very mindful of that."

"Alright then. I am going now to tap wine and then proceed to the farm" He took his machete and went into the house for his palm wine gourds.

Seven days after setting and boiling the pots of herb, Bondaa washed his son in a ritual which only he can conduct on his son. This must be done at full day break. He himself took the large pot of herbs which has been slightly warmed, as it has been intermittently boiled with the addition of more water for six days. He took it to a special makeshift wash booth which he had made just for this purpose, far away from the house. Nobody could see in from outside nor can anybody inside see what is outside except when the raffia mat hanging on the entrance is lifted. He also took a bucket of water and small enamel bowl to scoop the water and the liquid herbs in the pot. He asked Makalay to give him some black soap also made from special herbs.

In the booth was a stone which he had brought from under the village stream which no one has sat upon or used for laundry. Bondaa had also prepared a back-scrub fibre from a special spiral tree. Earlier he had taken in a bundle containing locally woven cotton cover cloth and some new clothes for Kewalie.

When everything was set, he summoned his son to the hut. But before he could enter the washing booth, he instructed him to take off all his clothes and leave them at the entrance. He should enter naked into the booth. When Kewalie entered Bondaa instructed him to sit on the stone. He then proceeded to conduct the ritual, first facing Kewalie he chanted a few incomprehensive words. When he ceased chanting, he scooped some of the brewed herbs twice and poured it into the bucket with water to dilute the potency. He then scooped some of that and slowly poured it over the head of Kewalie. He repeated these two more times and then took the back scrub and slightly soaked it with the diluted herb water and rubbed some black soap into it. When was satisfied that it has lathered enough, he then proceeded to scrub Kewalie from his head to the heels of his feet chanting again as he did so.

When he finished scrubbing him, he poured more of the water on him and asked him to wash off the black soap and it lather by rubbing himself as he poured the water. He asked him to wipe off the water using his hands. Satisfied that Kewalie's body was dry he took a green bottle that was leaning on the inside of the booth, shook it vigorously to ensure that the contents were well dissolved and mixed. As he was doing this he chanted again. He poured out an oily concoction into his right hand, set down the bottle gently and rubbed the concoction between his hands and rubbed them on Kewalie's head. He poured out more and rubbed it on the rest of his body. After that he took locally woven cotton cover cloth and wrapped him with it.

"We will repeat this for the next three days and you will stay here during those days." Bondaa told his son. "Nobody should see you except me. I will bring in your food and water. If you want to piss you can do it in the corner of the booth. However, if you want to ease yourself you will go to the adjacent booth also concealed from other people. I have arranged something special for that. I will bring you a mat to sleep on while you are here."

"How many days did you say I will be here?" Kewalie asked his father. "It will be cold at night. This is the harmattan season you know papa"

"That's why you have that thick woven cotton cover cloth. During the day even if you feel hot, don't remove the cloth over your body as it is part of the purification and fortification process."

"I guess I don't have a choice in this matter. I will endure as long as it is in the interest of the clan."

"I'm pleased to hear that son. I feel for you that you must endure this cold tortuous harmattan tonight. But I went through it too."

He left Kewalie to go about his daily work. Two days later he concluded the purification. One evening while Bondaa was relaxing in his hammock and sharing his youth escapades with his son, he asked his son what he would like to do as a youth growing up.

"I'm aware that the blacksmith shop is not always busy. Days pass when nobody shows up for any forge work.

"Add to that papa, some nights could be quite boring in the village especially when there is no moonshine. I want to do something that will lighten people in the evenings both during moonshine and darkness."

"Like what?"

"I observe that there is no drummer in this village. It is only the drummer *kothor* Mbaimba at Mabureh village who comes to beat his drum for us young boys to practice the *gbondokali*. When he is sick or something else prevents him, he will not show up and we can't practice."

"You're right my son because he does not regularly show up on the scheduled days for you boys to practice. This is the main reason why our boys in this village are not good *gbondokali* dancers during the male circumcision and society initiation dances."

"I observed that two years ago during the last dance, boys from the other villages were so good and impressive dancers but our boys were a disaster. So, to end this shameful and laughable situation of our village I want to be a drummer also as an additional career to the blacksmith workshop. I want to learn to beat the drum under the tutelage of *kothor* Mbaimba."

"That is a brilliant proposition. It will be an honour to him to be his student. A drummer of his calibre and standing will not want his artistic skills to fade away on his death. I am sure he will be happy to teach you."

"How soon are you going to see him about this?"

"Tomorrow evening, after I've returned from tapping my palm wine. I won't delay it"

"One thing more Papa."

"What is it again Kewalie-Hanwa?"

"You know that I can't practice without a drum. Can you make one for me please?"

"Indeed, you need a drum. But I can't make you one just soon as it takes some time to make one. I'm sure you do not want to wait that long until I finish making the drum, as it appears to me that you are anxious to start soonest from my observation. But don't worry. I'll also talk it over with Mbaimba because I know as a fact that every professional drum- normally has at least two extra drums because one could get burst while drumming."

The next day he left earlier than usual to tap his palm wine and he told Kewalie to wait for him at a point on the road to Mbaimba's village. After tapping, he met Kewalie at the rendezvous and they went to see Mbaimba who was surprised to see Bondaa with his son that moment.

"Mbaimba, I have come with a big request to you, and I hope you will consider it favourably."

"Pa Bondaa, since I do not know what your request is I cannot say that I will consider it favourably or not."

"I have brought my son to so that you can teach him to become a professional drummer like yourself."

"Thank you, Pa Bondaa. I consider it an honour to consider me to teach your son. But my experience with teaching boys has not been conclusive and profitable to either party. Some behaved badly that I had to ask their fathers to take them back. Others were unteachable and still others just did not show up after a week or two. So, I had decided not to take any more boys."

"I see your reason and I agree with you to a point. I will ask you one question and your answer will be final with me: Would you want your talent and your profession to die with you or do you want to leave a legacy for the chiefdom which could be passed on to willing learners as you were?"

Mbaimba bowed his head in meditation and did not respond for a few moments and then lifted his head.

"Pa Bondaa, nobody has ever asked me this question although it was something that bothered me. Your question is quite pertinent especially when I reflect that I left my profession for several years to go to Makeni to seek a paying job. Since we lost our son, my wife and I have tried to have another son but have not yet been blessed with one.

"So, what do you intend to do?"

"I think I have to rethink my decision. You are right. I do not want my talent and profession to fade with my death. Somebody has to take over from me and hopefully pass it on to another."

"So, are you in effect saying that you accept my proposal?"

"Yes, I do so gladly because I know who you are and what your clan is in this chiefdom.

"Thank you Mbaimba. Let me allay one important concern you may have for my son. He is willing to learn because it was, he who suggested this to me, and he has my total support."

"I'm happy to hear that. Maybe some of those earlier boys were unwilling brought by their fathers against their will and so were not interested in learning."

"I have one more request to make. I'm pleading that you allow my son to use one of your spare drums until I make one for him".

"I have no problem with that but with one condition that the drum busting rules will apply. Whenever he bursts the drum, he must replace the skin."

"That's but fair knowing that cow hides are expensive."

"One more condition though and that is that he becomes my second mate in dance festivals after he's mastered several beats."

"I don't think that is an unreasonable condition, especially when we know that he will learn more from such festivals"

For the next three months Kewalie spent two or three nights with Mbaimba learning drumbeats. He returned early in the morning to join the rest of the family for farm work or to attend customers in the smithy.

Other nights when he was not at Mbaimba's, Kewalie practiced at home and his peers gather to watch him and dance to his beats. During days when he had less farm work to do and didn't have to go to Mbaimba, he invited his village male youth peers to go to the *gbondokali* dance practicing grounds and practice. Here they practiced dancing and also wrestled among themselves so as to participate in the chiefdom's annual wrestling competition.

Kewalie's learning progress was phenomenally rapid that he soon became Mbaimba's supporting drummer in drumming performances where his boss was invited. He accompanied his tutor to distances far from his village. On one such travel, Mbaimba was invited to a joint performance at Magbogitha with another prominent drummer. Mbaimba knew that the other drummer was Ndawaa, the best in his chiefdom and that he had some unique drum beats. He decided to take Kewalie along so he too can pick up this other drummer's beats and moves and also to demonstrate how fast he has been learning.

During this joint performance Kewalie observed that the other drummer was moving around his drum while drumming to the rhythm. He never missed a beat. Ndawaa made some funny grimaces and gesticulations that attracted the attention of the speculators and dancers alike. Mbaimba did not make such moves or gesticulations. He was always steady by his drum beating his best tunes. Kewalie observed that because this other drummer made these moves and funny faces, he received great applause from the crowd and his was showered with money. He realized that indeed drumming is an entertainment for the people to dance and feel happy. Thus, in his next practice in his village, he started practicing what he learnt from Ndawaa.

Such practices continued and, in the process, he added a beat in which he has a conversation with his drum and on-lookers and dancers were fascinated by this. But when he went to his teacher to practice, he knew he was there to learn the beats and not to show off what he has been learning on his own lately. However, he had the opportunity do so when Mbaimba was invited to another joint drumming performance in a village of chiefdom. He did not only ecstatically entertain the dancers and spectators but dramatized the drumming that all eyes were glued on him and may be to the envy of the other drummers including Mbaimba. He displayed such prowess that he would have been mistaken to be the lead drummer but for his youthful age and stature. When the performance was completed Mbaimba proudly hugged him.

"My boy this was great and a surprise to me. Who taught you to play? Who is this teacher that I don't know?"

"*Korthor* Mbaimba nobody taught me. I decided to do this from the night we first had the joint performance at Magbogitha with drummer Ndawaa. When I saw him do all the movements around his drum yet never missed the beat, I decided I will learn to do likewise. I have been practicing at the village in the observance of my village folk and my peers."

"That was great and entertaining. I'm proud of you, my boy."

When he returned home, he reported to his father the wonderful and spectacular appreciation he received from dancers and spectators alike when he performed with his boss. He explained that he literally took the limelight off his boss. He believes that even though Mbaimba commended him on his performance he would not be comfortable performing with him again and be the centre of attraction.

"Papa I don't think I should continue to eclipse *Korthor* Mbaimba in performances. It is like humiliating him. So, I want to end my apprenticeship now to save further embarrassment because I will not cease entertaining dancers. Please go to him to thank him and express our appreciation for the wonderful, unreserved and frank training he bequeathed me."

"Yes, you're right. Your tutor is to show you what he knows. But it is the tutored that should show his skills and build upon what he has been taught. But I will not go alone as you seem to suggest. This time we are going to appreciate him for his wholesome tutoring. You must go with me. It is you who should show your gratitude and appreciation."

"Papa I agree with you. But how am I going to do this? I don't want us to express just verbal appreciation. You know that is not of our custom."

"That's true. But what do you have to demonstrate your appreciation? You have nothing to show."

"That is where you come in. But you are not totally correct to say that I have nothing."

"You don't even have a leone on you to buy a cock."

"Oh yes I have something. I have seventy Leones. I saved money showered on me during performances with *kothor* Mbaimba... I will give you the sixty and I will keep the rest. Will that help?"

"What my son? You have that much? I don't even have money now since few people come to the workshop because it's the dry season when farm work is at its lowest. But sixty Leones will be more than enough to buy a small he-goat and a gallon of palm oil. Whatever remains we will give it as cash to him."

"When are we going, as I have got an invitation to take part in performance at Makai in a few days' time? I don't want to accept the invitation before I show my appreciation to Mbaimba. It will be regarded as ingratitude."

"Give me the money first thing in the morning before I go to tap my palm wine."

"Let me go for it right now." Kewalie left to bring the money. He returned and gave the money to his father.

"Early in the morning, I will go to Ngadiya and buy the goat. The palm oil we can get from Yongaa. I know that he has not yet sold the palm oil he recently processed from the palm fruits he harvested. If I get the goat tomorrow, then we'll visit Mbaimba the following evening."

Indeed, the following afternoon just before sunset, Bondaa and son set out to express their gratitude to Mbaimba. Just as they approached Kewalie Hanwa heard the voice of Mbaimba close to the road. He called out "*korthor* Mbaimba."

"Who is calling? Is that the voice of Kewalie?" Mbaimba answered back.

"Yes, it's me. I'm here with papa."

"I am coming out," and a few moments he emerged from behind them.

"Greetings to you, Pa Bondaa. There must be something special to take you out from your village at this hour. And I see Kewalie behind you with a goat. Are you passing through?"

"How are you *Korthor* Mbaimba?" Kewalie greeted his boss.

"There is nothing in particular to move me from my village" said Bondaa. "But certain things have to be done properly otherwise people will consider you ungrateful. No, I am not passing through. We have come to you."

"Oh! What have I done wrong?"

"You have done nothing wrong."

"Does this visit concern Kewalie then?"

"Let's go to your house and we shall finish our discussions there but not in this bush." So, they followed him to his house. He ushered them to seats in the veranda while he sat in his special chair.

"Please call Majo to join us because she is equally worthy to hear what I'm about to say. I want to talk to you both." Mbaimba shouted to his wife to leave everything she was doing and come immediately to the veranda.

"Before you say why you came to me, please share with me my palm wine. It might not be much to your taste because it is ageing now, and I need to tap a fresh palm tree."

"Anybody of your age definitely knows when palm wine is too strong. I am sure I will relish it because my son has often praised the good taste of your palm wine."

So, after drinking the first cup, he poured out a cup for Bondaa and poured a second cup for Kewalie and a third for his wife. Immediately when the gourd was emptied Bondaa came to the purpose of their visit. He reached into his chest pocket of his agbada and took out his red handkerchief. He untied the knot at one corner and took out ten Leones and gave them to Mbaimba's wife.

"I am here to see you and your husband. Don't be apprehensive because we are here to express our appreciation and thanks to you good people. Almost two years ago I asked your husband to teach my son drumming skills. After an initial reluctance, he later had second thoughts about it accepted to my request."

"I was glad to have him because I was burning with intent desire to teach a successor."

"We can see from what he does at home that Kewalie has mastered the skill of playing the *gbodo- kali* drums from the training he's received from you. We also highly appreciate the fact that you lodged and fed him when he is here for practice. I sent nothing to you for help, but you extended your hospitality and training because of the long and good standing relationship between our two-family clans."

"If you had sent anything with him, we would not have accepted it because of what you've just said." Majo said.

"Thank you so much." Majo thanked Bondaa and passed over the message to her husband. He in turn thanked Bondaa and said "It was good you never sent anything with Kewalie. You saved me the embarrassment of returning it to you."

"Mbaimba, your student thinks he has learnt considerably from your training and wants to practice what you have taught him on his own. I have come to ask you if you have any objection to that or if there are more beats he needs to learn."

"Pa Bondaa, how can I object when the young man wants to build a profession in drumming? Candidly your son was such a fast learner that he learnt beats and moves that I can't even do.

For you to wonder whether I have more beats to him is an understatement of your son's ability and prowess. There is nothing more to teach Kewalie on drums."

"I am elated to hear that, and I appreciate it so much. Kewalie bring the half bag of parboiled rice and hand it over to Majo."

Bondaa took out a twenty Leone notes and gave them to Majo. "I have come to express my deep appreciation and special thanks to Mbaimba for training my son to be an excellent drummer. Also, there is half bag of parboil-ed rice and a gallon of palm oil. And please hold these twenty Leones to represent the rope tied to the goat. It is my way of expressing my high appreciation. I know that you do not want me to do this. But I have to do this so that what Kewalie has learnt from you will be blessed and prove rewarding to him."

Majo thanked Bondaa and passed the message to her husband.

"Pa Bondaa, you made a statement about reward and blessing. Therefore, refusing your token of thanks and appreciation will amount to not wishing the young man success in his quest to be a professional drummer. However, you have gone totally beyond my expecta-ation for such training. Frankly I was expecting just a gourd of good palm wine and a few kola nuts from Kewalie himself."

"No, I could not let Kewalie come alone when in the first place, I brought him to you as is father. It's but fitting that I should come to express my appreciation for a wonderful job well done."

"My dear husband," Majo butted in. "Bondaa is the only father that has exhibited material appreciation in this way. How many of the fathers of the few young boys you extraneously trained in drumming have ever come back to thank you?

"Majo, you are absolutely right. This is the first time a father has come to show gratitude and thankfulness. Pa Bondaa, I don't have words to express my accept-ance of your thankful gesture. But I a few words for Kewalie.

"What I have taught you son are just the rudiments of drumming. It's up to you to build on those rudiments by creating new tunes and rhythms; I know that you have added a new element to your drumming by your comical movements and funning laughable grimaces to the onlookers and dancers alike. The future is wide open for you. And the way I have seen you perform; I see you going to places where your father and I have never trodden our feet. Be humble and you will be lifted by those for whom you perform. Remember to beat tunes that people will appreciate and dance to and not to exhibit your prowess. I won't warn you about women before you marry, because if you fool around your father will be paying the 'woman palaver' money or you will be mortgaging your future to ruthless money lenders. I want you to outclass my talents. My wish is that you become the greatest of all drummers in this our chiefdom and beyond. That is what I wish for you Kewalie'"

Kewalie moved to face Mbaimba and stooped before him. *"Korthor* Mbaimba, I do not have adequate words to express my thanks and appreciation for your patience and understanding in training me. At first, I thought I couldn't make it, but you were patient and you constantly encouraged me to persevere. Today I can say that I have become a proven drummer because of you. Thank you very much and I promise you that I will do my very best not to disappoint you."

"Mbaimba, I thank you for the advice given to yet another graduate from your training. You have heard what he has promised you as his trainer and mentor. We must leave now. I want to thank you once more for training my son."

"Before you leave, please go into that room opposite you," Majo said. "I will bring in something for you to eat. I will not let you return with just Mbaimba's palm wine in your stomach. I will not feel hospitable and comfortable to let you return without a meal."

Immediately after the meal Bondaa and Kewalie returned to Magoronwa.

CHAPTER SIXTEEN

Several months have elapsed since the return of Bondaa and Kewalie from Mbaimba's village. No activity of merriment took place because it was the period when farming and other cultivation activities preoccupy the attention of the people in the chiefdom. In order not to forget the rhythms he has learned and the dancing skills he has acquired, Kewalie would take his drum at night after meals and beat to entertain the villagers especially after a hard day's work on their farms. Festivities take place after harvest and grains are stored in barns or boxes. Before, then no drumming or other festivities took place as everybody was busy with farm work. It was on one of these nights when Kewalie was entertaining a small gathering of young boys of his age that the sound of the village crier's horn was clearly heard.

"Booooooo, booooooo, booooooo." On hearing that sound Kewalie promptly stopped his drumming and there was total silence. The horn sounded a second time. The silence became eerie. It sounded for the third time to ensure that everybody in the entire village could hear what the horn blower was about to announce.

"Elders of Magoronwa, fathers, mothers, uncles, aunts, sisters, brothers and all strangers visiting Magoronwa, good evening."

The crier commenced his announcement while pacing through the centre of the village from one end to the other.

"You certainly know that when you hear the sound of my horn, I have an important announcement from either the paramount chief or our head man. Well, it is not announcement from the paramount chief concerning mandatory work on his farm work. He has not yet sent his messenger. However, we must prepare for that as we know it's soon coming. This announcement is from your diligent and hardworking headman, Pa Kombolo. He has asked me to announce that the elders of the village have met and consulted and have reached a decision about the next initiation into the male circumcision society. The message is this:

'Two months after harvest of this year, all boys from twelve years and over will enter into the society bush to undergo circumcision and initiation into the *Gbangbani* society. That will be the time they dance *gbondokali*. This is also the period of manhood training which lasts for three months. Therefore, he advises all fathers whose children qualify to prepare for this occasion as he is aware that this will not be easy but expensive. He has suggested that qualified fathers should increase their farmland to be cultivated this season to ensure that there will be enough food during the ceremonial period. Since this is an important event in the life of the households affected, he suggests that fathers and mothers of the boys should inform their distant relations not in Magoronwa so they too will partake of this joyous occasion. The elders have agreed that the fathers and mothers not affected should go the extra mile to assist their fellow village compatriots as they would want a good gesture to be returned when it is their turn. If anybody has any concerns or questions let him or her go and express that to the headman.'

At the end of the announcement, he had reached the other end of the village. However, to ensure that everybody gets the message, he repeated it while pacing back to the beginning,

"*Lontha*. Here ends the message" he concluded. "Thank you all for listening and have a peaceful and restful sleep from today's hard work."

Kewalie did not resume his drumming as this announcement donned on him. It meant that he will be an initiate in the soon coming ceremony. His contemporaries, who were in this small dance group, immediately rushed and surrounded him as if to scold him.

"Hey fellows! Why do you menacingly look at me like this? This announcement is a total surprise to me. I had not the slightest indication."

"Do you want us to believe that with all your travels to beat drums in dances all over the chiefdom nobody whispered anything of the sort?" one boy expressed some scepticism of his statement.

"No boys. I did not. This is the sincere truth"

"But why do you beat the drums so often at night so that we could practice dancing the *gbodokali* if you had no idea?" Asked another

"I do so because I do not want to forget the beats I have learnt and wish to create new ones. Look fellows, are you not happy to hear this announcement? I'm glad because I do not want to pass this age without going through the ceremony. There are certain things we cannot do in the society because we are unini-tiated." Certain things are taboos to us until we are initiated."

"I guess you're right," said a third boy. There are many things that initiated men do which we cannot

303

venture to do. Sometimes we are ostracized from their gatherings, nor can we participate in their discussions as they often talk in codes unfamiliar to us."

"Now that we know, we have to prepare ourselves mentally and physically for the occasion," said the first boy.

"That is the spirit boys. We should be healthy, robust, vigorous, and strong for our initiation. We should learn to master the *gbodokali* dance to be first in this year's *gbodokali* dance competition which we know is usually organized before the initiation. I can assure you that I will teach you my beats and you can instruct me which beat you will prefer when you are on the dance floor. So, let's start right now."

With that he sounded a different beat which he had never sounded in the village except when he was on engagement to other villages. The boys immediately made a dance circle and one of them jumped into it and started dancing acrobatic steps. He danced until he was exhausted, and another immediately jumped in. They danced in turns until every eligible boy danced his special steps. Then Kewalie jumped in with his drum to the cheering of the boys and all dancing and watching. He danced with his drum strung by his side and beating one of his favourite tunes. He performed a summersault dance with the drum at his back to the admiration of his watchers. He danced out of the circle to conserve his energy because he had to continue drumming for the boys to practice until the night was far gone. Satisfied that they've had a good first night's practice after this announcement, the boys all retired for the night.

In the morning everything was normal to Kewalie, and he went with his father to continue brushing the swamp which they have been cleaning three days ago. They brushed until it was almost sun set to allow them adequate time to go tap their palm wine. During their work neither Bondaa nor Kewalie mentioned anything about the announcement last night. The father refusing to say a word as the workplace was the wrong environment to discuss such a sensitive issue to his son. The son on the other hand knows it is not his appropriate place to bring up a topic concerning his initiation to the father who knows it's his responsibility to ensure that he is initiated. So, in the evening just after the evening meal, Bondaa summoned his entire family including his nephew Yongaa to a meeting in the house veranda.

"Is everybody here?" Bondaa asked.

"Uncle Yongaa is not here yet. But he sent a message that he will be here shortly" Kewalie proffered to assure his father as he knows that Bondaa never discusses anything concerning the family without Yongaa being present.

"Kewalie, I am sure that you brought some palm wine after having some at the tapping site" Bondaa opined. "I brought some myself. Let's bring the gourds out and drink with the rest of family while we wait for Yongaa."

Father and son left the veranda and disappeared into their rooms where they emerged each holding a gourd. Kewalie took his father's gourd and went to his bench. The tradition dictates that the youngest male pours the wine in a gathering of elders. He put down the gourd and fetched four drinking cups from his room. He poured out from his gourd the first cup and drank that bottom up. He set it down, poured it full and handed it to his father. As the father was having that, he poured into the other three cups. Yongaa walked in as he was about giving one of the filled cups to Hogaii,

"Good evening and peace be to everybody in this house. Good evening, Uncle Bondaa. I hope you're well and fine as I haven't seen you for the past two days. I guess the swamp brushing is keeping you and Kewalie too busy."

"I'm fine Yongaa. Thanks for the concern. But I look forward to seeing you at the swamp to help us finish brushing as we might get late for the next activity. But why are you still standing? Somebody please give him a bench."

As he sat down Kewalie gave him a cupful of palm wine. He took three gulps of it and stopped. "This is good palm wine. It is your palm wine uncle Bon- daa, am I right?"

"No. It is my palm wine." Kewalie answered proudly.

"Well, it now seems to me that you are not only learning to be an excellent blacksmith but also an excellent palm wine tapper."

He proceeded to finish the cup as the other members of the family received their turn according to age. Satisfied that everybody has had a cup of palm wine, Bondaa lifted himself from the hammock where he was reclining and sat with his legs dangling. As it is typical of him when he wants everybody to pay attention, he cleared his throat loudly so that everybody will hear him when he speaks.

"I have called this meeting because it touches everybody some way or the other. The issue I am bringing before you is what we heard the village crier announce last night. It touches our family as we have the only other male member of this family as a candidate for the next initiation ceremony. I believe that you all heard what the village announcer said about every affected family doubling its efforts to initiate their son. I have decided to farm the haybuda and to work on the mango swamp. Those two should yield us enough rice to meet the needs of what is ahead of us through the grace of God giving us favourable weather and no pests to consume what we shall plant. What do you think should be our approach Yongaa as you are the most qualified male next to me in this family?"

"Uncle Bondaa it is a great proposal to me. I think those two areas you have chosen have been fallow for more five years, and therefore promise good yields in the assumption that we have good weather and no outbreak of those veracious grasshoppers. I will also expand my farm this year to help you in getting the needs for this occasion."

"Thank you for the thought of help. What about you Kewalie? What have you to say since you are in the centre of this? I think I should seek your thoughts however trivial they may be"

"Papa I know that I am the focal point. But what can I say but to agree with you and to say that I will ensure that we have the help from my peers in this and surrounding villages to work on the farm and swamp?"

"But don't forget that some of them will also be initiates."

"So much the reason we should join forces to help each other's family to get what is necessary to have a successful initiation."

"Uncle I agree with Kewalie on this. The youths in the village have already been thinking along those lines."

"I see a point there. What do you women think as mothers?"

"Makalay what do you suggest as Kewalie is from your womb although he is our son also?" Asked Hogaii as the senior wife.

"*Tha* Hogaii I will support whatever additional proposals you and Tha Bendihe may have that will be feasible with the time frame we have."

"What about you Bendihe?" Hogaii asked.

"I have often told you that in matters affecting the family, I give you the first option to speak and make suggestion, and they have in most cases been the right one. There is no reason I should change this time especially when Makalay had given us the honour to proper suggestions"

"Here is what I think we women should do: I want us to get the womenfolk of this village and the surrounding ones to help us cultivate the pepper that we have been nursing over the last month. You both know how much the village women often pester us to give a few to spice their foods. When we pick it, we'll dry it. During the initiation time, when pepper is scare and not easy to obtain and when each affected family must cook food twice a day for his son, we will sell it or barter it for something that will help us in our sufficiency needs."

"That's a brilliant idea. Now Makalay you see the reason I always let her have a first say in suggesting solutions to issues we have."

"I agree with you, and I believe we shall get the support of the women as they know they eventually need the pepper."

"Bondaa, you've heard what we have discussed and agreed upon. Will that be alright with you?" Hogaii asked.

Bondaa who has been listening to his wives without a comment said "I see nothing controversial with that. I think it is an excellent idea as any excess resources from this will be to our benefits. I only hope that the work time for the pepper will not coincide with the weeding period as that is the time women are most highly engaged in weeding their family farms."

"You know that we usually plant the pepper two months after the rice is sowed on the field or replanted in the swamp. So, there is no time collision between the pepper planting and rice field weeding."

"Alright then. The next thing we must do is to inform all our other relatives. I must go with you to your parents to give them the good news and to seek their support. We should do so before we start all farming activities because when we start, we may not have that luxury of time to waste as every farming activity has it specific timeframe. I intend to go first to Gargbow to inform Sandima and Kargor that their grandson will be initiated in the next group of initiates. The next place is Mindorwa to Hogaii's parents as that distance is further that Dendehun, Bendihe your village. How do you see that schedule?"

"We accept as it is you that knows your prepared-ness for these visits" Hogaii said on behalf of the others."

"In which case Makalay be prepared to go with me in the next two days. When we return, I will plan when to go to Mindorwa and then to Dendehun. Yongaa I will also send you to my uncles in Soonhun and aunts in Kagbebeh to give them also the news lest they bear a grudge against me in not taking part in the joy that involves initiating a son into the Gbodokali society. So, we all know our various roles we must play in this big ceremony that faces us in nine months' time. I thank you all for your meaningful suggestions and have a good night."

Three months elapsed since Bondaa, and his family started farming activities and they were far ahead of most farmers in the village. Bondaa decided to start earlier than most people in the village so that he could get the maximum village labour to work when others are not working on theirs. Satisfied that the rice fields are growing nice and green, he decided to take the first visit to the in-laws at Gargbow. One evening he called his wives and Kewalie to the veranda after the evening meal.

"I have decided to go to Gargbow in two days' time. Makalay and Kewalie you will come with me. Kewalie, for this journey you will provide the palm wine that we will take to your grandparents. If your palm wine is now strong make sure that you get good one from your friends because presently, I do not know how good your palm wine is because it's been some weeks since you brought some for me or your mothers.

"Papa, it is because I have just tapped another tree a week ago. Certainly, you know the quality of a fresh cut palm tree wine. It is not one that you would like to share with people as you know it just tastes like coconut water. I need not tell you this as you have been tapping palm wine since you were my age, I guess. But as you have suggested I will ask *korthor* Yongaa who has been inviting to his site to partake of his sweet palm wine. I am sure he will oblige us a gourd."

"Make sure you tell him tomorrow so that if he has any plans for his palm wine, he will shift those plans to another day to accommodate us.

"I hear you papa. What else do I need to do before the journey?"

"Nothing else. You just make sure you get that palm wine as the shame will be on you to visit your grand-parents without a gourd of palm wine. You certainly would not want that."

"Certainly not. In fact, I'm going right now to korthor Yongaa to tell him before it is too late." Kewalie left his parents to go to Yongaa. Left alone with her husband, Makalay asked, "And me? What am I to do?"

"I don't think you have anything to do before we depart. But when we are at Gargbow you must visit your friends and tell them to join you during the dance before the initiation. They all know what this involves, and they may be inclined to come to your assistance in various forms. So, you do not want to ignore anybody."

"I may have to go to Bowarah my best friend who you know is now married to Fayrah at Kortorhun. She is the most important of all my friends and she will love to be with me. It will mean that we'll spend another day so that I could tell. I cannot certainly see myself walking from Kortorhun to Magoronwa in one day."

"Makalay, are you trying to suggest that I am unreasonable as not to understand that?"

"No, I did not mean that would be the infer-ence from what I just said. It's just the truth that your strides are not equal to mine. Your pace is faster than mine. How many times do you have to wait for me to keep up with you when we travel? Besides I think that Kewalie should have at least one clear day with his grandparents as it's been six months since he visited them."

"You've justified your extra day. So, we'll return two days later." Bondaa conceded.

"Thank you. That makes a lot of sense to me."

"Well, this is all I wanted to discuss with you ladies." The wives left him and went in. As it is his usual relaxation after each day's hard work and a review of pending farm activities and events with his family, he took his pipe and scooped out the ashes from it and replenished it with fresh *Sangotho*. He lit it and drew some puffs before reclining back on his hammock.

In the morning of the second day, he asked Kewalie "were you able to secure the palm wine from Yongaa? If you did then we should be ready to depart for Gargbow as soon as possible."

"Papa, I told him the very night we discussed this, and he was more than willing to give me a gourd. I will go to him right now so that he and I will go to tap the wine."

"Make it fast as I want to cover more than half the journey to reach Gargbow before it is midday as I hate to sweat under the hot sun."

"I will be back as soon as I get the gourd." Immediately he left, Bondaa called Makalay who was at the back yard cooking cassava as the family morning meal.

"I hope you have not forgotten that it is today we are going to your parents?"

"No. I haven't. In fact, I was cooking some cassava so that we can have something in our stomachs before we start our journey."

That's fine and thoughtful. As soon as your son returns with the palm wine from Yongaa we should be on our way."

"I hear you. Let me go back and finish what I'm doing, and I will be ready." Makalay returned and removed the pot from the fire as the cassava had almost over boiled. She ground some hot pepper with raw *samu* salt in a calabash. She put some of the cassava in a basin and poured some red palm oil on it. She scooped some of the pepper and placed it on one the side of the basin, then took it with a cupful of water to Bondaa.

"I have brought you some boiled cassava with red hot pepper in palm oil for you and Kewalie. You have always told us that it is not good to start a long journey on an empty stomach"

"Thank you. I don't think I will wait for Kewalie. I'll eat some and he will eat what I leave for him when he comes. I hope you are ready because as soon as Kewalie returns and finishes eating his cassava we'll head for Gargbow."

"I'm ready as there is not much to carry. Well, I think we will soon leave as I see Kewalie approaching.

"I see. Then we'll leave shortly after we have eaten our cassava breakfast." Sure, enough after Bondaa and Kewalie finished their meal they commenced their journey to Gargbow. They reached around midday only to find that Sandima and Kargor had travelled to Gbombu to the settlement of a family dispute as they as they were told by Makalay's siblings who were in the house.

"I know that such family disputes take a lot of explaining and are often protracted. They may even adjourn to resume the following morning." Bondaa observed. "So, let's take a chance and go there."

"Can you not wait a little so that I could cook something for you to eat before you continue your journey," Makalay's sister, Memuna offered?

"Thank you Memuna but this is more important and urgent to us that we have to leave right now lest we should miss this opportunity." Makalay replied. "Do your cooking at the usual time and we shall eat when we return. But for now, we must be going."

So Bondaa, Makalay and Kewalie headed for Gbombu. There was no mistake as to where the meeting was convened as evidenced by the amount of people who were gathered in the veranda of one house. They went straight towards the house. As they approached, they were immediately recognized by Makalay's younger female relatives who ran to meet them before they came closer. As they entered the veranda, all proceedings ceased so that the newcomers could exchange handshake greeting with all present. When all the greetings and handshakes ended there was some quiet.

"Bondaa, on behalf of the family assembled here, you are welcome to Gbombu," said Bawunda, Makalay's uncle. "You never informed us earlier of your coming. Nevertheless, we welcome you in our midst as an in-law is part of the larger family."

"Coming unannounced means that something important is upcoming" observed Bawunda. "Sandima with your permission may I ask Bondaa what brought him accompanied by his wife and his only son."

"You have my full permission as you were fore-front in their marriage ceremony" replied Sandima.

"Bondaa, may we know why you are here so we can decide whether we could continue deliberating on the palaver before us or discuss what you have to tell us?"

"*Kayneh* Bawunda, I thank you for asking me. Let me profusely apologize for intruding and moment-arily stopping your deliberation on issues that are vital to the family." After that the apology he beckoned to Kewalie to bring his gourd of palm wine. He then dipped into his front pocket of his gown and took as usual his red handkerchief which he untied to reveal the money.

"This money together with an additional gourd of palm wine represent our handshake as I didn't anti-cipate that I will find many of my in-laws here."

"We thank you and appreciate your respect for the marriage traditions. It also indicates that our daughter is a good obedient wife to you."

"Your daughter's humility and obedience are unquestionable. If she wasn't, you would have seen me here much frequently to complain or may have returned her long ago to her parents. But neither of these has brought me here Gbombu. Instead Gargbow is my final stop."

He again dipped into his pocket for his handkerchief and took out sixty leones and handed them to Bawunda. "This money is a token to inform you that my son by your daughter has reached the age for initiation into the men's circumcision society. He will also be initiated into the gbangbani society. He will be among the next batch of young men to be initiated in Magoronwa and the surrounding villages. We certainly cannot proceed with such an important ceremony without informing the grandparents and other important members of the family. Because of the joy it brings to you all I do not want to lose face by receiving a reprimand for not telling you."

"That's certainly cheerful news to us. There is not much to discuss here. I will pass the message directly now to Sandima and Kargor your immediate in-laws." He moved to Sandima and handed him the money.

"Your son-in-law wants to initiate your grandson into the men's circumcision and gbangbani societies. What say you?" Bawunda asked them.

"Bawunda what do you expect us to say with such good news, but to say we are happy to hear it and that we all here will be there to support them with all we can. Do I have the concurrence of everybody?

"Sandima, do you expect this gathering to say otherwise?" said Bawunda on behalf of all. "Is there anybody who is not happy to hear the news?" The entire veranda seemed in agreement with Bawunda voice as there was no contrary voice.

"I thank you all for the promise and we hope to see not only this gathering but more members of the family and friends alike. We'll leave now for Gargbow to spend the night as we will return tomorrow"

"Why not wait and take part in the family deliberation as you and your wife are part of this family." Said Bawunda. We are not deliberating on anything secret otherwise we would have gathered in a secret place. We are seeking to resolve disputes between family members, and we all have our inputs in such discussions. Besides we all learn from resolutions of disputes so that we who are present will seek to avoid the pitfalls that bring about the disputes. Peaceful conflict resolution is a learning process in life."

"You are absolutely right; we will wait and participate."

So Bondaa and wife waited until it was all over and later returned to Gargbow with Sandima and Kargor for the night.

CHAPTER SEVENTEEN

In the morning Makalay left with Kewalie to visit her friend, Bowara, at Kortorhun to give her and her husband the news, as she promised she would. When they arrived, they were informed by a young girl that Bowara has gone to brush the plot of land where she wants to plant her groundnuts. Fayrah, her husband, they were informed had gone to help a friend making cassava heaps.

"Who are you, beautiful girl? Are you Bowara's daughter Yawa?"

"Yes ma"

"Well, I'm glad to meet you. I am Makalay. I am sure your mother has mentioned my name to you before"

"Yes, she did, and she always mentions how you two were so close to each other.

"I will run and tell her that you are here as the place is not far from here."

She left immediately. Shortly after Bowara was seen fast approaching as if running towards the house. When the two met they fondly embraced each other and exchanged broad laughs that the neighbour wondered what that could mean. Makalay and Bowara had not seen each other since Makalay joined Bondaa. Makalay was not able to attend the wedding ceremony of Bowara as she was in hiding with his son. She would have loved to be present, but she could not afford to expose her cover

"This young man standing here is the reason I was not able to attend your wedding even though I received the good news. I had to go into hiding for two years two months after he was born. That was the time I received the message about your wedding through Bondaa, the only person who knew where we were.

"What a good-looking Youngman. What is your name?"

"Kewalie, auntie"

"Is this the young drummer whose famous performances are admired everywhere he had been with his trainer? We understand that he has even eclipsed his mentor?"

"Auntie, I just make people laugh and happy while I play the drum"

"Well, that has made you a star you know."

"Thank you, Auntie,"

"I have seen your beautiful daughter. How old is she?" Bowara asked.

"She's eleven and of course in the next two or three years she will be ready for initiation into the Bondo society."

"Talking about initiation, this is the reason I am here. Kewalie will be in the next batch of initiates into the men's *gbondokali* society after the harvest season. I cannot have such an important festive occasion as this without telling you and your husband. I did not want you to hear it through a third party but directly from me as that is the proper thing to do."

"Well, that is great news. Fayrah told me he was going to help a friend making heaps. I do not know when he will be back. I am sure he will be here as soon as they finish. Normally they are off by mid-day. While we wait for him let me prepare something quick for you to eat. How about *Pehmahun*? It will be the fastest to cook."

"You know I love it with grounded sesame powder and *Kaynda.*"

"Yes, I do, and will certainly serve it with some garden eggs and spicy hot pepper." The two friends went through the house unto the back yard. Bowara set a fire and started to prepare the *pehmahun.* While she was cooking the two chatted about their youth days and their experience as wives.

"Makalay, how do you cope with two mates?" Bowara asked.

"I try my best not to think that I am sharing a husband. Besides I have the most extraordinary mates. Even though we do have minor misunderstandings sometimes, yet they treat me with the greatest civility and respect. I too take them as my elder sisters, though they are mates, and I give them the respect they deserve. As for Bondaa, I know he loves me as the youngest wife but his emotions or actions he suppresses so as not displease my mates as they agreed to help him solve his succession predicament."

"Frankly our childhood upbringing is a factor to what you are saying." Bowara commended

"I respect Bondaa and honour him for what he does for me and my mates. But don't get me wrong. Sometimes we get on the wrong side of each other. And that is normal in human relations. However, issues are quickly and easily resolved. I know you can't comprehend this. Your experience so far is being the only wife to Fayrah."

"Now, I do Makalay. But I am beginning to suspect that he's thinking about another wife as he seems to be edgy these days. You know that Yawa is the only child we have. Since then, I have had several miscarriages. I have consulted elderly women in and around the village who have given me various reasons for my miscarriages. I have even consulted the village *thor-thorgbeh* man who has told me that I may not have another child except I carried out an awful and outrageous sacrifice which I do not think I should perform."

"What would you say about me? I have experienced the same thing since I had Kewalie. But we are still young and at the childbearing age. We shouldn't be discouraged neither should we be desperate as desperation often leads to disaster. I am hopeful that I will have another child. You should also have that same hope. All we need to do is to keep healthy and honour our bedchamber roles."

"Your consoling words I have missed over the years since we last saw each other. I wish I could have that positive attitude that you possess. But I agree with you. I am still young, and I certainly consider this as a temporary delay." She went to look at the rice cooking.

"I think the rice is almost ready. I'll go pluck some sweet potato leaves from the heaps over there to make the *pehmahum*."

"Oh! No. I will go and pluck them, and you patch the sesame." Makalay went to pluck the potato leaves and Bowara climbed up to the attic of the house to take some sesame, some fermented and dried locust seeds she preserved in a gourd against weevils.

Makalay returns with three ties of potato leaves, put them in a bowl and washed them. She then cut them into very small strips and placed all on the rice still in the pot. She covered the pot to allow rice to simmer.

As they waited, they continued to reminisce on their childhood days in Gargbow. Then Makalay pointed at the veranda where Kewalie and Yawa were talking and laughing as two youngsters who have known each other for many years. "They seem to like each other's company." She spoke; Bowara agreed.

When the *pehmahun* was ready Bowara called Yawa to come and wash the dishes. Yawa brought three bowls and set them before her mother. Bowara dished out first into her husband's bowl and then into another for herself and Makalay and into a third bowl for Kewalie. He left some in the pot for her daughter because after eating she must wash the pot.

"I observed that you and Kewalie were having fun because you were both laughing. Well, go and give him something to eat because I know that he is hungry after the journey here." Bowara told Yawa. She then gave Kewalie's bowl to take to him. Halfway through their meals Bowara heard the voice of her husband greeting somebody loudly.

"Good morning Ngonbu-goro. How is your cassava farm doing? The last time I passed through it was just beginning to sprout out." Fayrah recalled.

"Good morning Fayrah" Ngonbu-goro responded. "The farm has germinated very well, and you'll love to see the young green foliage. It is beautiful to see. I pray that we don't have a swam of grasshoppers to devour everything including the young stems"

"That is always our concern whenever we plant and other crops. Last year we did not have many grass hoppers. We only hope and pray that they did not lay many eggs which will hatch in another month."

"I hope so too. It looks like you got strangers in your house. I saw a woman and a young man enter the house this morning and I don't think they have left yet."

"Well then I must hasten home." And he headed home. As he approached his house, he saw Kewalie eating in the veranda

As he entered the veranda the Kewalie stopped eating and humbly greeted Fayrah.

"How are you, young man? What's your name?"

"Kewalie, sir. I am the son of Bondaa and Makalay."

"Wh-a-a-t? If my thinking is correct, you were crawling when I first saw you. I think that was the first and last time I saw you... Now I see a handsome youth standing before me. You're welcome to our house. Did you come alone from Magoronwa?"

"I came with my father and mother to Gargbow. Papa stayed behind and I'm here with my mother."

"Let me see her then. Finish your meal and you can join us later". Farah said to Kewalie as he approached the door to the house. As he was about to exit to the back he said "I understand that I have a stranger in my house called Makalay"

"Yes Fayrah" Makalay answered." I decided to visit you and your wife to give you some good news." She loosened one end of her Lapps which she had tucked to tie it around her waist and took out twenty Leones and gave it to Bowara.

"Please take this as token of our voice to inform you good people that the boy you last saw crawling is to be circumcised and initiated into the *Gbangbani* society. He is one of the boys to be circumcised and initiated during the next ceremony." She gave the money to Fayrah.

"Makalay, you didn't have to do this, your presence here is enough. But I thank you for your respect you have for us. Fayrah my friend says that their son is getting circumcised next ceremony."

"I agree with Bowara. We're too close to tell us about your son's circumcision with a token."

Kewalie joined them at this juncture.

"Thank you, auntie, Bowara, and thank you also uncle Fayrah for that delicious *Pehmahun* auntie Bowara, and thank you also uncle Fayrah for that delicious *Pehmahun.*"

"Your mother has given us the good news that you will soon join the noble Gbangbani society. Of course, you know that your father being the blacksmith of this chiefdom is automatically the head of the society.

"He has never told me this."

"Boy! It is against the society codes to go about broadcasting any position in the society to a non-member. I am telling you this now because his only son and I believe that you are already being groomed to succeed him at the smithy."

"That's true sir and I love to hit those red-hot irons to shape them into working tools."

"It is good indeed to hear that. I understand from the boy that Bondaa is at Gargbow?

"True, he is there to inform his in-laws about this upcoming event. However, I decided that my child-hood friend and her husband should be equally informed."

"That's good but it also tells us that our daughter will soon be initiated into the bondo society because we know that she is growing faster than her age." Bowara observed.

"Well, it means that have to start preparing for the day." Replied Fayrah. "Makalay let me assure you that my family will be at Magoronwa to support you, your husband and family."

"That will be great because your absence will be a great void in my celebrations."

"Are you staying for the night?" Asked Bowara.

"Sorry we have to go back to Gargbow as we return to Magoronwa tomorrow morning."

"Oh, how I wish you had stayed for the night so that we could reminisce about our childhood days. Bowara expressed a wish for more old days talk with her friend.

"You know what? We'll have a lot to talk about when you come for the ceremony."

"That's quite right. And as Fayrah said we'll be there to add grace to the occasion. Well, you'd better start your return journey to Gargbow."

"Kewalie, I know that you are looking forward to the big day." Fayrah turned to the boy to give him assurance and confidence. "When I was to be initiated, I was equally eager and anxious though also a little timid because of the unbelievable ordeal stories your uncircumcised peers and friend tell you when you are in the society bush though they themselves have not been there. But let me tell you this: when you are in there, you'll do all you can to become a member of the *gbangbani* society and that means you earn respect in the community and especially from women. The *gbangani* society is a noble society that every man in this chiefdom is anxious to be initiated into. I believe you are also anxious."

"Yes, uncle Fayrah, I am, and I hope to come out with special recognition." Kewalie answered positively.

"You can't even afford to let your father down in that bush. You have a point to prove as the son of the local chiefdom *gbangbani*. Remember the society members and the rest of the chiefdom will expect great things from you. As I see it, you are physically fit, and I believe you are also mentally alert. So, expect us to be there for you on the ceremonial dance day. You two should be going now before night fall."

Makalay and Kewalie bade their final farewells and departed   from Kortorhun. The   following morning Bondaa and his family returned to Magoronwa.

A few days later Bondaa decided that because of the close distance to Dendehun, the next visit should be to Bendihe's family. Two days later he and his wives accompanied by Kewalie proceeded to Dendehun to inform Bendihe's family and solicit their presence. After presenting his reasons for their presence Bondaa said:

"Dendehun folks, don't forget that my grand-mother was from here. So, I am confident that I will have a good representation from you."

"Bondaa, we have never forgotten that you are our grandson," Was the response from Pa Yeemeh-Chorgoh, Bendihe's father. "Don't you think that we are proud to have a grandson like you who is the only blacksmith in the entire chiefdom? We are, so be assured that my family and confidently say, many of the Dendehum folk will be there to fully support you. Please send us a reminder say twenty days before the D-day."

"That I will certainly do knowing that various things happen every day and people sometimes forget certain engagements."

Ten days later Bondaa Hogaii, Makalay and Kewalie were on their way to Mindorma to also inform Hogaii's family. Upon arrival late in the afternoon, they found nobody in Fundorwa's compound except the dogs which barked at them and Hogaii calmed them down. Shortly a little boy who was spinning cone shaped yoyo noisily burst in.

"I am sorry auntie Hogaii I did not expect anybody to be here at this time" the boy apologized.

"I understand perfectly Hapagolo. But where is everybody?"

"They're all gone to the farm to thresh grandpa's rice and they won't be back until evening time."

"Well, it means that you have to go and tell Papa that we are here, and they should come home earlier."

"Okay auntie I'll run there right now," and he took off at top speed.

CHAPTER EIGHTEEN

Fundorwa and his family returned home from the farm not too long after the boy left to call them.

"Bondaa, you are welcome. But why didn't you send a message that you're coming. You have taken us unawares." Fundorwa complained.

"My apologies *komaneh* Fundorwa, but you will understand why, when we discuss the purpose of our visit". Bondaa apologized.

"That will be after our evening meals. Meanwhile, Sangeetha, your brother-in-law gave a gourd of palm wine for you. We'll be drinking that while we wait for the women finish cooking."

Indeed, after the meal the family gathered at the veranda to listen to Bondaa. After performing the usual customary greetings, Bondaa proceeded to give the reason of their visit to Mindorwa.

"*Komaneh* Fundorwa I was here with Hogaii and Bendihe a little over twelve years ago to seek your blessing for to marry another wife. You and your family reasoned with me and endorsed Hogaii's decision to allow me to take another wife. The other woman with us this evening is Makalay, my third wife. She has given me a son seated over there." Pointing at Kewalie. "He has now reached the male circumcision age and to be initiated into the gbangbani society. It will disrespectful and discourteous for me to proceed without informing you and your relatives. This is the purpose of our coming here today."

"Papa, we have gone to Bendihe's father family to inform them, and they were not only very receptive but promised to be present and give their support too." Hogaii buttressed her husband's statement.

"It's good to hear that. As head of this family and considering the importance of male circumcision in Landorgor land I don't think I will respond otherwise than to say we are happy for you Bondaa. I Promise that the family will be adequately represented during the celebrations. Where is the young candidate?" Fundorwa asked for Kewalie.

"I'm here grandpa" the boy answered.

"Come close to me. I want to feel you and to talk to you as a grandfather as to what we will expect from you when you in that society bush."

"I certainly will appreciate your elderly wise advice grandpa." He went and stood facing the old man

"When you are in there, just remember that what you will be taught is to shape and build you to be a responsible man. Responsible, primarily to your clan and to the society. It is not a place to give up or give in. It is a place of determination to succeed. Giving up any task is a non-starter for success. Your *shayma*, will be your overseer in the bush. He will represent your father and will seek your interest. If you let down your *shayma* you have also failed your father. It also means that you failed the Nwoingoha clan especially when you are the heir apparent to that clan."

"I hear you loud and clear grandpa. I promise to do my utmost not to disappoint my family." Kewalie promised.

"You have to pass the *gbogboila* test. It's the highest accolade in the society and succeeding in that test goes with enormous amount of respect, honour, and privileges. But that will also make your father proud of you."

"I promise not to fail. If I fail, it will mean that I have failed the Nwoingoha clan, and I cannot be a successful heir of the clan."

"I'm proud to hear that promise, son and I hope you will accomplish your promise. Your father excelled when he was in the society bush." Fundorwa added.

"Thank you *komaneh* Fundorwa for your wise advice. I have not even told him about me and what to expect in the bush. It is for him to experience it himself." Bondaa said.

"Bondaa, let me say here that we give you our fullest support and we will be represented at the ceremony. Let me say it again, I may not make it." Fundorwa concluded

"Thank you, sir, and will highly appreciate your presence" Bondaa expressed. "We will leave very early in the morning. We will not wake you in the morning when leaving. Thank you, very much and good night." With that the gathering dispersed. In the early hours of the morning Bondaa and his entourage left for their return to Magoronwa.

Two months before the harvest and the next male circumcision ceremony, it is the custom for the can-didates to travel around and visit their other relatives in other villages. The visits are to inform their relatives about their pending initiation and to solicit their presence and support. Kewalie must make these trips to inform not only relatives but also friends of his parents.

To identify him on his travels as the next candidate, he had to wear a unique attire only worn by male circumcision candidates. Around his waist was a skirt just above his knees but decorated with several colourful braided cloths hanging from the waist band to knee length. As a top covering, a piece of colourful cloth about three inches wide was tucked under the skirt from the right back to the left front and tucked under the skirt. A similar cloth with a different colour was adorned in the opposite direction. The two cloths, the width of the palm made an X at the back and front. The skirt was tied tightly by a raffia belt about two inches wide. A beautiful bandana was tied round his head holding a series of brightly coloured tiny bead strings hanging from his forehead but not covering his eyes. His neck was decked with a necklace planted with of colourful tiny beads. On his arms he wore amulets that the *thortorgbeh* man made for his protection against witchcraft on his travels. He wore on each ankle three anklets of beads of three different colours. On his writs he wore a silver bracelet which depicted his father's standing in the society.

Kewalie went oftentimes alone but in other instances he went with other candidates from village to village to invite them to the ceremony. In doing so they are indirectly soliciting their material support for their parents. On one tour he was to visit Pa Dawaa, his father's friend at Gababara. He must pass through Hunduwa, one of the largest villages in the chiefdom. He reached Hunduwa by mid-day with the intent or reaching Gababra village before nightfall. Hunduwa village is known to have a considerable number of youths who organize wrestling competitions, and it is also famous for having good wrestlers. As he was passing through the village, he noticed several youths following him. He thought to himself that they were admiring his attire as it noticeably colourful and unique. But the youths continued to follow him to the end of the village.

"Hello boys, do you fancy my attire?" He asked.

"We do, but we also want to escort you through this thick and weird forest. We do not want any harm to befall you while you are through." The tallest among the boys answered.

"That's kind of you boys because this is my first time in your village. And yet, I have heard so many things about this your village."

"Negative ones?"

"Oh no. Certainly not"

"Have no fear. We'll see you through."

The culture in the chiefdom was that youths passing through one village to another were offered an escort through the forest closest to the village to protect against wild animals. It was to challenge a passer to a wrestling match at the end of the forest. The challeng-er was not usually the size of the passer but some much older and probably much stronger than the passer. The intention was to humiliate the passer and to instil fear in him for the next time he will pass through their village. Kewalie pleaded with the fellows to allow him to go through because was on a mission to announce his pending initiation.

"So much more you have to prove that you're a qualified candidate by wrestling with Daloma our champion that you are strong to go through the rigours in the bush."

"But how do you know about rigours in the initia-tion bush when none of you has been initiated?"

"That is certainly a blatant lie as an initiated man can never renege on his secret oath to reveal the secrets that are concealed in that bush. That bit I know because my father told me so. If you want me to believe that, it means that your relatives who have been initiated are oath breakers, then I will accept what you've said. I get it. Or you're envious because you see me dressed as a candidate for initiation."

"We are not," replied Daloma. "We will be in that type of dress next year. As you can see, we are almost of the same age as you. The challenge is a question of honour for what you are about to be"

"In that case I willingly accept the challenge. But you boys know I can't wrestle in this nice attire. So, you have to wait until I get rid of my dress."

He was thinking of sprinting from them as fast as he could because he knows Daloma was certainly looked tougher than him. But he thought that he is also the wrestling champion of his peers in Magoronwa. He decided to face the challenge and test his skills on a strange challenger.

"Make it fast or are you finding a pretext run away," said the challenger. "But if you do, you have no other route to return to your village except through here. To escape us you must travel at midnight when we are asleep. And let's face it; you don't want to risk attacks of wild animals and spells of witches and wizards at night."

"Are you calling me a coward?"

"You show us that you're not, by wrestling with me" said Daloma.

"Okay, tall boy I accept your challenge."

Kewalie carefully divested himself of all his clothes so that they could not be ripped during the wresting. He also took off his beads on his neck, wrists, and ankles lest they break. He did not take off the amulets on his arm because he was never to take them off until he goes into the initiation bush. He unwrapped the cover cloth, with which he covers himself at night. He tied one end tightly round his waist and folded the other end, passed it between his legs and tied it tightly round his waist. He could hardly finish this when Daloma charged him with the intention of knocking him down. Kewalie escaped him slightly on the right side and grabbed his right foot as he was about to fall and spurned him round.

"Get up Daloma and knock this weakling down" one of the boys spurred him on.

He regained his ground and swept Kewalie off his feet with his left foot and fell upon Kewalie. Both rolled over each other twice and then suddenly Kewalie was sitting on his challenger's chest.

"Wrap your feet around him and free yourself," another boy shouted to Daloma who raised up his legs and wrap them round Kewalie to force him off his chest and succeeded. The two boys hurriedly rose on their feet and grabbed each other in a real wrestling mode. Each tried his own trick to knock down his opponent on the ground. This went on for several anxious moments.

"Go for his leg and spin him round," a third boy suggested to Daloma.

Indeed, he grabbed Kewalie's right leg with both hands and almost tripped him down. But Kewalie looped his hands round his neck and squeezed hard to choke him. Daloma let go of his leg. As he was panting to catch his breath Kewalie took the opportunity to spring on him with his remaining strength. He bumped him off his feet and staggered backwards. He bumped him a second time and as Daloma was going down Kewalie fell on top of him and pinned him down by sitting on his chest and holding his hands pressed on the ground.

"Hey! Daloma, have you forgotten your skills to free yourself from such a position? Use your skill, man, and get up from the ground." His friend reminded him.

But he was in no position to do just that because Kewalie leaned forward to avoid him repeat wrapping his legs on his chest. Each time he tried to get up, Kewalie pushed him back forcefully on the ground. To weaken him, Kewalie would raise his buttocks up and thud with force on his stomach. Kewalie repeatedly hit Daloma's chest with his buttocks several times to weaken him. Daloma was gasping for breath. He was unable to get rid of Kewalie off his chest because his hands were firmly pressed down. He looked at his friends as if to say, "Get this fellow off my chest." The other boys realized that their champion has been defeated. Three boys had to pull Kewalie off from his chest. He slowly got up and sat for a moment because could not stand up on his feet.

"Now what do you say?" Kewalie asked. "Am I qualified and strong enough to face the rigours you say are in the society bush where you have never been?" There was total silence among the boys as they now feel embarrassed.

"Listen boys, we are all young men growing up and our chiefdom is so small that we never know when and where we might meet again. These challenges do not build up lasting friendships. It may be that one day I might want to marry one of your sisters. So, let's forget that this ever happened. So, are we friends?" Kewalie asked his challengers.

"Yes. Let us keep as a secret all that has happened here." Daloma said.

"When are you returning to your village?" One boy asked.

"Why, are you planning to escort me a second time on my return with another challenger?

"Now I can continue my journey uninterrupted."

"Sure, you should" said the youngest of the boys.

"You are brave to travel alone on your own between villages. I guess you have encountered similar challenges before reaching our village?" He asked.

"Not really. This is the first challenge I have faced. Most of the villages I have passed through are closer connected to our village. The young boys like you in those villages come to our village in the evening to practice *Gbondokali* to my drumming."

"What is your name if we may ask?" asked one boy.

"My name is Kewalie Meleh

"Are you Kewalie the gbondokali drummer?" Another boy asked.

"Yes I am."

"What? You're Kewalie; the famous drummer we hear was trained by Pa Baimba the renowned drummer of Mabureh village?" Daloma asked.

"Oh yes I am. You see, you boys never bothered first to know my name or where I came from. You barely wanted to molest me in my attire."

"Our mistake." Daloma admitted. "We profusely apologize for our behaviour. We regret our actions. We the boys who are to be initiated next year have agreed that you will be our gbondokali dance drummer. Now we have treated you unworthily. On hindsight we should have asked for your name and village. Again, our apologies."

"Apologies accepted with one condition: that you will welcome me back with a gourd of sweet palm wine as your peace offering.

"Agreed. We'll keep a gourd of palm wine on your return tomorrow."

"I do not know when my uncle will release me. I will suggest you keep a gourd every day for me. If I don't come, I know you fellows will drink it anyway. I suggest that you do this in turns so that no one person feels unfairly treated for my sake."

"That condition is accepted, not so boys" Daloma shouted to the boys who accepted in unison.

"Okay friends, I will dress up and continue my journey. I hope the rest of the day will be nice for all of us. Goodbye for now until I come." The boys filed back into their village humiliated and left Kewalie to dress up.

Kewalie wiped off the dust from his back and painfully dressed up though not as neatly as when Yongaa helped him to dress before he left. He picked up his raffia bag and continued his journey to Gababara. The interruption of his journey by the Hunduwa boys made him to arrive almost at sun set. At the entrance of the village, he asked at the first house for Pa Dawaa's house as this was his first time to the village. He went straight to the house pointed out to him. A young man sitting at the veranda greeted him and introduced himself.

"My name is Kewalie Meleh from Magoronwa, son of Pa Bondaa, the Blacksmith."

"Ah yes. Pa Bondaa is my father's best friend. He often talked about him. I am Deelow, his son. But why are you here if I may ask?"

"I have come to visit Pa Dawaa. I was informed that this is his house. I have a message for him from his friend."

"Well papa is not here yet. He has gone on debt collection at the next village. He will be back tonight but when, I cannot tell. Please come and have a seat. I will go to the back to tell mama that she has a stranger." Deelow went and told his mother who came to meet Kewalie.

"Kayneh Dawaa went to the next village. He told me he will not be long and that he will be back shortly." Deelow's mother reported. "You are in good hands with Deelow until his father returns. Meanwhile let me go back and finish cooking." She returned to the back.

"From your dress you are a candidate for the next circumcision." Deelow observed. "I know this because I also wore that before my initiation. But you know what? Let's go to my palm wine site and let me tap my palm wine so we can have some while we wait for the old man to return." Deelow offered.

"That will be great with me."

Kewalie followed Deelow to his site and after tapping his two palm trees, they sat down and drank two cups each before heading home. When they reached, they found Pa Dawaa in his hammock swinging slightly from left to right.

"Good evening papa. I guess mama has told you that you have a stranger from your friend Bondaa?"

"Yes, indeed she has. Not seeing him, I presumed that you have taken him to your palm wine site" Pa Dawaa replied.

"Kewalie you are most welcome to your other home." Kewalie went to shake hands with Pa Dawaa.

"Thank you, sir. I bring sincere greetings from your dear friend. He has sent me here to meet you and at the same time bring you a message."

"I can tell the message by your dress. So, you are a candidate for the next circumcision ceremony at Magoronwa?"

"Yes sir. It will be twenty-five days from today."

Okay. I hope I will not forget the day. Deelow please take note of the days and constantly remind me. How is your father doing?"

"I have been away from almost twenty-five days. But before I left, he was healthy and a little busy in his smithy."

"Well since you have been away that long, you will return tomorrow so that he will not be worried about you. Tell your father that I will certainly be at Magoronwa all things being well. Deelow please remember what I said: constantly remind me as the days close nearer. Have you already lodged him?"

"Not yet papa but I will fix the outside room for him for the night. After our meal papa, I have a gourd of my palm for you and the stranger."

Indeed, after the meal Deelow poured out the palm wine for everybody including his mother as his only three female siblings have gone to their husbands' villages. At the exhaustion of the palm wine, Kewalie asked to be released so that he can have an early start of his return journey. He bid goodbye to Pa Dawaa and wife as he wouldn't want to wake them up too early before his departure.

On his return journey his tormentors at Hunduwa welcomed him and they indeed fulfilled the peace condition. Not all the boys were present but Daloma and three were present in Daloma's veranda where they drank the palm wine, they had reserved for him. They told youth stories and got more acquainted with each other. When the wine was finished Kewalie bid farewell. But Daloma prevailed on him to stay over and leave early in the morning.

Mindful of the distance to the next village he accepted the invitation. At dawn the following morning, he departed for his return trek to Magoronwa.

CHAPTER NINETEEN

His parents were getting worried about his physical health as this is vital for endurance in the society bush. They have not heard a word from him or news about him from the other boys who were on similar tours. They also did not receive any message from those whom he'd visited. Two days after he left his uncle, he surprised them when he showed up late in the evening. The entire family was happy to see him especially his mother who was so happy that she embraced him warmly.

"My son, we were getting a bit worried about you not knowing where you were. You did not even send a message to state where you were and how you were coping with the journeys." She said with some satisfaction. "Nevertheless, we are glad to see you looking healthier than before you left because you have gained some weight. I believe your various aunties must have fed you with such nourishing food. I appreciate what they have done to make you get your puffed jaws."

"I haven't put on that much weight mama" Kewalie replied.

"If you had stayed another month, we would not have recognized you when you come back because you're now more plumb than before you departed." Hogaii said.

"I almost asked: who is this man?" Bendihe said. "But your voice betrayed you."

"It's good that you're back because if you had stayed another month, you may not be that agile to dance with the weight you have gained" his father commented. "It is good because by the time the ceremony actually commences you would have pulled down a bit because we have a few pending jobs to do. So, brace yourself because you've had enough rest from work in the farm and around the house. How was the trip anyway?"

"Papa it was great and rewarding. I got to know several villages and met people, especially some *Nwoi goha* clan members in villages you had specifically mentioned before. And they were happy to know that I was your son. Now that I am back, I want to know whether any date has been set when the ceremonies will start. I believe that several of my village friends have returned."

"That's true. In fact, you were the last to return because you had more villages and family members to inform. Yes, indeed a date has been set for the ceremonies to begin, and that will be twenty-two days from yesterday. It's good you're back. We have a few more important things to do before that time"

The next day Bondaa and Kewalie went to the bush to cut some sticks to build the dancing platform and stand. This is where he and his *Shayma* will be staying for the two nights that the ceremonial dance will be conducted as they cannot go back to their houses the moment the ceremony starts. They went to the nearest bush belonging to Bondaa as it's not customarily lawful to cut bush sticks from another villager's bush without his permission. Kewalie has cut down a few sticks and stripped off the branches when he heard an unusual a weird squeaking sound close by. He stood quiet for a moment holding the stick in his two hands raised up in defensive readiness to know the direction of the sound. The sound came from right behind his back. He spurned around and saw a wild boar charging towards him. His first impulse was to run but noticed that he was in a thick bush, and it was not easy to run away from the boar which knows the terrain. So, he backed up a bit to get some space between himself and the beast. As the boar charged, he raised the stick higher and smote the boar to one side. But he stumbled against a stump and fell. The boar sprang on him and tore some flesh off his right foot. As he tried to get up the boar charged again aiming at the other foot. Kewalie took a short stick close to him and swung it on the boar and warded it off. He got up badly shaken and hurt and rushed and picked up the stick which had fallen away from him. The boar again charged and Kewalie swung the stick as hard with his remaining strength and hit the boar that fell on its back and struggled to get up. Kewalie hit it again and again while shouting at the boar until his was sure that it was dead. He slumped down hitting a stone with his butt which hurt him even more. He looked at his hurting foot and he saw a big gash and he was bleeding profusely. His father came rushing to the site on hearing the unusual loud shouts of Kewalie and found him seated on the stone and bleeding. Then he saw the boar not far from his son.

"What happened here?" He asked. "Did you chase it, or did it attack you."

"Papa, the damned boar attacked me from behind. Although I heard the sound, at first, I could not decipher it or guess from where it came. The next moment I heard the sound it was right at my back. When I turned around the animal was close to me. I hit it but then I fell, and the boar charged again and tore my leg. I struggled to get up and it tried again to charge on me. I took the stick lying next to it and hit it several times and I think that was when you must have heard my shouts,"

"I'm glad that you were able to overcome this evil animal. Let me find some herbs to put unto the torn flesh and stop that bleeding."

He went to the bush and shortly after he brought some herbs and the back of a tree. He shredded the leaves and put them on a flat rock and took another stone to grind both the shredded herbs and the tree back together into a slimy pulp. Then he took his cutlass and cut a shrub from which gushed out some whitish sap and poured that sap on his torn flesh. Kewalie screamed as the sap burnt and effervesced on the wound. However, it stopped the bleeding immediately. Bondaa then took the slimy pulp and smeared it on the surface of the wound and covered it with some broad leaves which he had brought along with the other herbs. Then he plucked some palm fronds, tied six from edge to edge to make a rope and bound the leg with the leaves.

"This will keep it up for the next three days when we will lose it and redress it. I'm sure you can stand and walk."

"Thank you, Papa. But do you think this will heal before the beginning of the ceremonies. If my leg hurts, I will not be able to drum and dance. I am worried because if it does not heal it means waiting for another year."

"We will see. It will heal but not completely before the ceremonies begin. However, you will be able to drum and dance. So, don't be too worried about it. Some evil spirit wants to derail my succession and it has failed because you killed it. One thing though that I know is that a boar never attacks a human unless it is threatened."

Bondaa went to examine the boar. He noticed that the nipples of the boar were tout indicating either this boar was pregnant, or it had already littered.

"From which direction did it attack you?"

Kewalie pointed the direction close to where Bondaa was standing. Bondaa went in the direction slowly and quietly with his cutlass raised up.

As he advanced, he heard piglets. He searched further to the direction of the sounds. He found ten piglets about six to ten days old.

"I've found the reason why the boar attacked you" Bondaa shouted to Kewalie "She was protecting her litter from you."

"How many?"

"Ten tiny ones" was the response.

"Well, we have to take them home and rear them at the back yard. They will be meat for us in the future. Their mother has already provided us some pork for some days," Kewalie said.

"That is so true." His father replied. "Don't bother yourself to cut more sticks since you are hurt and in pain. I will cut the sticks we need. Why not cut a stick to support your walk to the village while I cut the rest of the sticks. Ask Yongaa to come and help me. Tell him to bring a basket to carry the piglets."

Kewalie cut a stick with a fork. He used that to support his right foot and wriggled his way back to the village. When his mother saw him limping with a stick under his right arm, she ran to him to help him the rest of the way to the house asking what happened.

"Mama let's get home and I will explain everything."

As they approached the house, the stepmothers, and his only sister now in the house, also came to accompany him to the house. They sat with him in the veranda and his mother took off her head tie and fanned him as he was sweating. When he had taken a good rest, he carefully narrated the entire incident to the rest of the family.

"Papa treated my wound and told me to come to the house. He has stayed to cut the sticks and to make sure nobody takes the piglets" Is uncle Yongaa in his house? Please send somebody to call him because Papa wants his help." Bendihe immediately sent a young boy who was standing by and curious to know what was wrong with Kewalie. The lad sprinted realizing the urgency of the message. Soon Yongaa came looking worried.

"Kewalie, what happened?" Yongaa asked. Again, he explained to Yongaa all that had occurred.

"Papa wants you to go to the *haybuda* bush and help him bring out the sticks he stayed to cut. But please also take a basket that will take ten piglets belonging to the boar I killed. He is expecting you now."

Yongaa went immediately to the aid of Bondaa and sooner he and Bondaa came back. He toted the basket containing the piglets and Bondaa with a bundle of sticks which he placed at the site where the dancing platform will be constructed. They both took two baskets and went back to the forest to skin and cut into pieces the carcass of the boar but also to fetch the rest of the sticks.

When they returned Bondaa told nephew that since the initiation ceremonies were to begin in eighteen days' time, the family should meet after the evening meals to discuss relevant matters pertaining to the ceremonies. Things must be re-arranged immediately as Kewalie is wounded and temporarily incapacitated.

Yongaa came over to house after having his evening meal as agreed bringing a gourd of palm wine. Bondaa and his immediate family gathered in the veranda the usual venue for family meetings. Yongaa passed the first round of palm wine while discussing the village gossip of the day.

"I have summoned this meeting so that I could assign tasks to everybody before the ceremonies start." Bondaa opened the meeting.

"Remember that much more is expected from this family than any other because of the positions I hold: the chiefdom's blacksmith, the head of the gbangbani society and the much respected and honoured Nwoingoha clan. This expectation is not only from this village but much so from the other participating villages."

"Uncle Bondaa, the task allocation is less the person in the centre of all this. There isn't much that Kewalie can do with that serious wound on his leg. In the next few days that foot is sure going to hurt badly." Yongaa Immediately tried to remind Bondaa of the limitations.

"That's precisely the reason I have called this meeting"

"Yongaa is right papa. Right now, I can't even move the foot. Maybe it is because the wound is still fresh. But let's see what happens in the next two days. "Kewalie said.

"Bondaa, I suggest that you go to Gargbow to request my cousin to come here and assist in constructing the booth that will accommodate our family guests and other invitees." Makalay suggested. "You have but a few more days before the ceremonies commence."

"That will certainly be a great relief if he agrees to come." Bondaa said.

"But he will be here anyway for the ceremonies. It will only mean that he comes days earlier to be with us and assist." Makalay said to strengthen her suggestion.

"Then make the journey tomorrow"

Bondaa instructed.

"But when you go, please tell him, being a good hunter, that on his way here he should pass through the bush and hunt for meat which we can fire cure for cooking during the days that Kewalie will be in the society bush."

"I am sure he will love to do that for his nephew. But we have to give him some money for the cartridges "

"Tell him that will be part of his help to you."

"Hogaii and I have already cleaned up and cut the pork into parts so that it can be easily smoke-dried." Bendihe informed the gathering.

"Thank you both. Hogaii you and your two mates will have to go fishing with your *baybays* in the streams around this village and the neighbouring ones to get some fish and crabs in addition to the pork that we already have. Although we might expect our relatives and friends to bring some chicken and may be smoked fish, yet I will give you money to buy more chicken and smoked fish"

"This is like reminding us of our given respons-ibilities." Hogaii commented. "At any rate considering the crowd we are expecting, we alone will not be able to catch enough fish for those we anticipate. We will certainly have to seek the help of some village women to join us so that we could have a reasonable quantity."

"Yongaa, since you are going to be the *shayma* for Kewalie you will design the dancing booth and the accommodation in the society bush. I know that you are a man that likes uniqueness and therefore I have assigned you this task."

"But uncle you know that building those two structures needs several hands. You and I can't build them well before the ceremonies start. And certainly, you don't want to acerbate the Kewalie's pain that will delay the healing process. We should think about soliciting help from two youths from the next village. I will also ask my friend Bombaii to help."

"I agree with you. So why not go there tomorrow and see who you can get. Kewalie, you know that your drum has been silent for quite some time now. You know your drum more than any of us. So, I don't need to tell you what to do with it. But you must fashion your dancing costumes that befits the son of Nwoingoha Blacksmith. I have already put together all the materials that you need while you were on your tour. You will find them tucked under your bed if you have not already seen them."

"No papa, because I have never placed anything under my bed. I did not notice anything unusual. But thank you and I will look at them in the morning" Kewalie replied.

"My task is to secure more rice and *kodogbala* (dried cassava) that will last beyond not only the three days dancing ceremonies but also for the rest of the days that Kewalie will be in the society bush. But the other task will be to construct the temporary accommodations for the family and friends we hope will come. I have already secured help from several men who have volunteered to come in the next four days to start the work. So, we all now know our various responsibilities and let us keep in mind that Nwoing-oha has an honour and reputation in this chiefdom to safeguard. Do we agree on that? Bondaa" asked

"Yes, we do." Yongaa answered on behalf of the rest. "We cannot afford to let that reputation to diminish under your leadership uncle."

"Fine then. If nobody has a question, thank you and we'll see in the morning"

CHAPTER TWENTY

Magoronwa youth were aware of the enormous task ahead of them in the next ten days. They knew that each family that had a candidate for this year's initiation must construct a dancing platform for its son and there are twelve candidates in the village in addition to another five from the surrounding villages. The construction task is intensified by the fact that these platforms should be completed three days prior to the start of the ceremonies, because the sticks and palm fronds used for walls and thatch must still be raw during the three days dance period.

The justification for this is minimizing the danger that they could easily be gutted by fire if they are dried.

Secondly it would be a shame and disgrace for the platform to collapse with your dancer because the sticks and palm fronds are dry.

Each participating household provided a youth. Then as a group they fetched all the materials for two platforms in one day and constructed the two platforms completely the following day.

Bondaa who had assigned himself the construction of the temporary booth to house the invited family members and guest, secured the help of some village men and Makalay's cousin from Gargbow accomplish his assignment. The back of the house was cleared, and ten palm fronts booths were erected and partitioned to accommodate ten plus couples. Other two structures with no partitions were also erected to lodge spinsters and bachelors separately. Each accommodation had a makeshift bed made from sticks and overlaid with dried grass and rice straw and covered with raffia mat. A fourth structure to serve as a bath place was also constructed and divided into two for male and female.

Kewalie had a much more intricate assignment. Assembling his dancing gear and refitting and decorating his rum proved more complicated. Indeed, his father had gathered all the material he needed as if he foreknew what will befall his son when he returns from visiting the relatives. He was aware that the attire which he wore on his trip to inform relatives and family friend about his pending initiation will basically remain for the big occasion, but several modifications and additions must be made.

He pieced together two one-yard lengths of beautiful *Fanti* cotton cloth that will be used as a sleeveless shirt. His skirt which should be just above his knees will remain but the colours of the braided cloths to hand from the waist band he changed to brighter and more fanciful colours. To add strength and beauty to the shirt, he hand-sewed a piece of colourful cloth, about three inches wide, that will be tucked above the skirt from the right back to the left front and tucked under the skirt. He also sewed a similar cloth with a different colour for the same purpose but on the other side. When so dressed the two cloths will cross each other and make an X at the back and front. He retained his raffia belt that tightly secured his skirt so that the skirt does not fall off while he per- forms somersault dancing. His mother had bought a beautiful bandana that will adorn his forehead. He changed the colours of the tiny bead strings that will be tied to forehead. He strung a new colourful necklace of tiny beads that will deck his neck. On his return from the visits, he had removed amulets from his arms but will be worn from the night of the dance until the day he graduates. He has also strung two sets of anklets of beads of three different colours to wear on his ankles.

He hadn't played his drum for several months. It had been hanging in the house veranda since he last played it. To his chagrin and annoyance, he discovered that rats had eaten part of the leather. The strings were weak and bristle. Bugs had gnawed the wooden frame. With hindsight he thought if only he had put it in a jute bag and stored in the attic, this wouldn't have happened. He had however preserved some hides in the attic. He climbed up the ladder to the attic to retrieve the bag of hides. Fortunately for him these hides were untouched by rats or any destructive insects. The hides were so dry that he had to soak these in a liquid of roots and leaves for two days to loosen them. During the waiting period he had to make two mummified monkey (without the head) knapsack that will be secured at his back with a special cloth that will loop in his chest.

In the morning of the two days after soaking the hides, he processed them. Before removing the hides from the liquid, he rubbed them several times between his hands to soften them further. He replaced the liquid with fresh water and again rubbed them. That too was drained. He submerged them in a basin containing a special concoction of soaked roots and leaves which gave them the texture for a good drum sound. From this basin he gently squeezed the hides and hung them on a drying rope in the fence behind his room. He ensured that no woman would touch them as it is taboo for a woman to do so. It is believed that if a woman touched the hides, the drum won't be melodious enough and its sound will not go far. Towards mid-day he brought the drum frame to his fence. He placed one hide (though not fully dry) on each side of the frame and strung them tightly with a special rope that has been treated to resist easy breakage. He left the drum under the sun, so that as the hides dry, so it sounds sharpened. He intermittently tested the sound.

The village youth had put up the basic platform structure for Yongaa. However, since he had designed a special platform for Kewalie, he had an extra day to complete it. He, therefore, solicited the help of Bombaii from the next village to assist him do the finishing touches. In three days, they both worked hard to finish it. It became the envy of the others.

Three days before the D-day all the initiated young men should go to the society bush to construct the temporary dwelling that will house all the initiates. It is an enclosure with no partitions to teach the initiates the essence of communal living and sharing. During the construction period nobody went to the village for anything. It was believed that whosoever went back to the village will be accompanied by evil forces on his return to the bush. These forces it was believed cause chaos, misunderstanding and confusion during the initiation period. Food and water brought for them while at work were left at a designated place and the women will shout out that food has been brought. When the women received acknowledgement from the men, they departed and should not be seen by the men. It took the young men three days to complete the construction of the booth and equip it adequately for the period the initiates will be in the bush. At dawn of the third day when work complete, they trouped to the village singing and dancing thus signifying that the society bush is ready to receive the initiates. The entire village men, not joined by women as this is a male affair, will join this jubilation till it is time for the evening meal.

After he was certain that every household has had its meal, the town crier came out to announce the formal declaration for the ceremonies. He blew his horn three times as usual to draw everybody's attention.

"My village brothers and sister, almost nine months ago I was directed by the head man Pa Kombolo to announce that at the end of this year's harvest all male boys from the age of twelve and will go into the male society bush for circumcision and initiation into the gbangbani society. I am certain that parents with boys within the ages specified have been working diligently and tirelessly towards the fulfilment of that announcement. The village has been involved in various ways towards the fulfilment of this occasion. This is manifested by the construction of platforms we see at the main open space of the village. The village has been gladly swamped and inundated by well-wishers all over the chicfdom. This evening the men welcomed the young men back from the society bush, thus signalling the readiness of the bush to receive the boys. Pa Kombolo wishes to thank all parents and well-wishers to usher us to this moment. It is his hope that ceremonies will be joyous and harmonious and to the liking of everyone. He now declares the ceremonies to begin in two days from tonight. We pray that the Almighty God will bless and guide the ceremonies from beginning to end. That is the end of the message from Pa Kombolo. If any family has any issues or proposals regarding the smooth performance of the ceremonies, please feel free to come to Pa Kombolo tomorrow before mid-day or immediately after the evening meal."

On hearing this announcement, the entire village was on the final notice for the commencement of the ceremonies. This was the moment every family with a candidate should have completed all preparations for the occasion.

So Bondaa summoned a family meeting that same evening to review all aspects of the preparations.

"Let me start by thanking everybody in the execution of the assignments I allotted out. I am aware that it has not been easy but that we must do as a family. Yongaa what can you tell us?"

"Well as you will see close to the house, I had completed the platform six days ago with the help of Bombai and it is no doubt the talk of the village because of its uniqueness. Of course, I joined the other village youths in the construction of the initiates' accommodation
in the society bush"

"That is considerate of you Yongaa. Thank you. What about you my Hogaii?" Bondaa asked.

"I will speak also on behalf of the other two mates. I am sure you were noticing that for the past ten days our compound was stinking with smoked fish and pork smell. The deer that Makalay's cousin hunted on his way here added much to the cooking needs. I want to report also that all our relatives who have come to celebrate with us brought one or two live chickens and a quart-bottle of palm oil. Some brought peeled groundnuts for cooking and pepper in addition. We have also assembled enough condiments that will last for the period your son will be in the society bush. We'll make sure that with all these Kewalie and his *shayma* get food twice a day until they graduate from the bush. That will be our duty as mothers"

"It is obvious to everyone that the back of the house has virtually been converted to a temporary living quarter for our invited relatives and friend some of whom have already come in. For your information Yongaa, because my wives already know, I was able to purchase three bags of clean parboiled rice, a bag of millet and a bag of *kondogbala* (parboiled and dried cassava) from the proceeds of the blacksmith work. I also bought two 5-gallon containers of palm oil. We are aware that we have in store eight bags of husk rice and when it is parboiled and milled it will give us at least five bags of clean rice. I believe that the eight bags of husk rice, the bag of millet and the bag of kondogbala will certainly see us through the next four months when we believe everything would have been over and done with."

"What can you report to us Kewalie, the man of the occasion?" Bondaa asked his son.

"I want to start by saying that my foot is much better now, and I don't think it will be much of a hindrance for me during two days of the dancing ceremonies. It still hurts a bit, but I don't want anybody to get worried over it. If anybody should be concerned it's me. I have changed the hides on the drum and completely strung it afresh and by the day the ceremonies start it will sound much better than before. For the rest of my dancing regalia, I think the best person to determine whether I have done a good job on it will be uncle Yongaa. I would ask you uncle that you examine them now and report to the rest of the family."

On that invitation Yongaa and Kewalie left the meeting and went into Kewalie's room for the assessment. He took out every bit of the dress and laid them on the bed. When Yongaa saw what was before him, he was not only very impressed but surprised how Kewalie could have put all these together without his input.

"I have to report that what I have seen is sure will be the eye-catching regalia of the occasion." Yongaa reported.

"I am glad to hear that report and and I'm sure your assessment will will make us proud on that day," Bondaa said.

"Well, it seems to me that everything is set and that we are ready for the occasion. I thank you all for accomplishing your various assignments. You know that several relatives have arrived, and many have been accommodated in the booths at the Back of the house and many more are on their way here. I hope we will be able to lodge them all here so that we do not have to encroach on somebody's convenience."

"I made a small booth at the side of my house that could accommodate at least three couples and may be three singles." Yongaa informed his uncle.

"That was thoughtful of you. Thank you. You have averted a possible embarrassment of begging for accommodation for relatives we believe are still on their way here. I hope we will be able to lodge them all here so that we do not have to encroach on somebody's convenience."

Well, it seems to me that everything so far has been set for our son's initiation. As tomorrow is the beginning of the celebrations, we should all retire to bed early so that we wake up in the morning refreshed to do our various tasks." With that the meeting ended with a great sigh of great relief for having accomplished their assigned tasks.

The village was awake earlier than usual because there is excitement in the air. People were already going about their chores for the beginning of the ceremonies just immediately after the first cock crow. At about mid-day the parents and their candidate sons gathered at the village centre for the traditional gathering bringing various articles and elements for peace offering to the village ancestors. All the articles and elements were put at the centre and the parents, and the candidates squatted around the articles and elements holding hands and making a big circle. Pa Kombolo the village headman and Sao-Gbo the *Thothogbeh* man were standing at the centre very close to the elements. They both offered prayers to the departed ancestors seeking their blessings and protection on the boys who are about to enter the society bush. Pa Kombolo joined the circle and left Sago-Gbo alone in the centre. He held a small calabash in hand containing some concoction of various herbs over his head and slowly walked his way around the sacrifice elements audibly chanting and invoking the presence of the prominent ancestors of the village to be with the candidates. When he rounded the elements the rest of the circle rose, and the women led singing an old praise-song to the ancestors. The congregation circled the elements on their right three times and repeated it to the left as they sang. At the end of the third time, the singing stopped and everybody stood still for moment. Then Pa Kombolo addressed the gathering:

'This is the last act of customary processes which you parents and sons have just performed. All that remains is the dance which should start this evening. I believe that the fathers and their households have done what is needed for their son's initiation and it's now up to you the mothers to ensure that your sons have the best nourishing food you can cook for them. I can sense a feeling of unity and comradely in the village which is an indication of a successful celebrations. So, l declare the celebrations should begin at the sound of the town crier horn.'

When he ended the fathers and their sons departed but the mothers remained, and all squatted again without holding hands. Pa Kombolo, Sago-Gbo and Bondaa remained standing. These three being the most prominent men in the village, carry the onus of sharing the elements just offered as sacrifice. The three shared the elements making certain that every household in the village, irrespective whether that household had a candidate or not, had something. It was to ensure that every household participated in unity and harmony for the success of the initiation from beginning to graduation. The customary practice in the village was that every household that does not have a candidate materially assists every household that has candidates. Then the women were asked to pick up a pile. The mothers or guardians were told to prepare a special meal for their sons and his *shayma* as the sacrifice elements have been blessed by the ancestors. This is the last meal each candidate should eat before the dance begins. The mothers or guardians were to taste the food while preparing it but should not eat it nor should it be eaten by any other woman because all the elements have been consecrated by the spirits of the society bush. Any excess food should be eaten only by initiated males.

When he gauged that everybody would have had their evening meal, the town crier blew his horn thus announcing the commencement of the ceremonies. With that every candidate and his entourage should be out to their platforms very shortly. Yongaa dressed his nephew in the dancing regalia. This was almost the same, except with a few adjustments and additions, as the one he wore when he was on his tour visiting relatives: a necklace braided with of colourful tiny beads decked his neck. His chest was covered with a beautiful floral cloth. At his back two mummified monkeys back packs (without the heads but with the tails) were tied securely to the cloths that crisscrossed his chest and back. This ensured that when he somersaulted the backpacks remained secure and did not fall off. (Thus, the dance is called *gbond-okali* monkey dance.) On his head he wore an oval-shaped hat made from a specially woven cotton cloth. It was decorated with white cowries riveted at the edges of the oval shaped rim of the hat. A blue and red bandana was tied round this hat also securing a series of brightly coloured tiny bead strings hanging to his forehead but not obstructing his view. He wore the arm amulets that the *thortorgbeh* man made for his protection against witchcraft. On each ankle were three jingles made from tin scraps and sewn on a soft goat skin. On his right wrist he wore a silver bracelet, a loving gift from his mother. Noting that the dance entailed somersaulting and tumbling, he wore a pair of skin-tight pants made from woven cotton cloth dyed in a combination special leaves and ground kola nuts. He was given three handkerchiefs and a whistle tied with a string on his chest but easily accessible to his mouth. He danced barefooted as shoes or sandals have never been part of his normal dress and therefore could be uncomfortable if he should wear any.

Shortly afterwards, all the candidates and their entourage converged at the centre of the village. Each candidate came to the centre with his hired drummer and *Kaylen player* with women singing as they approach. Kewalie, now the leading drummer in the chiefdom, led his entourage. Although each candidate had his supporters, yet there was only one lead singer for these entire ceremonial festivities. The lead singer composed songs and choruses that embrace the ceremonies' theme of unity and support for the parents and the boys. However, the songs were more praise songs for the boys. When all have converged at the centre, the rest of the crowd withdrew to the edges and the candidates were left to themselves to embrace each other. It was a show of jubilation, motivation, and brotherliness. Each candidate went to his platform to join the rest of his entourage. Pa Kombolo emerged from the direction of his house and took centre stage to address the crowd:

"Greetings to you all. Special greetings to our visiting relatives, well-wishers and friends who have come from far away and surrounding villages to join us in Magoronwa to participate in this dance before the initiation of our boys to circumcision and the *Gbang-bani* society. This village is proud to have so many initiates this year. We are also pleased that our brothers in our surrounding villages have decided to bring their sons to join ours in these ceremonies. I want to thank them for believing in us at Magoronwa and we promise that we will treat them with all sincerity as our own sons. The fathers of the initiates have asked me to express their appreciation and thanks to those who in diverse and sundry ways have helped them in undertaking this must-do task. They are however, appealing to you all to pursue positive ways to ensure a smooth and successful transition of the boys from adolescence to manhood while in the bush including fighting evil forces by all necessary means. To the *shaymas*, who will be surrogate fathers of the boys in the bush, the success or failure of the boys will be a reflection on you. So do your utmost as your own *shaymas* did for you while you were in bush. To the mothers it is my conviction that the fathers have adequately provided the necessary victuals for feeding of their sons while in the bush. I want to encourage you that this is the time you must prepare much tastier and nourishing dishes than ever before for the health of your sons. Now to the candidates: I am sure your fathers and *shaymas* have given you the basics of what you will expect just as ours did when we were about to go in. I am confident that none of you will graduate without successfully overcoming the gbogboinla *which* is the centre of graduation. The instructions and training you will receive is to build you up to face the real world when you graduate. So, my advice to you is to be attentive and ask your *shaymas* as many quest- ions as you can. That is one basic way to learn what you don't know. The society bush is also a place of camaraderie where you can make new and maybe everlasting friendships. Let me conclude by saying that on behalf of all and sundry gathered here this night, be safe and enjoy your days in the bush. So let the dancing begin."

CHAPTER TWENTY-ONE

Suddenly drums were sounding, and all the candidates and their entourages were at the village centre forming a big crowd of singers and dancers dancing in a circle to the rhythms of the drums and *Kaylen*. This continued for a while until the lead singer stopped and everybody will come to a complete halt. Then candidates and their entourage returned to their platforms to facilitate candidates show their skills in the *gbodonkali* dance. Since Kewalie was the leading drummer in the chiefdom and will lead the rest of the drummers in this dance, he had to perform his dance first. He picked up his drum and started moving to the centre while beating the drum followed by the *Kaylen* player and the lead singer. The rest of his entourage remained at the platform. At the centre the lead singer pitched a song that the rest of the crowd joined in at a chorus. Kewalie picked up his drum and strung it on his left shoulder and started a beat which all the drummers picked up in rhythm. The drumming and singing continued for a reasonable period and Kewalie signalled to the rest of the drummers to gradually slow down the beat until it died down completely.

He put his drum and beckoned another drummer to join him at the centre with his drum. As the drummer joined him, he asked him to start a beat to which he can dance his *gbondokali*. He made forward and sideway flips with the whistle sound from his mouth at the end of each flip. His *shayma* brought him his special short stick which he used to do sideway flips.

His hands did not touch the ground while he flipped and made several such flips. He dropped the stick and made several backward flips all to the rhythm of drum and the melody of the singing. Then he raced before the *Kaylen* player and danced to the rhythmic beat of the *Kaylen*. Several women joined him from his platform as they praised and applauded his performance. He suddenly left the *Kaylen* dancing and went back to his drum and picked it up and set it up on his left shoulder and started a beat. All the drummers joined. He went on beating the drum making a stop at the stand of each candidate.

On completing the rounds, he returned to the other drummer in the circle and set his drum close to him. He made a sign to the other drummer and together they drummed a beat that synchronized with the *Kaylen* music. The singing did not cease during this performance. The rest of the drummers picked the beat and moved towards the two at the centre beating their drums under their left arms. As they reached Kewalie, he arranged them in two semi circles with equal number of drummers facing each other at a distance. He took his drum and set himself at an almost equal distance from the semi circles. With a simple sign from him all the drummers in unison sounded a melodious but harmonious rhythm to the delight and admiration of crowd which danced excitingly to the beating of the drums.

The drumming and dancing continued for some time until Kewalie made another sign, and the drummers changed the rhythm to a slower beat and the dancing equally slowed to the rhythm of the drums. The drumming faded gradually until it came to a complete stop. Suddenly the drummers surrounded

Kewalie with their backs against him and their drums strung on their left shoulders. Kewalie sounded a note, and this was picked up by the rest. They marched away from Kewalie towards the crowd in an army-march fashion. As soon as they neared the crowd, they turned about face with drums raised over their heads but still beating to the rhythm. The crowd delightfully shouted in a loud applause. The mo- ment they drew closer to Kewalie, he gave yet another note and the two semi circles formed a single circle holding their drums under their left arm and drumming the new note. The crowd though thrilled by the drummers' performance, never stopped the singing and dancing.

The drummers reformed the circle but this time facing Kewalie and the drums at their backs yet still beating. They marched away from him and formed their semi circles in almost the exact position as before. Still drumming at the centre Kewalie beckoned on one semi-circle to beat with him a particular beat but changed the beat when the other semi-circle joined him. Kewalie took his drum and placed it on his shoulder and made several somersaults with his drum held tightly in his two hands. Then came to dance at his *Kaylen* man music. He moved back to the centre and beckoned two drummers from each semi-circle to join him. The five formed a circle with their drums touching each other. They stepped away from their drums a distance off and they too formed a circle. Then at a signal from Kewalie they danced round in circles twice at the sound of the other drummers and *Kaylen* playing. At another signal they ran to the drums and together they rhythmically beat their drums to a captivating melodious sound to which again the crowd roared in delight and ecstasy. They picked up their drums as they beat them and made a straight line and danced towards the crowd facing them. They made an about-face-turn and again danced towards the other side of the crowd. They performed this dance twice. The rest of the drummers finally retreated to their respective platforms, but Kewalie remained at the centre.

He slung his drum on his left shoulder and danced in the circle, formed by the crowd, to the rhythm of his *Kaylen* while he beats his drum in rhythm with the rest of the drummers. He made funny monkey face gestures towards the crowd while beating his drum and performing a beautiful but very delicate dance. This performance pleased the crowd so much that many paltered him with coins of money as an appreciation of the amusement which his *shayma* picked up. Finally, he beckoned his *Kaylen* player to join him at the centre. He signalled to the other drummers to silence their drums for this singular performance. He whispered to *Kaylen* player what tune he should beat so that he could synchronize it with his drumming. The two harmoniously played a strange beat that surprised the other drummers and *Kaylen* players. The two beat and danced in the circle close to the crowd so the crowd can appreciate the sound better. When Kewalie and the Kaylen man reached their platform, they suddenly stopped drumming and dancing. The rest of the drummers drummed up a beat and this continued until Pa Kombolo again emerged from among the crowd and announced that the dancing should continue with the candidates taking their turns in the circle.

As each candidate took his turn, his drummer stepped forward several yards away from the centre so as not to obstruct his candidate's dance performance.

Using his whistle, the candidate called the beat each time he changed the dance. To give an equal opportunity to all, each candidate was allowed five changes and he retired to waits for the second round as the dancing continued throughout the night until the rooster's second crow. After each candidate's performance, he retired to a special corner of his booth so that his regalia could be straightened up and what had fallen off during dancing could be fixed again or replaced. As this goes on, he is given two full cups of palm wine reserved purposely to refresh him after each dance.

At the start of the second round of dancing, the last candidate went first until all the candidates completed their turns in showing their various skills in the *gbondokali* dance. At the last step of the last dancer, all the candidate converged at the centre with their drummers and Kaylen players. The rest of the crowd stayed put. At convergence, Kewalie again took centre stage in leading the drumming and dancing until second crow of the rooster when Pa Kombolo came and joined them. Pa Kombolo gave a sign to the drummers and *Kaylen* players, and everything came to a complete standstill.

"Thank you, thank you, thank you every body. This has been a great celebration like none that I have ever witnessed before. Not even the day when we did our own dance. This has been a unique dance having watched the exciting and entertaining performance of the dancers led by Kewalie. The boys have shown their skills in the gbondokali dance and many of us marvelled at the way they somersaulted and flipped their bodies as if they were monkeys. They have entertained us, and we have danced enough. We now need to release them to go rest for the next four months in the society bush. So, I declare the end of this marvellous celebration."

On his announcement all the *shaymas* toted their candidates seated on the backs of their necks and shoulders and danced towards the society bush. The singing and dancing continued until the last *shayma,* and his candidate disappeared, and the drums faded away. However, the crowd did not disperse waiting to hear gun shots from the bush. After a while a gunshot was fired to signal the successful circumcision of a candidate. So, the crowd, especially the immediate relatives of the boys, anxiously counted every gun shot fired. As the number of gun shots corresponded to the number of boys, the crowd roared in excitement and dancing resumed in expression of joy. The dancing continued until noon when many relatives and well-wishers later returned to their various villages.

In the evening the *shaymas* met with all the adult males at Pa Kombolo's house and reported on the non-secretive aspects of the day's activities in the bush. Every adult male that wished to know the secret aspects noted that it is only in the bush that these could be dis- cussed. Such meetings were held every day for twenty days as the tradition dictated. Fathers and other adult male relatives on a daily routine basis visited the initiates for they were partners in the boys' training process.

Part of the boys' training was scouting and getting acquainted with surrounding forests, bushes, and grass- lands. Whenever they want to go on their sojourns an announcement was made at the village so that women and young girls should avoid certain specific regions of Magoronwa and the participating villages. It was forbidden and a taboo for women to see the boys while they were still undergoing the society rituals. It was not only forbidden but distasteful for women to see them as it was believed that the ritual spells will affect their conception. To ensure that women did not see them whilst in training, they sounded turtle shells at intervals to indicate their presence in an area. Whenever women heard the sound, they avoided or moved away from the area.

For four months the boys undertook vigorous mental, intellectual, and physical training to equip them for the task of being a male child in the family and man among equals. They endured various mental and physical tests, and they were graded according to their performance. Special names were assigned for each grade which recognized the recipient's position or level in the group. But the best all-round performer in their group was given a unique name. This name was like a title and became a prefix to the actual name of the recipient. Family members were proud when their sons graduated with names of high significance.

The final phase of the initiation is the graduation from the society bush. The graduation ceremony was not as elaborate as the pre-initiation dance, but the boys should wear graduation apparels. Bondaa knew that Kewalie must wear graduation apparels. He, therefore, went to tailor Siddie at Royiema to sew some not only for Kewalie but also for himself and his three wives. He knew that this graduation is of special to the *Nwoingoha* clan. Next, he went to Rokulan and purchased two different pairs of leather moccasins from Sulaimani, the cobbler. He used his own foot to select the size as Kewalie stature was almost like his.

He also bought two hats which Kewalie could interchange to match the clothes sewed by tailor Siddie.

The night before the graduation, when it's believed that every house has had its evening meal, the town crier came to announce the good news. As usual he sounded his horn three times to draw the attention of everybody in the town.

"Hello, hello, hello parents, men and women and everybody else in Magoronwa. Pa Kombolo has instructed me to announce that the graduation of our boys from the society bush will be in five days' time from this night. He has asked that the cooperation and united participation of everybody in the pre-initiation dance be manifested again in receiving our boys from the bush. He is fully aware that this time only relatives of the boys will be at this graduation. It therefore means that the grandeur of this occasion rests entire on us at Magoronwa even if you don't have a boy in the bush. It is our commitment to communal giving and receiving, material or moral that unites this town and makes it the envy of the chiefdom. Therefore, he is appealing to everybody to do everything in our material and physical ability to celebrate in grand style this graduation. He is asking all the parents of the boys to meet him tomorrow night immediately after you have had your evening meals to discuss issues pertaining to this graduation. This is the end of this announcement, and everybody sleep well tonight."

Two days before the graduation relatives from the other village started coming in and by the day of the celebration the village was again busy but not as it was at the last dance when friends and well-wishers were all invited. Even though Bowara and her husband were not relatives to either Bondaa or Makalay, yet Makalay cannot afford to leave out her best friend and her family from this celebration. So, they had invited them to come.

The parents and immediate relatives of the three wives also showed up in full force not leaving anybody of importance. In front of every house where a graduate was to come, a palm fronds canopy supported by sticks was constructed to serve as a sunshade for the occasion.

The night of the graduation, celebration commenced immediately after evening meals. This time drum sounds were absent but the elegant sounds of the *kondi, kokoma* and the *Kaylen* making a blend of beautiful rhythm. The occasion called for practically low but graceful music. Every song sang was personified praise song for the boys, their *shaymas* and parents who have done so much to reach this graduation day. The dancing lasted up until a little over midnight and everybody retired early to conserve energy for the graduation dance by midday immediately the boys are out.

Early in the morning white smoke was seen over the bush where the boys were camped, signifying the end of things in the bush. People came out to see the smoke and when it subsided, the graduation commenced. Some stood watching, while others went to prepare to welcome home the graduates. Suddenly they heard the village horn from the direction of the road leading to the bush. The match from the bush started when the town crier blew his horn. The graduates formed a single line according to their rank in the bush and each *shaymas* matched by the side of his graduate. The horn blower led the procession to the village in precise choreographic steps and chanting a new song that has been composed in the bush. As they gracefully advanced towards the village, the celebration picked up at the village with singing and dancing. When they reached the village centre, the graduates went directly to their respective houses where they were warmly welcomed with hugs and embraces. Relatives with gifts presented these to the graduates. When the emotional welcome ended the *shaymas* formally presented their new graduates with their new titles to the parents. Yongaa at this moment kindly asked the crowd in Bondaa's booth to allow him to present his graduate to his parents.

"Uncle Bondaa and *Thara* Hogaii, Bendihe and Makalay, you believed in me and entrusted me with your son to guide him through the society camp." He began. "He did not disappoint me nor you, the parents. He performed so marvellously well in all categories of tests that he was crowned the champion and advocate for the group. He was revered and respected by his peers and the *shaymas* for his proven skills and capabilities in the various spheres. He proved himself to be a resolute and unwavering chip from the *Nwoingoha* block. His health was excellent except one occasion when he experienced vomiting and frequent bowel movements from eating some wild fruits. As you can see, he gained weight which can only be explained as the result of extra snacks you mothers sent in addition to delicious bowls of rice, millet and *kondogbala* porridge. I appreciate your confidence in me and your son. I am glad to present to you *Hindowa* Kewalie Meleh."

"Thanks to be to God our benefactor and provider of all good and perfect things for successfully going through all the various phases in the bush and your achievements." Bondaa expressed his appreciation. "Yongaa, you have proved yourself to be a reliable, trustworthy and dependable nephew who has unhesitatingly offered himself in times when the family needs support and backing. have proved yourself to be a reliable, trustworthy and dependable nephew who has unhesitatingly offered himself in times when the family needs support and backing. I thank you wholeheartedly on behalf of all present and absent family relatives for your dedicated service to the *Nwoingoha* clan but particularly to your cousin. I pray that someday somebody will stand up to meet your urgent needs as you have done for me."

"May I add Bondaa," Pa Fundorwa Hogai's father stepped in. "Yongaa is in many ways your first son. He's been with you through several ordeals including this and I don't believe he ever grumbled to you. That is the hallmark of a dedicated and obedient nephew. What Kewalie achieved in the bush is direct manifestation of Yongaa's dedication to the *Nwoingoha* clan."

"Thank you, Pa Fundowa, for your sincere comment. Makalay this is certainly your happiest moment" Bondaa said. "Do you have anything to say to your graduate son and his guardian *shayma?*"

"My heart is full of joy and at this time I cannot express my happiness in words, Makalay said.

"But wait" and she rushed into the house leaving the gathering and brought back a beautiful cotton cloth that has been woven by the best weaver in the chiefdom. "Yongaa for being the guiding chaperon to my son please accept this as my humble appreciation of your dedication to directing and advising my son while he was in your total care. Thank you so much. *Tha* Hogaii your son is back, and I hand him over to you and *Tha* Bendihe."

"Makalay thank you for the honour you have given to me," Hogai responded. "This family is proud to

374

have a son as Kewalie whose demeanour and sense of responsibility have over-showed every one of his peers in Magoronwa and even the surrounding towns and villages. Now that he has become an adult there are several things, we as a family should begin to contemplate for him".

"I share your sincere sentiments Hogaii," Bendihe commented. "The solution to the dilemma for lack of a male child which this family agonized over for several years before he was born is being solidified by Kewalie's graduation as champion and advocate for his group. We are very much elated by his achievements."

"Kewalie my grandson, you have made Kargor and I very happy and proud to be your grandparents," Sandima said. If my memory serves me right Pa Fundorwa and Bondaa, it's been a long time anybody graduated as Hindowa also being a champion and advocate. Some of us have even believed that the present-day sons do not develop themselves to achieve that while in camp. But Kewalie has has proved my scepticism wrong, and I am definitely happy that it is you that has broken the impasse."

"Let's hear what our graduate has to say to us," Bondaa said.

With a wide smile Kewalie who was standing close to his mother, went over to Yongaa and took his right hand with his and lifted it up.

"This is my hero, mentor and champion. He's been my role model since I was a toddler. I can remember him bringing ripe mangos and other fruits for me in their seasons. He taught me how to climb palm trees and of course how to tap palm wine. He showed me how to set traps for small animals and birds. But that was the beginning of his mentorship. He continued to a greater earnestness in the bush. What I achieved there was a direct result of his mentoring, tutoring and encouragement. I will for ever be obliged and grateful to you uncle Yongaa. I promise you that when I have children, they will know who shepherded their father from childhood to adulthood. Thank you. I pray that someone will in the future render comparable mentoring to your children. To you my parents and grandparents you have more than adequately perform-ed you sacred parental duties. All I can say is, thank you and to all those who in various ways contributed to this ceremony from beginning to end. Having graduated from the society means that I am now an adult, and I must commence doing things which adults are supposed to do. So, I will ask you all to help and guide me through this adulthood journey."

"We hear you clearly son. We promise to do what our fathers did when we also graduated from the society," Bondaa promised. "Let us celebrate."

The kondi and Kaylen beaters resume playing and so was the dancing. The whole village was filled with music and dancing which continued until after midnight.

CHAPTER TWENTY-TWO

Early in the morning well-wishers were streaming out of Nwagoronwa returning to their various homes and Bowara came with Fayrah and her daughter, Yawa to bid farewell to Bondaa and family.

"My dear Yawa, I did not notice you yesterday because I was overjoyed and busy entertaining guests". Makalay said. "How are you doing? You are growing up fast and becoming such a beautiful girl. Is she joining the *bondo* society this season, Bowara?" Makalay asked.

"That depends on his father's decision." Replied Bowara.

"Whether we have a good harvest or not she cannot miss the next initiation." Her father replied. "So that is a standing invitation to you and your mates."

"We'll be there certainly, only let us get the date well in advance." Hogaii said"

"We beg to leave now as the journey is long and we want to get home early before the sun gets hot." Fayrah asked for leave.

"Thank you so much my in-laws for coming to witness Kewalie's graduation." Bondaa said. "We hope to be at Garbow someday to witness a similar graduation. I appreciate very highly you're witnessing the graduation of your grandson. Thank you so much for being with us. It shows how much you love your daughter and grandson. Please have a safe journey back to Garbow. Fayrah and his family stepped out of the house.

"Farewell and have a safe travel back home." Makalay hugged her friend.

Then Pa Fundowa turned to Bondaa and asked to leave with his family.

"I cannot stress the fact that our journey is longer than going to Kkortohun. We also want to leave now."

"Pa Fundowa! Why not spend the night so that you can start early in the morning?" Bondaa suggested. "I don't think it's advisable to start your return at this time of day considering your age and stamina. Please stay for the night."

"Papa, I certainly share Bondaa's concerns." Hogaii supported her husband. "I agree that you stay for tonight and depart early in the morning."

"Actually, there's nothing pressing at Mindorwa. We can afford another night, and this will give me an opportunity to share some of my life experiences with Kewalie."

Three days after the graduation, Magoronwa was back to normal. All who came for the graduation had returned to their various villages. Several days after the graduation, Kewalie left for various villages to thank and appreciate relatives for their material support to his parents and their presence on both occasions. Kewalie did no forget to visit Uncle Pa Dawaa at Gababara who was unable to attend both occasions. *En route* to Gababara he was surprisingly welcomed by the youths who had confronted him on his earlier journey. This time, the escort was friendly as the boys were curious to know about the pre-initiation dance and the graduation ceremonies. Kewalie was glad to explain to them.

"I believe that you boys will have a better experience than I had in the initiation bush and after. Of course, you know that every male child when he reaches the initiation age must go through it. In our society it is not a choice. And often no boy wants to miss the year for his initiation. Is that not so Daloma?"

"My brother, Korkorbeh and I will hate to miss the next initiation. We are, therefore, preparing for this by helping our father cultivate a bigger farm and work our two swamps. It will be a shame to see younger boys initiated and we are left behind" Daloma replied.

"I certainly agree with you." Kewalie concurred.

"We have told our father that you will be our drummer when the time comes, and he has agreed to that."

"I appreciate your decision. But make sure you do the right thing well in advance as I have had indications of being engaged"

"We will remember that."

"Okay fellows I must be going as you know that the distance to Gababara is a bit of a stretch from here and the sun is getting hotter"

"Are you coming back tomorrow so that we can keep a gourd of palm wine for you on your return?

"No. I'll spend two days with uncle Dawaa and return on the third day."

"That is not a problem. Your gourd will be ready when you come. We'll secure it under a thicket to keep it cool until you come.

"Alright fellows I will see you then in three days."

The parties parted and Kewalie continued his journey to Gababara. Three days later he was on his return journey to Magoronwa. True to their promise, the Hunduwa boys, based on their knowledge of the distance between Hunduwa and Gababara, gathered at Daloma's house just before midday when they believe Kewalie will be arriving from Gababra. It was not long waiting when they saw him approaching at the end of the road from the direction of Gababara. Daloma told Korkorbeh to bring the palm wine chilling from under the thicket in the bush near the village.

"Hey fellows I thought you're joking when you said that you'll keep a gourd for me." Kewalie said on reaching the group in the veranda.

"In our village, boys like us don't renege on our promises. If you do, you will be ostracized and detested by all. So, we extend this to strangers like you. Korkorbeh please pour out the wine and after your first drink, serve our guest."

As the cup was going round, Kewalie shared with the boys the non-secret experiences of his days in the bush and the boys were all ears to his stories. Each time a boy asked about an issue that fringes on secret issues he will answer "I'm not able to say but when you go in, your questions will no doubt be answered. I must go fellows as the distance is long and I do not to travel through the wilderness between Magurubow and Mathamba when in the dark. Thank you Daloma and all you fellows. I hope this is the beginning of friendship between us Daloma?" He got up and shook the hands of every boy and departed.

Three months after the aura surrounding the initiation and graduation has waned, the village returned to normal though with gratification on its achievements. Farming activities will soon commence and that means men and women must get prepared by having their implements ready. Thus, it also meant that for the next four months Bondaa being the chiefdom blacksmith and his son will be busiest in making new farming implements and repairing others. After the evening meal Bondaa summoned his family including Yongaa to a meeting.

"I am sure that you all know that the farming season starts soon and that means I have to get myself ready to serve the famers' needs of forging and repairing their implements. But I have decided that Kewalie should now take over the blacksmith hut because there is nothing more to teach him about forging implements."

"I know that you have been working in the smithy since I was born, and you definitely want to hand over to Kewalie. But uncle you know that the next four or more months are the busiest in the hut and although Kewalie may have known how to forge machetes, hoes, knives and what not, yet he has not the agility for now." Yongaa tried to caution his uncle.

"I certainly agree with *Korthor* yongaa." Kewalie agreed.

"That is precisely the point Yongaa. He has to be in control so that he could acquire that agility you are talking about."

"I think *Kayneh* Bondaa that you should assist him in the hut for the first month to build his confidence.

"Hogaii suggested.

"That is a brilliant suggestion *Thai* Hogaii. *Kayneh* Bondaa don't give him control without guidance." Makalay said.

"I want to believe that his grandfather showed you how to interact with the clients. You certainly do want me to believe that you do not want to impart that too to the boy" Bendihe contributed to the discussions.

"I see your points, people, and they are in place. I will be with him continuously for the first few months and thereafter I will occasionally keep his company.

However, I must do the necessary rituals first to comply with my father's instructions before I hand over. I will enter the bush tomorrow and get the necessary herbs for the ceremony. Makalay, we must give a cooked food sacrifice to the village children as part of the ritual. You, as the mother, have to spearhead this with the help of your mates."

By midday Bondaa prepared the various herbs and roots in a wooden oval-shaped bath with a flat base and concocted some herbs into a portion in a small calabash. He told Kewalie to prepare himself for the ritual. Shortly Kewalie came out naked from head to waist. He had tied around his waist a worn-out cotton cloth holding clean clothes in his hands.

"Please hang your clothes in the wash yard and help me take this bath in there and we will do the rest of the ritual in it also."

They both conveyed the bath into the wash yard and remained in there for some considerable time. Meanwhile the women at the backyard had far advanced in preparation of the sacrificial meal for the children. So, when Bondaa and his son emerged later the food preparation was almost complete. Shortly thereafter they summoned the village children gathered in the front of Bondaa's compound. Makalay and her mates brought out the rice dished in seven round wooden bowls and made the children sit around each bowl in groups of ten or less. They brought a bowl with clean water for the children to wash their hands. Bondaa beckoned Yongaa to administer the sacrificial rituals as he is the only the other important and significant male in the family. Besides he was Kewalie's *shayma* and mentor. After children had their fill, they washed their hands and wiped their mouths in the same bowl of water as they dispersed. Bondaa took the bowl spilled the water gently at the frontage of his house while chanting some ritual chants. He then invited Kewalie and Yongaa to follow him to the wash yard where again he performed another ritual on Kewalie.

The night before Bondaa handed over his smithy to his son he invited all the male elders in village to gather at the blacksmith booth to witness his handing over to Kewalie. This was in recognition of the fact that the blacksmith booth was vitally significant and the life blood of farming activities of Magoronwa and the chiefdom. All the men who were present in the village at the time responded to the invitation for two reasons: first, Bondaa was the blacksmith of Magoronwa and the entire chiefdom; second, he was the head of their gbangbani society. These were the most important reasons why they should attend to his invitation.

"Pa Kombolo, I am happy that you and the village men honoured my invitation." He commenced to tell them the purpose of his invitation.

"I have not invited you to arrange for another *gbangbani* dance nor to tell you that there is a pending initiation into the society."

"Do you intend to travel for many days that we should be worried about who will attend to our need at the smithy?" Pa Kombolo asked.

"No, I don't intend to"

"What is it then that you have summoned us here knowing that we cannot ignore your call?" Sago-Gbo followed with another question.

"We know the cost of scrap iron has increased lately. Have you called us to inform us that your charges will change henceforth?" His friend Fokogbo asked

"That too is not the reason Fokogbo, because if you bring your scrap iron to forge an instrument, I will charge my normal fee according to the implement I forge for you. But if I buy the scrap for you, then of course the price will change according to the cost of the iron. But no, that is not my reason for inviting you. I believe you all have noticed that I do not now have the strength and agility as before because we all age."

"How can you not age faster with less dexterity with three wives" Korthorbeh teased Bondaa as he was the only male in the village with three wives.

"That is certainly a minor factor Korthorbeh. Don't forget that I'm much older than you. So, assess me as the blacksmith by the fire nearly every day and hitting molten irons with those hammers with a single hand"

"I think uncle Bondaa has something very pertinent to the Nwoingoha clan which he probably wants you all to know" Yongaa tried to draw the attention of the meeting by the mention of the clan.

"Pa Kombolo, my nephew, Yongaa has mentioned the Nwoingoha clan partly because he belongs to the clan but partly also because he knows what he and I go through in our clan. I have bidden you here to tell you that I want to hand over the operations of the smithy to my son, Kewalie, two days from now. You know I have been training him for some time now and you have seen his handiwork.

"Yes, we have. I am particularly pleased at the marvellous way he forged my sword which is always by side on my business trips" commented Yeemor the trader.

"Passing over the blacksmith is one thing. But it automatically means handing over the leadership of the *Gbangbani* society to which you are members. Don't you think these are valid reasons why I should call you and appraise you?"

"It is Bondaa, and we are pleased to be here and to hear it for the first time from you than from rumours." Pa Kombolo commented. "My people, we all will agree that the next two days will be witnessing an important occasion for the Nwoingoha clan but particularly so for our village"

"We have no doubts whatsoever about Pa Kombolo." Kothorbeh emphatically said.

"So, we all know then what that means. For us the men of the village this is purely a men's affair. The *gbangbani* society has to grace the occasion."

"To celebrate the occasion let us remind ourselves that we need three fat he-goats: one for the *gbangbani* head and the others will be for us as the society rules stipulate." Korwaa reminded the gathering.

"Let us meet this evening after our meals. But please don't forget to bring along your contribution for the purchase of the goats." Pa Kombolo reminded them.

The men indeed met, and everybody brought some money for the goat that they had more than enough for the purpose. Early in the morning three young adults were dispatched to Ngadiya to purchase the goats.

In the morning of the day of the hand over, the messenger of the *gbangbani* went to the usual secret spots to sound his tortoise shell. All women, girls and uncircumcised boys who clearly hear the sound knew that it was an announcement that the gbangbani society will be in the village shortly after midday. They also knew that the next time they hear the town crier blew the horn and the tortoise shell was sounded every woman, girl, uncircumcised boy, and uninitiated man must go into hiding in their houses or any enclosed structure. All doors, windows and openings must be shut and remain closed until the *gbangbani* dance was over before they could emerge.

The men started streaming towards the smith hut. The three goats were brought to the gathering point close to the smithy. Sago-Gbo, Pa Kombolo and Bondaa performed the absolutions and rituals for Kewalie and his father. The goats were prepared according to the society specifications for the men to partake. Everybody was comfortably seated on wooden planks and bamboo benches and the younger folks who had each brought a gourd poured the palm wine and served everybody.

Shortly thereafter they began singing *gbangbani* ritual songs. The town crier blew his horn, and the tortoise shell sounded so that all those who are to go into hiding should do so immediately. When the *gbangbani* was out, its chilling voice was heard as far as it could go. The village was weirdly quiet except the dancing, singing weird voice of the *gbangbani*. The dancing rituals went on for the whole afternoon and it ceased at sunset when the horn sounded again to announce the end of the ceremonies.

Before retreating each male ensured that he secured a container of mixed of herbs and water specially concocted by the *gbangbani* chiefs for his household. This was left at the front door of every house. Every person who hid should pour some of this mixture into his or her palm and rub it on the face, head, arms, and feet to forestall any witches and other evil forces.

When the doors were opened there was a rush to the containers as rubbing the mixture, they believed dispelled evil spells. At the end of all dancing and rituals Bondaa addressed the men.

"Pa Kombolo, Sogo-Gbo and all you worthy men of Magoronwa, I want to thank you all profusely for gracing this never-to-be-forgotten hand over. This certainly surpassed mine when my father passed over the touch to me. This ceremony also ended my active participated in the blacksmith booth. I will occasionally pop in to share the fun and the rumours in the chiefdom. Kewalie is now the master blacksmith of the village and the chiefdom and head of the *gbangbani* society." With that they dispersed as it was time for many to go tap their palm wine.

Bondaa called a family meeting to appraise them what the crucial thing that took place at the blacksmith hut.

"So Kewalie will from now assume the role as head of this family. He will also be the head of the gbangbani society." He informed them.

"If I may speak on behalf of myself and my mates, we are so happy that Kewalie has now taken over your hard but rewarding job at the booth. We now have a much younger man at the helm of the family affairs. Do you Bendihe and Makalay agree with me?"

"There is nothing so gratifying than to have your son assume family responsibilities as Kewalie which we expect Kewalie will soon do. I agree with you Hogaii." Bendihe said.

"Is there anything else I need to add to what you two have said?" Makalay responded? "I sincerely don't think so except that we need to hear from Yongaa and the man himself."

"I'm happy for uncle Bondaa" Yongaa said. "I realized of late that your agility is much slower than before and hammering in forging at the blacksmith is much weaker and slower. I want Kewalie to know that I will be at his behest anytime he needs my help in any aspect of his new responsibilities."

"What say you Kewalie?" Bondaa asked.

"Well, well. You all have put me in tight corner that I have very little space for me to wriggle out. But I will try. First Papa, I thank you for having confidence in me and giving me this great obligation of jealously guarding the reputation and dignity of the *Nwoingoha* clan but also assuming the responsibility of the blacksmith booth. The latter is greater for the fact that the entire chiefdom's forgery for its farm implements is here in Magoronwa. I'm sure that I can count on you my immediate family for support. But Papa I believe that I will need somebody by my side as my help meet. Is that too much for me to wish? Is it too much a task for you and your wives to think about that?"

"So soon my son?

"Papa you have off loaded so much responsibility on me. You, my parents, are getting older every day and you are fully aware that inheriting the Nwoingoha clan isn't a light responsibility."

"That is a legitimate wish my son and certainly it deserves a priority treatment. I think this is a task for your mother and her mates."

"Bondaa, let's call things by their proper names." Said Hogaii. "The boy wants a wife by his side which is the normal next step to manhood. I and my mates will address this issue appropriately. I think that we already have a girl in mind. Kewalie, you have met this

388

girl and I am sure you will love our suggestion. Don't you agree with me Bendihe and Makalay?"

"It appears that you women have been thinking about this. I'm sure you don't want your son to be snared by some girl that will not fit well into this family. That is very thoughtful of you ladies. Thank you for your foresight. Please proceed. You have my full support, because in the end it will be a good choice to the liking of your son."

"Bondaa, you too know the girl", interjected Makalay. She is the daughter of Bowara, wife of Fayrah. We are talking about Yawa. She has grown into a beautiful girl, and you remember that she recently went through the bondo society. So, what do you two men say about our choice?"

"You mean the Yawa I met when we visited auntie Bowara at Khortohun before my initiation?" Kewalie asked her mother."

"Yes, she is. You remember her now, right?"

"Yes, I do"

"Alright then what say you to our choice?"

"I may like her, but it all will depend on if she and her parents will like the idea."

"My dear son, you think I was not eyeing you when you and Yawa were intimately talking to each other when we were at their house?" Makalay said. "It was at that moment I made up my mind to suggest to my mates that I would like Yawa to be our choice for you and we are in agreement."

"Okay, mama you got me there."

"If you and your father are with us, we will make the necessary approach" Hogaii suggested.

"You can proceed. I think I'll love that." Kewalie consented.

"I knew the parents of Fayrah." Bondaa said. "They were the most respected in Khortohun and were quite resourceful just as is their son. I think I agree that you make the approach."

"What have to say Yongaa?" Bendihe asked.

"Who am I to say otherwise when uncle and the man concerned have given you the go ahead." Yongaa replied. "I'm looking forward to the day when l will join the delegation to Khortohun."

Ten days after these discussions Makalay and Bendihe set out to Khortohun to take the first step towards getting the Bowara's daughter to be Kewalie's wife. This step is an all-women's affair. Makalay and Bendihe arrival around mid-day and put up with Bowara who was surprised to see them.

"What has brought you here with Bendihe?" She asked.

"Don't worry your mind." Makalay answered.

"We are here at the behest of the rest of the family." Bendihe added. "We would like to have a short but important discussion with you and daughter in the house YaBuffu after the evening meal."

"Bowara, you know that your auntie YaBuffu counsels the Khortohun womenfolk on several issues ranging from pre-marriage and marriage to childbearing worries." After the meal they asked Fayrah to excuse them.

"We are going to auntie YaBuffu to discuss some famine issues. We will not be long. We'll be back soon"

YaBuffu was quite surprised to see Bowara and entourage without any prior notification.

"What has Fayrah done to you Bowara that you should come to me this hour without any prior message?" YaBuffu expressed concern. "You have never come to me at this time of the night without first telling me that you will show up. This must be a very serious issue."

"Auntie YaBuffu, it is not anything relating to me. It's my friend Makalay and her mate just showed up this afternoon and requested this meeting. You'll have to ask them."

"Makalay the daughter of Kargor and Sandima?"

"Yes auntie?"

"How are they doing? "She asked Makalay.

"I guess they are doing fine although it's been some time since I heard from them. As the saying goes 'No news is good news'. This is my mate, Bendihe, Bondaa's second wife. I give her the right to talk first as the tradition dictates."

Bendihe loosed the edge of her wrap lappa and untied a knot at its edge and took our five Leones and handed it to YaBuffu.

"I bring greetings from our husband and our first mate. They have sent us on this mission as age is beginning to tell on them. We are here to tell you that Makalay's biological son, Kewalie, who is also our son, recently graduated from the male initiation and *gbangbani* society. Now he wants a partner by his side to inherit the *Nwoingoha* clan and the black-smithy from his father."

"Everybody in the family has agreed to have Yawa as Kewalie's wife. But as we all know the most important step is this one." Makalay added.

We are here to inform you that we love Yawa to be our son's wife. But we can only come forward for a formal engagement if we have a positive answer from Yawa. We know that it is the woman who

391

ultimately must go to the marriage home. Not the mother or sister."

"We could think of no lovelier girl than the daughter of my childhood friend." Makalay added.

"You remember when he and I last visited you, we watched them closely conversing with hearty laughter. So, I figured out from that moment that they will be good for each other."

"I thank you Makalay for the gesture Makalay." Yabuffu said. "I very much appreciate the honour coming to me. But this is a matter for Bowara and her daughter. So, I will turn over the issue to them."

"Auntie in as much as you say this is a matter for me and my daughter, but the truth is marriage is a matter so vital to Yawa than me. Makalay, you are right that we observed a chemistry between them when they first met. So, my dear daughter what have you to say to the wishes of Makalay?"

"Mama, I'm sure that when you were at my age, your greatest desire was for a man to come to your parents and propose for your hand in marriage. This is my desire right now at this moment of my life. When Kewalie and I first met, he made me laugh so much. It was then I knew that he was the famous drummer in our chiefdom. And when papa found us chatting, he did not scold us but merely demanded to know who he was. He simply said 'I am the son of mama Makalay' with a broad smile. I think that disarmed him of any reproach he had for us. So, if you ask me if I want to be the life partner of the amazing Kewalie, the answer is yes." Upon this surprised response, Makalay and Bendihe got up and both warmly embraced Yawa. Makalay took twenty Leones from the knot of her wrap lappa and gave it to Yawa as token of her son's love for her.

"May I suggest Bowara that the outcome of this meeting should not be disclosed neither to your husband nor any other relative?" Bendihe cautioned. "We will also limit it within our family and nobody else. The family will notify Fayrah when it will come to perform the traditional engagement and marriage process."

"I support Bendihe on the secrecy of this meeting from your husband and relatives because there are bad people among us." Yabuffu said. "Well, I look forward to the big occasion. Have a safe trip back to Magoronwa Makalay and Bendihe."

CHAPTER TWENTY-THREE

It was a very happy evening for the rest of Bondaa's family especially Kewalie, when Bendihe reported the positive outcome of their mission.

"We however, advised Bowara to keep this from Fayrah and other relatives and we also promised that our family will hold this a secret until we are ready to go to *Kortorhun* for the ceremony."

"That was a brilliant after-thought." Bondaa said. "I think everybody here knows the importance of the secrecy of this. We will shortly begin the process so that we resolve this issue sooner."

"I have something to say uncle Bondaa." Said Yongaa.

"What?" Bondaa asked.

"Yesterday, I had a surprisingly visit from Yakonie, wife of your best village friend Fokogbo." Yongaa said. "She showed up in my house last night just after the evening meal. She said since our families have been very close, it would be essential to further reinforce this relationship with a marriage. She suggested that her niece, Yebu-yanday, the daughter of her younger sister whose husband is Sunkor-sunkor, be married to Kewalie. I told her that it was a nice idea, and I will make it known to the rest of the family. I would have told you if we hadn't called this meeting. I'm now informing you all about this."

"Are you talking about Yenor-yehule's daughter, whom we know had some issues in the Bondo society?" Hogaii asked.

"I have no idea what you are talking about. I guess you women are more informed of what goes on in your society than we the men." Yongaa replied.

"Yes, she is a beautiful girl no doubt." Hogaii interjected. "But in our society when certain events or issues occur during the initiation, it is a notice to mothers present to take caution about their daughters. I understand that she is still trying to combat that issue."

"A similar situation happened years back at our village bondo society initiation." Bendihe joined in. "The girl was my cousin and up till now as far as I know she has not become pregnant.

"At Mindorma bondo society three years ago a similar thing happened." Makalay added to the concern. "And the information I have received from my sisters about another girl at home over five years ago is the same as Bendihe has told us. Do we want that situation in this family?"

"Although nobody knows the actual reasons for these situations, yet three experiences are adequate indications as to guard our son against such." Makalay expressed deep concern. "I would hesitate to go along with the proposal especially hearing what my senior mates have said."

"What say you Kewalie?" Bondaa asked.

"Papa I don't know the girl. Yawa, I have met. I would rather go with what I have seen and is probable than with the uncertain."

"Well, that settles it then. Hogaii and I will visit my friend Fokogbo and his wife and discreetly explain our stand for now. However, I don't think we should hold on longer to do the necessary. Yongaa when we are ready you will take a message to Fayrah that he should expect an entourage of well-wishers at his home a month from the day you deliver the message."

"That will be great," Hogaii said. "Bendihe and Makalay, we'll start preparing for the occasion tomorrow. I don't think we should delay this further than the beginning of the *swesweh* month."

"Hogaii, I don't think I will be financially prepared to secure all that is necessary for the occasion by that time." Bondaa said. "Let's push it to the end of the *mua-dayhun* month. From now on to the end of that month Kewalie will be fully engaged at black-smith work. I expect that by then he would have earned enough dowry money for his betrothal. You also know that is the month when rice harvesting starts, and we do not want to create unnecessary burden for Fayrah and ourselves as we know this will involve some expense on both parties."

"In as much as I need a wife as early as it is possible," Kewalie said, "I certainly agree with papa because I want him to have what is necessary to live up to the Nwoingoha clan reputation in the chiefdom. And don't forget that I am the acclaimed drummer and now the blacksmith of this and the surrounding chiefdoms. The value of the dowry means a lot to the clan and to me."

"Well! I think it seems that I am more anxious to see this concluded soon. But you have a very good reason for the slight delay." Hogaii conceded. "You will give us the time when we should start preparing."

"While we are all gathered here now, I want to remind ourselves about the good news we received three days ago that Hopanda safely delivered a healthy baby boy. We have to attend the naming ceremony at Magayloma seven days from today." Bondaa reminded the family. "So, let's start tomorrow putting together what is necessary to grace the occasion.

A month and a half after their return from the child naming ceremony, Yangaa was dispatched to *Kortorhun* to inform Fayrah of the pending visit. He arrived in Kortorhun in good time and headed straight to Fayrah's house. After exchanging greetings Yongaa asked Bowara: "Is *korthor* Fayrah around?"

"Fayrah was urgently summoned to another village. I cannot tell the purpose of the urgent call because he himself did not know why he was urgently summoned. But I am hopeful that he will return in the evening."

If he doesn't return before sunset, it means that I cannot return today as I had intended. I have an important message for both of you. I cannot deliver it to one person."

"My advice is to stay overnight, and you can deliver the message in the morning."

"I agree with you as we both do not know when he will be back."

"In that case, I will tell Yawa to get water for you to have a bath before your meal. I will prepare the outside room for you."

Fayrah returned when the village was already asleep, that Yongaa had no alternative but to deliver the message in the morning. This he could only to do so after Fayrah had returned tapping his palm wine. They both sat at the veranda and Fayrah poured out a cupful of palm wine to Yongaa after he had drowned the first cup.

"*Korthor* Fayrah, my uncle Bondaa of Magoronwa sent me to deliver a message to you and your wife. So, I will be happy if you could kindly call her to join us."

"Alright then. Bowara." He paused waiting for an answer. "Bowara-eh" he hollered a little louder to his wife.

"Naa Ye." Bowara answered from the back veranda where she was preparing food for her stranger before he departs on his return journey.

"Can you come to the veranda for just a moment? Fetch a bench as you come."

Bowara came with a bench and sat not too far from her husband.

"Yongaa says he has a message from Bondaa, for both of us."

"He told me that when he came and asked for you." Bowara confirmed.

"Yongaa you can proceed with your message."

Yongaa took out two ten-Leones notes from his pocket and gave it to Bowara.

"Before I say any word, I give you greetings from uncle Bondaa and his wives. They extend their greetings to you and hope that all you and your family are well."

"Thank you Yongaa for this gesture and please convey our thanks and deep appreciation to Bondaa and his wives. You can now proceed with the message." Fayrah told him.

"Uncle Bondaa is aware that you are the most respected and resourceful people and that you maintain a good reputation in the village."

Yongaa began to present his message.

"Thank you for the compliment."

"He is also aware that you have a very beautiful daughter. When I saw her yesterday, I confirmed Makalay's description of her. He is also mindful that you both gracefully attended the recent graduation of his son, Kewalie from the *gbondokali and gbang-bani* societies.

"We couldn't afford to ignore such an honourable invitation from him, especially for the sake of Makalay my dear friend." Bowara said

"Kewalie wants a wife which is the normal next step of a graduate from the societies. The family has agreed to ask for the hand of your daughter, Yawa, to be Kewalie's wife and partner. He prays for an indication of positive response to his wish. And to end this message, he sends these fifty Leones to give weight to his voice."

He handed over the money to Bowara who blessed and thanked Yongaa and passed on the money to Fayrah.

"Fayrah we're not expecting such an early proposal for Yawa. But these are the workings of the creator and it's your duty to respond to Bondaa's message." Bowara told her husband.

"Yongaa, I thank you for bringing this unexpected but good message from your uncle." Fayrah spoke slowly. "There's little doubt that when parents receive any marriage proposal for their daughter, they are not only pleased but proud that their daughter will be married and hopefully have a happy home."

"That's true indeed *korthor* Fayrah." Yongaa agreed.

"Tell Bondaa we have received his message. Since the ultimate decision to invite him and his family to come depends on our daughter, please inform him that Bowara and I will discuss this with Yawa and other key family members. We shall get back to him as soon as possible. I assure you that 'as soon as possible' means without delay."

"Thank you *Korthor* Fayrah." Yongaa said. "That is an encouraging message I will gladly convey. Well, I should be leaving now as the distance tells me to start early."

"After you have eaten the *pehmahun* I am preparing for you." Bowara said. So, wait a little while I dish out."

Yongaa set off on his return journey immediately after having a good morning meal. Before he reached the town, he decided to see what happened to his palm wine since he totally forgot to tell Kewalie to tap it in his absence. He found his gourd overflowing as he would expect. He climbed up, removed the gourd and when he tasted the palm wine it wasn't bad as he had expected especially after a day without tapping. He emptied the palm wine into another gourd and climbed down. He sat on his make-shift bamboo bench and gulped a couple of cupsful before moving off. On reaching home his wife told him that she had warmed some water for him to take a warm bath. Indeed, he took a much-needed warm bath after the two days walk to and from Kortorhun and changed his clothes. After having his meal, he went to deliver Fayrah's message to Bondaa and the rest of the family.

Bondaa and his family had expected that Yongaa would return from Kortorhun the day after and certainly they expect him to report in the evening. So, it was not surprising that Yongaa found everyone in the veranda except Kewalie.

"Where is Kewalie?" he asked.

"He has gone to deliver some hoes and cutlasses he had forged for his good friend." Bondaa answered. "But he said that he will be back shortly as he expects you to be back this evening".

Even before he could settle down on his bench, Kewalie entered.

"Good evening uncle Yongaa. How was your trek to Kortorhun?" Kewalie asked.

"I had a safe and uninterrupted travel." Yongaa replied. "Of course, we know that it's been really hot these past two days. You can imagine the amount of sweating we experience on our long journey. But as I have always said, I will do anything possible for you"

"Thank you, uncle. I highly appreciate all that you do for me. I hope that one day I shall be able to show my appreciation."

"Don't you worry yourself, there's plenty of time between you and me by the grace of the creator. Besides I am only repaying the enormous goodness uncle Bondaa showed to my father. I am aware of many of those deeds."

"Yongaa, I want to state that this is what family is all about, supporting members in the clan so that they will retain their dignity in this society." Bondaa said. "When a member of the clan is in difficulty and needs any help, those in a position to render it should support and succour that member."

"You have done that since I became aware as a teenager. Now for my report on my mission: I arrived safely on time at Kortorhun but *korthor* Fayrah was at another village and did not return until late that night. So, I had to wait until the morning to deliver your message over drinks of his palm wine. Your message was well received by both *Korthor* Fayrah and Bowara. Their message is this: 'since the entire issue surrounds our daughter, we will discuss this with Yawa and other key family members. We shall get on to him as soon as possible. I assure you that 'as

401

soon as possible' means without delay'. His message ended. *Korthor* Fayrah emphasized that 'as soon as possible' means "without delay." This is the outcome of my trip to Kortorhun." Yongaa concluded.

"We thank you Yongaa for the trip and we understand Fayrah's message. However, we already know the answer because Bendihe and Makalay secured that before we sent you. I think we should immediately start preparing for the nuptial journey to Kortorhun because Fayrah says we will hear from them without delay."

"Papa, during the past two months or so I have been able to earn some money for a significant and notable dowry to Yawa. I will give it to you tomorrow." Kewalie said.

"In that case, we already have the most important item for our preparation." Bondaa said. "What have you ladies to say?

"You should know that we were only awaiting the message, because we have been ready for almost a month since our initial discussion. Am I right Bendihe and Makalay?" Responded Hogaii.

"That's certainly the case" Bendihe replied.

"The only person more anxious than me is Kewalie. Yes, we are ready." Makalay responded.

A few days after the return of Yongaa, a relative of Fayrah arrived in the evening in Magoronwa to deliver a message to Bondaa.

"Bondaa, I bring greetings from Fayrah and his wife Bowara and the rest of the family to you and your family." The messenger addressed the family. "Fayrah sent a message to you that he will respond to yours without delay. His message is this: The family is looking forward to gladly receive your entourage at

Kortorhun on what you propose to do." The messenger concluded.

"Thank you for your journey to bring this pleasant message." Bondaa expressed gratitude to the messenger. "God bless you the bearer of this good message and may you return safely as you came. Please tell Fayrah and the family to expect us ten days from today. I hope that is not too short notice?"

"I don't think so. It seems a reasonable period to prepare to welcome you and your entourage. I will leave early in the morning so that I can reach early to escape from the excessive heat experience especially after mid-day."

"Yes, but after you've had sips of some of my palm wine." Kewalie suggested.

"And I will make sure that you have something to eat to set you off on your journey." Makalay said. "I'm fully aware of the distance to Kortorhun and the intense heat of the past few days."

Within four days after receiving the message, Bondaa and his family made the final arrangements for their travel to Khotorhun. All that they required to make a marriage proposal for Yawa had been put together. The wives made sure they plaited their hair for the occasion. In the morning before the journey Bondaa had gone to pick some fresh kola nuts in the forest for the occasion. Four days ago, he had dispatched Yongaa to select a hefty he-goat from Ngadiya. With mortar and pestle the wives cleaned rice to secure a full bag. They filled a five-gallon tin with richly coloured palm oil, the best. Makalay went to the local market at Pelewala to purchase the calabash and other items symbolizing the elements of a positive and fruitful marriage. Kewalie, the *orkor*, had gone to Siddie, the family tailor, to sew himself an attractive *tontonla* for the day.

CHAPTER TWENTY-FOUR

On the day fixed for the entourage to journey to Kortorhun, the wives were the first to leave as the men had to tap their palm wines before they left. Palm wine is an integral part of a marriage ceremony, and the proposing suitor provides at least two full large gourds. On arriving the entourage lodged in the compound of Bondaa's cousin Bombai who had been informed early about their upcoming visit to Kortorhun. The ceremony is formally performed in the evening after the meal. Indeed, immediately after the meal, Bombai headed Bondaa's troupe for Fayrah's compound. In such situations Bombai formally introduced them. The calabash was carried by young virgin girl dressed in white clothes from head to leg ankles to signify the genuineness and purity of what is being taken to the ceremony. As the troupe headed to the compound the women chanted a known community song depicting the occasion. The walked slowly deliberately but rhythmically according to song.

A short distance from their destination they stopped singing and they walked quietly to the compound gate. They found out it has been freshly barricaded with a makeshift bamboo fence. Mbombai was a bit confused. This was unusual to him because the Fayrah's compound is always open even at night. But this time the fence was erected not only to restrict unwanted intruders from disrupting the ceremony but also to create a deliberate huddle to test the determination of the intending suitors. They must prove here that they are genuinely desperate for the marriage. At this gate the entourage will be taunted and sometimes ridiculed as a way of assessing their love and determination to marry the woman.

"Knock, Knock, Knock" Mbombai knocked and shouted so that it could be heard.

But there was total silence within. After a while he shouted again, "Knock, Knock, Knock. Can anybody hear me in this compound?"

Again, there was no response, and the silence was even more deafening. But Bondaa and Mbombai did not give up as they knew this was all part of the procedure and practice.

"If anybody is living in this compound, please open this gate?" He shouted once more.

"Hey! Hey! Who is that trying to crash my fence? "What do you want? At this beginning of the night when you should be resting or discussing your family issues." A came voice from within the compound at last.

"We are strangers from Magoronwa to visit the family in this compound". Mbombai replied.

"Sorry mister whoever you are. Even though it is just nightfall, we do not open our gate for strangers, not even from Magoronwa. You could be a thief or violent person.

"It is quite the opposite, sir. I am here with women and children. Why would a thief go with children and women to do his havoc? Please slightly open the gate and let's see our faces. We can still recognize each other even though it is just nightfall."

"Am I an idiot to do that? If I do that you will have an opportunity to knock me off and have easy access".

"I think I recognize this voice. It seems to be that of Massa in this village."

"Mister whoever you are. Yours is strange to me. I don't know yours,"

"Massa, this is Mbombai talking to you."

"I refuse to remember voices at night because I don't want those voices to keep me awake at night."

"That's understandable Massa. But I am your neighbour so please open the gate. I am here with an entourage of men, women and children with a message of love."

"But why come at this time of the night?"

"It's the appropriate time when most people would be home and would have had their meals. You told me a few moments ago that I should be resting or discussing family issues at this time. Yes, it is this time when families sit together to review and plan farm work. It is also the time family grievances and complaints are settled. Massa this is the most appropriate time when sincere messengers are received into audience. I tell you what, I am one such messenger with a message that you cannot resist."

"But you said that you came with women and children. Why come with them if you have a message?"

"I need them to grace the message presentation and to be witnesses"

"Alright Mbombai, I will reluctantly open the gate for you and your entourage. But know that your time is short. You don't have the whole night here. We have pending family matters to settle. So be brief with your message."

"Massa this is not a brief message. It is a message delivered stage by stage"

"Whatever it is, enter."

Massa slowly opened the gate and stood holding it while scrutinizing Mbombai and his followers.

As they entered, they noticed that several people were seated.

After the traditional exchanges at the compound gate the entourage was finally admitted access. The men were immediate offered seats on long wooden benches close to the men who were already in the compound. The women joined the females who were on the opposite side of the men. Bowara who was in a special dress for this joyous night, was prominently seated among them. But Yawa who was the focus the occasion was visibly absent. During this ceremony the betrothed woman should not be out with the people. She was hidden from site in a room in the house dressed in complete white from head down to toes.

Mbombai and his followers were comfortably seated after the handshakes, hugs and laughter between visitors and hosts. There was silence for some moments as if to suggest who will speak first.

Bondaa signaled to Yongaa who walked to him and gave Bondaa a small wrap of kola nuts. Bondaa whispered to him to fetch the three gourds of palm wine that Kewalie had provided for this purpose. Then he beckoned to Bombai to approach him. He handed the items to him.

From earlier arrangements, Bombai was to do the preliminary procedures and introduce Bondaa. Bombai signaled Massa to approach him.

"I thought you and I were finished at the gate. Now why are you motioning to me?"

"I told you that I have good news for this compound. Was that not the reason you allowed me and entourage in?"

"I think you are trying to tease me."

"It is not my intention when I want something from you. But come and let's start the process."

Massa walked reluctantly but reached Bombai anyway.

"You know who I am but tonight I stand to introduce the man who I believe every adult male in this chiefdom knows. He is Bondaa the gifted and renowned blacksmith who forges and repairs all our farming implements. He brought this delegation to Kortorhun and informed me that they are strangers for the Fayrah family with a goodwill message."

Bondaa got up from his chair and moved two steps forward. "But before he says anything, please receive these unwrapped kola nuts as a manifestation of his peaceful mission. These are accompanied with the three gourds of palm wine to refresh the hearts of those who will hear this message this evening. Krikoma, he pointed at some youth, "kindly bring the gourds near Bondaa."

When the gourds were brought, he took twenty Leones and gave them to Massa

"This is a symbol of the gourds as they still have to be poured by the youth." Bombai said

"I thank you Bombai and by extension Bondaa. We pray for a happy ending to all that we will hear from you this evening." He handed the items to Pa Fahawaa, Fayrah's uncle. Both were seated close to each other. "I need not repeat Bombai's words. I'm sure you heard him" Massa said. "I pass this message to you for Fayrah."

"I share your thanks to Bondaa" Pa Fahawaa replied. "We are anxious to hear from him. But before that," he bowed down and picked up by his side a cup filled with drinking water containing two red and two white kola nuts and handed it over to Massa, "give this to Bondaa. The strangers are heartily welcome to our house and the water is to quench their thirst after their long journey." Massa in turn handed over the cup and its contents to Bombai who in turn handed the cup over to Bondaa.

"We pray that as we drink this water to quench our thirst, there will always be water of peace and love to quench any fires of discord and disruption in this home." Bombai prayed. "Please stand close to me Massa because I want to send special greetings through you to various people gathered here. Let me start with you as the man whom I believe is the *Sababu,* the intermediary rep- resenting your family. These twenty Leones are for your intermediation."

Massa thanked Bondda as he put the money in his pocket.

"Standing here I do not want to breach any tradition in this village. As strangers, we have no intention of con- ducting any important event without paying our respects to the headman of Kortorhun. To guard against such possibility, take these ten Leones to report our presence in this village. For the pastor and imam, the moral and spiritual guardians in this village, here are ten Leones for each."

"We'll pass the message to them in the morning as they are not present here this evening," Massa responded.

"Here is five Leones to greet all the little children in this house because they are not only a joy to their parents, but they do all the little chores. Ten Leones are for the young boys and girls in this house who sweep the house and fetch clean water for the house and for strangers like us to drink and wash. To the young men and women in this house who contribute to the farm work and other more difficult chores, here are twenty Leones. The mature men and women I greet them forty Leones. I've bombarded you with so many greetings. I will stop here for now to know if they are around for responses."

"I am happy to receive all these moneys on behalf of all those you have greeted. Thank you so much. However, I cannot response on their behalf. I pass them all over to our elder Pa Fahawaa." He turned round to face Pa Fahawaa and handed over the moneys.

"Bondaa, I want to thank you on behalf of all the people you have greeted." Pa Fahawaa responded. "On their behalf I express their gratitude. We pray that where these moneys were taken be never empty with money. We appreciate all these greetings, but can I ask Bondaa, what is your mission here tonight? Please speak aloud so that both the living and the dead will hear you."

"Massa, I am here to ask for the hand of a beautiful young lady in Fayrah's family for Kewalie, my son. I do believe that everybody in this chiefdom has either danced to his melodious drumming or has heard about it. Let me quickly add that he has succeeded me in the blacksmith shop. Customers have commented that he is a faster and better iron forger than me. Suddenly he has become the most known and respected young man in the chiefdom."

"Good to hear that you want to have Fayrah's daughter for your son, Kewalie. Now that we know, please proceed with the rest of your message." Massa said.

Again, Bondaa beckoned Massa to come closer to him.

"I have not finished greeting all the immediate relatives. Take these thirty Leones as our greetings to the sisters and brothers.

"Are you done?"

"No. These eighty Leones are for the uncles and aunties. We cannot forget the unknown distance relatives on the paternal and the maternal sides of this beautiful woman. I give you forty Leones for each side. However, for us to show up in this compound and not greet the grandfather and grandmother will be most dishonourable. We adults know as a fact that grandparents are caretakers of the children when the parents and all the grownups are busy on the farm or on a trip. Convey our special greetings to them with these hundred Leones. I will wait to continue when you pass on these greetings."

"Don't tell me that you have more greeting to send" Massa wondered.

"Yes, Massa I do have more.

Massa passed the moneys over to Fayrah's uncle.

"We continue to thank you and your followers." Fahawaa said. "You can now tell us the crux of your mission?"

"I totally agree with you Fahawaa. But I can't omit to greet two critical people that are paramount this all. I said earlier that, I am here to ask for the hand of a beautiful young lady in Fayrah's family for my son. With a humble heart I extend greetings to Fayrah with

412

two hundred Leones and the same amount to his wife? They did not only have this beautiful girl, but they cared and raised her to be so attractive that to my son wants her to be his wife. Pa Fahawaa, I end my greetings."

"May I ask, Bondaa? Who is this woman, because in this house we have several beautiful girls, and you don't want us to guess who she is?

"The one who has recently graduated from the bondo society. Her name is Yawa."

"Which Yawa, which Yawa?" Several loud voices came from the midst of the men hosts. Questions such as this often pop up from nowhere in such wedding ceremonies. Distant male relations usually pose such questions to get some money to shut them up.

"You mean my dear lovely 'wife' (*not really*) that I have nurtured since we were playmates?" The voice continued.

"You are not the only playmate husband of Yawa, I am her husband also," came another voice in the same area.

"Yaw's real playmate husband is me. You can't deny it Gbundeh. Pa Fayrah and Ya Bowara what am I hearing? Do you want to take my wife away from me to betroth her to another man?"

"Fayrah and Bowara those questions are not for you to answer," Bondaa interjected. "In this village I believe that there are many playmate husbands of Yawa. I also believe that they helped to groom this beautiful playmate. Over the years they probably picked and gave fruits and seeds which she could not get herself. It is also possible that at the time for her and her mother to prepare the back yard to plant some

413

vegetables these playmates obliged. Others I believe even brought palm wine to Fayrah. They were all in the background. But what I believe they did not do is show up as I have done this night to propose in public for Yawa. Nevertheless, Massa please ask them to let go and advise them that my son, a large love bug, has come to marry Yawa. Please thank all the playmate paramours. Plead with them with these sixty Leones to let go."

"Under our watchful and caring eyes as parents you all grew up together with Yawa." Fahawaa commented. "We cannot deny the fact that you made your various contributions to make Yawa an admired and good-looking woman. I am joining Bondaa to plead for your total understanding and release the parents from whatever favours you had made to Yawa or her parents. Bondaa offers these sixty leones as a token of his sincerity to thank you all." He walked over to Gbundeh and handed sixty Leones.

"Thank you, Fahawaa and Bondaa. On behalf of all the known and unknown playmate husbands I accept. I can freely say that there will be no interruptions and we ask you to proceed. Do you agree with me fake husbands?"

"We agree," was the unanimous response.

"Massa in that case can I continue?

"Yes, please do"

"Before the interruption by the fake husbands, I said that the woman my son wants to marry from this compound is Yawa. She is light skinned, medium height with lovely shining eyes. I am told that she is the belle and envy of this village. She has plenty of long hair and is in her mid-teen years. I also know that she is the first child of her parents."

"Do you mean my daughter who fetches water and warms it for me to bathe?" Fayrah spoke for the first time in the evening. "Are you saying Yawa who helps her mother with all the house chores and farm work? You want to create a grave handicap by taking her away from us?"

"Yes. Fayrah it is your daughter Yawa I want for my son, Kewalie" Bondaa answered. "You cannot hold on to your daughter when she is of age to marry. In your heart I believe that this is a momentous night for you and your wife. I also know that the ultimate choice is invariably Yawa's. But I believe that before we come to this point tonight some backroom softening of positions has been done."

"You are right, but as her father I would be expected to make such comments. They show that my daughter has been a very helpful and hard-working woman. At any rate proceed and we shall see."

As Massa went to his seat Bondaa conferred briefly with Bombai. Bondaa dipped his right hand into the front pocket of his gown and took out the dowry money tied in a white handkerchief. He turned to Makalay and motioned to her to bring the calabash. She handed it to Bombai. While it was still in Bombai's hands she meticulously untied it and slightly lifted the raffia fan covering the calabash to reveal the contents to Bombai and she tied it again. She returned to her seat leaving the calabash with Bombai. As this was going on the entire gathering watched without uttering a word except coughing and sneezing. Satisfied with the contents, Bombai stepped forward to Bondaa and gave him the calabash. Bondaa stood up and loudly cleared his throat so that everybody will know that this is the important moment.

"Massa, can you please come closer." Massa responded and stood facing Bondaa who was delicately holding the calabash. He stretched the calabash to Massa and said "please hold this bundle. This is our token of our love proposal to Yawa, daughter of Fayrah and Bowara, I ask her to marry my son Kewalie, who will be the successor the Nwoingoha clan Magoronwa after me." Bondaa stretched out the calabash to Massa.

But instead of receiving the calabash, Massa stepped back a few steps.

"Bondaa! I have received several items from you this night. But I cannot receive this tied bundle. I don't know nor have you told me what is in it. You don't expect me to receive a bundle with unknown contents. Even if I receive it, I will not hold on to it for long because it could contain some harmful device. I'll immediately take it off my hands and pass it on to Pa Fahawaa who will probably thank you because I can't as this bundle is suspicious."

"Let me assure you Massa that the calabash contains nothing dangerous or harmful other than precious things. It contains items that are usually presented to a bride. It contains nuggets for a successful and peaceful marriage.

"Despite that explanation I still will not hold on to it. Fahawaa please take this calabash tied in white cloth from my shaking hands. Massa says it is harmless and contains good things and it is a present for Yawa. As her uncle, you're competent to deliver this present to her not me."

He handed the calabash to Fahawaa in the same delicate and gentle manner as Bondaa handed it to him. Without any hesitation Fahawaa took the calabash confidently and set it on the ground before him.

"Thank you, Massa, for the bundle." Fahawaa said. "I do not doubt what Bondaa said. But a gift like this must be passed on to the father who will summon his daughter to receive it. So, I will pass on the message to you Fayrah"

Fayrah who has been seated close to Fahawaa got up and faced the two men who were still standing.

"Massa you expressed fear and suspicious over the bundle. But let me say this:" Fayrah said. "Bondaa standing there is a man of his word. He has often proved it to many of us who have been to his blacksmith shop. He has a clean reputation, and he heads a very important clan in this chiefdom, the Nwoingoha clan. I am sure he will not sacrifice all that at this moment, especially when he wants a woman for his son who will succeed him. I don't believe for one bit that he will bundle harmful items in a calabash and bring it as a present. I believe what he said, and I take his word. I know he means well and nothing less."

He turned to face Bondaa 'I want to thank you immensely Bondaa. I pray that you and your entourage will return in good health as you came. I pray that the blessings of your ancestors continue to increase and overflow to your children. I pray that all evil intentions against your family totally fail. Above all I pray that you achieve your objective here tonight. This is a great night for my family. I will reserve further comments afterwards."

He turned to his left where the women were seated. His wife, Bowara, was prominently seated in the front row.

"Bowara, we have a very pleasant message from Bondaa for Yawa. Is she in the house? If she is, please send someone to summon her to come immediately?

"I have my doubts because I have not seen her since nightfall." Bowara replied.

"Well, we have a present for her brought by Bondaa on behalf of his son to pick up. Please find her so that we will know whether she will pick up it up or not."

"Manjay," Bowara called her niece standing at the main entrance of the house. "Can you please find your cousin and tell her she has a present here."

"*Tha* Bowara, Yawa is not in the house," said Bowara a friend of Bowara "she told me this afternoon she will be going to Rogbalan to visit her friend. If you want me to go fetch her, I need transport to go there and bring her."

Fayrah and Bowara knew that this was not true because she was the centre of all this, and she was aware of the occasion. They also knew that Manjay wanted something from the proposer. It was practice to put the proposer in some uncertainty.

"Manjay as long as you can assure us that you will bring her in shortly, we will provide money for you to take the fastest means of transportation to Rogbalan". Bondaa said. "But let her not be sandwiched between young men in a *poda-poda*. Massa, please give her these twenty Leones to take whatever fastest means possible."

Massa gave the money to Fayrah who in turn handed it to his wife. Immediately Manjay received the money, she disappeared into the house. But moments later she returned to report.

"Uncle Fayrah the *okada* I hired ran out of petrol and indeed money to buy the gas as I was the first trip for the *okada* rider."

This again it was untrue. It was another strategy for more money as everybody knew that a bike rider will not take a passenger without ensuring that he has petrol. Another ten Leones were given and once more she disappeared. Everybody was anxiously looking out to see Manjay and Yawa. For some time neither the messenger nor Yawa appeared thus keeping everyone in suspense. Then suddenly Manjay surfaced running and panting for breath.

"This trip seems to have some jinx. Something seems wrong. We had good progress going, but about four miles to Rogbalan, the front tyre spouted but the rider skilfully brought the bike to a safe stop. Another rider brought me without paying him. The owner of the bike could not help when I told him what happened. The rider spent all money to pay for the tyre, but it was not enough. So, I need twenty Leones to help buy the tyre."

Again, this was another scheme and again she was given the money.

"Please pray for me to overcome all these obstacles on my way and we'll be here soon." She sprinted into the house once more.

A few moments later she appeared with a small girl with her face covered.

"I have brought Yawa. Here she is."

Bondaa approached the little girl and gently raised the cloth over her face.

"This Yawa is too young. No……no…...no. She is not the one I want. Here are two Leones little Yawa. I am sure your turn to marry is not too distant. So go wait."

Manjay returned with the girl only to come back with a tall fat woman with covered face and presented her as Yawa.

"This is your Yawa and don't tell me again she is not".

"Thank you Manjay. But this Yawa is too old to be my young son's wife. My son does not want a mama in his house, but a help mate of almost equal age. However, I will give her this advice with this ten Leones 'hold tight with all sincerity your present husband.'"

The gathering burst into laughter. Then Bondaa turned to Manjay and said "I believe that you may have more 'Yawas' in the house. Take these twenty Leones and hold back all the other Yawas in there and bring me the real one. I can tell you with all certainty that when my eyes fall on my Yawa, you will be surprised at what I will do. Can you to do that for me?"

"No. I can't promise you that. I'm not sure if I can. She might have slipped out again from the house." There was laughter when she said that.

"Alright, do whatever you can to trace and bring her. But please don't coerce her to come. If she doesn't want to just come back and tell me. Her decision will be acceptable."

"As I said, I won't promise you anything. I can only promise to do my best."

"I accept that."

Bondaa was left standing in anxious anticipation as everyone else. At this point Bondaa and his entourage focused all their eyes on the front door of the house. The thought was: "is Manjay dressing up another

Yawa." Indeed, she appeared holding the hand of another Yawa who had a manly feature and man-like gait and they stood facing Bondaa.

"I have brought Yawa to collect her present?"

"As usual I need to me see the beautiful face." Bondaa said. When he unveiled the face, the whole gathering erupted into laughter. The face was not even that of a woman but that of coarse bearded young man dressed in a woman's clothes with a beautiful head dress. Bondaa could not resist laughing and he said "as long as one lives one never ceases to see wonders. For the first time in my life, I have seen a woman's face covered with so much coarse beard and moustache. I have seen this spectacle because of you Manjay. Thank you for that. But give this fifteen Leones to this bearded woman to assist her buy a packet of blades so that she can trim her beard and moustache."

"Can you blame me? When I returned to the house, I found three more faces covered and I could not uncover any face as it will be an insult to uncover the faces. Obviously, I had to bring one next in line. That was the dilemma I faced in there. So, I have two more covered faces in there to choose for the next Yawa. So, pray hear that when I bring the next in line, she will be your Yawa. However, as I was bringing this last Yawa, we stumbled and almost fell as the inside of the house is dark. There is no light. The lamp in the house has run out of kerosene." Yet another trick to get more money.

"Here six Leones for three pints of kerosene. Make sure however, that this time you bring my Yawa."

"What? Is that a threat?"

"No-no-no. How can I threaten you the messenger who has done a marvellous job this evening in bringing several Yawas? I was just asking kindly that you please bring her this time."

"Do you really want me to bring your son's Yawa?"

"Yes Manjay. I am anxiously waiting for you to bring her"

"Demonstrate to me how prepared you're to receive her"

"You fetch her, and I will surprise you what you will see."

"No, no. Practice with me first. Show me how you will do so." Bondaa dipped his hand the pocket of his gown with reluctance and gave more money

"I promise that when I see her, you will have more."

"I have heard that you are a man of your word," she reminded Bondaa, and she left and went into the house. Moments later she came out holding the hand of a figure dressed in white lace from top to bottom and then slowly walked before her to where Bondaa was standing. The face could not be seen clearly even though it was covered with a transparent white veil. Slowly but with great dignity, gait, and poise the figure walked with Manjay by her side. They stopped right in front of Bondaa.

"I have brought you another covered face but this one is dressed in complete white. Can this be the one you're expecting me to bring?"

"As I have done with all the others before, I will lift the veil and make sure of that." He moved close to the figure and slowly but confidently lifted the veil.

"Yes. This is the right person I've been longing for you bring."

"So, are you happy now?"

"Yes Manjay. You have proved to be a diligent and devoted envoy. As I promised that I will do more when I see her, take these forty Leones for your shuttling between me and the house to bring Yawa. I want to express profound appreciation on behalf of my son. Now that I have seen her, I will return to my seat with complete satisfaction."

"*Tha* Bowara," Manjay turned and faced Bowara, "I have brought your daughter and she is standing right there before Pa Fahawaa. Now that I have done my assignment, I should withdraw and vanish." And she left.

"Fayrah, your daughter is here as you asked me to call her and appear before you."

Everybody knew that Yawa was in the house since the beginning of this ceremony. But what Manjay did was to spice some fun into this joyous occasion and not be too formal an event.

"I see her, and we thank our able messenger Manjay." He turned to face his daughter.

"Yawa before me on the floor is a present wrapped in white cloth. It has been brought for you by Bondaa the blacksmith of Magoronwa and head of the *Nwoingoha* clan. He says this present is from his son Kewalie and he is proposing to you.

"Do you know his son, Kewalie?"

"Yes sir. You remember papa that he and auntie Makalay came here to invite you and mama to his initiation to the male circumcision and the *Gbangban*i society about two years ago. You found us chatting in

423

the veranda in the morning when you returned from tapping your palm wine."

"Yes, I remember, and I asked who that young man was, and he boldly answered, 'I am the son of Mama Makalay.' What else did he say he was during your chat?"

"He told me that he was the proclaimed drummer in the chiefdom trained by Pa Baimba

"Anything else he told you?

"He said he is the next direct bloodline male of the Nwoingoha clan at Magoronwa."

"Well with all that you have said about this man, you must have created an amorous and affectionate impression on him that he has sent a present as a proposal to marry you." After a slight pause her father continued.

"If you want this young man to be your husband, take this calabash. It's all yours. You can do whatever you wish to do with it. Your dowry prize and all the elements that show you how to live a married life are all in it. Or you can reject the present and walk away. Your decision to reject or accept will be accepted. It's your absolute choice to make and we will in no way influence your decision."

Hearing this from her father, she stooped and gently picked up the Calabash and gave it to him. As she picked up the calabash and gave her father, Bondaa and his followers, except for the groom, rose from their seats and showered her with Leones notes thus expressing joy and appreciation for accepting the proposal.

When this was over the betrothal party were entertained to food and more palm wine. The party retired to Bombai's residence shortly before midnight.

CHAPTER TWENTY-FIVE

Fayrah and Bowara must now send Yawa to her husband immediately. This should be a few days after the return of the betrothal party.

"Bowara, we have to dispatch Yawa immediately to her husband. We cannot hold her here any longer." Fayrah said. "As is the custom we have to provide her with basic cooking utensils to begin her home should be. I think we should use some of the dowry to purchase some of these basic items."

"It's the practice and your suggestion are appropriate. She will need at least two pots some basins and a bucket to fetch water." Bowara agreed. "I will give her some of my new bowls that I don't need at the moment."

"I will ask Konda to make two durable mortars and pestles for her."

"They will be certainly necessary for her and thank you for the thought. I forgot that it is one prominent utensil that a home cannot lack." Bowara said. "My sister brought two nice straw mats. She also brought her some groundnuts, sesame seed, dried pepper and okra."

"We have rice and palm oil to give her too? Am I right?" Fayrah asked.

"Yes. We do have some clean rice, but we need to add a little more. The palm oil I reserved for the raining season we'll give her. She needs basic utensils just as my parents provided for me when they were sending me to you. Lack of these basic things often causes frustration and even friction between women."

425

"The calabash and all of the rest of the items in it, with the exception of the kola nuts, she will take along. It's hers and the contents have significant meaning of how to live a successful and peaceful marriage." Fayrah suggested. "Whatever remains from the dowry money she will retain."

"Do you think that you will be able to get all these things in the next three days so that we can dispatch her after that?" Fayrah asked Bowara.

"I believe so. You know that you and I cannot take her to Magoronwa as it is not the norm. We have to ask Bombai and his wife to do that on our behalf." Bowara suggested.

"That I know, and I have already asked Bombai and Habba and they are willing to do so."

Two days later Bowara told Fayrah that everything was ready and that she has sent a message to her friend, Makalay that she should expect her daughter-in-law any time from the day the message was delivered. On that information Fayrah summoned Bombai and Habba to come over after the evening meal to his house.

"Bombai, as I told you before neither me nor Bowara can take Yawa to her husband. You willingly accepted my request that you and your wife will do that on our behalf." Fayrah reminded Bombai. "We have been able to get the basic needs for her to start her new home. Everything is packed, bagged and ready. We therefore want you to take her tomorrow if that will be alright with you?"

"Fayrah, we told you when you asked us that we are honoured and proud to take my niece to her husband. We will make the journey tomorrow."

"Gbundeh and his friend have agreed to tote the load as their goodbye gesture to Yawa." Fayrah told Bombai. "When you hand her over, it will be you who will give the final address to Yawa. You will take my place to give her the advice citing among others her mother's humility and respect to emulate it. We have already addressed her as parents. But the advice that you two will give her will be remembered as you will be addressing her in the presence of the husband and all the in-laws."

"We can give all the good parental advice. It will be up to her to listen, accept and adopt the advice." Bowara commented.

"We hope and pray that she will decide to implement what we tell her." Habba hoped. "I express this hope because our children these days seem to have less humble attitudes which we cannot imagine in our early days. Yawa has so far not portrayed such an attitude over the years since she was born."

"Although that may be true now of Yawa, yet certain things might trigger some disobedience. We pray that does not happen to her." Fayrah prayed. "We also know that she is now married to a respected and revered clan. We pray that no evil influence will penetrate that family. Thank you for doing this for us and we let you go and have early sleep so that you can have an early start."

Early in the morning the escort company was ready. Fayrah and Bowara gave their final blessings and advice to Yawa before they departed.

"Don't forget that it takes two to quarrel. Don't be quick to answer but be quick to listen. Be slow to anger and rage. Unwarranted rage will yield nothing good. Contentious issues between you and your husband are best settled in your room." This was Bowara's final motherly advice to her daughter.

"Mama I hear you and I promise to do my best. You have been my role model and I pray that I won't let you down." Responded Yawa.

"My final words are clear; you must obey your husband and respect him at all times." Fayrah said. "Respect and obedience constitute powerful weapons to woo a man's heart. These have been your mother's greatest assets which you are aware of. Don't forget to honour the in-laws especially the older ones." Fayrah gave his own counselling.

Bombai and Habba came to get their instructions from Fayrah but there was none. Gbundeh and his friend toted the heavy stuff, and the lighter ones were shared among Bombai, Habba and Yawa. They reached Magoronwa just before sunset as they made an early good start. It was Makalay that spotted them as they approached the Nwoingoha house, and she walked to welcome them.

"You're welcome to Magoronwa and to the Nwoingoha family house. The men are not here as usual at this time of the day, but I will tell my mates that you've come." She greeted them as she ushered them into the house.

"Hogaii and Bendihe, Bombai and Habba are here with Yawa. They are in the veranda." Raising for them to hear.

"Well! It was good we started the cooking earlier than usual as we had received the message of their coming." Hogaii said. She and Bendihe got up from the cooking and went to greet the expected visitors.

"You are so welcome to our village and house." Hogaii said shaking the hand of each one of them.

"Bondaa, Yongaa and Kewalie are not here now. They've all gone to tap their palm wine. But we will get you settled before they come. Bombai let me show the room for you and your wife for the night. The two boys will be lodged by Yongaa when he comes."

The mates returned to their cooking accompanied by Yawa. Makalay put a bucket of water over a fire for Bombai and his wife to have warm water baths. When the water was warm enough, she told Bombai that the water was ready for him in the wash booth. Habba washed after her husband.

As Bondaa approached his house he noticed somebody was in his veranda. He wasn't surprised to find Bombai as he was expecting a delegation from Fayrah bringing his daughter-in-law. They exchanged pleasantries and Bondaa asked "how is Fayrah and his wife?"

"They are doing fine up to this morning when we left them. They send their greetings to you and the family. They have asked me to bring your daughter-in-law to her husband."

"You will formally hand her over at nightfall after we've have eaten." Bondaa advised Bombai. "Besides the *okor* is not here. He's gone to tap his palm wine and we know that when young men go wine tapping, they help themselves with some before they head home. But where is Yawa?"

"She is at the back with our wives." Bombai answered." It will be abnormal for her to sit here with me and not join the women at the back."

"It certainly will be. That is an indication of a woman who wants to assimilate and adapt. While we wait for the women to finish cooking and for the return of Kewalie we'll drink this small gourd of palm wine I brought."

He poured out a cupful and gulped that before pouring another for Bombai. Halfway through the gourd, Makalay came to announce that Bombai's dish was in the room he was lodged. She also told Bondaa that she will bring his if he wants it now.

"I think we will eat after finishing this palm wine. Thank you for telling us." Makalay returned to the back and the two continued to partake of the palm wine. Bombai looked in the direction they had come, and he saw Kewalie.

"Well here comes my son-in-law."

"He's early because he is expecting a delegation to bring his wife today."

"I will do the same if I were him." Bombai said. Kewalie walked in and shook Bombai's hand.

"How are you *Kothor*? Kewalie asked. "I'm glad to see you. I hope you had a safe travel to here?"

"It's a pleasure to be here at the behest of Fayrah and his wife of which you're aware." Bombai replied. "But we shall talk about this later as your father has already proposed."

"Then I will see you shortly I have a few things I have to put together before the talk." Kewalie left the Bombai and his father to continue drinking the palm wine. He went to inform Yongaa that Bombai has come to present his wife formally and that his presence is absolutely needed.

"I know they sent a message of their coming, but I didn't think it was today." Yongaa said. "It's good you came to tell me because I was preparing to go Dendehun to ask the young folks for help in making my cassava heaps. I will leave at the first cock crow in the morning. I hope you prepared yourself for this night?"

"Yes uncle. I've got two gourds of palm wine after everything is over. I hid them close by. I did not want anybody to see me bringing them in."

"Alright. But remember what you were taught in the society bush when your wife gets into your bed for the first time?"

"I do remember"

"Fine. We will know by the morning. You can go and get ready for the presentation."

Kewalie and Yongaa returned home. When he arrived, he found his food in his room, but he was not that hungry as he was ecstatic and overjoyed at the fact that he is getting a wife tonight. He took a few handfuls of the rice and cassava leaves sauce. He changed his farm clothes for more decent ones. When he came out, he found everybody was seated in the veranda except Yongaa.

"We were just wondering what's happened with you?" Bondaa asked.

"I went earlier to inform uncle Yongaa to be present and then I had my meal." Kewalie replied. "Can we hold on for a few moments for uncle to show up?" He pleaded.

"You know that we cannot proceed without his presence. So yes, we'll give him a few moments."

"Good evening, everybody, especially the visitors from Kortorhun." Yongaa greeted.

"Now that you're here, let's welcome visitors. Please take these kola nuts and these thirty Leones to usher them into our home with open hands and hearts. Also tell them that we are anxious to hear the message from Fayrah and his lovely wife." Yongaa took the items from Bondaa and gave them to Bombai.

"As you have heard from uncle Bondaa, you're most heartily welcome to the Nwoingoha family house. We are indeed eager to know your mission here."

"Thank you Bondaa for welcoming us. Surely everybody is yearning to know what I am going to say and do. You recently received a message from Fayrah to expect visitors. I'm here to represent him this evening to bring his daughter to her husband. Yawa come forward." Yawa came from inside the house and knelt before Bombai.

"Am I right to say that you accepted the calabash which Bondaa presented to you as a marriage proposal from his son, Kewalie?"

"Yes uncle."

"And you said that you want to be Kewalie's wife?"

"Yes uncle. I have not changed my mind. I still want to."

"You have no idea what marriage is like until you enter into it?"

"Although I have no idea, yet I am prepared to learn what it involves when I get in."

"I am happy to hear that. I pray that you will assimilate and adapt into good and peaceful marriage life."

He unwrapped kola nuts from a bundle wrapped in green leaves and gave them to Yongaa. "We all have heard what Yawa has just said. With that Yongaa please take these kola nuts as token from Fayrah and Bowara to hand their daughter unconditionally to Bondaa on behalf of his son. They also gave me a message for Bondaa and that is: Take Yawa first as your daughter and treat her as you'll treat anyone of your daughters and then as a daughter-in-law. To your wives: Bowara says you now have a daughter who replaces those that have left you and gone to their married homes."

Yongaa took the kola nuts and thanked Bombai.

"I am so overwhelmed with happiness that I have very little to say because I know what this means to the *Nwoingoha* clan. Uncle Bondaa I will handover to you."

"God bless you Yongaa. But before I say anything I want to hear from Hogaii and her mates." Bondaa responded.

"In all previous family meetings, I have been given the honour by my mates to speak first." Hogaii said. "But this night I give the privilege to Makalay as I believe this is her moment of joy and happiness."

"I bless you Hogaii. Indeed, it is a night of delight and gladness." Makalay said. "Bombai please tell Bowara that she has just cemented our friendship by sending her daughter to me to take care of her. Tell her that I will not treat Yawa as a daughter-in-law but as my own daughter because I believe that the orange fruit does not fall far from the tree. We pray that she will outlive us the older ones. We also pray that she and her husband and their children will take over the family clan. All I can say to Yawa is, welcome to another home."

"I think you have said it all Makalay." Bendihe remarked. "Hogaii, do we have anything to add to what she has said?"

"No, I don't. We know that our daughters are all with their husbands and to have Yawa is indeed a blessing. We'll listen to you Bondaa."

"It's a delight to me in all this. Bombai please tell Fayrah and wife that their message is received with a clear heart. We will do all we can to assist the couple in forging their marriage. We pray and hope that Yawa will be obedient and humble to her husband and that Kewalie will love his wife. That is the only way marriage can work peacefully and successfully. Tell Fayrah that it means so much to him to give a daughter to marriage as I have experienced with six daughters. Thank them immensely. Kewalie please come forward." Kewalie who has been silent since the beginning of the presentation rose from his seat and approached his father. At that same moment Bombai rose and took Yawa by the hand and led her towards Bondaa and Kewalie. He formally handed Yawa to Bondaa and returned to his seat.

"Kewalie take these kola nuts from Fayrah as a token of his unconditional handover of his daughter to you as your wife. Standing before you in person is your wife, Yawa."

Kewalie took the kola nuts from his father and stretched out his hand to Yawa and they embraced for the first time.

"Papa, uncle Yongaa and my mothers, my heart is overwhelmed with happiness and joy. No doubt this is the most memorable night in my life. I want to thank you all for the different roles you played make this happen. I want *Kothor* Bombai to thank my in-laws and to tell them that what they have given is an egg. I will take the greatest care of it as long as the egg does not roll away from where it should be. To you Yawa: I hope the attraction we had for each other the first time we met will continue to flourish between us as you join me here in Magoronwa. You are most welcome to my home."

Yawa smiled and bowed her heads in shy happiness as her husband continued.

"To celebrate this unforgettable night, we shall all have some palm wine before I show my wife to our room."

GLOSSARY

Ashoyebi	a uniform dress to identify a group of people
Baybay	fishing net tied on a circular wooden twig used only by women.
Baii	a special rope for climbing palm trees .
Boraa	a valuable token for greeting.
Chakabula	locally made musket (gun)
Jackitomboi	grounded cassava leaves cooked as a sauce to eat with cooked rice.
Gbangbani	men's secret society
Gbodokali	Loko youths' somersault dance.
Gbongboinla	the most difficult manhood test in the male circumcision society.
Haybuda	the entrance of an elephant hole.
Hindolo	a strong young man.
Kaylen	a dug out wooden gong.
Kayneh	a title used to address a respected and older male.
Komaneh	father or brother-in-law
Kondi	a musical instrument made from 4 x 6 inches tin with nine small flat iron tongs tied at the center.
Kongoma	a musical instrument made from a square wooden box with a hole in the center on top on which are three small flat iron tongs tie to it.
Kondogbala	parboiled and dried cassava.
Kothor	title of respect for an older brother or male.

Lappa	a cloth wrap that women tie from waist down covering their legs well below the knee.
Landorgor	the Loko people and dialect.
Lontha	the end for everybody to heed
Manadbesse	chewing stick for brushing teeth.
Muemibdehu	month of September.
Nyanday	beautiful (girl/woman)
Okor	the groom.
Paybayli	a broad hoe for Ploughing or swamp work.
Poda-poda	local mini bus.
Pehmahun	fast cooked rice eaten with sweet potato leaves, benniseed, garden eggs and ground dried fermented locust seed (kaynda).
Ronko	a half gown made from locally woven cotton cloth dyed brown.
Sababu	an intermediary.
Sangotho	smoking weed but not cannabis.
Shayma	the mentor or caretaker of a boy while in the society bush,
Sukublai	a round basket made of straw and raffia.
Swesweh	month of July.
Thara	title of respect for an older sister or female.
Tha	the shortened form of thara.
Thorthorbeh	the seer or sorcerer.
Taymulay	female top blouse-like dress with frills down to the waistline.
Tontola	a male sleeveless gown.
Yaywore	mother-in-law.
Yenki	handsome well-dressed young man

Compiled by the
WLTF Literary Agency
http://www.winstonfordebooks.com

Made in the USA
Middletown, DE
23 July 2023

35617865R00265